THE DEACON'S DEMISE

The Deacon's Demise

A PINE COUNTY MYSTERY

Dean L Hovey

Moose Town Press

Dedicated to Raymond and Hildur Lund
My favorite (and only) in-laws

CHAPTER 1

PINE BROOK, MINNESOTA

The early evening aromas of perking coffee and floor wax had given way to the acrid odor of perspiration as the deacons' board meeting dragged into its second hour. Although the windows were open, the only moving air was provided by the deacons fanning themselves with copies of the proposed budget. After discussion of the last budget line, Edith Anderson brought the meeting back to order with a rap of her gavel. As their side conversations ended, the two dozen deacons refocused their attention on the chairperson.

With the group's full attention Edith said, "We've been through every line of the budget for the next fiscal year. I'd like a motion for a budget vote."

Three hands shot up and a rumble of, "So moved," came from several committee members. The stifling heat and hard chairs provided motivation to end the already overly long meeting.

"Seconded," said Claire Waldemarsen, sitting near the back, her plump face flush from the heat.

"The acceptance of the budget has been moved and seconded. I assume there is no further discussion." Edith's words were spoken with authority, which made it clear she wanted to get the budget approved and the meeting adjourned. She tugged at her blouse as a trickle of sweat ran past her ear and under her collar.

"I have a few words I'd like to say before the vote is taken."

A groan rose from the membership as George Brown rose to his feet. An imposing figure, tall with close-cropped salt and pepper hair, George commanded respect. His bass voice anchored the choir every Sunday and was often heard at church meetings.

"My grandparents helped build this church after the Hinckley fire. My parents' money kept this church's doors open during the Great Depression." He scanned the room to make sure all the eyes were staring at him. Every face was solemn. "My grandparents and parents are buried in the church cemetery. My children and grandchildren attend Sunday school and make up half the choir." Unsaid but known to all was the fact that half the current budget was largely based on Brown family pledges.

George let his words steep in the stagnant air as chairs creaked and eyes rolled. He studied each of the faces seated around him. Outside the church, a car door slammed and the sound reverberated through the silence. He went on. "I don't like this budget. I don't like it one bit. In the history of this church we have never approved a budget to spend more than was pledged. If my calculations are correct, this budget is twelve percent over pledges. On top of that, there is this

Mexican mission project." George paused and took a deep breath, revealing his discomfort with the topic. "Don't get me wrong, I think we should participate in mission projects. We should be committed to the spreading of Christ's word. But I don't see how a little church like this can take on a project to build a whole new church. The money isn't there and I don't think it should be done." George had rolled his copy of the budget into a tube. He ended his statements by twisting the tube and ripping it in half. He left no one wondering if he would waffle on the topic.

Edith nodded to George, acknowledging his comments as the secretary scrambled to catch the essence of the monologue. Edith asked, "Is there any other discussion?"

Ed Abbott, the pastor, raised his hand, and then spoke from his chair with a carefully modulated voice meant to remove some of the tension from the air. "George has compelling arguments. However, offering plate collections have been running nearly twenty percent over pledges for quite awhile and I don't feel bad about approving a budget that includes actual collections rather than pledges as the base." He paused to collect his thoughts. "As for the mission project, it has been a really great focal point for the youth of this church. Our monthly trips have included virtually every teen from this congregation, including three of George's grandchildren. One of George's granddaughters is in Mexico right now with our work group. The kids and the chaperones are taking great pride in the project and the progress. I think the enthusiasm this project has brought to this congregation is the seed that has brought the increased level of collections. I think that's healthy."

The heads of several younger board members nodded their assent. A side conversation broke out in the back row and Edith used the gavel to bring the meeting back to order again. She glanced nervously at her watch. It was nearly ten o'clock.

"All right then," Edith took control and attempted to summarize. "We've heard arguments for and against the budget. I would like to have the deacons' vote. All those in favor, please signify by saying aye."

A chorus of "Ayes" filled the room.

"All those opposed, say nay."

The room was silent except for one, "Nay!" offered emphatically by a deep bass voice.

George Brown rose from his chair and glared at the board members. His face was the color of overcooked beets and the veins bulged in his neck. "The rest of you can do as you please, but there are things going on we don't fully understand. You can spend *your* money any way you'd like." He paused for effect. "But I'll rot in hell before I let you spend any more of *my* money on this mission project."

George turned and his heels clicked on the hundred-year-old hardwood planks as he stomped out of the room and down the hall. The sound of his steps died and the front door slammed, leaving the board members staring at the empty door.

Edith looked at the astonished faces of the deacons' board. "Well, I guess we don't have to wonder where George stands on the budget." A titter of nervous laughs was punctuated by the sound of George's car door slamming outside the open windows.

Claire Waldemarsen rose from her chair. "In spite of George's concerns, I know in my heart we are doing the right thing with this budget and the Mexican mission project." Her endorsement was greeted with nods of assent. "I will personally increase my pledge to help cover the budget, and I plan to go to Mexico next month as a chaperone."

The building shuddered as the shock wave from the explosion passed over the church. Shards of glass showered the room as a blinding flash lit the parking lot. There were cries and shouts as the board members took account of themselves and each other. Art Richardson, a volunteer fireman, ran for the door as the others tried to assist the elderly deacons. Claire Waldemarsen had been flung onto the laps of the people sitting behind her. Claire, and a number of others, had cuts on their faces and arms from the flying glass. One woman lay on the floor moaning.

Art Richardson rushed back and stuck his head in the door with his cell phone in hand. "George's car blew up!" He hesitated for one second to survey the damage inside the room, and then added. "I called 911."

• • •

Floyd Swenson, a Pine County Sheriff's Department sergeant, was parked on a gravel road west of Hinckley. With more than thirty years in the department, he was the most senior deputy, the training officer, and unofficial counselor. He was slender but wiry and was famous for being able to talk to anyone about any topic. The previous sheriff had once described Floyd as stern but fair.

Floyd had a bench warrant to arrest Ronny Benson for nonpayment of child support. He'd spent several nights in the same gap in the brush, just down the road from the farmhouse Ronny had been sharing with his girlfriend. He was beginning to suspect that Ronny had gotten word about the warrant and had skipped town. He made a mental note to request a warrant to look through the house for something that might tell him where Ronny was hiding.

The tones sounded on his radio for the Pine Brook and Hinckley volunteer fire departments, followed by the tones for the Pine City ambulance. The dispatcher's voice followed the tones. "All fire units respond to an explosion at the Pine Brook Free Church. Pine County Sheriff's deputies, please call with your availability."

Floyd turned on his flashing lights as he pulled onto the road. "608 is responding to the fire call," he announced as he pushed the accelerator to the floor.

Floyd raced down a back road to downtown Hinckley where he turned south, parallel to I-35. Both of the other Pine County deputies were at a domestic dispute near Denham, in the furthest northwest corner of Pine County, nearly an hour away from the fire.

Floyd slowed through downtown Hinckley, meeting several volunteer firemen driving to the fire station with their 4-way flashers pulsing. Past downtown, he quickly accelerated to over 100-miles-an-hour down old highway 61. By the time Floyd reached highway 23, he could see flames lighting the western sky. He accelerated hard down the empty highway and reached the church well ahead of the firemen.

The car fire lit the parking lot and the west side of the church like daylight. About twenty people were watching as two men sprayed water from a garden hose on the cars nearest the fire. Most of the remaining cars had been driven away from the fire, but those immediately adjacent to the fire couldn't be moved. Their paint was already blistering from the heat and their tires smoldering. The smell of burning oil and plastic filled the night air as a plume of black smoke rolled from the flames over the cars.

Art Richardson raced to Floyd's cruiser. "I think it's George Brown's car. He left our meeting in a huff and then 'Boom!' The explosion broke the windows and rattled the whole building. By the time I got outside, the roof of the car was peeled back and the engine compartment was already engulfed in flames. Someone was in the driver's seat and I could see he was in bad shape. The fire was already too hot for me get him out."

As they watched, the fire spread to the full interior of the car and the tires were burning, adding the stink of burning rubber to the smoke. The garden hose was having little effect, the weak stream of water vaporizing as it hit the cars. Floyd looked at Art's hands, which were red and blistered in his attempt to save the man inside the car.

"Was it George?" Floyd asked.

Richardson ran the back of his hand over his sweaty face, leaving streaks of soot around his eyes and singed eyebrows. "I couldn't say. It's George's car and he'd just walked out." Art shrugged. "By the time I got to the car, the person inside wasn't recognizable."

The distant wail of sirens cut through the roar of the fire.

"A bunch of people were hurt inside the church, mostly from flying glass. But it looks like everyone is out here watching the fire."

Floyd nodded and lifted Art's hand. "You need to get someone to look at your hands. They look pretty bad."

Art was obviously pumped up on adrenaline. He looked at his blistered skin as if he was staring at someone else's hand. "I'll be darned. I guess I must've been closer to the fire than I realized." He let his hands fall to his sides. "I'll have one of the paramedics look at them after they check the other people. There are a couple of them with pretty bad cuts and it looks like Irene Paulson might have a concussion."

When Floyd got closer to the car, he could see the dark outline of a body engulfed in flames. He realized the hood was entirely missing and looked around the parking lot. The hood was lying in the grass about twenty yards beyond the parking lot. That certainly lent credence to the theory an explosion had taken place. Floyd walked to the hood and noted that it was deformed, but not burned. It had been thrown from the car before the fire started. The sirens of multiple fire trucks grew close as Floyd returned to the crowd, easing them further back from the burning cars in the parking lot.

"Excuse me." A man wearing a sport coat had his hand on Floyd's arm. "I'm Pastor Abbott."

Floyd nodded. "We've met. You presided at a couple of funerals I've attended. I'm Floyd Swenson, from the sheriff's department."

Recognition swept over the pastor. "Yes, I recognize you now. I'm terribly concerned about some of the injured people."

He pointed to the broken windows on the front of the church. "A number of the deacons were cut by flying glass.

Floyd assessed the pastor as being uninjured but shaken. "I think you'd better sit down for a second." He led the pastor to the building's steps and helped him sit down. Floyd guessed Ed Abbott to be about sixty years old. The evening was quickly aging him. "Are you okay?"

Pastor Abbott nodded his head. "This is terrible. I think George Brown was in the car when it caught fire."

Pine Brook's only fire truck rounded the corner and stopped at the edge of the parking lot. Two firemen jumped out and started pulling hose from a reel mounted on top of the truck as a third fireman adjusted the controls on the water pump. Within seconds, water poured on the car and the raging inferno roared as the water turned to steam. When the cool water hit the nearly molten steel it shrieked as if banshees were arriving to claim George Brown's eternal soul. A Hinckley fire truck arrived quickly and its hoses were added to the deluge. Within fifteen minutes a third fire truck arrived. As the flames died the parking lot returned to darkness.

Floyd and the pastor watched the firemen continue to spray water onto the smoldering cars. A Pine County Sheriff's department cruiser stopped outside the parking lot as another fire truck, with a huge tank, arrived from Hinckley with more water. Deputy Pam Ryan emerged from the squad and joined Floyd and the pastor.

The tires of the burned cars continued to smolder and steam even as firemen poured water onto them. A highway patrol car turned off highway 23 and preceded the Pine City ambulance to the church. Art Richardson met the ambulance at the driveway and directed them to the far side of the parking lot where the deacons were gathered.

Floyd tapped Pam on the shoulder and pointed to the hood of George Brown's car. "The hood was blown clear of the car. We need to secure the car hood before someone tampers with it. I want it tested for blast residue."

Pam got a roll of crime scene tape from the trunk and quickly strung it between a tree and some shrubs.

Pastor Abbott caught Floyd's words and slowly processed them. His eyes went wide with recognition. "You don't think this was an accident?"

Ignoring the pastor's question, Floyd gave Deputy Ryan additional instructions. "There's a body inside the car. It'll be awhile before the metal cools down. I want the St. Louis County Medical Examiner to remove the body and do the autopsy. Treat this as a murder scene and secure the area until we can recover evidence. Have the firemen put up the klieg lights and pull the deputies in from the next shift to do a grid search of the parking lot and the grass around the church for evidence."

Floyd and the Pastor watched in silence as the white column of steam from the car took on an eerie glow as it was backlit by the rising moon.

Pam was back in less than two minutes. "Sandy Maki is on the road tonight with me. We can probably pull Jack, the highway patrolman. He said he'd hang around unless there's a major accident on the interstate. The dispatcher is calling the night shift deputies."

Floyd nodded assent and turned his attention back to the pastor. "Pastor Abbott, could we move to your office?"

The pastor nodded and Floyd helped him stand up. "Please call me Pastor Ed. I prefer to be a little more informal." Abbott turned at the bottom of the steps and surveyed the broken windows. He shook his head. "The Lord works in strange ways." He walked up the steps and into the church.

Pastor Ed's office was small, barely large enough for his desk, a computer table, a bookcase, and a guest chair. "Have a seat." He started to sit, and then hesitated. "I think there is coffee left over from our meeting. I don't know about you, but I could use a cup."

Floyd nodded. "A cup of coffee would be great."

With the pastor gone, Floyd pulled out his cell phone. Noting that he'd missed a call, he dialed the sheriff's home phone number which was answered on the second ring. "John, this is Floyd. There was an explosion at the Pine Brook Free Church. It destroyed George Brown's car and there's a body inside we assume is George."

The sheriff's deep voice grunted. "Accidental?"

Floyd peeked into the hallway to make sure no one was listening. "I don't think so. The car was incinerated within minutes and the hood was blown yards from the parking lot. I asked Pam Ryan to secure the area around the hood and car. We may have lost some evidence when some deacons moved their cars away and as the firemen doused the flames. I hope we can find an ignition device in the debris once the car cools down."

The sheriff pondered the information in silence. "Who would want George dead?"

"I'm asking questions."

"You don't need me down there, do you?" The inflection made it clear the question was rhetorical.

"Not tonight, but you probably want to be ready for the media. They'll have trucks here by sunrise and you'll want to make a statement."

"I wonder if my wife picked up my white shirt from the dry cleaners?" the sheriff asked idly. Then said, "Sure. Do you have the resources you need at the scene?"

Floyd stared at the pastor's bookcase while he thought. "I've got enough people to keep the scene secure, and the evening shift deputies are coming to help search for evidence, but we need to make a call to ATF because of the explosion. They can probably send someone from Minneapolis and have them here by morning."

"I'll call them and the BCA, too. It's beneficial to look like we're team players, using all the resources available to us. It'll look good when the news cameras pan across the scene showing windbreakers with an alphabet of agency logos."

Pastor Ed returned with a tray as Floyd was putting his cell phone in a holster on his belt. The minister had two unmatched mugs full of steaming coffee and he'd set a few homemade chocolate chip cookies on a paper plate. "I couldn't find the cream or sugar, so I hope black coffee is okay."

"Black is fine." Floyd took a cup and one of the cookies. He jumped on the opportunity to catch the pastor before he spoke with other people. "Has someone been unhappy with George Brown lately? I mean, so unhappy they might want to see him dead?"

The pastor looked at Floyd like he was speaking in tongues. "I don't believe so. I mean, George speaks his mind and makes some people uncomfortable. But that's just George. We expect him to speak his mind."

Floyd pressed. "But, there was no one who especially disliked George?"

Pastor Abbott stared at Floyd, the recognition finally hitting him. "You still don't think this was an accident?" asked the pastor. Floyd shook his head. "You're asking me if I know who might have killed George?"

"It'll take days of investigation," Floyd said, "but I suspect someone put some type of explosive in George's car. A simple car fire doesn't cause an instant explosion that blows the hood out of the parking lot."

Pastor Ed sipped his coffee and stared at the top of his desk. "George and I aren't . . . weren't close friends. The only time we spoke was when he was informing me of a problem. He was a rather strong-willed man who was used to having his way." Pastor Ed looked up to make sure Floyd was getting the meaning in his words.

Floyd added. "Many powerful people are used to getting their way. But, they also tend to alienate others along the way."

"Well put," the pastor said, nodding in agreement. "George had a way of telling people what was right and what should be done. He didn't like to negotiate or compromise, nor did he want to be the person responsible for resolving the problem." The pastor weighed his next words. "Many great leaders are like that. But in a church, that's not how things get done. We have a representative democracy and the deacons' board makes the decisions. George was sometimes irritated because he gave a lot of money to the church, but only got one vote on the board."

Pam Ryan knocked lightly on the door frame. "Excuse me. The ambulance left with two people with the worst injuries. It looks like everyone else is rattled, but okay. The night-shift deputies are here and the fire department has the parking lot lit up like noon. The medical examiner is on his way and the coroner looked at the body in the car, declaring it human and definitely dead." Pam glanced from Floyd to the pastor, wondering if she should conclude her verbal report. Floyd didn't stop her, so she went on, "The body is burned beyond recognition. The coroner can't even tell if it was a man or a woman at this point. The front license plate was blown clear of the fire, but the car is registered to George Brown with an address in Pine City."

The pastor closed his eyes, clasped his hands, and whispered something to himself, probably a prayer.

"Talk to the people who were at the meeting," Floyd said. "See if anyone came late and may have seen someone tinkering with George's car, then drive down to Pine City and notify George's widow."

Pastor Ed straightened up. "Oh dear! That had completely slipped my mind in all the commotion. I have to come along when you go to see Bernice. She is a wonderful soul and she'll be shattered. She shouldn't get this news from a stranger."

"Before you leave, is there any *one* person who was particularly angry over George's attempts to direct things?"

Pastor Ed leaned back and thought. "Well, no one person in particular. I'd say George had irritated most everyone at one time or another. He didn't like to spend his own or the church's money. That had a number of people disgusted at different times." The pastor hesitated. "Just tonight he announced he wouldn't support the budget and he was going to stop contributing. I planned to visit him tomorrow at the hardware store and we would have smoothed things over. That's how it always went…George made some big threat, then I went back to him after he'd cooled down and we smoothed it over. That was just George's way."

• • •

Pastor Ed Abbott left to tell Bernice Brown about George's death. Floyd Swenson joined the grid search around the car as the last group of firemen wound their hoses back onto the truck. The metal of the car was still hot to the touch. The parking lot was a soupy mess of ash, broken glass, and gravel that crunched and squished under Floyd's feet. As Floyd approached the driver's side of the ruptured vehicle, the stink of burnt flesh reached his nose. Decades of law enforcement hadn't hardened him to that nauseating smell. He shone his aluminum flashlight into the shadows around the driver's seat which had been thrown back by the blast. The charred corpse of George Brown, or what was left of him, was in the back-seat, blown back as if he were reclining. A few glints of white glistened among the blackened interior of the car. Floyd walked over to the group of men who were having a discussion on the edge of the parking lot. Pam saw him approaching. "Chris Halvorson and his boy are going to pick up plywood to cover the broken church windows," she said. "They're driving Emil home. His car is the Chevy next to the burned out wreck."

Floyd nodded, then gestured toward the burned-out car and walked with Pam to the driver's door. "There was a bomb in the engine compartment." He shone the flashlight onto the dash. The pattern of force showed the expansion of gases had pushed the area near the steering column straight out, but the area to the right was pushed toward the passenger door. The engine compartment was bowed out in all directions. "Someone knew what they were doing. They put in just enough explosives to kill him. Amateurs tend to either use too much explosive and pieces of debris get spread over a square mile, or they use too little and there's a puff and bang, but little actual damage. I called the sheriff and asked him to contact the Bureau of Alcohol Tobacco and Firearms. We're going to need some help from the Feds to sort this out.

• • •

It was after midnight when Floyd left the church parking lot. He sat in his idling car and looked at the half dozen missed calls on his phone from Mary Jungers. He decided it was too late to return her calls and turned his cruiser toward his rural Sturgeon Lake home. He was on I-35 when the phone vibrated, signaling an incoming call. As he fumbled the phone, trying to answer, he hoped the call wasn't related to the George Brown case.

"Floyd," Mary said, the concern coming through her voice. "Where have you been? I've been leaving messages for hours and I was about ready to start calling hospitals."

"I've been . . . busy. I didn't see your calls until just a bit ago and it seemed too late to call."

"You always call about ten o'clock when you're on the afternoon shift. I thought something bad had happened."

"Well, something bad did happen," he said.

"And?"

"And it'll be on the morning news."

"That's only five hours from now. You can't tell me now?" she asked.

"Not until the family has been notified."

"Car accident?" she asked.

"Worse. Someone's car blew up," he said. "I really can't say anymore tonight."

Mary sensed the sadness leaking through Floyd's voice. "Was it someone you knew?"

"Not a friend, but an acquaintance. I have to leave it at that for now. Get some sleep. I'll call you in the morning."

"Will you be OK?" she asked.

"I'll be fine."

"I love you," she said tentatively, having not spoken those words before.

The phrase jarred Floyd and he hesitated. Were his butterflies love? He'd loved his wife and before she died he'd felt like they'd been two logs in a fire, feeding off each other's warmth. His feelings for Mary were different. Sometimes they were butterflies, and other times they were longing for Mary's companionship and touch.

"When I say those words, I want to be holding your hand and looking into your eyes," he said. "That's approaching, but I can't say those words for the first time over a cell phone. I hope you understand."

"You just said them, you old romantic," she replied. "Goodnight."

"I suppose I did," he said to himself, setting the phone on the dashboard.

CHAPTER 2

White Bear Lake, Minnesota
Tuesday morning

Tubby Lasoya threw another empty Coke can into the backseat of the car. It rattled as it settled among the other cans and junk-food bags littering the floor. While hunkered down he hid his face with a San Antonio Spurs cap, trying not to let his Hispanic features stand out in the White suburb. He watched people move through the parking lot of the strip mall with their carts of groceries. Ernie Gonzales was asleep in the passenger's seat, leaving Tubby to his lone vigil. The weekday morning activity was slow, the majority of the shoppers being senior citizens who moved in slow motion. None of them noticed a car with Texas license plates and two Hispanic men.

The radio weather forecast said the Twin Cities were experiencing a mild cold front with overnight temperatures in the 50s. Tubby thought to himself that the Minnesota cold was more penetrating than the worst south Texas winter he had ever experienced. Their windbreakers and sweatshirts were inadequate to deal with the cool spring temperatures without running the engine heater two or three times an hour. Tubby hoped the wind and the sound of the cars and trucks passing a quarter mile away on I-35 masked the engine sound.

In the quiet boredom Tubby dug another can of Coke from the back-seat and thought about his family. They had settled near the Mission San Antonio in the late 1700s in what was then northern Mexico.

A woman with gray hair sprouting from under a knit cap walked past, holding hands with a small child. It reminded him of trips to the store with his own grandmother. She used to tell him stories about how the Lasoya family had farmed the land near the San Antonio River. They had raised cattle for 50 years before the Texas independence movement. Tubby's great, great uncle, Toribio Lasoya, had fought alongside the Texans at the Alamo. Tubby's mother had named the small child without a father after the uncle in hopes it would inspire young "Torry" to great things.

He squirmed as he reflected on how cruel the other kids at school had been as "Torry" turned into "Tubby," as he became a chunky adolescent from the poorest part of south San Antonio. Young Tubby had realized quickly that being a Mexican-American descendent of the heroes of the Alamo did very little to provide opportunities in the Anglo dominated world of south central Texas. It was much easier to find jobs hustling drugs and burglarizing businesses than it was to get a job packing groceries at a store. The drug-running business was where he'd met Ernie.

Tubby and Ernie had spent the previous night in a motel a few miles east of I-35. The young girl at the registration desk had mistaken them for Native Americans instead of Mexican Americans. She'd been surprised and suspicious when they had signed in as brothers under the surname Ramirez after eleven o'clock. Ernie hated being identified as an "Indian" even though his heritage was a mixture of Spanish and Incan blood. The people in the South at least recognized the contributions of Mexican Americans to their culture. In the north, the native people were given welfare and treated as third class citizens deserving of nothing except cash grants and pity. Many were willing to wager their Social Security checks at the gaming tables and slot machines of the tribal casinos.

Tubby leaned over and poked Ernie in the ribs as a young woman approached. "Ernie, look at this one."

Ernie rubbed his eyes open and slid down in the seat. They watched a young mother wheel her shopping cart full of groceries to a red minivan. In the seat of the grocery cart was a child dressed in a blue snowsuit which braced him against the 50 degree temperature. The mother was oblivious to them, but the boy watched Tubby and Ernie curiously as the cart bounced across the pavement.

Ernie slid a little lower in his seat as a car passed. "He looks good to me. Blue jacket, it must be a boy, probably less than two. Let's give it a try."

They watched as the mother loaded eight bags of groceries into the rear of the van. She pushed the shopping cart to the side door and strapped the child into a car seat, then pushed the cart across the lot to a cart corral and walked back to the minivan. Tubby started the engine in the nondescript gray Oldsmobile. The car was totally unremarkable except for the lack of rust for a car of its vintage here in the rustbelt.

Tubby watched the van turn across I-35 and then followed a few car lengths back. The morning traffic was sparse so they easily followed the minivan into a residential area. The van turned onto a side street from the two-lane highway and drove past a park. Tubby followed a hundred yards back as it slowed and turned onto another quiet side street with a stop sign at the opposite end of the block. The van eased into a driveway and stopped. Tubby stopped just past the corner where they could see the van in the driveway clearly three houses down.

The mother opened the rear door of the van and carried two bags to the front door. She fumbled with her keys, then unlocked the door and carried her groceries into the house. Ernie looked at his watch then studied the surrounding houses. There was no sign of activity in any of them. In his mind this was a bedroom neighborhood where most mothers and fathers both worked and consigned the children to daycare or school during their working hours.

Ernie and Tubby had gone through the same drill five times that morning. Each of the previous times they had seen a neighbor looking out a window. In one case, a retired man walking a dog had looked at them too closely and they left. This time there was no evidence of any activity in any of the nearby houses.

The woman reappeared from the house. Ernie again looked at his watch. "Two minutes and 10 seconds from going in the door to coming back out. I bet the kitchen's in the back of the house and she has to carry the groceries a long way."

She opened the sliding door of the van to take the child out, and Tubby and Ernie held their breath. Apparently he was asleep and she decided to leave him until the groceries were in the house. She left the side door open and took two more bags out of the rear door of the van. Ernie looked at his watch again.

Ernie asked. "Can you make out the name on the mailbox?"

Tubby lifted a pair of binoculars from the seat and looked. "I think it says 'Martin.' The street name is Campbell."

Tubby punched the name and street into his smart phone and watched the 4G symbol pulsate as the woman walked back out of the house. Ernie lit a cigarette from the stub of the last one. He exhaled a huge cloud of smoke and said, "Only one minute and 20 seconds this time. Dial her now and I'll go as soon as she's out of sight."

The Martin phone number popped up on Tubby's phone and he touched the "Call" icon. The phone started to ring as he started the engine. The woman had two bags of groceries in her arms and was just starting up the steps. They noticed her speed pick up, probably responding to the ringing phone. As she hustled through the door Tubby dropped the car in gear and drove down Campbell Street, then stopped at the end of the Martin's driveway.

The phone line clicked as Mrs. Martin picked up. Ernie was out of the car door and racing toward the open side door of the minivan as Tubby heard a woman's voice say, "Hello."

Tubby put on his best Minnesota accent. "Mrs. Martin?"

"Yes, this is Mrs. Martin."

"Hello, this is Tom Roberts from the Sweepstakes Clearinghouse. Our records indicate you are one of the finalists for our 10 million dollar drawing. We haven't received your last set of entry forms and we just wanted to verify you returned them before the drawing deadline next week."

Tubby looked up to see Ernie lifting the sleeping child from the side of the minivan. He looked around to see if any activity was evident in the nearby houses. He clutched the sleeping child to his chest as he hurried back to the car.

Terri Martin sounded confused. "I don't think I've returned any of them. I think I threw them all away."

Tubby persisted. "Perhaps your husband has been filling them out. We've received all except the last one."

"I doubt that. He lets me handle the junk mail."

Ernie climbed into the car and eased the door shut. The little boy was sleeping soundly with his mouth open and a tiny smile on his face. Tubby took his foot off the brake and accelerated quickly down the block to the stop sign.

"This is very important Mrs. Martin. If you don't return those forms we can't enter you in the final drawing. I suggest you check immediately to see if you still have them. If you do, there is still time for them to get here before the drawing. Will you please check, for your own peace of mind? You are a finalist. This is not a joke." Tubby accelerated around the corner. By the time she started to respond, the gray Olds was driving toward I-35.

"I'm sorry, but I wouldn't even know where to look. I'll think about it and see if there's some place I might have set them aside, but I'm afraid they went with the trash. I don't even remember seeing them recently."

"Okay, but please make a serious effort. I'd hate to see you lose out now that you are in the major prize category." Tubby pushed the *end* button and threw the disposable pre-paid phone out his window as they passed a Goodyear tire store in front of a strip mall.

Terri Martin was a little baffled by the call. She stood staring at the cupboard for a moment trying to remember if she'd even seen anything from Sweepstakes Clearinghouse recently. She recalled hearing their radio ads encouraging everyone to return the forms, but she really could not come up with a memory of having handled them. She shrugged and walked to the back of the van for another load of groceries. She passed on the driver's side, carried another two bags into the house, and was still wrestling with the mystery of the Sweepstakes Clearinghouse when she went back for Tommy. By the time she realized Tommy wasn't in his car seat Tubby and Ernie were nearing "spaghetti junction" where I-94 meets I-35 on the edge of downtown St. Paul. They were ten minutes into a twenty-five-hour drive.

The "911" dispatcher's phone rang and an address on Campbell Street in White Bear Lake flashed on the screen as the dispatcher pressed the button to answer the call. The female caller was hysterical. "Please help me. My baby disappeared from the van in my driveway."

"What's your name?" The dispatcher asked in a carefully modulated voice.

"Terri Martin."

"You live on Campbell Street in White Bear?"

"Yes." Terri found the dispatcher's calm was infuriating. "Please help, my baby's gone."

"I'll contact the White Bear Police in a moment. How long has your child been missing?"

Terri Martin was at the breaking point. "About ten minutes."

The dispatcher hesitated as she typed a message into the computer for the White Bear Lake Police department. "I just sent a message to the White Bear Police dispatcher. They should have an officer at your house in a few minutes. Are you sure the child didn't wander away? Is it possible the child is playing in the yard or at a neighbor's house?"

The floodgates opened and Terri Martin sobbed. "He's only a toddler. He was asleep in his car seat. I left him sleeping while I unloaded groceries. He's been kidnapped!"

Terri Martin set the phone down without waiting for further instructions from the dispatcher and walked to the living room, dialing her husband's work phone number.

"Butch," she sobbed. "Someone took Tommy out of the van. He's gone!"

Butch Martin was stunned. "Have you called the police?"

"Yes. Yes. They're coming. Can you come home?"

"Give me a few minutes to shut down the computer and I'll be on my way."

She stared out the window for a second, and then collapsed onto the couch in tears. What had happened? Why Tommy?

She didn't hear the doorbell. The officer walked in through the open front door. "Ma'am? Are you here?" It was a moot question. He could hear her crying from the front door. He walked up the steps from the landing of the split entry house and walked over to Terri Martin where she was curled up on the couch.

He put a hand on her arm and knelt next to her. "Ma'am, I'm Officer Peltier. Can you tell me what's happened?"

Terri slowly uncurled and sat up on the couch. She was having a hard time stopping the spasms from her crying. Officer

Bob Peltier spotted a box of tissues on the end table and handed it to her. He looked at the living room strewn with children's toys and the normal litter of a busy family. When she finally caught her breath, she looked up. The pretty face was puffy and streaked from the tears. Her strawberry blonde hair was tousled and a few strands near her face were wet with tears.

Bob Peltier sat down next to her on the couch. "Can you tell me what happened?"

"I think so." She sniffed back some tears and wiped at her eyes with the tissue. "I came home from grocery shopping and was unloading groceries from the van. Tommy was sleeping so I left him in his car seat while I carried the groceries upstairs. It's easier when he's sleeping." Her voice rose an octave as she blurted out the last few words. "When I went down to get him the car seat was empty." She immediately broke into tears again and fell against the officer's shoulder, bumping her forehead on his portable radio.

"Are you sure Tommy was in the car seat?" The officer asked as he consoled her. "Is it possible you left him at the grocery store?"

"No!" She shot back. "He's not at the store. I strapped him into the car seat. When I got home, I checked to make sure he was sleeping before I started unloading the groceries."

Officer Peltier pulled out a small spiral notebook and started making notes as Terri Martin sat back up again. There were a few dark tear stains on his blue uniform shirt.

"How old is Tommy?"

"Nineteen months."

"He's old enough to get around by himself?"

"Sure. He walks around."

"Can he release himself from the car seat?"

Terri paused. "No, but I'd released the straps. He was soundly asleep though. It usually takes him a few minutes to wake up and if I'm not there when his eyes open he usually cries."

"How long was he alone?" Officer Martin asked. "Is it possible he woke up and wandered off?"

"Oh no. I was just running in bags of groceries and then I was back out again within a minute or two. He was never there alone for more than two minutes tops."

Suddenly a wave of realization and fear swept over Terri. "I had a phone call from Sweepstakes Clearinghouse. They called to tell me I was a finalist and reminded me to send in my forms. I might have been on the phone for 3 or 4 minutes with them."

Bob Peltier had a terrible sinking feeling. They had been briefed on several child abductions in the Midwest and this fit the profile. A mother distracted by a phone call while a young child disappeared from the yard. He tried to hide his personal fear and anger from her.

"Mrs. Martin. I'm going to call this in to start an Amber Alert. We'll get some officers to canvass the neighborhood. In the meanwhile, please don't touch anything in the van. We'll get some investigators here to check it over. I suggest you call your husband and let him know what's happened. Are any of your neighbors home during the day?"

Terri tried to focus on the question. It took a few seconds for her to answer. "Mrs. Finley lives across the street, two doors over. She's retired. And Mary Park lives on the corner of Third Street. She's home on maternity leave. That's about it."

Bob Peltier called for a sergeant from his radio. He walked to the van and carefully looked around. A child's blue snowsuit was still in car seat. On the floor were a number of pieces of paper, toys, and a couple of Dairy Queen napkins and spoons. On the driveway, next to the open side door, was a cigarette butt, which had burned to the filter without being stepped on. It appeared someone had been in a hurry to dispose of it. The ash on the asphalt indicated very little of it had been smoked before it was dropped. He sniffed the air in the van. No hint of stale cigarettes. His heart sank further.

Peltier heard the crunch of the sand under tires behind him as a second squad pulled up. Sergeant Bill Randall was a 24-year veteran of the White Bear Lake Police and a store-house of White Bear trivia. His family, starting with his great grandparents, had seen the community grow from a quaint village spawned as a resort for St. Paul to a booming suburb.

"What's up?" Randall asked as he approached the minivan.

"A 19-month-old boy disappeared from the child seat in this van. The mother never left him alone except to unload groceries . . . and then she got a call from Sweepstakes Clearinghouse about returning her prize forms. It looks like the parents don't smoke, but here's burned-out cigarettes butt." He pointed to the butt with the toe of his shoe.

The sergeant visually surveyed the interior of the van. "You're thinking about the baby kidnappers?"

Peltier nodded. "It fits. I called in an Amber Alert. I'll go ring some door bells to see if anyone saw anything. We need to get the detectives out here to check the van for prints and evidence. Maybe they can pull DNA off the cigarette butt."

CHAPTER 3

St, Paul, Minnesota

Laurie Lone Eagle's specialty was tracking down missing children for the Minnesota Bureau of Criminal Apprehension (BCA). When she arrived at her office an Amber Alert was flashing on her computer and a blinking light on her phone. She pulled up the Amber Alert information while she listened to the voicemail from Sergeant Bill Randall at the White Bear Lake Police Department asking her to call.

The non-emergency number at the White Bear Police Department rang several times before a female voice answered.

"This is Inspector Lone Eagle from the BCA. I have a message to call Sergeant Randall."

"Just a minute, Inspector. I'll try to reach him."

The line went dead for several seconds. She used that time to read the details of the Amber Alert, "19-month-old white boy, blue eyes and blonde hair, missing from a van outside his White Bear Lake home. Suspected stranger abduction."

The dispatcher's voice came back. "Inspector, please give me your number. He's going to call you from the cellular phone in his squad."

Two minutes later the phone rang on Laurie's desk. "Inspector Lone Eagle."

"Hello Inspector, this is Bill Randall from the White Bear Police. We have a missing child we think has been abducted."

"I just read the Amber Alert, I assume that's your case," Laurie said as she took out a pen and a yellow legal pad. "Go ahead, Sergeant."

He reviewed the details of the abduction and the follow up they had made since he'd left the voicemail. "Our detectives have pulled several sets of fingerprints from the van and are comparing them against the parents and grandparents. We found a cigarette butt in the driveway. It appeared to be fresh, and neither parent smokes. It was unremarkable outside of the fact the smoker liked Marlboros, the most popular brand in the U.S. That narrowed the possible perpetrators down to about 12 million people. Assuming it wasn't the paper delivery person or someone else who just happened by and tossed it in the driveway. It's packaged and we'll have it delivered to your lab for analysis."

The sergeant went on after flipping over a page of notes. "When Officer Peltier canvassed the neighborhood, he didn't find anyone home. He followed up later and spoke with a retired neighbor who'd been visiting a friend at the White Bear Care Center a few blocks away. There's a mother on maternity leave around the corner, but she'd been grabbing a few precious moments of sleep after spending the night up with the new baby who had his days and nights backwards."

Sergeant Randall finished reviewing his notes and closed up his notebook. "Inspector, what's eating all of us is the bulletin you sent out about Midwest child abductions. We don't have many of the details, and I'd hoped you could tell me if this fits the profile. It appears the mother may have been distracted by a phone call while the kid was taken. Because of the timing they must have had her in sight while she was running back and forth with loads of groceries."

"Hang on for a second while I pull something up on my computer," Laurie said as she spun in her chair and typed in a few key words and waited for a directory to come up. She clicked her mouse on an icon and waited for the information to come on the screen.

"We had one abduction in Owatonna, in southern Minnesota, late last summer. A little girl was playing in the backyard sandbox after a trip with Mom to the mall. Mom got a call about winning a local church raffle and when she got off the phone she looked outside and the girl was gone." Laurie leaned back in her chair and blew out a breath. "I'll call around to nearby states. I seem to recall bulletins about several other kids missing the same way. This one appears to be similar to some others I've noticed."

"Thanks Inspector. If you come up with anything, please give me a call."

"You do the same," replied Laurie. "I'm really curious to see if you find any unknown fingerprints. Owatonna found nothing. I'll call them back and ask about a cigarette butt."

Laurie opened a computer file of contacts in other states who either specialized in missing persons or had unbelievable memories. By the end of the day she'd spoken with people in

Wisconsin (one missing girl in Madison), North Dakota (nothing similar, probable non-custodial-parental abduction), South Dakota (one missing boy in Brookings), Nebraska (had nothing similar), Iowa (two missing; A boy from Ames and a girl from Des Moines).

In all the cases the abductions were during the day, in urban or suburban neighborhoods. The mother had been distracted by a phone call while the child was unattended. No fingerprints had ever been found and there was only one report where a neighbor had seen an unusual dark-colored car in the neighborhood, but couldn't describe it because of cataracts. Every neighborhood that experienced an abduction was within a few minutes of a major interstate highway. All the children were white, with about an even split of boys and girls.

Laurie picked up the phone and called the psychologist the BCA used to profile criminals. He was in with a patient, but Laurie made an appointment to see him at three-thirty that afternoon. She decided to update her boss.

CHAPTER 4

PINE COUNTY TUESDAY EVENING

Floyd pulled into his driveway and a small terrier-mix dog came flying out from under the deck. She danced around until Floyd got out of the car, then circled his legs as he bent down to pet her head. Mary Junger's car was parked in his driveway and the lights were on in his kitchen.

Mary owned a flower shop and during the course of an earlier investigation, he'd found her to be funny, with shared interests, and common values. Once the investigation was closed, they'd started meeting for coffee, and over the following months Floyd found that she filled a void that had been haunting him since the death of his wife. They weren't cohabitating, but he'd cleared closet space for some of her clothes. She'd taken over a dresser drawer and had staked out space for herself in the bathroom medicine cabinet. She'd given him a key to her house, but he'd only left a toothbrush there, so far.

He could smell pork chops frying when he reached the door.

"How did you know I'd be home now?" he asked as he hung his uniform jacket on a coat tree behind the door.

"I talked to Jodi, the dispatcher, and asked her to give me a call when you were on your way home," Mary replied as she drained boiling water from a pot of potatoes.

"You know the dispatchers are there to handle emergency calls, not for checking up on the deputies."

"Jodi said it was quiet and we talked for quite awhile," Mary said with a shrug. "She's quite a chatterbox. She and I got caught up on all kinds of news."

"You heard about the explosion at the Pine Brook church."

Mary put a dollop of butter and splash of milk into the potatoes, pulled a potato masher from the drawer and made quick work of the mashed potatoes before scooping them into a bowl. "Jodi didn't have many details, other than they had the fire department out and they asked for the coroner. I assume that was the excitement you couldn't tell me about last night."

Floyd took plates from the cupboard and set the table with silverware. "I guess you know it all," he said.

After putting a fried pork chop on each plate Mary set out a dish of brown gravy, and took two lettuce salads out of the refrigerator. "You're not getting off that easy," she said as she sat down. "I want details."

"Well, we had a body…" Floyd said as he cut his pork chop.

"Whoa!" Mary said, putting up her hands. "You know the rules; no discussions about blood or body fluids."

"There was no blood involved," he replied. "Someone was trapped inside a burning car…"

"Uh uh," Mary said, her hands still up. "I'm declaring another forbidden topic — burned bodies."

Floyd ate silently as Mary waited for him. "What?" he asked.

"I'm waiting for more," she said, pushing lettuce around in the bowl.

"You just forbid anything I can tell you," he said with a smile.

"What caused the fire?"

"Probably a bomb."

"What?" Mary asked, setting down her utensils. "There was a bomb in a car?"

Floyd nodded.

"Where?"

"At the Pine Brook Church. If you'd been at the flower shop you would've heard the windows rattle."

"Who was in the car?"

"I imagine you'll start getting flower orders for George Brown's funeral in a day or two."

"Oh dear," she said. She opened her mouth, but words escaped her. The Pine City/Pine Brook/Hinckley area Chamber of Commerce was a close-knit group of business owners and George Brown had served as the president for a number of years. Mary knew him well. Tears welled in her eyes and she stood up, pulling some tissues from a box on the kitchen counter. Once she composed herself she sat down.

"George was a pillar of the community. Do you think he was the intended target of the bomb?"

"At this point, that's our working theory."

"But why would someone want George dead?" She asked.

"That's the question."

• • •

On I-35 near Duluth, Minnesota Wednesday Morning

At the start of his shift Floyd Swenson was briefed on the Amber Alert from the White Bear Police and a recent burglary in Sturgeon Lake. He listened politely, but his thoughts were consumed by the explosion at the Pine Brook Church. He couldn't discern a motive for the bombing, so he let his mind wander as the mile markers flew past him on I-35. Everyone he, or the deputies, had spoken with had shared their surprise at the vehemence of George Brown's outburst during the church meeting although several mentioned his short fuse, none seemed personally annoyed with him. Most had said he was a pillar of the church and the community. Several expressed admiration for his willingness to stand up to the other deacons on matters of fiscal responsibility, when they agreed with him themselves, but were unwilling to stand up and speak their minds.

I-35 broke over the Proctor hill and the west end of Duluth lay below with a spectacular view of St. Louis Bay and Duluth harbor. It was another cool day in Duluth but the usual spring mist didn't shroud St. Louis Bay. The muddy waters of the river blended to murky greens in the harbor. They stood in stark contrast to the sapphire blue of Lake Superior where it lay beyond the historical Duluth Lift Bridge and Minnesota Point, then spread to the horizon.

Floyd cruised past the huge ore-loading docks along the interstate and took the Superior Avenue exit that led him through the brick streets of the reborn downtown. At a stoplight he looked at a girl and boy walking along the sidewalk. The boy had orange, green, and yellow hair. A huge earring dangled from one ear. The girl had spiked platinum blonde hair and was wearing a studded biker jacket. They looked strangely out of place among the tourists who were making their way to the train museum. The guy gave Floyd's unmarked squad a look of disdain. The girl mouthed the word "pig" at him as they passed. Floyd smiled his best official smile and pulled ahead as the traffic started to move. "Freaks," was the word which came to his mind as he turned up the hill toward St. Luke's hospital. Life was somewhat simpler in a small town where the fringes of society find it hard to find kindred spirits he thought. The downside was that high school kids moved to the Twin Cities to find jobs, or go to college, and most don't return. There weren't a lot of jobs in the small towns of Pine County except the prison, the casino, or in a restaurant. There were always online job openings, but the salaries in mostly rural Pine County lagged the Minnesota average and the unemployment rate was higher than the average.

He found a parking spot near the loading dock on the backside of the hospital and walked through the loading dock to the morgue. Even before he passed through the morgue doors he caught the smell of burned flesh, despite the negative air pressure and air filtration systems in the morgue.

There was a scarred wooden desk in front of the morgue entrance, with a couple of empty vinyl-covered guest chairs, but no one was there. He ignored the sign on the desk that said visitors should ring the bell for assistance and pushed the heavy door into the morgue, following his nose to the autopsy room. Strong odors of antiseptics, death, and charred flesh filled the air. Two people, dressed in green surgical scrubs, face shields and surgical masks, were leaning over a charred corpse lying on a stainless steel table.

Air rushed into the room as Floyd opened and closed the door. Tony Oresek, the St. Louis County medical examiner, looked up to see who had arrived. At six-foot six, Oresek was almost a foot taller than his assistant, Eddie, although they weighed about the same. Oresek once told Floyd he was often so engrossed in the job he would simply forget to eat for a day at a time. Eddie, on the other hand, hadn't missed many meals since his days as a soldier in Viet Nam.

"Hi, Floyd," said Tony. "We were just getting started on your blast victim."

Eddie Paulson looked over his shoulder and gave Floyd a nod before going back to his work, carefully examining the surface of the body through a large lighted magnifying lens articulated on a flexible arm. Eddie's salt and pepper ponytail stuck out from the back of his surgical cap. It was a throwback to Eddie's life before Viet Nam, before his exposure to combat had pushed him over the edge and put him in a Vet's hospital psych ward. Oresek had rescued Eddie to serve as his morgue assistant. It had been a risk, but Eddie had risen to the challenge and slowly put his life back together. They were a perfect pair: Both meticulous to a fault and neither had a life other than the medical examiner's office.

Eddie pushed the magnifying glass aside and started peeling back layers of what appeared to be charred clothing, placing them into a basin next to the body.

"It appears the victim was wearing a polyester shirt," Eddie observed. "It melted onto the skin before burning. Most of it has been consumed in the fire. What's was left had been against the car seat."

Floyd edged to the table and surveyed the grisly form. The skin was charred over the whole body and the face was burned into a grotesque black mask that appeared to be smiling because its lips had burned away. The teeth were exposed, but most looked like they had been broken off near the gum line. Floyd had to look away and take a deep breath of less putrid air.

Eddie noted Floyd's discomfort and suggested, "There's a bottle of 'Vaporub' on the desk. If you put a little on your top lip it overpowers the stink." Floyd backed away and took a large glob of Vaporub on his finger. He liberally applied it to his top lip and wiped the remainder on a tissue.

Oresek was examining the victim's head under the magnifying glass when Floyd came back. "It was one hell of a fire," the medical examiner observed. "The gas tank must have ruptured for the flames to get so hot." He pointed to the mouth. "The pulp in the teeth boiled and shattered the teeth. We won't be able to do a dental comparison for identification unless I can find a bridge or a tooth with a porcelain filling."

Eddie continued with his work on the torso as he explained, "His back and buttocks had less damage because they were protected from the flames by the seat. His wallet was in a back pocket and that's pretty much intact. It had a driver's license, some credit cards, and a fishing license which all said George Brown, with an address in Pine City. There was also a card indicating he had a pacemaker. The pacemaker should be intact and we can pull a serial number and compare it to the manufacturer and hospital records."

Floyd watched the autopsy for the next two hours. Tony opened the chest cavity. "Massive chest trauma: Undoubtedly instantaneous death due to the blast wave from the explosion. I don't know that it'll be a lot of consolation to the family, but the victim died instantly."

Eddie was removing lung tissue and putting it into a plastic cup. He stopped and fished a tiny fragment, the size of a fingernail, from the bloody chest cavity.

"Bingo!" He said and put what looked like a silver watch fob into a stainless steel pan and took it to the sink. After a brief rinse he brought it back to the exam table and showed it to the medical examiner. As they looked through the magnifying lens, Floyd excused himself, knowing the serial number on the pacemaker would provide positive identification that the body was George Brown.

CHAPTER 5

Floyd turned north from Sturgeon Lake and followed the east frontage road of I-35 to Island Lake. He made a slow circuit around the lake, inspecting the driveways leading to the summer cabins while he formulated an investigation plan for George Brown's murder. A starting point would be to interview all the people at the church meeting now that their adrenaline rushes had passed. He made a mental note to check the books at Brown's hardware store to see if there was anyone far in arrears on their account. Another avenue would be to see if George had terminated any employees in the recent past. Occasionally a disgruntled former employee would come back to get revenge. It was more common in the big cities, but even small towns like Pine Brook and Pine City had their share of hotheads, drug users . . . and idiots.

Floyd continued his circuit of Island Lake, checking the driveways of the seasonal cabins for fresh tire tracks. Every spring a rash of cabin burglaries were reported. The burglars mostly took guns, booze, electronics, and outboard motors, which could easily be fenced for cash. Some cabin owners had installed burglar alarms, the more stoic carried everything back and forth with them every weekend and left the door unlocked in an effort to minimize the cost of repairing and replacing doors.

Floyd hoped to catch the burglars in the act someday but there were a thousand cabins spread around the 1,411 square miles of Pine County. Arrests were usually made when someone sold stolen goods to an informant or a pawn shop. Most items were sold to private parties who were happy to get a big-screen TV at a rock bottom price, and weren't too concerned with the provenance.

He saw tire tracks in the soft soil where it was shaded by the balsam firs. He backed up to the driveway.

He announced his location to the dispatcher and pulled into the driveway, slowly rolling down the driveway rutted by the runoff from the melting snow. As he came over a rise the narrow path through the trees opened up and he saw a very large man, and a woman only slightly smaller. He estimated them both to be in their 70s. They were having a heated discussion next to an old Ford pickup. They were close to blows and seemed oblivious to his approach. He put the squad in park and opened the door. When he slammed the door, the two stopped and looked at him as he approached.

"Is there something wrong?" he asked.

They both started talking at once and the volume and intensity of their explanations were apparently related to their credibility, at least in their minds.

"Please, please. One at a time. You first, ma'am." He gestured for the man to be quiet.

She huffed and then went into a tirade. "We drove up here from Eagan, down south of the Cities, to open the cabin. But the brain surgeon here," she pointed to the man with her thumb, "forgot the keys and we can't get in."

The husband was turning red and at the phrase "brain surgeon" started to protest. "I didn't forget the damned keys. I told you to grab them out of the cupboard when I carried the cooler to the car!"

The woman was so mad spittle flew from her mouth as she protested. "You didn't tell me nothin'! You know I always have to pee before we go on a trip and I didn't hear anything from the bathroom." She shook her head and explained, "It's the water pills."

The man gestured wildly with his arms. "What's the matter? Does the water back up and plug your ears?"

Floyd put his hands into the air to stop them. "Enough! If you two calm down a little bit, you can see the locksmith in Moose Lake. Otherwise, you can drive back home and get the keys. But you've got to quit fighting. Okay?"

The two stared at each other and said nothing. Finally Swenson broke the silence. "I have to call my dispatcher. You two decide what you're going to do and let me know when I get back."

He walked to the squad shaking his head. He told the dispatcher he'd be clearing the location shortly. By the time he got back, the husband was still protesting but in a lower tone and with more civility.

"So," Floyd asked, "what's the plan."

The wife looked at Floyd and back at her husband. "We're going to the locksmith, but we can't decide who's going to pay."

Floyd rolled his eyes. "It's going to cost you about ten bucks. Why don't you each put in a five?"

The husband was suddenly resistant. "I ain't putting up five dollars for something that wasn't my fault."

Swenson started to reach for his handcuffs. "Okay. Then I have to take you to jail." At five-eight and weighing about 150 pounds, Floyd was a less than imposing figure, but he projected authority beyond his stature.

The husband's resolve melted when he saw the chrome-plated handcuffs. His voice came out in a whine. "For what?"

Floyd opened one side of the handcuffs, stalling. "Domestic assault."

"She's assaulting me too." He pointed at the woman.

"Yeah, but you're bigger. You could hurt her worse." Swenson was standing with the handcuffs dangling from his right index finger.

The man looked broken. "All right. I'll put up five. But if it's more than that, she pays."

Swenson smiled inside at his winning bluff. "Try the Ace Hardware on old 61 before you get to downtown."

They nodded and started for their pickup. Swenson noted the entire back end of the truck was stuffed with food and bedding. It looked like they were provisioned to stay for a month.

Swenson backed out of the driveway and called the dispatcher to clear from the scene. He waited for the truck to come out of the driveway and he followed them until County Line Road crossed I-35 turning toward Moose Lake.

The domestic spat was a pleasant diversion from George Brown's autopsy. However, it also put into perspective the low threshold some people had before they resorted to physical abuse and assault. Alcohol and drugs lowered that threshold even further. Maybe they'd have to canvass the local bars for several nights to see if anyone had been complaining about how George Brown had treated them. One more thing to add to his "to do" list.

• • •

SAN ANTONIO, TEXAS

Tubby and Ernie had restocked their supplies of junk food and disposable diapers in Kansas and again near Dallas. Now on the outskirts of San Antonio, they were oblivious to the piles of Coke cans, potato chip bags, and fast food wrappers littering the floor of the Olds. On the back-seat sat an open box of Pampers diapers. Dirty diapers and wet wipes lined the interstate highway ditches from Minnesota to Texas. Ernie's job had been to keep the kid quiet and alive until they dropped him in San Antonio. Mostly that involved changing a diaper occasionally and feeding the kid anything that tasted good, then throwing the residue out the car window. They had no concerns about the long-term nutritional content of the sugar and sodium laden food the kid had been happy to stuff into his face. When all else failed, a spoonful of children's Benadryl guaranteed two hundred miles of silence.

They pulled off at the Alamodome exit and worked their way east through a commercial district and then into a neighborhood of blue collar homes, well maintained by the proud

Mexican-Americans who lived there. Neither Ernie nor Tubby had the benefits of that lifestyle. They had been raised by single mothers, aunts, uncles, grandmothers and grandfathers at different times through their lives.

Ernie grew up in tight quarters with extended family members who slept in shifts on mattresses strewn on the floor. The families had no cash to spend on niceties, nor energy for cleaning the transient apartments they occupied. They worked rotating shifts at night on cleaning crews, as cooks and as day laborers. His only peers were tough kids on the streets who belonged to gangs or who were "running errands" for the gangs. He'd been educated in the school of hard knocks where failures, or any signs of weakness, were punished with a beating. He was street-wise and stood up to anyone of any size.

Tubby had the advantage of being raised on the U.S. side of the Rio Grande where he went to school and his family found menial jobs that provided shelter and regular meals. He'd been a shy mediocre student, picked on by the other children, and always last when choosing teams for any sport. Pitting acne added to his junior high school angst. By the time he reached high school he'd become withdrawn and chose solitude over social interaction. He'd never been to a dance, a football game, or on a date. He grew up in front of a television showing an idyllic outside world he'd never experienced.

Ernie's relationship with Tubby was a matter of convenience. Tubby had a driver's license and spoke unaccented English, which allowed them to travel with ease and comfort. Ernie was small, wiry, and ruthless. He was the Yin to Tubby's Yang, the balance that made them successful in a harsh and risky business. They'd watched their friends live large, spend money like drunken sailors, then die young. Neither Tubby, nor Ernie, spoke of long-term plans. Each knew there might not be a tomorrow. One mistake or wrong word could bring the gunshot that would bring their lives to an abrupt end, as both had seen happen to their friends.

They pulled in front of a medium-sized house with slightly better paint than its neighbors. The yards were covered with brown grass, burned by years of drought and watering bans. Some yards had children's toys strewn randomly and each front porch had a few chairs where the residents spent evenings sipping sweet tea or beer.

Tubby picked up the little boy and carried him to the front door. Ernie rang the bell. Both of them were dead tired but buzzing from "speed" and caffeine. With the kid delivered, they would return to their own apartments and crash for two or three days when the speed wore off.

A middle-aged white man, wearing a gaudy Hawaiian-style shirt, answered the door. Half of the shirt buttons were open exposing a mat of graying chest hairs and several gold chains so thick they could be used to tow a truck.

"Ah, boys. Come in. You made a fast trip this time." He took the little boy from Tubby and hoisted him into the air. "What a cute little fellow you are. Your new mommy and daddy will be very happy."

The man walked down a hallway that led to a kitchen. He strapped the little boy in a high chair, opened a cupboard and pulled a white envelope from a shelf. He handed it to Tubby.

"Good job, boys," the man said. "My clients will be very pleased. I'll call you in a day or two. I have another order from one of my clients and you can do some shopping for me. Same arrangement as usual."

Tubby held the top of the envelope open and fanned the stack of bills with his thumb, sure the count was as promised. Ernie looked at the stack of $50 and $100 bills and smiled, exposing chipped and decaying teeth.

"Give us a couple of days to get some rest," Tubby said. "Maybe next week we can go again."

The genial smile left the man's face. "You'll go when I have a customer."

Ernie and Tubby walked to the door without responding and let themselves out. Mr. Applewhite opened the refrigerator freezer, took out a Popsicle, and unwrapped it. The little boy watched in fascination until it was handed to him. The man pulled up the contract list on his smartphone and touched the number he wanted. The call was answered on the second ring

"Hello Mr. Peters. This is Mr. Applewhite, from the adoption agency. I am very pleased to tell you that we have found a lovely little boy for you. We did incur some extra expense making the transaction, but I'm sure you and your wife will be very happy with the total package. Will you be home this evening? I can bring him to you, and we'll sign the adoption papers."

CHAPTER 6

St. Paul BCA Office

Wednesday morning

L aurie Lone Eagle had been reviewing cases on the National Center for Missing and Exploited Children website for hours. She quickly skipped the reports of children over five years old, and used the NCMEC filters to note the cases fitting the pattern of the White Bear Lake abduction. Most kidnapping were abductions by a non-custodial parent. Those abductions, while frustrating and emotional, were usually solved quickly. She was amazed at the lack of evidence accumulated on any of the other kids who were still missing due to apparent stranger abductions. She was making notes when the phone rang, breaking her concentration.

She composed herself, shifted her focus, and picked up the phone before the second ring. "Inspector Lone Eagle."

"Hello, Inspector. This is Bob Randall from the White Bear Lake Police. I have some news for you."

Laurie let out a sigh as she stared at the files she hadn't reviewed yet. "I hope it's good news. I've been going through the NCMEC database, looking for similar kidnappings and any cases that look similar, date back up to two years and are still open. It looks like we're dealing with some real professionals or else some amateurs who are really lucky."

"My people examined the van and picked up a lot of prints. Most were from the parents. I imagine most of the remaining prints are from a grandma or the guys at Rapid Oil Change. I'm running them through the National Crime Information Computer. One unknown print on the door frame appears to be a match with a partial print from the cigarette butt the investigating officer found in the driveway."

Laurie's attitude picked up. "Now we have to hope that the owner of that print is in the NCIC." She paused and ran her hand through her short black hair. "If there is any way I can help, let me know. I spoke with the bureau chief and he told me to run with it. The BCA can bring a lot of resources to bear. I just haven't seen an opportunity to make use of them yet."

Randall was surprised. The BCA investigators were busy with rural investigations and didn't often offer to help a metropolitan department that had their own investigative resources. "I don't know where you could help. But if I come up with any ideas I'll give you a call."

"Give me a call anyway." Laurie suggested. "I might be able to spot a tie-in with one of the cases from outside Minnesota." She paused, then added, "Check with Michelle Post. She's our DNA expert and she has had some success pulling DNA from saliva on the cigarette butts. Maybe we could get a match two ways."

Randall scribbled a note. "I'll give her a call, but the DNA testing takes so long. I hope we have this solved long before we'd get a DNA match."

"Granted." Laurie agreed. "But if you touch her heart, and she starts the test immediately, you might get results in a week. If you just get in line, it will be five or six weeks later. Besides, you'll need the DNA evidence if this crime ever goes to trial. Juries are inundated with television CSI shows and they all expect to see a DNA match as part of the trial evidence."

Laurie had just hung up when the phone rang again. "Inspector Lone Eagle."

"Laurie, your father is very sick. Can you come home?" She recognized her mother's frail voice.

Laurie picked up a pencil and started tapping it on the desktop. Her mother hated talking on the phone so things had to be dire. "What's the matter, Mom?"

"The doctor in Cloquet says he isn't sure. He wants to send Dad to Duluth to have some tests done by a specialist there." By the tone of her voice, Laurie could tell her mother was very unhappy with the doctor's plan.

"What kind of symptoms does he have?"

"He can't keep food in his stomach." Laurie's mother explained. "It's been getting worse. He used to be able to eat a little bit and then rest and eat a little more. Now he can't even drink and keep it down."

Laurie set the pencil aside and stared at the pages of notes she'd taken while reviewing the NCMEC database and let out a sigh. "I'll talk to the director and make arrangements to work remotely. I'll be home tonight."

After Laurie hung up, she had a sinking feeling. Her family was very close, including aunts, uncles, and cousins. It was a cultural matter when illness arose in the family. Relatives would come from across the nation and long vigils would be held for the very ill and dying.

It was difficult for her co-workers to understand that it was mandatory to pack up and be with sick extended family members. Her friends and associates believed in medical doctors and prescription medicines. They found it odd when she talked about relatives packing up to spend a two or three month vigil with an ill relative. Most employers weren't sensitive to the Native American culture, and as a result, careers had been cut short to fulfill the cultural family requirements. Laurie lived in both worlds and respected modern medicine, but she felt the strong bonds of family and the need to be with her mother and father in this crisis. She also felt a strong bond to her job with the BCA and she wasn't about to let her family interfere with her commitment to investigate child abductions.

She packed her notes and files into a backpack and removed her HP laptop from the docking station. "What a jump between centuries," she said to herself, "taking a laptop computer to a healing vigil."

● ● ●

STURGEON LAKE, MINNESOTA

When Floyd Swenson called in, the dispatcher passed along a message from the sheriff requesting a three-thirty meeting. After accepting, he took a leisurely drive around the back roads of the county, arriving at the Pine City Courthouse five minutes early. The sheriff's car was in his reserved spot, and Floyd found an open spot next to the first floor entrance to the law enforcement offices in the courthouse.

The Pine County Courthouse was a stark concrete building on the northern outskirts of Pine City. The upper levels housed the courts and county offices, and the lower level, facing I-35, contained the county jail and the sheriff's department. A large garage door marked "Sally Port," used for secure loading and unloading prisoners, faced the lower parking lot where half a dozen patrol cars were parked.

He waved to the dispatcher, who electronically released the security latch for him, and he went to the ready room to get a cup of coffee. He needed a caffeine infusion to prepare himself for the meeting with the sheriff.

Pam Ryan was sitting at a computer in the back corner of the ready room. When Floyd stepped into the room, she looked up and stretched. Floyd had been amazed she had been with the department for nearly three years and had performed her duties admirably in some very threatening situations. The male deputies sometimes had physical confrontations during arrests, but Pam had managed to defuse nearly all tense situations with her calm demeanor. She had been especially effective in domestic situations where several male deputies had suffered minor injuries trying to break up fights between spouses or partners. Pam had often stepped between the combatants and the fight ended.

Floyd poured himself a cup of coffee. "Did you check the bars to see if anyone had been mouthing off about George Brown?" he asked.

Pam pointed to the computer terminal on the desk. "I was just writing a report. I stopped off at the Pine Brook Inn, both bars in Pine City, and the Beroun bar. The bartenders hadn't heard anything and the few patrons I spoke with didn't offer anything either. I left my business card with all the bartenders and asked them to call if anything came up."

Floyd smiled. "How many guys hit on you as you made the rounds?"

A slight blush crossed Pam's face. "Two guys asked me to come back to the Pine Brook Inn when I got through with my shift. I told them the bar had better be closed by the time I got off or I'd arrest the bartender. That seemed to end the discussion."

"Touché!" Floyd held up his cup in a salute. "What's up for tonight?"

Pam shrugged. "The usual. A couple of court papers to serve. Hours of mind-numbing boredom maybe interspersed with a high-speed chase. Maybe a domestic." Pam considered the last comment. "Probably not a domestic on a Wednesday night. They seem to occur more on the weekends when one or both of the partners are drunk or high."

Floyd looked at the clock and realized he was late for his meeting with the sheriff. "I've got to run.

"If it's quiet," Pam said, "I'll stop at the bars in Duquette, Cloverton, and Duxbury, then check back with the first bars to see if the clientele changed."

The smell of cigar smoke lingered as Floyd neared the sheriff's office. Officially, there was no smoking in all public buildings. However, the sheriff loved his cigars and often closed his door to smoke in the privacy of his office. Who was going to tell him to stop?

Sheriff John Sepanen was reviewing budget information in preparation for a meeting with the county commissioners. He was stocky, with a booming bass voice. He was wearing what he referred to as his unofficial uniform — a golf shirt with an embroidered gold badge and khaki pants. His dark hair was liberally doused with gel that made his pate look perpetually wet. When Swenson knocked the sheriff waved him in.

"Floyd, come on in." The sheriff rounded the desk and gave Swenson a hearty handshake. Floyd was surprised, because he usually got a head nod at best. Of course, this was an election year and Floyd was a Pine County voter.

The sheriff directed Floyd to a guest chair, then walked to the door and closed it. That too was unusual. In a culture of open meetings with public accolades and private reprimands, a closed door usually meant something bad. The sheriff smiled. It was strange.

"Floyd. I want you to direct 100% of your efforts into the George Brown murder case. I've had calls with offers of assistance from the BCA, FBI, and ATF. I told them we appreciate their offers but we will lead the investigation ourselves."

"What? Why? They have lots of people to throw into this to get this case solved quickly. We need the ATF to track down the source of the explosives. The FBI has interstate connections. We could use the BCA to scour Minnesota for the source of the explosives and to check through hundreds of files for known bombers. All I can do is canvass the neighborhood again to see if anyone saw a person putting a bomb into

George's car." He added, "And we've done that twice since the bombing."

"Calm down. I said we would lead the investigation, not handle it alone." The sheriff rolled back in his chair and rubbed his chin. He had a sly expression on his face as he moved the unlit cigar from the left corner of his mouth to the right. "Do you want the official or unofficial reason first?"

Swenson raised his eyebrows. "Official."

The sheriff rolled forward and rested his forearms on the desktop. "You're the senior deputy in Pine County. You were the senior deputy on the scene and you have experience dealing with the FBI and the BCA. All of those are necessary assets for this investigation."

"What's the unofficial reason?"

The sheriff leaned back and stared into Swenson eyes. "I need to have your word nothing said in this office today ever leaves. Not to the deputies. Not to your Mary. Not to a living soul. I promise that everything I say will be perfectly legal and moral . . . in a political sense."

Swenson shook his head with annoyance. "You're the sheriff. If that's the way you want it, then that's the way it is."

The sheriff glowed. "The election is coming up in a matter of days and it would be a big feather in the department's cap if we solved George's murder."

Swenson's head was spinning. "Well, that's great *if* we solve the case. If we run this and fail, we'll look like a bunch of idiots." Floyd paused and closed his eyes, searching for the right words. "What if you're not re-elected? My job isn't worth a plug nickel if we botch an investigation because we didn't fully utilize the resources available to us. The FBI likes to be the lead agency and I think they'll be reluctant to take direction from me." Floyd paused when he saw the sheriff smile. "It's the retirement thing again, isn't it?"

"You're still a civil service employee, Floyd. You can't be fired, but you can retire if this goes south on us." The sheriff paused and considered his next words carefully. "Besides, I think this is going to be an open and shut case. If we let the Feds or BCA lead, they'll use all of our evidence, share nothing, and claim credit for everything. If it turns out to be tougher than I think, I'll call them back and eat crow. I'll say we didn't have enough reach beyond the county to properly execute the investigation."

"Reading between the lines, 'tougher than we thought,' means we didn't solve it before the election."

Sepanen replied with a shrug.

"We're already past 48 hours since the explosion," he said acknowledging that most murders are solved in the first 48 hours or they go unsolved.

The sheriff nodded. "Most murders are committed by spouses or someone very close to the deceased. I don't see that here. Do you?"

Floyd shook his head and stood. "No." He took a deep breath and let it out. "I suppose if the investigation goes too badly it would be expedient to have a lead investigator who could be the scapegoat and retire." Swenson walked out of the office without waiting for the answer.

CHAPTER 7

Sandstone, Minnesota

Floyd Swenson asked the dispatcher to have Pam Ryan meet him for supper at Amy's Country Café in downtown Sandstone. He parked, then found a booth overlooking the street. At first, the weekday evening traffic consisted of a few people going home from work. A sudden stream of newer pickups signaled the shift change at the Sandstone Federal Prison, one of the few employers in Pine County paying middle-class wages and offering benefits.

Sanford "Sandy" Maki, a newlywed deputy, walked in the front door and spotted Floyd. At twenty-nine, only Pam Ryan was younger and less senior. Sandy had dark hair from his Finnish relatives and stayed trim regardless of his diet. As he slid into the booth Floyd asked, "Anything new with the explosion investigation?"

A minute later, Pam Ryan walked into the restaurant and sat next to Sandy. At five-foot five-inches, Pam was the smallest deputy and the youngest. She moved to Pine County from

Southwestern Minnesota and embraced the woods and lakes over the open farm fields of her parents' prairie home. She wore her blonde hair short and had endured all types of dumb blonde jokes while routinely refuting the blonde stereotype through her actions.

"Pine Brook is crawling with Feds," Sandy said. "They've been at Ben's garage with the BATF team looking at the car, they're searching around the church's lawn on hands and knees with magnifying glasses, and they're screaming at the sheriff for letting the medical examiner move the corpse before they had a chance to view it in-situ. Now, they're demanding that the Medical Examiner release the body to them."

Pam's face cracked a smile. "I'll bet Tony Oresek is holding his own. He has enough presence to deal with J. Edgar Hoover himself," she said, referring to the medical examiner in Duluth.

"Yeah," Floyd agreed. "Doctor Oresek will put them in their place."

The waitress came with glasses of water and took their drink orders.

When she was out of earshot Sandy said, "The Sheriff had a press conference and he spoke of all the help we were going to get before the Feds showed up. Now he's getting jerked around with the Feds telling him how to run the investigation or telling him they're running the investigation and he should just step back. BATF wants him to turn over all the evidence we've recovered from the scene of the explosion. The courthouse phones are ringing off the hooks with media people who want exclusive interviews. The sheriff, who usually revels in the media attention, is ducking and running for cover most of the time because he doesn't have anything new to tell them."

The waitress returned with three cups of coffee and a small bowl holding individual coffee creamers. "Are you ready to order now?" she asked.

They each made a dinner selection from the specials posted near the kitchen. When the waitress left they went on with the discussion.

"The sheriff asked the Bureau of Criminal Apprehension for investigative help," Sandy said as he poured a tiny cup of French vanilla creamer in his coffee. "He hopes they will prevent the rest of the Feds from walking all over us or shipping the blast evidence to Washington D.C."

"That ought to be interesting," Pam said with a smile. "I hear the BATF and the BCA are fighting to see who gets to test the car for blast residue. Last I heard, the ATF was shipping the car hood to Washington D.C. and the BCA was planning to tow the burned-out car chassis to their lab in St. Paul. I hope they get the same answer."

Their dinners came and Sandy and Floyd dove into the fried chicken they had both chosen over the meat loaf special. Pam had opted for a chef's salad, without the hard-boiled egg.

"I watched the Brown autopsy this afternoon." Floyd said as he dove into his dinner. "They should have a positive I.D. on George Brown this afternoon."

Pam looked surprised, stopping a forkful of salad halfway to her mouth. "How?"

"The victim had a pacemaker and they can trace the serial number. The M.E. also pulled fragments of an electronic circuit board from George's chest. He thinks the FBI or BATF should be able to trace the detonator source and buyer of the materials. That should get us close to the murderer."

Sandy's facial expression showed he was impressed. He wiped gravy from his chin, catching it before it ran onto his uniform shirt, then said, "We sure haven't been able to come up with anything by canvassing the neighborhood. No one saw anything. No one heard anything. And, there isn't a soul who would kill George, with the possible exception of the deacons at the church last night."

"It seems odd for someone to get killed over the church budget," Pam said. "Doesn't it?"

Floyd put up his hands defensively. "I'm just repeating what I was told. More people have been killed in the name of religion than any other cause. Look at the Crusades."

Pam shrugged. "I talked to all the deacons last night and they seem like a pretty mellow bunch. They told me their church accepts everyone with open arms, unlike some churches where it's my way or the highway."

"When Barb and I decided to get married," Sandy said, "I talked with a minister in Pine City. There was no way he would even consider marrying us until we'd shown him baptism certificates, joined his church, and attended for a year. We decided to be married by a judge."

They finished their meals and paid the bills.

As they stood at the cash register Floyd said to Pam. "I had a thought on the way here. Check with the bars close to Pine Brook again and see if anyone overheard someone complaining about George Brown. Maybe the clientele will have changed since the last time you were around."

Pam nodded. "I don't think there's a lot of overlap between the church deacons and the bar crowd, but chatting up the Pine Brook Inn bartender beats driving around on a quiet shift, waiting for something to happen."

Floyd checked in with the dispatcher and drove back to his hidden spot on highway 70. Maybe tonight would be the night he'd catch Ronny Benson.

● ● ●

After reading the Cabela's spring catalog for 20 minutes, Floyd saw headlights approaching. Several cars had gone by earlier. None had been Ronny Benson and none had been excessively over the speed limit. Benson's car sped into view and continued west. Swenson set the catalog aside and shifted into "Drive." By the time he got onto the road, Ronny's car was out of sight. He accelerated hard, squealing the tires, and then turning on the red and blue flashing lights.

As Swenson rounded a curve he saw the taillights of Benson's car disappear further ahead. Swenson was still accelerating and was up to 95 miles an hour when he reached the point he'd last seen the car. Benson didn't even realize he was being chased.

The car slowed to turn onto a side road. Floyd sounded a single "whoop" of the siren. The brake lights came on and Benson made a right turn onto the smaller road. Floyd swung wide, then slowed through the turn. Benson turned into a driveway leading to an old farmhouse. Beyond the house were a fallen down barn and some out buildings badly in need of paint. Floyd turned off the flashers and followed Benson's car into the barnyard and parked, blocking Ronny's car.

Ronny looked disgusted. "Floyd. I didn't see you until I turned the corner. Was I speeding?"

Swenson smiled. No one ever admitted to speeding. "You were speeding and failed to signal two turns. However, that's not why I'm here. I have a warrant for your arrest."

Ronny's face turned pale. "My arrest? For what?"

A young woman appeared at the farmhouse door. She was supporting a baby on her hip. The woman's T-shirt was ragged and her jeans worn through. Her brown hair was tied back in a ponytail. Her appearance matched the general state of the farm buildings.

"Judge Johnson issued an arrest warrant for contempt after your ex-wife's attorney filed papers for non-payment of child support."

Ronny shook his head in disbelief. "Geez. That old fart just doesn't get it. My ex left me and packed the kids off. I used to work for my father-in-law, but he fired me when we split. I've been cutting pulpwood and doing odd jobs to buy groceries. I moved in with Polly but I don't pay her any rent because there isn't any money for it. Getting child support out of me is like trying to get blood out of a rutabaga." Benson threw his hands up in disgust.

"Sorry Ronny, I just serve the warrants and make the arrests. You'll get a chance to explain it all to the judge." Floyd didn't say what he knew: old Judge Johnson was a sucker for a tear-filled female eye. Ronny wouldn't have a chance when his ex-wife started to cry.

"Turn around and lean on the car while I frisk you." Swenson patted him down and put the handcuffs on Ronny's wrists. They walked to the back-seat of the squad and Swenson eased him into the seat and closed the door.

The young woman walked across the yard. "I heard what you said. Is Ronny in big trouble?"

"Not if he can come up with some back child support payments." Swenson looked at the woman. She was possibly in her late teens. Her cheeks were hollow and the clothes hung on her frame. It appeared she had missed a few meals lately. His concern moved quickly to the baby in the girl's arms.

The baby seemed chubby and content. Its face was round and clean. The baby's clothes were clean and looked like they were adequate, although well-worn. He guessed they'd come from a rummage sale.

"Will Ronny be back tonight?" the girl asked. "We were going grocery shopping. He delivered some wood to the mill today and got paid."

Swenson's heart sank. "Do you drive?"

The young mother nodded her head. "But I don't own a car."

Swenson walked to the back of the squad and opened the door. He squatted down. Eye to eye, he spoke to Ronny in a whisper. "She says you were going to buy groceries tonight."

Ronny nodded. "I was, but I didn't get to the store yet."

"Are there any groceries in the house now?"

Ronny blew out a breath. "Probably not anything but formula for the baby. We make sure she gets what she needs, but Polly and I go a little lean sometimes."

Swenson shook his head and leaned close to Ronny. "You're going to stand up, and she's going to kiss you good-bye while I look away. Make sure she gets the car keys and money out of your pocket. If anyone asks, I didn't get here until after you gave her the money, or we'll both be in deep shit."

Swenson motioned the young mother to the squad car. "Ronny wants to kiss you goodbye." He turned away from the car and stared at the dilapidated barn for a moment.

"Thanks deputy." Ten seconds later Swenson turned and looked at the young mother. In the arm supporting the baby, she clutched cash and car keys.

Floyd walked over to the woman and touched the baby's nose with the tip of his finger. He got a big smile in return. "You have keys for Ronny's car?"

The girl nodded. "I'll drive into town to get groceries."

"Do you have a social worker?" he asked.

She shook her head.

"I'll have someone come out and talk to you. They may be able to help you stretch those grocery dollars."

The woman shook her head emphatically. "Thanks, but I don't beg money off the county. I wasn't raised to take charity."

Swenson smiled. "When was the last time you had the baby to a doctor?"

The young mother looked at the baby. "When she was born, about 8 months ago. I'm paying on the bill."

Floyd grimaced internally. "She needs to get vaccinated, have hearing tests and other stuff I don't even know about. Please talk to the social worker. Just to help you until you get on your feet."

Polly shrugged. "I guess we can talk."

Swenson smiled and made a note in his notebook after he got back to the squad. Then he drove Ronny Benson to the Pine County jail and booked him. At least Ronny would get a meal, even if it was jail food.

After the booking he left a voicemail for social services and drove to the Pine Brook Free Church to see how the repairs were progressing. Much to his surprise, the lights were on and a number of cars were in the parking lot. Two men were busily re-glazing the windows on the parking lot side of the church while a teenaged boy watched. Swenson recognized Emil Peterson. The younger man looked familiar but his name escaped him.

The teenager looked up and smiled. "Deputy Swenson, I'm Andy Peterson. I was in one of the drug awareness programs you did when I was in grade school." The boy walked over and shook Floyd's hand. Over the years Floyd learned that most of the kids were pleased to see the law enforcement officers who came to the schools and they formed a bond which stuck for many years.

"Hi Andy. You helping out?"

The older two men looked up and stopped their efforts at smoothing the glazing compound, edging the last repaired window.

"I'm supposed to be learning, 'cause I'm going to Mexico to help build a church when school is out this summer. But Art and Dad won't let me do much except watch and lift heavy stuff. I don't know how they expect me to get good if I can't do any of the work."

The first responder from the night of the explosion waved a gauze-wrapped hand. "I'm Art Richardson. We met in the parking lot the other night. Andy wants to do everything, but the deacons aren't very receptive to having the youth practice their skills on this building. It's okay for them to build a church in Mexico though," Art joked.

Floyd looked at the gauze covering Art's hands. "How bad were the burns?"

Art gave a weak smile. "You know, after the adrenaline wore off, they hurt like hell. The doctor in the emergency room put some goop on them and the pain stopped right away. I guess I should've known better than to try to reach through the flames. I was pretty sure George was dead anyway. Luckily, they're just second-degree burns and they'll heal over time."

Swenson turned to Emil Peterson. "You're letting Andy go to Mexico? Who are you going to hire to help around the farm?"

Emil laughed. "You notice he's not going until school is done, in June. That's after all my planting is done and before we start haying. We've got other groups going every few weeks until then. I figure the timing will be just about right for Andy to be glazing windows in Mexico because the construction should just about be complete."

"Sounds like you folks have taken on quite a project."

Emil smiled. "I'm really proud of the congregation. We found a community in Mexico who wanted a church and was willing to embrace us. The congregation here has pitched in with time and money to make this happen. Going to Mexico has been a real revelation for us and a lot of closed wallets have opened up when they see the poverty there and the faces of the people in the town as the building has gone up."

Art was just about bursting to jump in. "And it has really revitalized the congregation. Sunday attendance is up and collections have gone through the roof. We've got more money coming in than we've ever seen before."

Floyd said, "I heard that was part of the argument at the meeting the other night. George Brown didn't like the way the money was being spent."

The three workers turned very somber. Emil spoke up. "George wasn't much of a visionary. He liked things the way they've been and was pretty uncomfortable with a lot of the new things we've been doing."

"Sometimes change is hard for people. I'll let you get back to work." Floyd waved and walked back to the squad. He sat and thought about Emil's comments.

"I wonder what else made George Brown uncomfortable?" Floyd asked himself.

CHAPTER 8

SAN MIGUEL, MEXICO

Tom Knight, the associate pastor of the Pine Brook Free Church, and Judy Arendt, a parent, were the chaperones for the church group's trip to San Miguel. The drive to Mexico in the church's van had been exhausting, with Tom doing most of the driving. The old van held together without a major problem. They had arrived in San Miguel on Monday afternoon, tired and ready to be out of the van.

The group spent their first day checking out the partially enclosed structure that would soon be the church, and setting up a primitive camping arrangement on the packed dirt floor inside the church walls. The boys and Tom Knight slept in a small office off the side of the sanctuary. They covered the door opening with a small tarp. The six girls and Judy Arendt rolled out their sleeping bags in what would eventually be the sanctuary. By Tuesday, they had managed to put rafters over half the sanctuary and covered them with rough-sawn boards. They stapled tarpaper over the boards making the structure weathertight. The night was windless and the interior so hot no one fell asleep in the stillness and stifling humidity. Minnesota had heat and humidity, but the evenings usually cooled off. The Mexican adobe walls and packed clay held the heat like an oven all night long.

As a treat, Wednesday evening, Tom had the group put on their bathing suits and he drove them to a small pool in a nearby stream. They brought bars of soap and bottles of shampoo, and had a wonderful time frothing the water with their soap, while getting their first "bath" since leaving the church in Oklahoma where they'd spent one night on the trip down. The teens slept like babies that night, having spent all their energy on the roof project, then cooling off by splashing in the stream.

● ● ●

San Antonio, Texas

Tubby Lasoya's one-bedroom apartment was a mix of high-priced electronics, cheap furniture, and clutter. It smelled of spilled beer and dirty laundry with a hint of taco seasoning for background. Tubby was parked in his favorite recliner in front of the 96-inch plasma television. When the phone rang he was watching *Lethal Weapon 2* on-demand, waiting for the toilet to blow up under Danny Glover.

Tubby swore briefly as he reached for the phone. "Yeah."

"Tubby, this is Applewhite. I have another package for you and Ernesto to pick up. It'll be ready Saturday. Can you handle it?"

Tubby punched the "mute" button on the remote control. "Already? We just got home." Danny Glover was pleading with Mel Gibson as Glover sat on a toilet filled with explosives rigged to blow when Glover stood up.

"I know it's quick, but I've got waiting customers. Everything will be exactly the same. After the San Antonio pick-up, you'll make a road trip to make the delivery. Then I'll need you to pick up another adoption candidate on the return trip. A girl this time."

Danny Glover's bathroom window exploded as he and Mel Gibson were propelled into the bathtub. The special effects were mediocre compared to watching George Brown's car explode from a block away. Tubby stopped the DVD again, trying to talk seriously with his employer.

"Listen, we've been lucky the last two trips. No problems with the deliveries, but I'd rather lie low on the adoption stuff for a while. It makes me nervous. I definitely don't want to hit any of the same towns again for a long time. Ernie and I stick out too much up North. Somebody is going to notice us and put it all together."

"Don't worry," Applewhite said, trying to ease Tubby's anxiety. "I've got an idea for a new town. Big city, but not too big. A couple Indian reservations nearby so you guys will blend in. It'll let you boys see some more country."

Tubby cringed. "People don't call them Indians anymore. The correct term is Natives or Native Americans."

"What's your point?" Applewhite asked.

"I'll talk to Ernie. Call back in a couple of days."

● ● ●

PINE CITY, MINNESOTA

Floyd Swenson stopped at the dispatcher's cube on the way out of the door. "I'm out of service for the rest of the evening." He drove to his home past downtown Sturgeon Lake.

Mary Jungers, Floyd's lady friend, dressed in a long sweat-shirt that covered her hips, which she felt were a little too wide, was warming leftover meatloaf for dinner when she heard tires on the gravel driveway and looked out the kitchen window. She was concerned when she saw the squad in the driveway. She knew Floyd hardly ever came home during a shift unless he was sick or unless something very bad had happened.

She wiped her hands on a dish towel and opened the kitchen door to meet him. Thinking back to a night just after they'd met when Floyd had been called to a fatal accident. He'd come to her house late at night badly shaken.

A drunk had fallen asleep behind the wheel and veered into an oncoming vehicle. The young couple he hit head-on were driving home from the prom in the boy's recently re-stored 1953 Ford pickup. The boy had been impaled on the steering wheel and was dead before Floyd arrived. He helped the firemen extract the girl from the truck but her injuries were too severe and cutting through the wreckage took too long. Floyd had to tell both sets of parents their children were dead. The girl would have been the class valedictorian. The boy was a track star and had a full scholarship to the University of Wisconsin-Superior. The drunk spent one night in the hospital and, on the advice of his lawyer, pled guilty to vehicular homi-cide in exchange for a six month sentence in the county jail. As he was being led from the courtroom, he asked his lawyer how he could be held responsible for something he couldn't even remember. The years of similar experiences had left Floyd cyn-ical and bitter about lawyers and the courts.

Floyd was walking down the sidewalk with the same look he'd had after the drunk had been sentenced. He ignored Penny, who was circling his legs, and walked to the house with purpose. He walked in the door, pecked Mary's cheek and went to the refrigerator. He pulled out a Michelob, unscrewed the cap, and carried it to his chair. Penny circled his chair, then curled up next to his feet.

After a long drink of beer and a deep breath he asked, "Would you like to go out for supper?"

She was surprised. "I can feed the meatloaf to the dog. What's the occasion?"

"I'm off early. Isn't that enough of an occasion?" He finished off the beer with a second long swallow and went into the bedroom to change clothes.

The May opening of the walleye fishing season rejuvenated the tourist trade and the roads were crowded with vehicles towing boat trailers. They drove in silence to a small resort on Hanging Horn Lake, which had been a music camp until the 1960s. The sunset faded into twilight as they wound down the long driveway past a chapel and old cabins. A few people were standing around the parking lot, sipping beer, and watching a man fillet walleyes. The parking lot had one open spot on this weeknight. It was the beginning of the Minnesota tourist invasion. The smell of cedar and grilled steak and the hum of laughter greeted them as they opened the door. Robin, the owner, met them at the door. Her face was always cherubic.

"Floyd and Mary, it's nice to see you. We're packed tonight." Robin said, gesturing toward the mass of busy tables with a nod of her head.

Robin led them to the one empty booth near the bar and gave them menus. They sat under a British Union Jack. Floyd ordered a Double Diamond Ale and Mary an Amaretto sour.

They looked over the menu of American steaks and British pub selections.

Robin brought their drinks and pulled out an order pad. "So, what'll it be?" she asked with her pen poised over the pad.

Mary looked over the top of the menu at the bar. "Is it always this busy during the week?"

Robin smiled. "We don't carry much staff during the off-season. I take orders and Lou cooks. But when the summer folks show up, we're packed every night, with a waiting line on the weekends."

Mary nodded and handed the menu to Robin. "I'll have the shepherd's pie," she said, trying to make herself heard over the cacophony.

Floyd's gaze seemed fixed on the boar's head mounted on the wall. Mary turned to see what held his attention. The wild boar's head went through seasonal costumes. The patrons who changed the decorations hadn't been back since Valentine's Day, so the pig was in a pink bonnet with heart shaped sunglasses.

Floyd handed his menu to Robin. "I'll have the rib eye with hash browns and onion soup."

Robin made notes. "Medium rare?"

Floyd nodded and Robin was gone. He looked up, staring at the pig. "Last year they had the pig in shamrocks for St. Patrick's Day. They must be slacking off. We're months past Valentine's Day."

Floyd took a sip of the semisweet ale, stared at Mary and thought she had aged gracefully. Mary's face had crow's feet that crinkled in the corners of her eyes when she smiled, but she had the same pretty features as the picture she's shown him in her high school yearbook. He had no regrets about the three decades he'd been married to Ginny, whose bout with cancer had left him a widower, but he felt truly blessed he'd met Mary. He smiled to himself as he stared at this woman who said she loved him. Sometimes he found it scary that she read his thoughts almost better than he did. She knew the right questions, and too often knew his answers before he did.

Mary looked at his silent stare with concern. "There's something eating you, isn't there?"

"There's no mystery there." Floyd stared into the dark ale. "I come stomping home when I'm supposed to be working. Then I drag you out for supper without giving a word of explanation."

"Did something happen at the courthouse?" Mary asked.

Floyd pondered his answer for a few seconds. "The sheriff wants me to catch the person who bombed George Brown's car."

Mary looked at him quizzically. "That's your job."

Floyd looked into her eyes. "He told me to lead the investigation. He doesn't want the Feds to take it over and cut us out."

Mary leaned close across the table. "Do you have a suspect?"

Floyd took a deep breath. "No suspects. No leads. Just the sheriff's great faith I will be able to solve the crime."

Mary reached across the table and put her left hand on his left. "Why would he do that? It seems so . . ."

Floyd gave a snorting laugh. "Because it's an election year and he doesn't want us to be an also-ran when the Feds call a news conference to announce that *they* solved the crime. He wants me to solve it so he looks good to the voters."

They stopped talking as Robin delivered two bowls of French onion soup, saying, "Mary didn't order any soup, but I didn't want Floyd to eat alone." She set the bowls on the table and straightened up. "Looks like your drinks are fine. I'll see if Lou has taken the bread out of the oven yet. Enjoy!"

Mary pushed the soup aside and wrinkled her nose. "I don't care much for onions," she said. Then she leaned across the table again. "I suppose you should be flattered that the sheriff has such faith in you."

Floyd scooped up soup and watched the cheese string down from the spoon. He held it up, letting it cool. "It's not flattery. It's plain stupidity. Sepanen should grab every re-source he can get his hands on to solve this crime. We're a dinky department. We can't bring nearly the resources a couple of agencies like the BCA and FBI could offer. It's stu-pid to leave me chasing this by myself when more bodies might break it sooner." He set the spoon back into the soup and stirred. "I can't even talk about it anymore. How was your day?"

Floyd took another spoonful of soup into his mouth with-out letting it cool. He quickly swilled a quarter of his beer, try-ing to quench the burning on his tongue.

Mary watched with amusement. "I got eight flower orders for George Brown's funeral and Heather Reynolds came in to choose flowers for her wedding."

Floyd felt embarrassed he had taken center stage with his job concerns over her flower shop business.

Mary pulled the soup bowl back and peeled the melted cheese off with her spoon. "Robbie Peterson is almost done with the shelving in the gift area. I have a few people who stop by every week to see the progress and I think remodeling the flower shop will bring a significant increase in business if I have a grand re-opening party.

Floyd nodded. "It must be terrible being an optimist hanging around with a pessimist."

Mary just shook her head. "George Brown's obituary was in the newspaper today. The visitation is tomorrow night at Johnson's Funeral Home with the funeral Friday at the Pine Brook Free Church.

Floyd nodded. "I suppose I'll have to go to both."

The kitchen door opened and Robyn brought out the steaming shepherd's pie and a sizzling steak. "Be careful," she said. "The plates are really hot."

CHAPTER 9

Floyd Swenson was sitting at his desk reading Pam Ryan's reports when he heard Sheriff Sepanen's bass voice greeting the dispatcher from fifty feet down the hallway. Floyd finished Pam's notes, walked down the hall to the sheriff's office and knocked on the door frame.

"Come on in," The sheriff had a smile which looked like he already knew Floyd would agree to lead the bombing investigation.

"I thought about your suggestion last night." Floyd closed the sheriff's door and stayed standing. "I'd like to clarify a couple of things before I take on the entire investigation."

Sepanen leaned back, taking a sip from his SuperAmerica disposable cup. "Fair enough."

"This investigation may be big. I would like to be able to pull in a couple of deputies to do legwork. At least for a week."

"Sure. I'll authorize the overtime to cover their other work."

"If I hit the wall on this, I can walk in here and we make nice with the Feds and BCA, then take all the help they offer."

The sheriff sipped his coffee and contemplated the top of his desk. When he looked up he said, "I'll agree, but only after you brief me on all you've done and why you have no other avenues to pursue."

Floyd nodded. "Fair enough." As he walked away he decided it was time to talk to Bernice Brown.

● ● ●

San Antonio, Texas

Tubby Lasoya was playing the *Zombie Invasion* game on his computer while drinking his third can of Coke. Playing on the big screen television made the characters over three-feet tall, adding a touch of realism to the upgraded graphics. The knock on the door broke his concentration and he missed an easy shot as Ernie let himself in.

Tubby greeted his partner. "Como esta?" He tried to make the greeting sound earnest, but he really didn't like Ernie. Theirs was a partnership of convenience and neither would have chosen the other as a friend. Ernie, being an illegal alien, courted Tubby's tolerance to ensure he had a safe haven when the INS agents made their periodic raids of his usual haunts and to make sure he was included in Tubby's next job so he had cash. Ernie brushed past Tubby. A zombie was frozen in his fall on the television.

"Tubby," Ernie said with obvious disgust, "why do you play this kid's stuff? We got money and we got drugs. We could be very popular with women."

Tubby turned sour and shut down the game. "You could be very popular. They fall all over you. Women look at me like I'm a fat leper."

Ernie smiled, knowing he had Tubby's attention. He put an arm around Tubby's broad shoulders and said, "It's all an illusion, Tubby. Women believe what you project. I project money and confidence. You project a fat belly and insecurity. You've got to change your approach. Be tough. Be strong. Be in control."

"Be skinny." Tubby uttered under his breath. He took a long drink from the Coke and tossed the empty can into the corner where it bounced off the wall before tumbling into the 5-gallon metal pail in the corner. The wall behind the pail was chipped and splattered with dried Coke.

Tubby started toward the kitchen in search of another soda when Ernie grabbed his arm from behind. "Come on. I got a couple of places where the girls like a little meat on their men. They come from homes where a little fat is a sign of prosperity. Not like here where everyone is trying to lose weight until their ribs show."

Tubby reluctantly locked up the apartment and drove to an older area of San Antonio where Mexican immigrants lived in small houses with extended families. Sometimes three generations lived in the same two-bedroom house, the grandparents providing daycare when the parents worked. They joked about the inter-generational daycare, calling it, "Mexican Social Security." The yards were brown and littered with toys. Several old men were deep in discussion on a porch, smoke curling from the cigarettes as they gestured emphatically.

At Ernie's direction, Tubby parked the car in front of a small bar with a "Lone Star Beer" sign in the window. The inside of the bar reeked of spilled beer and a hint of marijuana. The lighting was so dim Tubby could barely make out the arrangement of table and chairs until his eyes adjusted from the sunlight. Selena's voice blared a Tejano song from hidden speakers. Several young Hispanic men stared at them briefly before returning to their beer. Each had a very young girl hanging from his arm.

The middle-aged bartender with salt-and-pepper hair and a body builder's physique slipped from behind the bar and exchanged handshakes with Ernie and Tubby. "Roberto, this is my friend Tubby," Ernie said. The three of them moved to a corner booth.

Ernie leaned across the table and spoke to Roberto. "We would like some company for a while, maybe two of your new girls. Some without too much . . . um . . . experience. How much?"

The bartender made a helpless gesture with his arms. "What do you want? An hour, a day, a week? Hey, I got three who just came in last night. You pay for their trip, add something for my trouble, and you can have them for a few days. Maybe something like fifteen hundred each."

Ernie looked at Tubby, who had a very pained expression on his face. Ernie smiled. "My friend Tubby needs long-term help with his attitude. We'll take a look at them and see if we're interested."

"Fifteen hundred is a lot of money," Tubby said softly.

Roberto slid from the bench and disappeared down a hallway marked, "Restrooms."

"I don't like this, Ernie." Tubby whispered just loud enough to be heard over the pulsating music. "You can't buy a girl.

What do you think this is going to do for us? They'll fight us and run away. First thing you know, the cops are knocking on the door and we'll be in jail. I don't like it. It's kidnapping . . . or slavery, or something."

"Don't you worry." Ernie was all smiles as he reassured Tubby. "They'll be really happy to come with us." Ernie swept his arm across the room. "They'll be giving up all this. See those girls at the bar? The girls go upstairs and they screw a different guy every 30 minutes for 16 hours a day. The only way they get away is if Roberto sells them to someone like us, or if the INS raids the place and takes them back to Mexico. These girls will think we're heroes. Shh. Here they come."

Roberto walked toward them with the three young girls. All wore cotton print dresses and were a little dirty, like they'd just come from the floor of a truck. Sweat made tiny rivulets through the dust on their necks. Tubby, who'd never been on a date, was speechless. He'd seen an online story about trafficking of illegal aliens, but it seemed irrelevant. Now he was witnessing it firsthand and he was at a loss for words.

The first girl had a wide-eyed look of terror and appeared to be barely 12 years old. She was terribly skinny, to the point of looking malnourished. She stared at Tubby and Ernie with undisguised fear. Roberto introduced her as Maria. She shuddered every few moments as if she might be running a fever and was having chills. If she wasn't ill, she'd just come to an understanding of what was expected of her in return for her passage to Texas.

The second and third girls appeared to be well into their teens or even older. With poor nutrition some young Mexicans tended to look immature until they suddenly looked very old.

Roberto introduced the second girl. "This is Roberta." She stared at Tubby. Her eyes were so dark they appeared almost black and behind the dirty face he saw natural beauty. Her cheekbones were high and she had a slight cleft in her chin. Ernie's interest was aroused and he surveyed her figure, mentally undressing her. Roberto smiled, knowing this sale was going to be easy.

Tubby was put off by the apparent youth of the first girl. It was obvious Ernie wanted the second girl. Tubby looked at the third girl. She was chunkier than the others. Her dress was too small and the seams stretched to breaking across her breasts. She smiled at Tubby.

"What's your name?" Tubby asked.

She quickly looked back to the floor, nervously clasping and unclasping her fingers. "My name is Dolores." He was surprised that she understood English. Her reply was in English, although her Mexican accent was very strong.

Roberto quickly realized Tubby was a native Texan and he might have some language barriers dealing with most of the girls. He also saw Tubby needed a nudge. He said, "Dolores has better English than any of the other girls." Roberto gave Dolores a push. "Ask him something."

"What's your name?" Dolores asked, continuing to stare at the floor.

"I'm Toribio," He replied. "My friends call me Tubby."

Ernie winked. Roberto took the waif by the arm and disappeared down the hallway past the restrooms. The other two girls stood by the booth uneasily. Ernie patted the seat and Roberta sat next to him. Dolores moved next to Tubby, but didn't sit. Ernie explained to them, in Spanish, that he and Tubby were willing to pay for their passage to Texas. In return, they would have to be "friendly" to them and would be expected to do some cleaning and cooking. After a few months, they could decide to stay or leave.

Roberta and Dolores nodded assent. The "experienced" girls in the bar had explained the nature of their obligation to Roberto, the bartender. If they stayed in the bar, their lives would involve servicing any man who chose them until they ran away, came down with some visible signs of disease, or got pregnant. If they ran away and were caught, they'd be beaten until they were unconscious. And Mexican gangs would take them and they'd never be seen again. Going with Ernie and Tubby seemed like the best option. Tubby and Ernie were well-dressed, clean, and polite. The possibility of being free after a few months was tantalizing.

When Dolores saw Roberto returning she immediately parked herself in Tubby's lap. She wrapped her arms around his neck and assumed a pose that made it appear it would take a crowbar to remove her from Tubby's possession.

Roberto smiled and said, "It appears you have made your choices."

Ernie slid out of the booth and whispered something in Roberta's ear. She slid back into the booth while Ernie walked to the hallway with Roberto. The men talked, their words lost in the blaring music. After some protesting from Roberto, and arm waving from Ernie, they both nodded. Ernie pulled a roll of bills from his pocket and peeled off bills that amounted to most of the roll. Roberto acted like he was unhappy with the payment, but he was smiling at the end.

Ernie nodded at the door and tucked away his bankroll. He threw his arm over Roberta's shoulders and announced, "It's done." All four looked happy as they climbed into the Olds and drove back to Tubby's apartment.

At Tubby's apartment, Ernie rushed to the bathroom. The girls started talking to each other in Spanish. Tubby was having a problem keeping up with the rapid-fire conversation and started to think they were planning an escape. He relaxed when he understood that the girls had never seen such luxury. Roberta and Dolores quickly set to work clearing the soda cans and food wrappers from the chairs and floor. Tubby was too amazed to say anything and just watched.

When Ernie came out of the bathroom, he stood in awe. "They really think we want them to clean and cook!" After Roberta took a load of food wrappers to the kitchen garbage he led her to the bathroom and closed the door behind them. Dolores stared at the door until she heard the shower water.

Dolores dove back into cleaning. After a few minutes, Ernie walked out of the bathroom with a towel wrapped around his waist, the shower still running behind him. He went into Tubby's bedroom, reappeared with a wrinkled T-shirt, and returned to the bathroom. A moment later, the shower stopped. Ernie and Roberta came out of the bathroom with wet hair. Roberta was wearing Tubby's shirt like a long nightgown as she scampered to the spare bedroom looking guilty.

Ernie nodded toward the bathroom. "Tubby, show Dolores how the shower works."

CHAPTER 10

PINE CITY, MINNESOTA

The Minnesota weather took a turn for the worse. Lightening lit the sky and rain drove in torrents. The entirety of northeastern Minnesota was under a thunderstorm warning with a chance of tornadoes. Floyd drove past a pair of motorcyclists waiting out the storm under an I-35 bridge. The defrosters were barely able to keep the windshield clear.

Floyd took the County Road 11 exit off the interstate hoping low spots on the side roads weren't under water. As he drove past the gas station and McDonald's, the radio sounded the tones for the Pine City ambulance and fire. There was an accident near Bruno, in the northeast corner of the 1,400 square mile county. He considered assisting, then heard that the State Patrol was on the scene. Floyd decided he had put off the interview with Bernice Brown long enough.

Pam Ryan had interviewed Bernice briefly on the evening of George's death and he'd read the report. Pam had not pressed Bernice. That left him with the task of asking Bernice Brown some difficult questions, and he didn't relish the task.

Threading through town gave him a chance to mull the words of condolence he had to offer Mrs. Brown before asking the definitive questions about her husband's death. The timing was bad for Bernice, with a visitation the same afternoon and the funeral tomorrow. He hoped she might give him frank answers she hadn't had time to think over. He also had to assess her grief. Nine out of ten homicides are committed by someone known to the deceased. Spouses and lovers topped the list of murderers. Bernice, with her slender build and quiet personality, hardly seemed like a murderer and explosives were rarely a woman's weapon of choice. Still, the questions had to be asked.

Floyd passed slowly through downtown Pine City before turning onto 10th street. Brown's boulevard was lined with old oak and ash trees, which shaded the old money family homes in Pine City. This is where the bank president, the judge, the owner of the feed mill, and the Browns lived, where those families had always lived.

Floyd pulled in front of the two-story brick house and parked at the curb. After a moment's hesitation to call himself out of service, he walked up the front steps. Within a minute Bernice Brown answered his knock.

A strained smile pulled the corners of Bernice's mouth as she struggled to remember Floyd's name. "Umm, Floyd. Floyd Swenson." Pine City is a small town and all of the deputies had dealings with George and Bernice Brown at the hardware store, church, or in some philanthropic organization.

Floyd fidgeted with a cap in his hands. "Mrs. Brown, I'm terribly sorry about what happened to George, but I need to ask you a few questions. May I come in?"

"Sure, but I've already told that cute deputy, Pam Ryan, everything I know." She remembered Floyd, recalling him picking up building supplies with his father.

In small towns, like Pine City, people grow up together and know virtually everyone in town before they're out of grade school. It has advantages, because people really watch out for each other. It also has disadvantages. Once someone has a bad reputation, it's impossible to change it without moving away, as many unwed mothers have discovered over the years.

Bernice invited Floyd into the entryway of the house and closed the door behind him. Although it was one of the largest residences in Pine City, the Brown's house was not ostentatious. The structure dated back to the turn of the century, when the last big fire gutted the town. The house smelled musty, the woodwork dark and dreary. The wall colors were uninspired, making Swenson think they had used paint people had returned to the hardware store. George was noted for his frugality.

Bernice led Floyd down the hallway and invited him into the living room where a huge fireplace and mantel dominated one wall. The room was furnished with an old-fashioned wing-backed chair and two sofas with wooden legs carved in the shape of lion's feet. The Chintz covers were well worn. A coffee table was littered with magazines and unopened mail. A large picture window looked over the street. Swenson had expected something a little classier from the man who owned the only hardware store in town.

Bernice sat on a corner of the nearest couch and left the chair for Floyd, He settled uneasily onto the seat and said, "Are you doing okay?"

"It's hard," Bernice said with a sniffle. "The church brought cookies and casseroles, but I don't feel much like eating."

"It takes time," said Floyd. "I thought my world had ended when Ginny died, but I dove into my job and got my footing back. She still has a place in my heart, but I'm living my life."

"I suppose I'll cope, but it's just too soon to look forward."

"It's clear George was murdered and we're trying to find a motive. Did George have any enemies?"

Bernice's eyes filled with tears and her breathing grew shallow. "George was a good man. He gave credit to people who did *not* deserve it. When I tried to push people to pay up their accounts, he shushed me and told them it was okay and told them to pay when they could. Some of those people live better than we do, but George didn't press it. I can't think of a single person who's lived in this town, including your family, who hasn't received money or goods from George when they had a tough go of it." Bernice's voice broke and she raised a handkerchief to dab the tears from her eyes.

Floyd took in the scene and assessed Bernice as genuinely grieving. The disarray, the wilting flower arrangements, the undisturbed plates of cookies wrapped in Saran, and unopened mail told him she wasn't coping with day-to-day issues. Her bubble had burst and it was evident she held George in high esteem.

"At the church meeting George was agitated about something. You told Pam Ryan he was seeing a lawyer about the spending at the church. Do you know anything about that?"

Bernice shook her head slightly. "Something had happened at the church but George wasn't one to make accusations without having all the facts." Bernice paused and she stared into a corner of the ceiling. "George and I were married in that church, and we probably put up half the money to expand that building. George felt like he had the right to make the decisions about the spending. Until the last year, he pretty much had his way. Then the church started to get more money than it had before and everyone was in a rush to spend it. George thought it should be put away for a rainy day, but he was overruled by the board. They bought a computer. George thought the idea was stupid since the church's finances were simpler than the accounts at the store and we still do those by hand. Then, they started to build this mission church in Mexico. George was furious. We have hungry people here in Pine County, but we're sending money and people to build a church in Mexico." As she spoke, Bernice Brown got more animated. She started to wave her hands around with a handkerchief flagging through the air like the tail of a kite.

Floyd took out a notebook and made a few notes. When Bernice stopped he asked, "You said George had contacted a lawyer. What did he find out? Was everything legal?"

Bernice started wringing the handkerchief. "I don't know. He was very upset by the meetings. He said there was something that wasn't right, but he wasn't quite sure what it was. Last week he got very bitter about the whole Mexican church deal and he was talking about hiring an auditor to go over the church's books. It was a matter of principle for him. Not something anyone would get *killed* over."

Floyd nodded as he jotted the words *Mexican church* in his notebook. "What lawyer did he see?"

Bernice paused for a second. "We've been using Janet Ames for all the work on the store. She's that lawyer who used to have an office near the old courthouse. I'm sure he saw her."

Swenson shifted in his chair. Janet Ames had been involved as the appointed public defender on several cases in the past. On her last case, she and Floyd had a difference of opinion about the guilt of her client. The client had eventually been found guilty and had been killed in prison. Janet hadn't accepted any criminal cases since.

"Thank you Bernice," Floyd said as he stood and put his cap on. "I'm going to see Janet Ames. Maybe George told her something that can tie this together." They walked to the front door together.

Bernice opened the door, then put a hand on Floyd's arm. "There is one thing you need to know." She hesitated as she chose her words. "George hated Tom Knight, the youth minister. George called him the Pied Piper. George really disliked the way the kids followed Tom around like little lost puppies. George said they were too dependent on Tom. I don't think it means anything because even our own grandchildren love Tom. It was just George."

"Thanks, Bernice."

Floyd jogged to the squad as sleet pellets turned to a heavy rain. He slipped on some ice halfway down the sidewalk, then slowed his pace for the last few yards. He sat in the squad and made a few notes in his notebook while waiting for the defroster to clear the windshield. He wrote Tom Knight's name in his notebook, followed by "Pied Piper." He circled the phrase.

● ● ●

DULUTH, MINNESOTA

Janet Ames' law practice had been in Pine City for over 10 years. Because of her refusal to accept public defender cases, her workload had dwindled so she moved to Duluth to generate enough billable hours to pay the rent. Janet answered the telephone herself, indicating the sorry state of her law practice. She reluctantly agreed to talk to Swenson but they agreed to meet at 3:00 that afternoon.

Floyd made the hour and a half drive to Janet's office through intermittent rain showers. The police radio was alive with car accidents as the unpredictable Minnesota spring weather hovered at the freezing point, alternating rain showers with sleet, with hundreds of fender-benders and the highway ditches strewn with cars. He turned off I-35 at Lake Avenue. Instead of turning right toward the refurbished areas along Minnesota Point and the lift bridge, he turned left and went up the hill into the low-rent areas. Janet's office was on the second floor of a historic brick building that was exempt from ADA standards requiring wheelchair access. Swenson climbed the wooden steps and was at Janet's office door exactly at three. He knocked once and didn't wait for a response before entering what he assumed to be the anteroom.

He entered the sorriest law office in northern Minnesota. The office consisted of one room with a desk covered with papers. The only clear spot on the desk supported the overflowing ashtray. An old rusty file cabinet stood in one corner with dog-eared folders sticking out of the drawers and a pile of papers on the floor awaiting filing. Janet sat at the desk reading with her head propped up on one hand holding a burning cigarette. The walls were yellowed from the residue of the smoke from thousands of cigarettes and the air reeked of cigarette smoke despite an open window behind the desk. Floyd knocked again and said, "Miss Ames?"

She lifted her head and tried to focus on Swenson. Floyd was shocked. There were dark bags under her eyes and her face had aged 20 years since he had seen her a year and a half earlier.

"Come in Sergeant Swenson." Her voice was tired.

Swenson walked into the office and looked around for an empty guest chair but both were covered with papers. Janet rose slowly from the desk and moved a pile from one chair to the floor next to the file cabinet. She sat back down in the creaking desk chair and stubbed her cigarette out in the ashtray. Janet was dressed in khaki slacks and a light green cotton blouse, a far cry from the fashionable women's suits with silk blouses and colorful scarves Floyd remembered. He guessed she had also gained ten pounds.

Janet asked, "What can I do for you? You mentioned George Brown's death when you called."

Floyd sat uneasily in the chair, trying not to step on any files. "You'd heard about George's death before I called?"

Janet nodded, picked up a manila folder and set it on her lap. "I was going over George's file when you came in. There isn't much here other than he asked me to remove the Pine Brook Free Church bequest from his will two weeks ago. I was trying to remember the discussion. There isn't anything in the file that gives me any indication why."

Floyd perked up, thinking someone might have tried to cause George's death before the new will was signed. "Did you make the change?"

Janet nodded. "Yes, I had it changed the same day. I sent the revised will to George and Bernice. They signed it, had it witnessed and notarized, and I got it back within the week."

Floyd let out a deep breath. "Did he originally have a large bequest to the Church?"

Janet closed the file and set it back on top of the desk. "I'm not really at liberty to share the details of the new or old will with you. It will be read to his heirs in a couple of weeks. I can say the amount was modest. Certainly not an amount I'd kill someone over. As a matter of fact, I'd say the change was more symbolic than punitive."

"Tell me, who are the biggest beneficiaries in the revised will?"

Janet shifted uncomfortably in her chair. She took a deep breath and closed her eyes. "I guess I can say, in general terms, that his family members are the primary beneficiaries. Most goes to his wife and each of his children gets a modest bequest. He set up a trust to provide college funds for his grandchildren. "

"How about the store?" Floyd asked.

Janet scratched her nose before answering. "Bernice gets the store. He set up a life insurance policy to cover the inheritance taxes so it is free and clear. Beyond that, there weren't any million dollar insurance policies or anything that will make anyone rich now or in the future." She paused, then added.

"George was very frugal. He felt quite strongly that it would be wrong to drop a load of cash on any of his heirs. He wanted them to succeed due to their own initiative. Consequently, his funds are tied up in trusts. Bernice gets the store with a trust that grants her a comfortable monthly stipend."

Floyd pushed on. "Did he say why he made the change in the bequest to the church?"

"I'm sorry," Janet said, shaking her head. "I really can't remember him stating a reason."

Swenson pulled out his notebook and flipped through the pages. He hoped to find some key which might jar Janet's memory. "Did George mention anything about Tom Knight? I understand George referred to him as the Pied Piper."

Janet gave a sign of recognition. "That sounds familiar. George talked about the Pied Piper. Is he the guy who's working with the youth groups?"

Floyd said, "Bernice referred to him as the youth minister. I think he's also the one who's been the guiding influence on the mission church they're building in Mexico."

Janet sat bolt upright at the mention of the Mexican church. "That's it! George didn't like something about the Mexico deal. He said it didn't smell right to him." Janet stared out the window for a few seconds, then added, "There's something more about the Pied Piper. George hinted he might be having an affair with someone, but he never gave me any details."

Swenson scribbled in his notebook. "Do you think the Pied Piper was having a relationship with one of the children?"

"If that had been the case," Janet said, "I think he would've called you. If there was an affair, and I emphasize *if*, I'm sure it must've been an adult. If George had proof there was an affair, I'm sure he'd have taken it to the pastor or the church elders."

"Thanks. That gives me a couple leads to follow." Floyd flipped back through his notes and stopped at the page from the night of the murder. "I've got one other question for you. George hinted that he'd been checking the legality of some of the spending the church had been doing. Is that correct?"

Janet shrugged and said, "We had a discussion about that, too. I told him the church rules are not necessarily law. The Catholic Church has a whole area called canon law with canon lawyers who do nothing but make interpretations. I told George if the deacons' board voted on spending, and it was documented, then even if he didn't agree with it, there was nothing he could do in a court of law unless fraud was involved."

Swenson scribbled more notes, then closed the notebook, and looked up at Janet. She was slightly more composed than when he'd arrived. "Are you okay, Janet? We've known each other professionally for a few years and you look a little . . ."

She smiled. "Thanks. I didn't think law enforcement people worried about slime-sucking lawyers."

Swenson smiled. "In general, we tend to foster an adversarial relationship. It keeps everyone on his or her toes. But I never like to see one of my honored opponents get out of form. Who knows when I might need someone to challenge my wits?"

Janet shook her head. "Business is a little tough right now. Some of my clients followed me from Pine City, but I lost a lot. The new business isn't steady yet and since I won't do criminal cases any more, I have a lot of people who just go elsewhere."

The conversation was wearing thin and Swenson rose to leave. "If you think of something else relevant to George's death, please call the courthouse and leave a message."

"Sure." Her response lacked sincerity.

CHAPTER 11

STURGEON LAKE

Floyd could see Mary through the kitchen windows as he pulled in the driveway. The dog had been hiding from the rain in the doghouse under the deck but upon hearing the sound of Floyd's tires on the gravel, she raced out to meet him. The temperature had dropped a few degrees as the sun set and the rain turned to sleet.

Floyd turned off the car and patted the dog on the head before jogging to the front door. He slipped in, leaving the dog bouncing on the deck. Mary gave him a peck on the cheek as he shook the water off his jacket.

"Supper will be ready in a few minutes," Mary said as she lifted the lid on a pot. "Change into some dry clothes while I set the table."

Floyd slipped off his shoes and set them on the mat. "I could use a beer." He slipped the holster off his belt and set it on the table.

Mary started for the refrigerator, then hesitated. "I thought you were going to George Brown's visitation tonight. Do you want to go to the funeral home with beer on your breath?"

Floyd shook his head. "Yeah. I'd forgotten the visitation." He put his holster on the closet shelf. "I'll throw on some dry pants and be right back."

When he returned, Mary was dishing up steamed broccoli and tuna casserole. "Oh boy! It's my favorite, broccoli." He sat down and poured a glass of milk for each of them.

Mary wrinkled her nose as she replied, "You know vegetables are good for you. It is my job to make sure you get a few in your diet. Would you rather have beets, or perhaps spinach?"

Floyd made a gagging sound in reply before asking, "Where's the cheese sauce for the broccoli?"

Mary sprinkled some lemon juice on her broccoli. "No cheese sauce tonight. Try a little lemon on it."

Floyd grimaced. "No thanks. I'll just gag it down like this."

"Any breakthrough on the George Brown case today?"

Floyd waited until he had swallowed a large bite of casserole before answering. "It looks more and more like there is a link to the church. I spoke to Bernice Brown and to George's lawyer. Both of them made comments about George's unhappiness with the church and the way the money was being spent. They both mentioned the youth minister and how George thought he was up to something. The lawyer even said George thought the youth minister was having an affair with someone."

Mary pondered those thoughts while she chewed. "But why would someone get killed over problems at a church, on

the other hand, even if the youth minister is having an affair..."
She let the last thought dangle.

Floyd nodded and replied, "Every church has some level of dissent among the members. They argue about all kinds of stuff, but in the end they either come to an agreement or the dissatisfied parishioners move to a different church.

"The Browns couldn't move." Mary replied. "The family founded the church."

Floyd nodded. "True. George liked to remind people of that fact. I guess that is one point, which keeps sticking in my mind. The Browns were always big contributors and because of that, George pretty much called the shots. Lately, there has been more money coming in and spending George wouldn't approve. He had lost his influence and he didn't like that. Not one bit."

"It sounds more like George might have been the murderer rather than the victim. He apparently saw things he didn't like and moved to resolve them."

Floyd smiled at the simplicity of Mary's analysis. "That may be the key. In trying to resolve whatever problems George saw, he made someone so angry they killed him."

Floyd finished his food and picked up the plates. "I don't suppose you would like to come along to the visitation tonight?"

Mary shook her head. "I think I'll go home and get some rest. The flower shop has been nuts lately and I'm worn out."

• • •

San Miguel, Mexico
The youth group was sweltering as they thatched the church roof. Pieces of thatch got everywhere. Everyone's arms were

scratched and they all itched where the sweat caught the palm debris and adhered it to their skin.

"This is like putting up hay," Jarrod Newquist said as he scratched his waistband. "The pieces get everywhere and itch."

"No!" shouted Hillary Schmidt, grabbing Emily Payson's hand. "Don't pull your underwear away from your skin," she said. "That lets all the seeds fall inside your underwear and that's even worse. Everyone who bales hay learns that quickly." She blushed bright red when she saw several of the boys laughing at her.

An aging pickup truck bounced down the road, leaving a trail of dust behind. It stopped in front of the church. A small man, wearing a clerical collar and black shirt, waved to the workers.

"Is one of you Pastor Knight?" He called from the base of the ladder.

Tom Knight waved and slid down to the ladder. He climbed down the rungs and offered his hand to the man. "I'm Tom Knight."

The man's white teeth glowed in contrast to his dark Mexican skin. "Pastor Knight, I am Pastor Jaime Romero."

Pastor Romero put his hand on Knight's upper arm and led him out of earshot. "I'm terribly sorry. You should have received this message two days ago, but I have been traveling and my truck broke down."

Tom Knight reassured the man. "Yes, yes. That's entirely understandable."

"The parish had a call on Wednesday morning. It was from your church." Romero unfolded a slip of paper torn from a notebook. He handed it to Knight. "It seems that someone named George Brown has passed away. It's a pity that we had this delay, because his grand-daughter is here with you and they wanted her to come home for the funeral."

Tom read the note, then looked up with a pained expression. "But the funeral is tomorrow."

Romero nodded. "Yes. That's the pity of it. There are no phones nearby, and I really wanted to personally deliver the news."

They turned together and looked at the teens, laughing while tying thatch to the roof. Tom said, "She's the one with the red T-shirt. Her name is Melissa."

Romero nodded. "You will tell her?"

Knight read the scribbled note again. "Yes, I will tell her. There is no point in rushing her back now. She's missed the funeral, and we return tomorrow anyway."

Romero nodded. "Yes. Perhaps she would like to ride back to the rectory with me to call from my telephone. It takes two hours to drive there."

Tom called Judy Arend and Melissa Brown down from the roof and gave them the news as Pastor Romero watched silently. Judy hugged Melissa as she cried, then took her inside the church. The others gathered around Tom Knight to hear the news. Soon afterward, Pastor Romero drove away with Melissa Brown and Judy Arend.

CHAPTER 12

PINE CITY THURSDAY EVENING

Floyd arrived at the funeral home about fifteen minutes after the start of the visitation. Cars were parked for blocks in both directions despite the drizzle. Floyd parked three blocks away from the funeral home and his coat was soaked by the time he reached the front door.

The entryway was jammed with people and they shuffled ahead to make room for Floyd. The air was overly warm and filled with the fragrance of hundreds of flowers. As the crowd edged forward, more people packed in behind. Floyd slowly made his way to a desk where all the guests were signing a book and dropping off cards of condolence.

Floyd greeted a few acquaintances as he made his way to the cloakroom. The throng of people seemed to represent every business in Pine City along with all of the civic leaders and other friends and family.

Gerry Brown, George's son, was standing next to the open doors to the visitation room. He recognized Floyd and grabbed him by the arm. "Floyd, how nice of you to stop by. Is this visit social or professional?"

Floyd shook Gerry's hand. "Some of each. I'm really sorry about the loss of your father."

"Thanks. I hear you talked to Mom today. She said it sounded like you weren't making much headway with the investigation."

"We've got leads, just no one in jail." Floyd said. Then he said, "Tell me about the youth minister and the Mexico church project. Is the youth minister here?"

Gerry shook his head. "No. He has a group of kids in Mexico this week, over spring break. They're due back on Sunday."

"It seems like your father was pretty down on this Mexican church deal. Do you have any idea why?"

Gerry surveyed the crowd and weighed his words before answering. "Dad was fiscally conservative and our church is pouring a lot of money into this Mexican building project. The pledges don't cover expenses. Even though the Sunday offering makes up the shortfall right now, Dad thought the church should live within its budget and bank the excess for a rainy day. Personally, I think he didn't like it because it was out of his control. No one else saw any problem with the cash flow."

Floyd nodded. "I know your dad was into control." Then he added, "Tell me about the youth minister. Your dad called him the Pied Piper. Why?"

Gerry smiled. "Dad hated Tom. I guess he's officially a seminary student who is serving as our youth pastor. He's the most inspirational youth leader we've ever had. The kids love him, and he's started all kinds of activities that have the kids energized and active. We've never had so many kids involved in the church and they seem to be driving a lot of adult attendance." Gerry turned solemn. "I think that irritated Dad too. He thought the deacons should be driving the church and here you have a bunch of kids who were suddenly having fundraisers, starting their own programs, and dragging their parents to church. Dad didn't think that was right."

Gerry spied someone across the room and waved. "Excuse me, Floyd. My cousins from Sleepy Eye are here."

Floyd moved into the sanctuary and considered how convenient it was that the man who was the most disliked by George Brown was in Mexico at the time of the funeral. "I wonder if they left before or after George's death?" Floyd asked himself as he worked his way through the crowd, shaking hands.

An elderly couple inquired about Mary's health and Floyd gave the standard Minnesota response, "She's fine." Floyd thought the health question was nothing more than an acknowledgement of his budding relationship with Mary, and less risky than asking if they were still seeing each other.

Floyd moved up to the closed casket. Bernice Brown looked frail and her eyes were red-rimmed. She wore a long black dress and had a white handkerchief in one hand.

"Oh, Floyd." She gave him a discreet hug. "It's so nice of you to come." Bernice's face was tear-stained and her makeup in disarray. She put her hand on Floyd's arm and whispered, "Did you talk to Janet Ames?"

"I caught her this afternoon," he said, leaning close. "She didn't have much to offer. She said George was very worried about the youth pastor."

Bernice nodded.

"I understand he is in Mexico tonight."

Bernice nodded. "Yes, the youth group left last Saturday for another round of building. I think they'll be back Sunday evening if you want to talk to him."

Tom Knight had the perfect alibi. He'd been a thousand miles away when George Brown died. Was it too much of a coincidence that the object of George's hatred was a thousand miles away? Floyd wondered.

CHAPTER 13

Tubby rolled over and bumped into something in the bed. He jerked his head up and saw a body with a mop of black hair lying next to him. He quietly settled in beside her and threw his arm gently over her side. His hand came to rest on her naked breast and he nervously moved it to her stomach.

She made a contented noise and he nestled up close behind her. His heartbeat started to rise and his body responded. He pressed his hips against her back in the hope she would feel his hardness but she continued to sleep.

He snuggled there waiting for her to stir until he had to run to the bathroom. Then he hoped she wouldn't awaken and see his portly body. She was still sleeping when he came out of the shower with a towel wrapped around his waist, so he quietly rummaged through the bedroom trying to find something to wear. In the closet he found a wrinkled Houston Astros shirt. In a laundry basket were clean boxer shorts, and on the floor a pair of jeans that weren't as dirty as some of the others.

He wandered into the kitchen and put strips of bacon into a frying pan. He got a can of Diet Coke from the refrigerator, hoping the caffeine would ease his headache. He had an alcohol buzz when they picked up the girl. They continued to drink all afternoon. Later they drank their way through his refrigerator, running the gamut from Corona beer to margaritas and then on to straight shots of Mescal.

"What happened to the worm in the Mescal bottle," he asked himself when he found the empty bottle on the floor next to the couch. The last thing he remembered was drinking from the bottle and passing a joint among the four of them. His stomach churned as he considered the demise of the worm.

The aroma of frying bacon pulled him back to the kitchen where he cracked four eggs on top of the bacon. After a few minutes he slid the bacon and greasy eggs onto a plate. His solace in all situations was food. He had a slice of Wonder Bread dangling from his mouth as he carried the plate, Tabasco sauce, and a fork to the table. He was about to sit down when Dolores leaned against the kitchen doorframe wrapped in the sheet that covered her breasts, but left a lot of her thigh exposed.

Tubby looked up from his plate with a mouthful of eggs and bread. She was staring at the plate of food and Tubby wondered how long it had been since her last meal.

He picked up the plate and set it on the opposite side of the table. "Here. You eat. I'll cook more."

He put more bacon into the frying pan. As it started to sizzle, he watched curiously as Dolores devoured the food like she was starving, mopping yolk with the bread before stuffing it in her mouth. She closed her eyes as she chewed like she was savoring fine cognac.

She opened her eyes and was suddenly embarrassed at having eaten so quickly. "Sorry, I was very hungry." Then she looked around the kitchen. "No tortillas?" she asked. Her English was understandable but her accent was thick, and her vocabulary limited.

Tubby shook his head. "No tortilla. Bread instead. I grew up in Texas and we eat differently. You'll get used to it." He picked up the loaf of Wonder bread and handed two slices to her. She eagerly mopped up the bacon grease from the plate until it looked as if it had been washed.

After wiping her mouth on the back of her hand, Dolores rolled the sheet at the top of her breasts so it wouldn't fall off. Then she started to gather the dirty dishes from the table while he cooked. Tubby watched as she moved several days of dishes from the table to the counter alongside the sink where dozens of dirty dishes were already piled. She ran hot water into the sink and squirted detergent into the water. Her body moved sensuously against the white cotton fabric and he found it terribly erotic. When she caught him staring at her breasts he turned away in embarrassment, nervously turning the bacon slices, which were starting to get overly brown. He cracked several eggs into the pan and they quickly formed a crusty edges in the hot bacon grease.

Dolores was suddenly at his side, wiping her hands on a paper towel and pushing him toward the table. "No. I cook for you. You get used to my cooking."

He laughed at her broken English as she ushered him to a chair. Tubby was moved by something other than the thought of food as she fried bacon and cracked eggs.

She slid the eggs and bacon onto a freshly washed plate and brought it to the table. As she set the plate in front of him he reached out for her hand and squeezed it. Her brown eyes sparkled with a mischievous glint as she leaned across the table to kiss him.

"My lovely Dolores," he said as he pulled her onto his lap and kissed her passionately. That moment was the first time Tubby had chosen any activity over eating.

• • •

Pine City

Floyd was at his desk when Pam Ryan walked into the office area they called the bullpen. She poured a cup of coffee from a carafe and sat in the chair next to Floyd's desk. "I checked a few more bars and still came up empty on George Brown's killers or anyone stealing explosives." She dropped into a guest chair as if her legs would no longer hold her up. "I did get one interesting comment though. Two Mexican guys sat in The Village Inn the night before George's murder. They didn't talk to anyone except the waitress, and the one spoke English very poorly. I checked around the local motels and learned they spent two nights at the motel in Rock Creek. They checked out the day after George's murder, they were registered as..." Pam pulled out her notebook. "Paulo and Rico Rodriguez. They paid their motel and restaurant bills in cash and the motel clerk said their car had Texas license plates and they didn't trash the room."

"I don't suppose they left behind any explosives or detonators?" Floyd asked with a smile.

Pam closed her notebook. "No. The room was clean except for some empty beer cans."

"I suppose all the beer cans are gone so we can't pull fingerprints."

"I had the same idea," Pam said, "but the room has been cleaned and the beer cans are long gone.

Floyd leaned back. "If they'd stuck around here everyone would be suspicious. We'd better be careful, or we'll get investigated for racial profiling."

Pam shrugged. "They weren't locals, so everyone remembered them. I don't think it had anything to do with race, they were just something out of the ordinary. When I asked about anything or anyone unusual, people remembered them."

Floyd nodded. "It's one more piece of data. File it with the others and if something points back that direction we can pursue it further."

"I'm off," Pam said, finishing her coffee.

● ● ●

Floyd drove to Pine Brook for the ten o'clock funeral service. The small church was jammed with people ten minutes before the funeral started, so an usher set up a folding chair in the back corner for him. Pastor Abbot read the eulogy. There were fewer civic leaders at the funeral than at the previous evening's visitation, but the full congregation of the Pine Brook Free Church attended. A pretty woman with a lovely soprano voice sang *The Old Rugged Cross* and the choir sang *Amazing Grace*. After a closing prayer, the pallbearers came forward and rolled George Brown's casket out of the church he had attended for sixty years as the organist played *Here I am Lord*.

The gray sky threatened rain as the walnut coffin was carried down the front steps. Floyd watched George's children assist their mother down the steps, followed by the throng of people. The cemetery was directly behind the church and the funeral procession walked the fifty yards to the gravesite. As the pallbearers set the casket on the supports over the open grave, drizzle moistened the air.

Pastor Abbott offered another prayer as the drizzle turned to a sprinkle and the sobs of the family filled the air. George's two sons placed wreaths on top of the casket and the droplets of rain started to gain size and force. Floyd surveyed the crowd for anyone who didn't seem to be as sad as the other mourners, or someone whose display of grief seemed inappropriate. All he saw were people who seemed genuinely sad about George Brown's passing.

After the final blessing, the sky opened with a deluge that sent the mourners scurrying for the church. George's oldest son held a black umbrella over his mother's head as she shuffled toward the church, still crying. The family huddled around their matriarch, guiding her to a side door leading to the church basement.

Floyd followed behind the Browns and was quickly engulfed in the basement activity. The large open room was arranged with two buffet tables. Two dozen smaller tables were set with silverware, coffee cups, and coffee carafes. The Browns, dripping with rain, were hustled to the head table where the funeral director held places for them. After a brief prayer, the Browns led the line of mourners to the first buffet table, which was covered with a wide array of hotdishes. The church women's club had turned out a buffet that would have fed an army. Hot casseroles, Jell-O salads, homemade rolls, pies, brownies, and cakes were jammed so closely together that there was barely room for serving utensils. The best cooks in Pine City and Pine Brook had turned out their finest fare to honor George Brown's passing.

Floyd watched as the funeral evolved into a reunion. The sorrow of the day turned into a celebration of life as old friends reminisced and family members talked about the future. There was not a murderer evident. Floyd shook hands and hugged old friends while he waited for his turn at the buffet table while listening to the whispers about George's murder.

CHAPTER 14

SAN MIGUEL, MEXICO

It had been a long tiring day for the Pine Brook Church volunteers. They were rousted from their sleeping bags at seven a.m., an ungodly hour even for pious teens. They ate a breakfast of corn tortillas piled with spiced eggs. Most of the teens liked huevos rancheros once they became accustomed to the burn from the ranchero sauce. The bulky tortillas provided the calories they needed to work through the morning.

The Mexican heat was oppressive compared to the brisk Minnesota spring weather. They all loved working under the sun and deepening the tans on their mostly pale Scandinavian bodies. Most of the boys worked without shirts on, their sweaty skin glistening. The girls who were daring wore their T-shirts rolled up, exposing bare midriffs. They were scandalized when Judy Arend showed up in a halter top and short shorts that morning.

Since it was their last night, some of the villagers honored the group by baking a goat. At first the Minnesotans were a little squeamish, but after Tom explained that these peasants had slaughtered the goat in their honor, they all felt compelled to try some. Although it had an unusual texture, mild seasoning mixed with the gamey flavor of the meat tasted great. When one of the boys said, "It tastes just like chicken," they all laughed. One of the girls said it tasted like venison and that resulted in a lot of nods. One of the other girls suddenly looked green and set her fork down.

After dinner, the oppressive daytime heat softened and they all started to feel tired. The Mexican family who brought the goat pulled it off the spit and carefully trimmed every scrap of meat from the bones, then threw the bones to the three village dogs who snarled and nipped at each other before each skulked away with a heavy bone. Then Judy Arend and the village adults washed dishes while Tom Knight broke out his guitar. He played some church camp favorites, *Kumbaya* and *Michael, Row the Boat Ashore*. One of the Mexican men borrowed the guitar and taught them *La Cucaracha*.

At ten o'clock, the villagers shook hands and thanked each of the volunteers, then left, and the party ground to a halt. Tom surveyed the array of sleeping bags arrayed on a sheet of plastic over the dirt floor. "All right. Everyone into a sleeping bag ... preferably your own." There were a few nervous laughs from the teens at Tom's feeble attempt at humor.

The dirt floor was still warm, but with the insulation of a yoga pad, they had all learned that within a couple hours of the sunset the air temperature dropped rapidly in the dry San Miguel air and they'd be able to sleep. It was not at all like the sweltering humidity of Minnesota summers.

As the last of the boys settled into his sleeping bag, Tom leaned against the door between the church office, where the boys were housed, and the sanctuary, where the girls were bedded.

"Knock, knock," he said softly. "It's the youth pastor and he's not ready to go to bed until he's sure all the kids are asleep."

There was a shuffling as Judy pulled on a pair of shorts inside her sleeping bag. "I'll meet you by the banana tree," she whispered.

Tom and Judy walked under the clear sky and the waning quarter moon. The evening was still warm as they walked down a packed path that led to the edge of the village. The villagers' thatched roof huts were all dark and the only sounds were insects humming. Tom pulled some of the fallen banana palm leaves together to make a spot to sit in the sand.

"I don't think I've ever seen this many stars in Minnesota," Judy said, leaning back on her elbows.

"Once you're away from the city lights they're much more visible," Tom replied. They sat silently looking at the sky.

"How is Melissa doing?' Tom asked.

Judy took a deep breath and looked back at the church. "She was upset after the minister picked us up. She talked with her mother, and after the call she was inconsolable. I think the dinner and camp songs helped a lot." Judy paused. "I haven't told anyone. George Brown was murdered."

Tom looked at Judy with surprise. "Murdered? When you said he'd died I assumed he'd had a heart attack."

"There was an explosion in the church parking lot. George was inside the car."

"At the church?" Tom asked. "Was anyone else hurt?"

"This is all second hand," Judy warned. "No one else was hurt badly, although several people were cut by flying glass. The church had a couple windows blown out, but no major damage. Melissa said they haven't found out who placed the bomb."

Tom shook his head. "Wow. That's incredible."

Judy looked back at the church again. "The kids quieted down quickly tonight."

"We worked them pretty hard today," Tom said, wrapping his arms around his knees. "I bet they sleep like little logs tonight."

Toby Hanson slipped out of his sleeping bag and padded barefoot to the outhouse behind the church building. After relieving himself, he slipped back into the building. As Toby passed the window, he watched Tom slip his arm around Judy Arend's shoulders. Toby poked his friend, Micah, who joined him at the window. With wide-eyed wonder, they watched Tom apparently nibble at Judy's ear against her playful protests. The bodies slowly rolled back onto the banana leaves and the boys could see the silhouette of a halter top lifted into the air and dropped to the side. There were muffled sounds of necking and the boys watched nervously. The silhouettes of the two bodies were occasionally visible and the boys were dying to get a better view, but didn't dare move out of the building.

Judy's voice floated through the silent evening air. "Oh, Tom . . ." she moaned softly.

The boys looked at each other. "Oh, Tom, what?" Toby whispered. They watched silently, trying to see a flash of bare skin or other voyeuristic delight. From the sanctuary they could hear the sound of Melissa Brown quietly crying on the other side of the door.

On the opposite side of the church building, two young men crept up to the church van. It was parked a dozen yards away from the church to keep the smell of the leaky gas tank away from the sleeping and eating quarters. One man slid under the bumper while the second handed him tools. There were a few scraping sounds, then a hand emerged from under the fender. Foil-wrapped bricks with an overwrap of thick plastic were passed from a backpack, then inserted carefully into a niche inside the gas tank. There were more scraping sounds from the tightening of rusty screws and then the man emerged from under the van. They quietly slipped back into the darkness.

Under the banana tree, the murmurs stopped and Tom Knight's sweaty torso sat up. A lingering kiss followed. The boys watched as he reached over and handed something to Judy, who sat up and slipped her halter back on. The boys caught a brief silhouette of bare breast and watched as the two figures squirmed, apparently donning the rest of their clothing. The boys were on top of their sleeping bags and feigning sleep by the time Tom and Judy returned to the building.

SAN ANTONIO

Fresh from the shower, Dolores washed her dress in the bathroom sink and hung it to dry over a towel rod. She rifled through Tubby's piles of clothes, searching for something to wear while he showered. She wandered the apartment in an oversized San Antonio Spurs jersey and shorts cut from a pair of gray sweatpants with the drawstring cinched tight, picking up beer cans and food wrappers.

Before Dolores' dress was dry, Tubby picked up his wallet and keys. "Come. We're going shopping."

"I can't shop wearing this," she said, sweeping her hand over the jersey and shorts.

"It's fine." She slipped into a pair of flip-flops and he led her to the parking lot.

They drove to the Outlet Center at New Braunfels, just north of San Antonio. The first stop was a shoe store where they bought sandals. At the Eddie Bauer store she tried on a variety of jeans, shirts, and shorts, choosing a half dozen of each. Dolores tried to drag Tubby into the Bali store to look at underwear, but he balked, giving her cash and waiting nervously outside the store. She was afraid Tubby might explode when pressed to do something uncomfortable, like so many of the men that she had dealt with in her short life, but he seemed resigned and didn't get angry. She found the restrooms and changed into her brand new outfit, the first of her life.

Returning to San Antonio, they drove through the narrow streets near the Alamo until they found a parking lot near the Hilton Palacio del Rio. Tubby led her down the steps to the Riverwalk and they walked hand-in-hand among the tourists along the edge of the river. Dolores had never experienced anything as beautiful and clean, or as opulent as the shops and restaurants along the river. People seemed relaxed and happy, which was a total change from her tense life in Mexico where she looked over her shoulder whenever she was in public, ready to duck for cover or run when gang-related gunfire broke out.

They walked through the lowest level of the Hyatt hotel, where the river ran through the lobby, then sat at an outside table at a little cantina. Tubby bought a pair of slushy drinks and set the blue drink in front of Dolores. He kept the one that looked like lemonade for himself.

Dolores watched Tubby take a long drink through the straw. She gingerly took a tiny sip, not knowing what to expect. The rich orange flavor filled her mouth as the ice pieces rattled against her teeth. Her eyes grew wide and she asked, "What do you call this?"

Tubby looked around furtively to see if anyone had reacted to her strong accent. He leaned close and answered, "It's called a Blue Hawaii. Do you like it?"

She took a long sip through the straw and closed her eyes. After she swallowed, she licked her lips. "Is wonderful."

As they sipped their second round of drinks, a gringo dressed in cowboy boots and a western style shirt pulled a guitar out of a case. Sitting on a barstool against the outside wall he started to sing country oldies *Crazy* and *Folsom Prison Blues* were a little old for Tubby's tastes, but the alcohol was making him mellow and Dolores was in awe of the whole experience.

Tubby slid his chair close to Dolores and put his arm over her shoulders. She snuggled into his embrace. He was troubled by her overt friendliness and asked, "Did you know what was expected from you when you made arrangements to come to the Texas?"

She shrugged. "I knew I would have to work to pay for my passage. I thought I would be a maid for a rich family. Or maybe a cook."

Tubby asked, "Were things so bad in Mexico?"

The alcohol made her words start to slur as she answered. "I have many brothers and sisters and there are no jobs. Everyone lived in the same apartment with mother, father, sisters, brothers, grandparents, and cousins all together. When someone got sick there was no money for a doctor. We ate tortilla and orzo because we had no money for meat. We heard that Texas was like . . . like this!" Dolores swept her arm around the surroundings. She drank the last sip of her second slushy and snuggled under Tubby's arm. "You're nice. You treat me very nice. I like working for you. It's not work. It's more like being . . . a wife."

"Being married?" The words hit Tubby like a hammer.

Dolores didn't react to his surprise. "Yes, only you are nicer to me than most men are to wives. I have friends with husbands and sometimes it is not good. When there is no money or when they drink, they hit their wives and children."

They sat quietly listening to the music while he considered her words. The alcohol mellowed him. A couple got up from a nearby table. As they passed the guitar player, they threw a few dollars into his open guitar case. Tubby drained his drink and took Dolores by the hand. "Come, I want to show you something."

Tubby dropped a ten-dollar bill into the guitar case as they passed and the musician nodded his thanks. They walked up the steps behind the bar and stopped in front of a life-sized bronze sculpture of a man holding a pistol and cape. The statue had Hispanic facial features and wore a bandana over its head. A plaque under the statue said, "Toribio Lasoya, An Unsung Hero of The Alamo."

"This was my great, great uncle. My mother named me after him in hopes that I would be a great hero too." Tubby paused and took a deep breath. "She called me Tori when I was little. I have been a disappointment to her."

"You are a very nice man. You saved me." Dolores said as she kissed him gently.

They walked hand-in-hand through the Hyatt and along the river. Tubby read the sign in front of a store and walked up a set of stairs. They walked into a shop where there were glass counters full of belt buckles, necklaces, and other jewelry.

Tubby flagged down a clerk and asked for something Dolores didn't understand. The clerk reached under the counter and took out a large hoop that had rings that increased in size in ½ steps. The man took Dolores' hand and slipped rings onto her ring finger until one slipped easily on and off. He unlocked a section of the counter and took out a tray of rings and indicated to Tubby which were the correct size.

As Dolores' alcohol-hazed eyes grew large with excitement, Tubby looked back and forth over the tray. Tubby pointed to one with a large clear stone.

The clerk picked it up. "This one is two-thousand-two-hundred dollars." He whispered discreetly as he handed it to Tubby.

Tubby lifted Dolores' hand and slipped it on her left ring finger. When he was satisfied it fit, he produced a huge roll of bills from his pocket. He peeled off forty $50 bills and handed them to the clerk. "I assume that if I pay cash you'll give me a discount."

The clerk nodded, looking at the pile of currency in his hand.

Tubby lifted Dolores' left hand and admired the ring. Dolores was overwhelmed. She pulled her hand back. "No

Tubby, do not joke with me. I am not to be made fun of." As she tried to pull the ring back off her finger Tubby put his hand over hers.

Tubby shook his head. He reached into his deep past for a word. In the gray alcohol mist his Spanish vocabulary escaped him, but finally it came out. "Novio! Dolores es mi novio."

"Novio?" Dolores asked. "Casar? Really?"

"Yes, really." Tubby assured her. "I want you to marry me. In English we say fiancée."

Dolores lunged at him and nearly knocked him over with her hug. "Oh Tubby. Si, Si!"

CHAPTER 15

L aurie Lone Eagle had been at her parents' home for two days. The house was crowded with relatives. She'd explained her role with the BCA several times, and also explained that she was married to her job and that was why she didn't have a husband or children. An elderly great uncle pointed out that she was nearly forty and on the verge of being a childless spinster. Her father had undergone extensive testing at Miller Dwan Hospital in Duluth where the doctors speculated that a restriction at the end of his stomach was cancer.

Laurie's family was characteristically stoic. In the corner of the family waiting room her mother and the other elders held lengthy discussions about the values of natural healing versus the exploratory operation the doctor suggested. Laurie sat to one side, trying to maintain the role of the quiet daughter while also trying to stay connected to her life as an influential law enforcement professional. The conflict was taking a toll on her stomach so she bought antacids at the hospital gift shop then escaped to the hospital lobby, where she connected her laptop to the hospital Wi-Fi and pulled up missingkids.com, the website for the National Center for Missing and Exploited Children (NCMEC). After scanning the site, she decided to physically separate herself from the family drama rather than stepping in and incurring her mother's ire. The family would do whatever the elders decided, regardless of her input.

Planning only to escape the family drama, she drove south on I-35. She thought about the missing child from White Bear and how little she'd heard since she left St. Paul. She was saddened when she recalled the statistic that 76% of murdered children are dead within 3 hours of their abduction. The White Bear abduction had occurred days ago. The NCMEC office, in Austin, Texas, had several similar kidnappings which had been virtually unnoticed because of the dispersed jurisdictions involved. She'd called them for some input and was informed they had assigned an investigator from Team Adam, a network of retired law enforcement officers, to the cases. She decided to call the FBI. She took the Moose Lake freeway exit and parked in the grocery store parking lot.

She stood next to her car searching for a contact on her cell phone when she heard a familiar voice.

"Laurie, what are you doing in Moose Lake?" Floyd Swenson asked. He was in uniform, carrying two plastic bags of groceries.

"My father's ill and the family is holding a vigil. The tests showed he has a duodenal obstruction that may be cancer and the doctor suggested exploratory surgery. The elders are having a long discussion about whether to go with the surgeon or to continue natural healing and prayer."

Floyd knew that Laurie took great pride in having knocked down racial and sexist barriers in the sheriff's department. She hadn't been as effective with her family.

"I take it you have an opinion and that may not mesh with the elders."

"You know me pretty well, Floyd."

Sensing no further point in pursuing the conversation about Laurie's family, Floyd asked, "What's new at the BCA?"

"Somebody's kidnapping toddlers."

"For ransom?" he asked.

"No, someone takes them and they're never seen again. We've had a couple in Minnesota, but there have been a number of similar abductions around the Midwest."

Floyd's face turned to a scowl. "Are we talking about a lot of kids?"

Laurie shrugged. "Five or six that we know about. Who knows how many others don't fit the profile I've been querying but are victims of the same person or persons. The NCMEC and FBI are involved now that I've shown there is an interstate pattern. I'm *sure* they will have it solved in no time." Her voice was laced with sarcasm as the topic of the FBI came out. She asked, "What's new in Pine County?"

"Well, we had a murder this week. Someone blew up the hardware store owner's car with him in it."

Laurie nodded recognition. "I read about that in the newspaper. That's big news for up here. It hardly made the second page after the Minneapolis gang violence news."

"Let's grab a cup of coffee at Art's Café. You fill me in on the kidnappings and I can tell you about the big explosion that killed George Brown."

As they locked their cars, Laurie studied the lake map painted on the side of the building. "It looks like they touched up the map a little."

Floyd chuckled. "Progress does come to Moose Lake. They refurbished the grocery store after the fire and you'll hardly recognize downtown. It seems like all the old store-fronts have changed over in the past ten years."

When they stepped into the café Laurie felt like she'd gone through a time warp. Art's was a throwback to the days when Moose Lake was a Highway 61 stopping place on the drive to Duluth. The murals painted on the plaster walls depicted a deer bounding over a fallen tree. Among the antique advertisements for Remington ammunition, mounted fish, and pictures painted on old saws were pictures of the "Triple Crown" winning Moose Lake girls' sports teams who won the Minnesota State Championships in basketball, softball, and volleyball during the `81-82 season.

Laurie took a menu from a holder on the table and a smile creased her face. "You know what I like about Art's?"

Floyd looked at her as if it was a trick question. "No."

"I can get comfort food here." Laurie held the menu toward him and pointed to a spot in the middle. "Look at this," she said. "Here's the meatloaf dinner with mashed potatoes and a vegetable. I bet it'll taste as good now as when I ate here as a kid. And it won't cost me a week's wages like the steak I had last week in Minneapolis."

Floyd ordered a hot beef sandwich with hash brown potatoes. While they ate, Floyd shared the history of George Brown's death and the BATF blast residue testing.

Laurie shared the story of Tommy Martin in White Bear Lake, kidnapped while his mother was distracted by a telephone call. Without a description of the kidnappers, or their car, the Amber Alert hadn't resulted in Tommy's recovery. The comfortable conversation between the former police partners made both of them feel better.

CHAPTER 16

PINE BROOK, FRIDAY AFTERNOON

Floyd Swenson canvassed the neighborhood around the Pine Brook Church. Two deputies made the same circuit the day after the explosion but Floyd had decided to talk to the neighbors again in case something new had arisen or someone who'd been at work could be contacted. By early evening most residents were home, but no one had seen or heard anything unusual Monday night except the explosion. The neighbors nearest the church reported regular traffic from the church parking lot most evenings. Aside from the explosion that rattled windows, nothing seemed particularly unusual on the night of the explosion compared to any other night. No one had seen anyone tinkering with the cars or acting furtive. He came up with dead end after dead end.

As he walked down the block nearest the church, Floyd reflected on how a detective from Minneapolis had told him investigative work was a lot like prospecting. You dig for weeks or months to come up with that one nugget that leads you to the mother lode. Most of the time, the nuggets you find that look like gold turn out to be fool's gold.

He walked up to an older two-story house that had been unoccupied earlier in the afternoon. This time a trim woman in her thirties, wearing a t-shirt and khaki shorts, responded to his knock. She had a dishtowel thrown over one shoulder when she opened the door. The aroma of frying chicken reminded Floyd that his last meal had been seven hours earlier and Mary was waiting for him to take her out for supper.

"I'm Floyd Swenson from the sheriff's department and I'm investigating the explosion at the church Monday night. I was wondering if you saw someone prowling around or an unfamiliar car that night." He wasn't very hopeful. This house was two blocks down and a block over from the church. As he spoke a small boy peeked between the banisters of the stairs.

She took a deep breath and thought hard. "Gee, I'm sorry deputy, but I really don't remember anything unusual. Maybe you should come back later and talk to my husband. He'll be home after eight."

A whisper came from the top of the stairs. "Mommy."

"I hope you find something." The woman ignored the boy and grasped the door handle.

"Mommy." The voice from the stairs was stronger the second time.

A look of exasperation swept the woman's face. She spoke over her shoulder to the boy. "Not now Jimmy. I'm talking to the deputy." She turned back to Floyd, "I'm sorry for the interruption."

Floyd nodded and held out a business card. "Please ask your husband to call if he remembers anything."

The woman opened the screen door and accepted the card. She studied it for a second and then said, "I hope you find whoever did this."

Floyd thanked her and walked down the driveway, thinking about trying a couple more houses before driving home to Mary. He had reached the street when the woman opened the door and called. "Deputy Swenson."

When he got back to the house the woman seemed a little uneasy. "Jimmy says he saw something. He's pretty trustworthy and you might want to hear what he has to say." She motioned the boy to join them. "Come here and tell Deputy Swenson what you told me."

Jimmy peeked around the post at the bottom of the banister. Floyd knelt down and looked at Jimmy at his eye level. He thought Jimmy looked about four years old. He asked, "Did you see something the night the car caught fire at the church?"

Jimmy nodded.

Floyd smiled and tried his friendliest demeanor. "That could be very important. Can you tell me what you saw?"

Jimmy nodded again, but didn't say a word.

Swenson looked helplessly at the mother. She shrugged. "We've told him not to talk to strangers."

She bent down too. "Jimmy, this is Deputy Swenson. He's a policeman and he is one of the people who helps us when there's trouble. If you get lost or are in trouble and Mommy and Daddy aren't around, I want you to talk to Deputy Swenson. He's a very nice man."

"All policemen and deputy sheriffs have badges like this. Lots of them wear uniforms and pin their badges to their uniform shirts, like this," he pointed to the badge pinned to his shirt. "Have you ever seen a policeman wearing a badge?'

Jimmy nodded.

"What did you see the night of the big explosion, Jimmy?"

Jimmy came out from behind the banister and stared at Swenson. "If you're nice, why do you have a gun?" he asked, staring at Floyd's holster.

Swenson smiled and looked down at the butt of his pistol. "Sometimes I have to deal with people who aren't very nice and I need it to protect other people."

Jimmy leaned forward so he could see the butt of the gun better. He asked, "Like when bad men rob a bank and shoot people?"

Floyd nodded. "That might be one time."

Jimmy nodded. "Okay."

Floyd asked Jimmy again, "What did you see the night of the explosion?"

Jimmy sat on the bottom step and answered. "A car stopped in front of our house and let a man out. He had a box and he carried it that way." Jimmy pointed in the direction of the church.

Floyd was surprised by Jimmy's comment and somewhat skeptical someone that young could even remember what had happened a few days before. He asked, "What did the package look like, Jimmy?"

Jimmy thought for a second before answering. "Like a loaf of bread." Jimmy held his hands apart about nine inches.

Floyd asked, "Was it anyone you know?"

Jimmy shook his head. "I couldn't see his face. He was just a man."

"Do you remember what the man was wearing?" Floyd asked.

"He had on jeans and a shirt." Jimmy answered, "And maybe a baseball cap."

"What color was the car?"

Again Jimmy paused to think. "It was dark. Maybe black. It wasn't shiny. They needed to wash it."

Floyd took out a notebook and started to take notes. He asked, "Did the car stay parked very long?"

"Uh uh. It just stopped for a second and then drove away after the man got out."

Floyd nodded. "Good work, Jimmy. Did you see the car again after that?"

Jimmy shook his head. "No. Mommy came back and yelled at me 'cause I was looking out the window."

Floyd looked at the woman who blushed bright red. "It was past his bedtime and he has been a little stinker about not staying in bed and going to sleep when he's supposed to."

Floyd cracked a smile and turned back to the boy. "Can you remember anything else Jimmy?"

Jimmy shrugged. "Nope."

Swenson stood back up. "That may be just the little lead we wanted to get going. If Jimmy is right, we know there was a man wearing jeans and carrying a package the size of a loaf of bread, and that there was a dark colored car that may have dropped him off. It's a start." He asked the woman, "Do you have any idea what time it might have been when Jimmy saw the car?"

She shrugged. "It must have been after eight. That's Jimmy's bedtime." She thought for another second and added. "It seems it was closer to nine now that I think about it."

Floyd nodded and made a note. "Thanks." Jimmy's observation was shortly before George's car blew up.

● ● ●

FOND DU LAC, MINNESOTA

The sound of Laurie's cell phone chirp was barely audible over the din in the Lone Eagle's kitchen. She walked down a hallway to get away from the noise before answering.

"Hi, this is Laurie." Her voice sounded tired and several conversations were going in the background making it hard to hear her.

"Inspector, this is Bill Randall, from the White Bear Lake Police. I hope that it's okay to call your personal phone. Your office gave me this number and said that I could reach you here."

Laurie looked at the half dozen relatives jammed into the tiny kitchen of the tract house. She pushed a finger into the ear opposite the phone and slipped out to the yard. "It's okay. We have a family thing going on, but I can take calls." The tone of her voice made it sound like she was happy to get the call.

Randall was reassured that he was not interrupting a family dinner. He said, "I thought you'd like to know that we've got a match on the fingerprint from the van where Tommy Martin was kidnapped. It belongs to an illegal alien named Ernesto Gonzales who's been returned to Mexico a number of times. The FBI is following up with the Immigration and

Naturalization Service but basically, they said that if INS knew where he was, he'd be on his way back to Mexico again."

"Hmm." Laurie paused while she considered the new information. "Any links to him locally?"

"I made an inquiry with a friend in West St. Paul where many of the Twin Cities Hispanics live. There's no Hispanic core community in the north metro area. A Mexican national would stand out here. White Bear Lake is pretty white."

Laurie nodded. "That may work to your advantage. I'd check around at some of the restaurants and motels to see if anyone noticed any Mexicans within a day or two of Tommy's disappearance."

"I'm following up on that. The FBI is checking with Mexican authorities to see if they know if Ernesto Gonzales has relatives in the U.S. My contact said that rarely produces much in the way of leads." Laurie could hear notebook pages flipping as Randall stopped talking for a moment. "I guess that's about it. Thanks for the support, Inspector. I'll get back to you if anything else turns up."

"Call if anything turns up."

Laurie ended the call and went into the bedroom in search of a quiet place to think. She pulled the door shut and took her laptop from a leather satchel. She made a few notes regarding the conversation with Bill Randall, then thought for a while. An illegal alien could fit the profile of the kidnapper. He'd stay close to the freeway because he wasn't familiar with the areas. He wouldn't be tied to one region or state. Most criminals strike within a few miles of their homes, but this person wasn't tethered by location. But why would a Mexican be kidnapping kids in the Midwest if not for ransom? Laurie's mind ran through some of the common motives. It obviously wasn't a parental custody dispute.

A chill ran over Laurie as she considered two other insidious possibilities. Could he be making a profit on it somehow? Selling them for adoption? No legitimate agency would touch them. Was he selling them into the black market for kiddy porn? Anyone with a video camera and Internet access could be selling kiddy porn all over the world from his or her home. The thought nauseated her.

She backed up and considered the geography. The kids were missing from the Midwest, but an illegal Mexican alien wouldn't suddenly drop into the Midwest. Bill Randall's comments stuck in her head: "White Bear Lake is pretty white." Where were the other towns that had children missing? He might have a place to dispose of the children where he was less obvious. Laurie typed in some thoughts and then considered her next step.

She pulled up her computer file of contacts and started making telephone calls. She suggested that each police department ask if anyone had seen an unknown Hispanic man in motels and restaurants the days around the kidnappings.

● ● ●

At the same time, Bill Randall was making a few calls of his own. He spoke with the manager of the White Bear Inn at the intersection of I-35E and highway 96, who didn't remember any Mexican customers in the hotel or the restaurant, but promised to interview the desk clerks and the wait staff. Randall also called the Emerald Inn and Best Western in nearby Maplewood since they were the only other nearby motels. He was starting to call restaurants and was speaking to Kurt, the owner of Ursula's Restaurant in downtown White Bear, when someone tapped him on the shoulder and pointed to a button on the telephone that was blinking.

He punched the blinking button after he got a negative response from Kurt. "Sergeant Randall."

"Sergeant, this is Bob Harris at the White Bear Inn. After we spoke, I checked the guest register for the nights around the date you gave me. We had a double room rented to someone registered under the name Ramirez the night before the kidnapping. They listed a Texas license plate on a gray Olds. The clerk who checked them in is not on again until tomorrow. I can give you her name and home number."

Randall scrambled to scribble down the name and license number, then the clerk's name and phone number. Confidence crept into his voice as he said, "Thanks, Mr. Harris. I think you've just given us a huge lead."

Bill Randall quickly punched the Texas plate number into the computer and waited. The computer indicated the car had been salvaged. The plates were probably taken off the car at a junkyard somewhere. "No surprise," he said to himself. Next, he called the motel clerk at home.

Tracy Pearson's brother answered the telephone. Her brother called out, "Tracy! The White Bear cops are on the phone for you."

Randall smirked as he imagined Tracy's reaction. He bet himself she would be either panicked or wouldn't believe her brother. Panic won. "Hello? Is this really the police?"

Randall put on his best reassuring demeanor. "Tracy, this is Sergeant Randall from the White Bear Police and I need your help." He paused to let her relax. "You checked in someone named Ramirez about a week ago when you were working at the White Bear Inn. Do you remember?"

Tracy's mind shifted back and the evening came back to her. "Sure. There were two guys together. They got upset because I thought they were Indians. They told me they were Americans named Ramirez. I got really embarrassed and apologized to them."

Randall's ears perked up and he asked, "There were two of them?"

"Yeah, both of them were about 25 or 30 years old."

Randall's pen was making quick notes as he asked, "Can you describe them to me?"

Tracy paused and closed her eyes. She said, "Sure. They both had kinda dark skin, with straight black hair. One was skinny and shorter. The other one was taller and fatter. The fat one did all the talking. They both wore jeans and denim jackets. They looked cold."

Randall asked, "How tall were they, and did they have any distinguishing features?"

Tracy thought before answering. "They were both taller than me, over five-two. But not much taller. The fat one had a bad complexion, as if he had really bad acne as a kid. But that's about all I remember about them." She paused for a second, then asked, "Did they do something bad? I mean, am I in trouble for checking them in? They paid their bill in cash, so I know they didn't skip out without paying for the room."

"You're not in trouble. We think they may have been involved in a crime unrelated to their stay at the Inn." Randall tapped his pen on the desktop and thought about the INS link. "If I can get some pictures of men that match the description you gave me, I'd like to bring them over and have you look at them."

Tracy's voice was timid and unsure. "I'm not very good at faces. Mexicans and Indians look the same to me."

"Thanks Tracy. I'd like to call you after I get some pictures."

His next call was to the FBI office in Minneapolis. The telephone rang twice before Special Agent Randi Pitt answered the telephone. Bill Randall had worked with Randi to break up a drug ring working the northern suburbs of St. Paul a few years previously and they had developed a mutual respect. They had exchanged a dozen calls about the Martin kidnapping. It had been Randi who called earlier with the INS news about Ernesto Gonzales' fingerprints.

"Randi, this is Bill Randall again. I got a solid lead. A clerk at the White Bear Inn reported two Hispanic men registered the night before the kidnapping. She gave me a description of the car and the license number. The license is from a junker in Texas, so nowhere to take it, except it points to Texas again. I spoke with the clerk who checked them in. She said one was fat and one was skinny. Beyond that, she couldn't help much other than to say that they were wearing jeans and denim jackets, and they looked cold. I think that if we could get a mug shot of Ernesto Gonzales from the INS, we might get her to make an I.D."

Randi Pitt was rapidly scribbling notes as Bill Randall spoke. "I'll call my contact at INS and have him send a booking picture. I'll also pass this along to our Midwest field offices asking them to follow up with the other cities reporting kidnappings. This may be enough to get us going. What kind of car was it?"

Randall flipped to the page of notes with the car description that the manager of the Inn had provided. "A gray Olds."

Randi made a note and replied, "Got it. Thanks Bill."

CHAPTER 17

SAN ANTONIO, FRIDAY NIGHT

Tubby and Dolores were snuggled together on the couch when Ernie and Roberta unlocked the apartment door and walked in. Both were in the same clothes from the previous day and both were high. Roberta immediately spotted the ring on Dolores's finger and their discussion flew back and forth so fast it sounded like Spanish gibberish.

Ernie spoke in a mixture of Spanish and English. He rattled off conversation while he paced back and forth.

Tubby grabbed Ernie by the arm. "Slow down. Are you guys on speed?"

"Hey." Ernie pushed Tubby's hand off his arm. "I can handle myself. A little speed helps me focus." He threw himself into a chair. "We made it three times last night. Every time she asks for another hit, I make her give me a little treat first. I'm getting so sore I can hardly even pee anymore." Ernie leaned back on the couch as if he were the king of the world.

Tubby shook his head. "You shouldn't bait her into sex if she doesn't want it. You're as bad as the guy in the bar."

Roberta pulled Ernie onto the couch and pulled his arm across her shoulders. She cooed in his ear, "I'm coming down a little. How about a little more?" She ran her hand over his crotch sensuously. "What do you want for a treat this time?"

Ernie grabbed her hand. "No more today. I gotta take it easy for a while."

Roberta pouted and moved to the other couch, next to Dolores.

Tubby shook his head in disgust and said, "We still got a job for Mister Applewhite tomorrow. Same deal as last time. We pick up the package in town tomorrow night. We deliver it up North in a UPS box."

"We should take the girls along on the trip. It would sure make the time go faster." Ernie blew a kiss to Roberta who smiled, unsure of what had been said, unable to keep up with the Spanglish discussion.

"Are you nuts?" Tubby said in horror. "If they get in on this, they could blow the deal. Let's leave them here and set them up with some food and stuff. They'll be okay."

Ernie shrugged. "Like I said, it would sure make the trip better. But you're the boss. Think about it." He turned to the girls, who were talking in hushed tones. "Come on, Roberta. We've got to go before these two bring us down."

Ernie pulled Roberta by the arm and they were on their way, leaving as quickly as they had swept in. Tubby settled down next to Dolores and put his arm round her shoulder. He asked, "You didn't tell Roberta we were getting married?"

Dolores shook her head. "Yes, but they were on drugs and I don't think she understood. They would not remember much tomorrow anyway. We can tell them later."

She ran her finger up Tubby's neck and around the edges of his ear. "What did Ernie say about a trip? He wanted us to go along and you said no."

Tubby pushed her hand away and rubbed his ear vigorously. "Ernie and I have to work. It wouldn't be fun. I think it would be best if you stayed here with Roberta. We'll be back in a few days."

A frown crossed Dolores' face. "How do you and Ernie make money? Ernie said something about a job. I have not seen you go to work."

Tubby thought for a second. "We're couriers. We deliver packages for people. We'll pick one up tomorrow and we'll take it to Minnesota. We'll pick up a package there and bring it back. When we get back we'll have lots of money again."

Dolores had little formal schooling and had never taken a geography class. She asked, "Where is Minnesota?"

"It's almost to Canada . . . way north." Tubby replied. "It takes more than a day to drive that far."

CHAPTER 18

SAN MIGUEL, SATURDAY MORNING

The church work group rose before the sun crept over the horizon. Friday had been their last day of work and the dinner put on by the villagers, and the aftermath for some, was the capstone on of the trip. In the pink morning twilight they stumbled around, rolling up sleeping bags, gathering belongings, and packing their bags in preparation for the long drive to Texas. Every time Micah or Toby looked at Judy Arend they smiled, then quickly looked away.

Judy spent much of the morning consoling Melissa Brown and motivating her to pack after a sleepless night interspersed with bouts of tears. Loading her own duffle bag into the van, Judy soon noticed the glances and giggles of the boys. She cornered Tom Knight who was carrying a Coleman stove to the van.

"Tom, the boys weren't asleep when you got back into the church last night." Judy whispered. "Toby can't look me in the eye and Micah blushes every time I look at him. I'm so embarrassed."

Tom, trying to act nonchalant, said, "You're paranoid Judy. They were all in their sleeping bags sawing lumber when I walked in."

He gave her a peck on the cheek and she looked around nervously. "Cut that out," she whispered as a blush spread over her cheeks. "It's bad enough we're fooling around when they're asleep." She quickly walked back to the building and made sure she wasn't alone with Tom before everyone loaded into the van.

The drive from San Miguel to the border took three hours over rough gravel roads. One of the boys jokingly suggested that the next group bring a road grader. By the time they reached Matamoros, they had all settled into their routines— some sleeping, some reading, and two playing "Go Fish" on the seat. The van joined a queue of cars, trucks, and vans, lined up blocks from Rio Grande Bridge.

They were waved through the Mexican barricades by a uniformed guard who didn't get out of his chair. On the American side of the river, a Customs agent waved the van into a lane away from the flow of truckers. Once they were committed to the lane, the van was quickly wedged between two cars and stopped.

A female agent walked to the driver's side window as Tom rolled it down. Her badge indicated that she was a U.S. Customs agent. She asked, "How long have you been in Mexico?" She peered at all the tired, grimy faces in the rear of the van while she waited for Tom's answer.

"Four days," he said, handing the stack of passports to her.

"What was the nature of your visit?" As she asked the question, the second agent finished with the car ahead of them and looked in the rear windows of the church van.

Judy suddenly became uncomfortable with the agent's casual inspection of the van's interior, including eyeing her from lap to hair.

"We were on a mission project to San Miguel for the Pine Brook Free Church in Minnesota. We've been building a church."

The second agent came to the driver's side and nodded to the rear of the van. The female agent took a step back from the door, still holding the stack of passports and said, "I'd like all of you to step out of the van. Please step around to the rear, remove your bags and stand next to them." A third agent matched a passport picture to each traveler and returned the passports after they were matched. She pointed to a window in the nearest building. The sign over the window said, Immigration and Naturalization Service. "Leave your gear here, and take your passport to the window."

Ann Perry, groaned and in a stage voice complained about harassment to one of the other girls. Tom quickly stepped to Ann and leaned close. In a firm voice he said, "These folks are doing their jobs. Let's not make it more difficult than it need be."

As a group, they took their passports to the INS window as an agent walked around the van with a mirror on a stick that allowed him to inspect the undercarriage.

Their passports were scanned, they each answered questions at the INS window, and then they returned to the van. The female agent was standing next to the pile of luggage from the van. When the group reassembled, she stood back from the pile of backpacks and suitcases. The Customs agent pointed to a long table next to the traffic lane and said, "Please bring your personal bags to the table and open them." As they trudged to the table, car after car was waved past the checkpoint, crossing without apparent delay.

A male agent looked at Tom and Judy's passports, then handed them back. "You two don't need to unpack your bags," he said, clearly focused on the teens and their bag inspections.

Another male agent approached them. "Do you own the van, sir?"

"The van belongs to our church," Judy blurted out. "Is there a problem?"

"Your gas tank has a leak," the agent replied. "Your gas mileage is probably terrible already and you've got gas dripping out, too."

"Thanks," Tom said.

The teens opened every suitcase and backpack under the watchful eyes of the customs agents. They were allowed to close the bags and they returned to the van. A few minutes later they were on the road.

As they pulled away from the border crossing Judy whispered, "Are they always that thorough? When we drove to Canada with my kids they hardly had us stop."

"You didn't have a vanload of teenagers," he replied. "Every time we cross back into the U.S. they almost take the van apart. I think they have a profile of drug smugglers and it must involve a van loaded with teenagers."

At five o'clock, the outskirts of San Antonio were visible. They got onto I-35 and passed the Sea World exit. Judy followed the highway to a sign for a Holiday Inn Express. When she parked at the motel, they were within sight of the Pearl brewery, which was being reincarnated as condos and an art museum.

Ann Perry climbed out first and stretched. "So, are we just going to crash here for the night, or do we actually get to see some of the town?"

Tom pulled open the back doors of the van and a backpack spilled out and nearly onto his feet. "Tell you what. You guys get checked in, cleaned up, and then we'll go down to the Riverwalk together. We'll walk around the Alamo, then eat in the mall food court. Let's meet in the lobby in 30 minutes."

With the mention of the Alamo, Toby perked up and said, "Cool!"

"There is no way four of us are sharing a room and being ready in 30 minutes. We have to each take a shower and blow out our hair!" Crystal Perkins said.

Judy took Melissa Brown aside and consoled her about the delayed return to Pine Brook. Melissa asked if they could drive straight through. "The plan has always been to stop in San Antonio for Saturday night. We all need a shower, and the rest of the drive will take almost twenty hours. The drivers need a break."

Melissa quickly resigned herself to the delay. "Can I call home again?"

"Sure."

They parked the van across from the Menger Hotel. After sorting out cameras and backpacks, they walked to the Alamo.

"Everyone listen up," Tom Knight said, pulling them together. "This place is a church and I expect you to act with reverence. Take off your caps, turn off your electronic devices, and whisper if you have to communicate." They joined the line and filed into the chapel.

The teens were intrigued by the history of the battle and enjoyed the museum. Judy Arend was overwhelmed by the feel of the chapel building and teared up as she looked into the room with dozens of flags representing the home countries of the martyrs who died in the battle.

Everyone voted for "real American hamburgers" in the food court. The Mexican food had been an adventure, but burgers were the top choice for the repatriated 'gringos and gringas'. By nine o'clock, they were back in the hotel and within minutes everyone was asleep.

CHAPTER 19

After four days of canvassing the neighborhood, Floyd had finally interviewed all the neighbors within two blocks of the church. Everyone heard the explosion, but the only lead had been the sighting of a man, wearing jeans and maybe a baseball cap, carrying a box the size of a bread loaf, from a dark colored car, all offered by a four-year-old boy. The child was at best a questionable witness.

He drove back to the courthouse and parked his squad. Seeing the Sheriff's car in its reserved spot, Floyd noted that it was nearly eight p.m. and uttered to himself, "The sheriff's keeping later hours than usual."

He passed through the outer security door and walked by the dispatcher's cubicle. She waved to him and released the electronic lock on the door. He stopped at the sheriff's corner office and stuck his head in the door. Sepanen was studying some papers, his head shrouded in a cloud of cigar smoke.

"Have you got a second, John?" Floyd asked.

John Sepanen looked up from the papers, then waved Floyd in with the hand holding the cigar. "Sure. What's up?"

Floyd sat down in the furthest guest chair to avoid the cloud of smoke as much as possible. "I just talked to the last of the neighbors in Pine Brook. Other than one report from a kid, I've come up dry on George Brown's murder. No one remembers anyone unusual in the neighborhood."

Sepanen set the papers down and considered Floyd's words before replying. "Have you been able to find a motive?"

Floyd shook his head. "Nothing that would justify murder. George was uncomfortable with the church mission project, but I suspect that may be more a fiscal matter than a murder motive. George didn't like to spend money."

Sepanen nodded. "Have you been using any outside agencies?"

Floyd took a deep breath. "Yeah. The BCA is looking at criminal files and they sent the hood of George's car to St. Paul for blast residue analysis. Tony Oresek, the medical examiner, removed a chip that may be part of a detonator. He turned it over to a BATF agent. If they can determine the manufacturers of the chip and explosives, we might be able to trace it to a company or person." Floyd ran his fingers through his hair. "Other than that, I don't have another avenue to pursue at the moment."

Sepanen raised his eyebrows. "I guess we'll hope for a lead that drops out of the sky."

"Sometimes they do. If you call the *St. Paul Pioneer Press* and *Minneapolis Star-Tribune* with a plea for help, the sky might open."

Sepanen reached across his desk, took a gold pen from its holder, and scribbled a few words on a Post-It notepad. "It's worth a try." He put the pen back and added, "I've had a good response when I talked to Channel 5 in St. Paul. Maybe they will run a "Crime Stoppers" segment for us. That usually generates a few calls."

"Thanks." Floyd got up from the chair and walked to Sepanen's office door where he stopped, "What's keeping you here so late?"

The sheriff held up a sheaf of papers. "The Pine Brook Free Church isn't the only group working on budgets."

A pink message slip lay on Floyd's desk. He peeled off his jacket and hung it on the chair while he read it. Andy Peterson left a telephone number. He mentally sorted through the local Peterson clans and then remembered Andy. "The kid from church," he said to himself. He mused for a second on how unusual it was for a teenager to call the sheriff's department as he dialed.

After four rings a male voice answered. "Hello."

"Hi. This is Floyd Swenson from the sheriff's department. I'm returning Andy Peterson's call from earlier today."

The voice picked up enthusiasm. "Yes sir. This is Andy. We talked when you stopped by the church the night we were reglazing the windows."

Floyd smiled. "I remember you, Andy."

"Well, it made me think about the DARE program in fourth grade when you came and talked to us about resisting drugs. You said that we could talk to you anytime." Andy paused while he considered his next words. "I have something I think

I want to tell you." He hesitated again. "Umm. There is this older guy selling drugs at the roller rink. It kinda seems like he's there every Wednesday night."

Swenson sat down and searched the desktop for a pen and scratch paper among the piles of reports and other papers that had accumulated on his desk. As he scribbled a note he asked, "The Willow River roller rink?"

"Yeah. Wednesday nights are reserved for people sixteen and older, so the little kids aren't around. There's been a guy who rents skates, but he never puts them on. He just sits in the back and talks to guys. I've seen them pass him some money and once I think I saw him passing something hidden in his hand."

Floyd considered the information, then asked, "Do you know his name?"

Andy let out a sigh. "No. I've never seen him anywhere but at the roller rink. He's a little older than me, so I wouldn't know him from school, but I've never seen him around town either."

"How old do you think he is?"

Andy considered his answer for a few seconds. "He's pretty old. Maybe 25. He has long dark hair in a ponytail and he's really skinny."

"How tall do you think he is?"

"I don't think I've ever seen him standing up. I guess I don't know." Andy replied.

"Have you seen him in a car?"

"Not really."

Floyd stared at the notes and tapped the pencil on the desktop. "Thanks for calling. I really appreciate you taking the time. Call me again if you can think of anything. And please don't mention this to anyone."

Andy barked out a nervous laugh. "Oh, don't worry about me telling anyone. I think I would get some heavy-duty grief if anyone at school knew I was squealing to you."

Floyd smiled at the thought of the peer pressure surrounding the use of drugs. Then another thought struck him. "Don't try to be a hero. You've given me enough information to follow up further on this. Keep yourself clear of this the guy and let me take care of it. Okay?"

"Sure." Andy's reply sounded like he was relieved.

Swenson leaned back in the chair and thought about the conversation. If this was legitimate, and he had no reason to believe it was not, he would need someone to go in undercover and make a buy. He pulled open the lap drawer of his desk and dug until he found the business card he needed. Then he picked up the telephone and called the chairman of the Northeastern Minnesota drug task force. The task force was a joint effort of ten sheriff departments and two dozen major police departments to coordinate drug investigations and to provide investigators that were not recognizable in other municipalities.

Swenson got a voicemail answer to his call and left a message for Cory James, the task force chairman, at his office in Duluth.

CHAPTER 20

SAN ANTONIO

At midnight, Ernie knocked at Tubby's apartment door. Tubby was just pulling on his windbreaker. He opened the door and walked out without looking through the peephole. They walked down the stairs without speaking.

Tubby's voice was tense. "I hate this shit. Of all the things we're paid to do, I dislike this the most."

Ernie struggled to keep up with Tubby's fast pace. He was irritated that Tubby was so uptight. "What are you complaining about, man? All you ever do is drive the car. I'm the one who takes all the risks. I grab the kids and run, and now I have to crawl under the van and pull the package."

"All you have to do is watch for cops and ride along. Don't give me any of your complaints. You just say the word and I'll switch with you . . ." Ernie suddenly stopped walking and laughed. "Oh, that's right. You wouldn't fit under the van to get the package."

Tubby stopped to glare at him. "Quit giving me shit about being fat. I got the car. I tuned it up and I take care of it. You haven't even got a license. So, fuck you, Ernie. If you don't like the arrangements you just let me know you want off this job and I'll find myself another flunky to do your job." Tubby started walking again and shouted over his shoulder. "Oh! Too bad you can't get another job because you're illegal. Sorry." The sarcasm dripped from his words as he unlocked the driver's side door.

Ernie rattled the door handle until Tubby finally unlocked it from the inside. Ernie climbed in and sat silently as they drove through the quiet back streets on their way to the motel parking lot. The lot was half-full of cars with the church van parked conveniently in a poorly lit back corner. After circling the block, Tubby parked the Olds a half block from the motel. Ernie stared out the windshield without making a move to open the door as two people pulled rolling suitcases across the parking lot and into the front door.

Tubby rolled his eyes in frustration. "So, what's the matter now?"

Ernie turned his head and glared at Tubby. If his eyes had been laser beams they would have drilled holes in Tubby's head. "I don't like your attitude. I work as hard as you and I deserve to be treated with respect." Ernie crossed his arms across his chest and stared out the windshield again.

Tubby's temper erupted. "You're mad at me? You call me fat all the time and make jokes about it. Then you get mad because I can replace you." Tubby slammed his palms on the steering wheel. "I can't believe this! Quit whining and get the package before some cop stops to ask why we're parked here." Tubby reached across Ernie's legs and pushed the door open.

Ernie gave Tubby another glare, then got out of the car and walked toward the van. Eight minutes later Ernie was back in the car and they were underway with gasoline fumes filling the car. Ernie slid a rust-covered shoebox from under his shirt and slipped it under his seat, then wiped his hands on his jeans. The grime and rust were part of the camouflage in case the gas tank seam slipped open. The whole underside of the van was as dusty and rusty as the package.

CHAPTER 21

SAN ANTONIO

After exploring the San Antonio Riverwalk, the group had retreated to the Holiday Inn. The girls called home and took turns luxuriating in the bathtub. Each girl emerged from the bathroom wrapped in a towel, cheeks rosy, and looking refreshed. Judy waited and took the last bathtub shift. When she emerged, the girls were all sound asleep.

The boys went to the pool where they did cannonballs and horsed around until the assistant manager asked them to quiet down. Tom, who was reading next to the pool, intervened when the noise started to rise again, herding the boys back to their rooms. It was well after midnight when they'd all showered and settled into bed.

The church group was up before sunrise and partook freely of the complimentary continental breakfast. Tom and Judy were tired and frazzled by the chaos of breakfast, suffering through burning toast that set off a smoke detector, a "bake your own" waffle that oozed out of the waffle iron then crept across the countertop, and the cacophony of voices that irritated a number of businesspeople who were trying to read newspapers and/or listen to the news on a big screen television. The boys were mostly oblivious to the scowls of the people around them or those who left looking for quieter seating. Tom, who was also reading a newspaper, set it aside to remind them about restaurant etiquette. The girls sat quietly at a separate table and Judy shook her head.

Done with breakfast, the thundering horde rushed to their rooms to retrieve their backpacks and suitcases. They assembled in the lobby while Tom settled the bill at checkout.

Tom managed to catch Judy alone, just outside the lobby. "You seem quiet this morning," he said.

Judy looked around nervously at the teens before whispering. "I feel so guilty. What we've done is so wrong. I can't face the kids." She crossed her arms across her chest and shivered in the morning twilight.

Tom reached out to hug her for warmth and she stepped away. "We can't do this, Tom. I have a husband and kids."

Tom put out a hand. "Do you love him?" he whispered.

Judy stared at his hand, arms still crossed, as tears welled in her eyes. "I love my children."

Ann rushed up to them and announced, "Everything is packed." She saw the tears in Judy's eyes and her enthusiasm quickly turned to concern. "Are you okay, Mrs. Arend?"

Judy wiped her eyes with her hands and nodded. "I'm fine, just a little sad about leaving."

● ● ●

Tubby set a package of toilet paper, bags of junk food, a case of Coke, and a 12-pack of beer on the kitchen counter. Those were the only grocery items that Tubby ever bought for himself so it never occurred to him that Dolores might want something else.

Dolores surveyed the contents as Tubby loaded the beer into the refrigerator. "Where are the tortillas? You didn't even buy pollo . . . I mean chicken." She threw her arms in the air. "I'll look like a watermelon if this is all I eat while you're gone. Take me with you to the store and I'll get some real food."

Tubby shrunk under the verbal barrage. He didn't want to anger her further by refusing to make another grocery run, but time was running out. "I don't have time. Ernie will be here any minute and we have to leave." He dug in his pocket and pulled out a wad of bills. "Here," he said, peeling off a dozen twenties. "Order Domino's pizza. The number is next to the phone and they will bring it to the door. All you have to do is pay them."

He grabbed her by the hand and dragged her into the kitchen. "Here's the phone number." The number was scribbled on the wall with a red permanent marker.

Tubby watched television while Dolores pouted. It was a scene that was becoming too familiar to Tubby. Although he professed to love her dearly, he was starting to tire of her constant company. She wanted to do things. He was happy sitting in front of the television playing *Mortal Combat* for hours at a time. They went out to eat often, but Dolores didn't like any of the food. She complained there were no "real" tortillas. The peppers were too mild and she found sandwiches and burgers disgusting. As time passed it became clear she really wanted to go somewhere else and considered herself a prisoner in a gilded cage. Tubby wouldn't let her go anywhere unless he was with her.

When Ernie and Roberta walked in, Tubby was taken aback. Roberta looked like a bedraggled waif. Her dress hadn't been changed or laundered in several days. Her skin was gray, her cheeks hollow, and there were dark bags under her eyes. In contrast, Dolores's fresh appearance and new clothing surprised Ernie. He pushed past Tubby and pulled a beer from the refrigerator while Roberta stood by the door looking lost. After taking a long swallow of Corona, Ernie pointed the neck of the bottle at Roberta.

"She's coming down. She'll be okay in a couple of hours." He quickly changed the topic. "Did you get the UPS uniform pressed?"

Tubby was still in a state of disbelief as Roberta walked past him and sat down on the couch. She started to shiver, pulled a pillow onto her lap, and clutched it like a security blanket while Dolores hugged her shoulders.

Ernie's question pulled Tubby away from his focus on Roberta. "Uh, yeah. I picked it up from the cleaners yesterday. It's hanging in the car. I made up a couple of new boxes too."

"Roberta has to stay here while I'm gone." Ernie said. "She's a little too strung out to be alone at my place. I figured the girls could keep each other company while we made the trip."

Tubby looked at Dolores with a questioning expression. She shrugged.

Ernie nodded and threw the beer bottle toward the wastebasket in the corner. The bottle hit the wall and fell to the floor. He ignored the bottle as it dribbled beer onto the carpet. "Good. Let's go." Ernie said with a belch. He walked to the door and held it open.

Tubby went to Dolores and gave her a peck on the cheek. She never let go of Roberta to return the kiss. "Look after Roberta. We'll be back in a few days. Then I'll take you to the grocery store and you can pick out groceries and cook for me." Her dour expression lightened a little, and she gave him a tentative peck on the cheek.

Tubby and Ernie drove through the residential area and onto the Interstate in silence. The brown Texas countryside rolled past, dotted with patches of green prickly pear cactus. Ernie was asleep within a few minutes of reaching I-35; he too appeared to be coming down from their drug binge. Tubby's mind wandered back to Dolores, unhappy and pouting in the apartment with Roberta, who was strung out and shaking.

"Will they be there when we come back? Do I care?"

• • •

DULUTH, MINNESOTA

Edmund Lone Eagle's condition deteriorated to the point that the elders succumbed to Laurie's demands that he be hospitalized. It was a hollow victory. Laurie feared that the cancer had invaded so much of his body that surgery, chemotherapy, and radiation might not be enough to save him.

The family waiting room at Miller-Dwan Hospital was starting to take on the appearance of a pow-wow. Several aunts and uncles had arrived from South Dakota and Minneapolis. They sat in small clutches like at a reunion, or a funeral, most dressed in jeans and casual shirts. Some talked, some played games, and one old man sat quietly in a corner meditating in a near trance-like state.

Laurie tried to continue her role as the dedicated daughter, but she avoided all the groups and sat alone in a corner, typing on her keyboard. Through the hospital Wi-Fi she was able to access the BCA e-mail system. She scanned hundreds of electronic messages and responded to questions.

The third e-mail was a note from the deputy director. As she read it, a chill ran over her body. She set the computer on the table and pulled out her cell phone. She glanced up at a sign that forbid the use of cell phones, then went in search of a spot that wasn't posted "No Cell phones."

● ● ●

PINE COUNTY

Driving directly to the Pine County Courthouse was still a strange feeling for Floyd Swenson. Conditioned by nearly three decades of patrolling the rural roads, he never realized how that helped him ease into his job. Entering the courthouse, the dispatcher handed him three pink message slips. The top one was from the sheriff. After hanging up his jacket he walked to the ready room and poured himself a cup of coffee that looked like it had been on the warmer for over eight hours. He read the other two messages as he sipped the hot, biting coffee. The second message was from Cory James, the head of the drug task force, and the third was from Emil Ogren, whose name Floyd recognized as a farmer east of Pine City. Floyd decided to deal with the sheriff first.

Floyd was surprised to see the sheriff was sitting in his office on a Sunday morning. He was studying spreadsheets on his computer when Swenson rapped a knuckle on the door frame. "Come in." The sheriff motioned him to a chair.

The sheriff set aside the computer and pulled a cigar out of the mahogany box that sat on top of his desk. He made a ceremony of removing the wrapper and lighting it with a match.

The sheriff's bass voice was unusually raspy. "I talked to a news producer from Channel 4 in the Cities. He's trying to free a reporter to do a follow-up story on George Brown's murder." The sheriff carefully blew a stream of smoke to the ceiling. "The Minneapolis *Star Tribune* had a big drug bust last night that's taking up most of the front page, so they may run something the day after tomorrow. The *Pioneer Press* is going to have a reporter call me back this morning."

Floyd nodded. "Great! Maybe that'll break something loose." He waved the pink note from the drug task force chairman. "We've got something else brewing too. I had a tip that there is a guy selling drugs in Willow River. I'm going to see if we can get an undercover officer from the drug task force to make a buy."

The sheriff rolled the cigar between his fingers, savoring the aroma of the smoke. "Can you handle the investigation? We could pull a deputy off the road to help for a week or two."

Floyd shrugged. "There's nothing new with the Brown murder. Unless we get a lot of leads from the media exposure, I should be able to handle it all."

The sheriff smirked, leaned back in his chair and stared at the ceiling. "Pam Ryan asked if she could get involved in more investigative work. I guess you really got her turned onto being an investigator with those cold cases last year."

Floyd smiled. "She's a fireball and she has a talent for sorting through streams of conflicting information."

The sheriff got up from his chair and closed the door. He sat in a guest chair so close that Floyd could smell the cigar smoke on his breath. "Pam is a great asset to this department. Her smiling face really charms people in our booth at the county fair and she's fabulous with the kids in the DARE program at the schools. I don't want to lose her. You're not going to be here forever, and I would like to groom her to be your successor. Do what you can to make use of her and help her hone those investigative skills." The sheriff stood, signaling the end of the conversation.

"That will cause some hard feelings among the older deputies," Floyd said. "Pam is the least senior deputy and many of the others would consider this a cherry assignment."

The sheriff stopped with his hand on the doorknob. "I don't think any of them has Pam's potential or charisma. Do you?"

Floyd hesitated and then said, "Sandy Maki is about the only one that's close. The rest are great road deputies, but I couldn't turn them loose on a major investigation without directing their every move."

The sheriff pointed the butt of his cigar at Floyd's chest. "Then we're in agreement. Make it happen."

Floyd walked back to his desk considering the impact of engaging Pam in his investigations. The sheriff had the final word on the assignment but the overall morale of the department shouldn't suffer either. He dialed the number for the drug task force and after holding for a few minutes got Cory James. While he waited he tried to find a way to sell the change to the more senior deputies.

"Cory, I need some help."

"Everyone who calls needs help, Floyd. Tell me more."

"I had a call from one of my DARE kids. He thinks there's a guy selling drugs at the Willow River roller rink. The Wednesday night crowd is older teens with a few around twenty. I don't have anyone in the department with an unfamiliar face, or who looks young enough to show up in that crowd."

Cory weighed the request. "Are you looking for an officer to attempt a buy, or are you trying to bust a major operation so you need a whole team?"

Floyd pondered the question before answering. "At this point, I think that we have one guy selling. There hasn't been too much drug activity around here, so I'm guessing that we've got someone from Minneapolis coming up once a week to sell to the Pine County hicks. Let's assume that he's a loner and take him down."

Cory agreed. "As long as there aren't a lot of sales around the area a single bust might work out. If we bust him here, we might be able to get him to turn in his sources too." Papers shuffled in the background. "I've got a Brainerd city officer that just finished a project in Aitkin. I think we could let him spend a couple Wednesday evenings with you."

The second call was to the farmer. When Emil Ogren answered the telephone Swenson could hear cattle noises in the background and he assumed Emil had a phone in the barn.

"Mister Ogren, this is Floyd Swenson from the sheriff's department. I had a message that you called. How can I help you?" Floyd pictured the old man standing in his barn wearing denim coveralls. Emil had emigrated from Sweden nearly sixty years ago, but his speech still had a strong accent.

Emil raised his voice to be heard over the clamor. "Yah. I called late last night. There were gunshots out back last night. I walked out to the field with my 30-30. There wasn't no one in my field, but I could hear an engine through the woods, so I walked back a ways. I could see two people guttin' a deer in the headlights. I told the dispatcher that I knew you seemed to be a helpful sort of fella, so I thought you'd want to know."

Swenson scribbled some notes on a sheet of paper. "I sure am glad you called. We've had a few people report gunshots but no one ever sees anything. Could you give me a description of the car and the men? A license number would be even better."

"There weren't no license number and only one of them was a man. It was Tom Emich and his wife. They weren't driving no car either. They was driving their John Deere tractor."

Floyd cracked a smile. "Are you sure it was them?"

"About as sure as my son's name is Matt," Emil replied. "They were here trying to sell me some of last year's moldy hay about two hours before."

Floyd agreed. "That's pretty sure. Thanks, Emil. I'll get in touch with the DNR and we'll check it out right away. If they're convicted you can collect a reward from the 'Turn in Poachers' program."

"I don't want no reward. I want them to stop shooting my deer. I don't approve of people shooting deer in the spring. They got fawns now, ya' know."

Swenson dialed the phone number of Ed Jennings, the officer from the Department of Natural Resources. He hoped to catch Ed at home, but with only one DNR enforcement officer covering the entire county, he often worked varying shifts and slept during the day. Jennings' wife answered the telephone and after a brief conversation rousted Ed from his sleep.

Ed's voice sounded sleepy. "Hi Floyd, Did I hear you got a line on our poacher?"

Floyd replied, "I got a tip from a disgruntled landowner. It sounds solid. How'd you like to meet me at the poacher's house?"

Ed yawned. "Sure. Give me a couple of minutes to shower and put on a uniform. Where am I going?"

Floyd looked at his watch, then guessed that it would take him almost ten minutes to make the drive. "I'll meet you at Ogren's house." Floyd gave him the rural Royalton Township address of their final destination. "I can hardly wait to see his face when we knock on the poacher's door together."

The drive to Ogren's took Floyd through the open fields and then into the broken woodlots and rocky pastures that make up most of the farms of northeastern Minnesota. Floyd waved to a farmer who was loading split oak firewood into the back of his pickup.

"I hope he's cutting that for next year, because that wood won't be dry enough to burn for months." Floyd said to himself, catching the scent of the freshly cut oak as it wafted through the car.

Swenson pulled into the Ogren's driveway and shut off the engine. Within a minute, Ed drove up and stepped out of his pickup, pulling a lightweight green coat over his bulletproof vest. The vest is standard apparel for all Minnesota Department of Natural Resources enforcement officers although it provides little protection against a deer rifle.

As they crossed the driveway, Swenson filled Ed Jennings in on the conversation with Emil Ogren and his sighting of the poachers in his woodlot. Emichs lived on the opposite side of the section of land from Ogrens.

Emil Ogren met the officers at his back door. After a brief conversation, he walked them to the spot where he'd seen the poachers. In a sparse patch of hazel brush, they found the head of a young buck, his antlers still growing under a coat of velvet, and a pile of entrails. Close by were deep ruts cut in the soft marshy ground by tractor tires. Jennings took pictures of the scene and got several shots of the deer's antlers.

"There's a special trophy depletion charge for shooting a buck illegally," Jennings explained as he put the camera away. "That's in addition to the penalty for shooting a deer out of season."

"As far as I'm concerned this is your bust. I'm just here to back you up," Floyd said as they walked down Ogren's driveway.

"You're certainly generous," Jennings said with a smile. "Don't have an arrest quota?"

"My only quota is keeping enough taxpayers happy to get the sheriff reelected," Floyd followed the conservation officer into Emich's driveway.

Jennings knocked on the door while Floyd stood out of sight. The sound of footsteps came down a hallway and the door opened. Marge Emich's face had a brief look of horror at the sight of a DNR officer on her doorstep. She regained her composure and put on a nervous smile.

"Officer, what can I do for you?" She turned and yelled over her shoulder. "Tom, the game warden is here."

"Could I come in and talk to you?" Jennings asked, pulling open the storm door.

Marge looked over her shoulder nervously and replied, "Uh, not right now . . . the house is a mess and . . . I wouldn't like you to see it like this." Tom Emich walked into the hallway wiping his hands on a dishtowel. His forehead glistened with sweat even though the temperature was cool inside the house.

"Then please show me your tractor," the DNR officer requested.

Marge quickly looked back toward her husband and then to Jennings. "I...uh...The tractor? I think it's in the shop. Isn't it dear?"

"Well. Let's walk to the barn and see." Jennings held the door and gestured for them to come outside.

When the couple stepped outside they were surprised to see Floyd. They walked in silence to the barn. Jennings stopped at the door waiting for the Emichs to open it and show them in. There was a brief moment of hesitation.

"We don't have to let you in unless you've got a search warrant," Tom Emich said, crossing his arms and blocking the door.

"You watch too much television," Jennings replied. "The DNR has broad powers of search and seizure. We also have an eyewitness to you two loading a poached deer into the bucket of your tractor last night. That amounts to probable cause. If you don't open the door for me, I will open it myself and the courts will stand behind me."

The Emichs hesitated and Jennings grabbed the handle of the door to pull it open, then hesitated. When he withdrew his hand he rubbed his fingers together and held them out for Floyd to see. "Floyd, doesn't this look like blood to you?" Swenson looked at Jennings' fingers and saw the rusty smear.

Floyd offered, "It's blood. Open the door."

Inside the barn, they found a deer hide rolled into a ball and tied with twine, lying alongside the tractor. The tractor's bucket was smeared with blood and there was a puddle of congealed blood on the bottom of the bucket.

"Would you show us where the meat is, or would you like me to search your freezer?" Jennings asked.

Tom Emich led them back to the house. The two officers and Marge followed him through the house and to the kitchen. The table was covered with an oilcloth tablecloth smeared with blood. On one side lay a cutting board and a fillet knife. On the other side was a roll of freezer paper. On the floor was a cooler filled with white paper packages.

Jennings pulled a citation book from his rear pocket and flipped it open. "I'm going to give you a citation for taking a deer out of season. You'll have to appear before the judge. He'll fine you and impose a trophy fee for taking a buck. Of course the real penalty is that we'll seize the tractor and auction it off after the trial."

Marge Emich looked nervously at her husband. "I thought you said it might cost us $35 if we got caught?" Her husband shrugged.

"It used to be that way," Floyd said, "but the legislature put some teeth into the game laws a couple of years ago because too many people were making economic decisions about wildlife. Now, prime beef is cheaper."

Jennings ripped out the ticket and handed it to Tom Emich. "There have been a number of other reports of deer being taken late at night in this area. Let's take a look at your freezer and see if there is any other venison without a license number on it."

Ten minutes later, Swenson and Jennings carried the cooler and several shopping bags of frozen venison to the pickup. "What are you going to do with all this?" Floyd asked.

"I'll drop the meat in the freezer in my garage. The food shelf distributes it to needy families and some goes to the Sturgeon Lake Volunteer Fire Department for their annual wild game feed. It won't go to waste."

Floyd thought of Polly Hanson sitting in a drafty farmhouse with the baby and no food in the cupboards. "Do you mind if I take a package of steaks to a charity case I know?"

"Help yourself to whatever you'd like," Jennings replied. "It makes no difference to me."

Floyd chose a package marked "chops," and another marked "steaks." He wrapped them in a blanket and set them in his trunk. Half an hour later Polly met him at the farmhouse door.

"I was helping the game warden and he confiscated some venison," he said, holding the white paper-wrapped packages out to her.

The girl turned the packages in her hand, looking at the writing. "Steak? Can I fry it up in a pan?"

"That'd work better with the chops," he said." The steaks are better if you cook them slow with some moisture and maybe some gravy."

The look in Polly's eyes told him her cooking skills might be limited to opening cans. He wanted to tell her to look for a recipe in a cookbook, or online, but he was sure she didn't have access to either. "Brown the steaks in a little grease, then put salt and pepper on them. Put a half cup of water over them, cover the pan, and turn the heat way down low. Make sure the liquid doesn't all cook off, you might have to add more water once in a while. Let them cook for at least an hour before you eat them."

"Sure!" she said. "And thank you. Ronny's been in jail and we haven't had much meat to eat for a while."

He drove away feeling sad and wondering what else he could do for Polly.

• • •

Duluth, Minnesota
Laurie Lone Eagle tried to reach the deputy director of the BCA several times throughout the day. She never made contact and he didn't return her calls. In desperation, she went back to the computer and typed him an emphatic e-mail message.

What do you mean the FBI has taken over the Tommy Martin investigation? I Will NOT drop it!! Laurie

• • •

I-35 IN SOUTHERN, MINNESOTA

Tom Knight called the church from the rest area outside Albert Lea, Minnesota. It would be another two or three hours before the group would be home, but he wanted to make sure the parents had a chance to make plans to pick up their kids. The teens raced to the restrooms and vending machines while he called. He was the first one back to the van.

Judy Arend was the second. "Was there someone at the church to start the phone chain?" she asked, as they watched the teens swarm around vending machines.

Tom stretched his tight muscles as he answered, "Yup. Hazel was putting the final touches on the newsletter in the church office. She said she'd make the first call and everyone will be notified." He rolled his head on his shoulders. "I suppose your husband will be there with the kids and you'll have some type of mushy homecoming welcome."

Judy tensed. "Actually, I kinda expect that he'll be there with the kids sleeping in the back-seat. It will be long after their bedtimes by the time we get to the church." She hesitated, then added, "He wasn't happy when I agreed to be a chaperone. I don't imagine he'll be any happier now that I've returned."

She watched the teens swapping snacks and drinking caffeinated soda pop that would keep them awake for hours.

"It's back to the apartment for a decent night's sleep for you, I suppose."

Tom considered that thought and replied, "I think it'll be a long hot bath first. Then about twenty hours of sleep." He gave her a playful hug and added, "I don't suppose you'd consider joining me?"

She glared at him, then started to say something, but the teens filed back from the vending machines with a variety of candy bars and soft drinks. Everyone loaded back into the van to start the final leg of their journey.

The church parking lot was a beehive of activity with parents, friends, and siblings. The girls were glued to the windows of the van, waving to friends and family while the boys became sullen. Tom stopped the van at the bottom of the church steps where it was quickly swarmed with people. The rear doors flew open and luggage was distributed to owners amid hugs and goodbyes. Family groups departed as stories of their Mexican adventure circulated.

With the last teens gone, Tom closed the back doors of the van. He found Judy standing on the steps next to her suitcase, sleeping bag, and make-up kit. She was staring down the road in the direction of the last departing car.

"Need a ride?" The playfulness was gone from his voice as he felt her disappointment.

"No," Judy said, shaking her head. "I'm sure something came up with the kids and he's just a little late." She avoided using her husband's name or looking at Tom while she answered.

Tom looked around to make sure they were alone, then said, "You know I was only kidding when I offered to share my hot bath."

"No, you weren't." The last set of taillights disappeared and Judy let out a sigh. "The problem is . . ." Tears streamed before the words came.

Tom took her gently in his arms. She buried her face in his shoulder and let the tears flow. He nuzzled her hair and said, "The problem is, I think you would prefer my bathtub to your husband's bed."

They stood in the cold moonlight in an uneasy embrace for several moments. When the hinges of the front door creaked, they stepped apart like kids caught kissing on the front step. Hazel Bergren stuck her head out the door.

"Judy, your husband called. One of the boys is sick and he just got home from the clinic. The newsletter is still running on the copier for a few more minutes. If you can wait a bit, I'll drive you home. Otherwise, if Tom can stay awake a little longer . . ."

Judy opened her mouth, but Tom cut her off.

"It's the opposite direction from your house, Hazel. I'll take her home."

The ride to the Arends' house was silent. They pulled up to the small rambler, built on an acre lot in what had once been a pasture. The lights were on inside the house and Judy stared at the shadows moving behind the curtains for a few seconds without moving as the engine idled.

Tom finally broke the silence. "Things aren't going well with Chuck?"

Judy couldn't bear to say the words, and just shook her head.

"So, it wasn't my animal magnetism that attracted you to me." He commented, rather than asked.

Judy looked at him and tried to smile. Instead, her smile turned into a frown and tears streamed down her cheeks again. She buried her face in his shoulder. It took her several minutes to regain her composure.

"I have to go." She leaned across the console and pecked him on the cheek. "You were just an impulsive fling. I hope you can deal with that." Her words came easily, but lacked sincerity. They both knew Judy's marriage was over.

She closed the door and walked to the house without taking her bags out of the van. Tom watched her go in the front door. When it closed behind her he got out and carried her bags to the house. He set them on the top step and left. As he drove away, he considered the time he had spent with Judy and the emotional pain he'd inflicted on her. As much as he wanted to be aloof, he felt a pang of regret. He considered her a bit frumpy and overweight, but he'd come to enjoy her company.

CHAPTER 22

SOUTHERN MINNESOTA, MONDAY MORNING

The fast food restaurants, car dealers, shopping centers, and warehouses of the southern Twin Cities suburbs cluttered the edges of the freeway before I-35 split into East and West, long before the St. Paul skyline came into view. The Olds crossed the Mississippi River and the speed limit slowed to 45 mph. Ernie sensed the slowing of the car and woke up as Tubby matched the speed of the cars around him. "Where are we?"

Tubby had been driving for twenty hours and his voice was tinged with irritation. "We're going through that stupid chunk of freeway in St. Paul that's only 45 mile an hour. A talk radio station was giving a traffic report, and they said there was a slowdown on 'the practice freeway.' I think they meant this piece of crap highway." Tubby slowed further to match the speed of the early commuters merging into the flow at every entrance ramp.

Ernie stretched and looked at the sound barrier walls that lined the edges of the freeway with bushes and trees buffering the view. "I wonder what dumb-shit came up with the bright idea that the only stretch of interstate in the entire U.S. with a 45 speed limit should be in this ugly trench? It's like they wanted everyone to slow down so they could get a good look at the sound barriers."

Tubby was concentrating, looking for the I-94 West exit while Ernie tried to look over the barriers at the passing neighborhoods. They came around a curve and saw a trooper standing next to his maroon State Patrol car writing a ticket to a millennial driving an ivory Acura sedan.

Ernie pointed at the trooper as they went past. "They probably lowered the speed limit here so the cops could make their monthly quota of speeding tickets. Every time we go through here they've got someone pulled over." Again, Ernie's observation got no response from Tubby.

Tubby took the I-94 West ramp and wound through "spaghetti junction" a snarl of intersecting St. Paul streets meeting at the crossroads of I-94 and I-35E. The traffic was even slower after the turn and Tubby started tapping his thumbs on the steering wheel as they crept along. He took the Snelling Avenue exit and turned north. A few blocks later he turned onto a familiar side street in a neighborhood of 1920s bungalows. It reminded Tubby of the neighborhood where he'd grown up. Some of the houses were neat and freshly painted, while others were run down.

They passed a Vietnamese grocery store advertising fresh tilapia and parked on a side street. Ernie pulled the brown uniform with a UPS logo from the hanger in the back-seat while Tubby opened the trunk. Tubby lifted out one of the repackaged two-kilo "bricks

" they'd removed from the church van in San Antonio. He'd put it into a clean, but slightly scuffed box that looked like it had been shuffled around during shipment. The return address indicated the package had been shipped from the Simer Pump Company. The pre-printed shipping label he'd attached said it weighed 4.5 pounds and was destined for Preston Pump Service on Snelling Ave in St. Paul, Minnesota.

Tubby finished taping the box and Ernie stepped around the back of the car wearing the brown UPS uniform. In the office of the Preston Pump Service a brown-haired teenage girl, dressed in a gray Hamline University sweatshirt and blue jeans, was typing invoices when the bell rang signaling Ernie's entrance. She looked up and rose to meet Ernie at the "will call" counter. He set the package on the ledge and turned to leave.

The girl called after him. "Don't you need to scan this to confirm delivery?"

Ernie spoke over his shoulder as he walked through the door. "Naw, I scanned it in the truck." He was out the door and gone before the girl looked back up from the label. She had barely seen his face.

Ernie climbed back into the car and within 10 minutes, they were checked into the Midway Motel. More than half of their job was completed, having made similar UPS deliveries in Kansas and Iowa on their way north.

Back at Preston Pump Service, the girl carried the box to Terry Preston's office. "The part from Simer Pumps was just delivered." She put the box on his desk and went back to her computer.

Terry Preston closed and locked his office door. He pulled out a box cutter and carefully slit through the sealing tape. He unwrapped layers, first of cardboard, then of rust encrusted plastic and finally aluminum foil, exposing two kilos of white powder in Saran Wrap. He licked the tip of a finger, touched it to some exposed powder and put it to his tongue. A broad smile spread across his face as he rewrapped the parcel, taped it, and locked it in the safe.

• • •

Floyd Swenson was going through his notes about the George Brown murder when Pam Ryan popped into the bullpen and sat on his guest chair. Something about her constantly upbeat demeanor tended to make people smile when she spoke to them. She made Floyd feel old, gray, and in need of a jolt of caffeine.

"The sheriff said you might have a special project for me," she said with obvious enthusiasm.

"Something isn't right with the George Brown investigation," Floyd said, gathering a stack of papers and tapping them on the desktop until they were a neat pile. "I keep sifting through my notes and then I re-run the interviews in my brain. Something just doesn't fit and I can't put my finger on it." Floyd held out the stack of notes to Pam.

"Can you give me a hint at what the problem is?" Pam asked as she glanced through the first page, notes from interviews Floyd had made while canvassing the Pine Brook neighborhood. Most said, "Saw nothing."

Floyd leaned back and stared at the ceiling. "We're missing the motive unless this was a terrorist attack, and I'd say terrorism is about as likely as an alien abduction. No one gets killed unless someone wants them dead."

"Unless they were killed accidentally," Pam said, jumping into the brainstorming. "I mean, what if the real target was someone else and George just happened to be in the wrong place at the wrong time…"

Floyd sat up and shrugged. "The bomb was no accident. I dismissed the prospect of someone else being the target quickly, maybe too quickly. That would mean the bomb was put into George's car by mistake." Floyd pondered that for a second and added, "We could check that out pretty easily. There were only about twenty people in the church that evening. If we look first at people whose cars look like George Brown's . . ."

Pam thought about the parking lot and the explosion. "Was there anyone whose car wasn't in the parking lot? If I was planning to blow up a car, I wouldn't park next to it."

Floyd smiled. "Unless you wanted to collect the insurance." They both laughed and he added, "I thought about that too. All the cars were in parked together that night. We've only eliminated the deacons. That leaves a few other suspects at the church and many who weren't."

Pam leafed through Floyd's notes. "I'll look through these to see if I can pick up the missing motive."

"Sure." Floyd thought for a second and said, "Why don't you do another round of interviews with the deacons to see if you hear something different. Try out the theory that George wasn't the target."

● ● ●

With Pam gone, the office suddenly seemed stifling. Floyd was barely out of the parking lot when a thought hit him.

He turned onto I-35 south. At highway 70 he exited west. After a few turns down gravel roads he pulled into the yard where he'd arrested Ronny Benson. As he opened the car door Polly, holding the baby, emerged from the house. She appeared to be wearing the same clothes he'd seen on her the night he'd taken Ronny into custody. In the daylight the girl looked even thinner than she'd seemed the night they'd met.

Floyd waved to her, thinking that she was hardly more than a girl and far too young to be raising a baby alone. "Hi! I thought I'd stop by to see how you were doing."

The girl smiled, apparently pleased to have company. "Please come in. I'll boil some coffee." Although Floyd didn't consider himself a coffee gourmand, the thought of boiling coffee gave him a shiver.

The kitchen was Spartan, with weathered cabinets and a flowered linoleum floor that was curled at the edges and worn thin in the center. The refrigerator was harvest gold, hinting at an origin older than the girl, and a chipped gas stove looked older than the refrigerator. The cabinets were a dark wood with checked shellac and the countertops were covered with the same linoleum as the floor.

Everything seemed to be clean and tidy. The girl swung the baby off her hip and she locked the tray onto a well-worn wooden high chair. She pulled a porcelain coffeepot from a cupboard and ran water into it as she spoke.

"The lady from social services came by yesterday." There was no hint of animosity in her voice.

The girl pulled out a can of Folger's coffee and measured two scoops of coffee grounds directly into the pot.

Swenson grimaced at the proportions and the thought of drinking unfiltered coffee. She struck a wooden match, lit one burner, then set the pot on it. "This might even be worse than the coffee in the ready room." Floyd thought to himself.

With the coffee pot warming, she pulled up a chair. "I don't think we were ever introduced. I'm Polly Hanson." She offered her hand for a handshake.

Floyd knew Polly's name from the reports on the Benson arrest, but acted like they'd just met. "I'm Floyd Swenson. I'm pleased to meet you." He looked at the cherubic face of the child who was totally intrigued by the stranger in the house. "What's the baby's name?"

Polly leaned close to the baby and stroked her blonde hair. "She's April. Looks like she's taken a shine to you, sir."

Floyd smiled. "Please don't call me sir. I prefer Floyd." He looked at the baby. "She's cute."

Polly fussed over April and asked, "You're not a grandpa?"

"My wife and I never had children." Then he asked, "Did you get April in to see a doctor?"

"Yup. We went and she's fine." Polly took both of April's hands in hers and patted them together. In a baby voice she said, "April's fine, isn't she?"

"Are you fine, too?"

There was a pause and Polly looked away at the coffee-pot. "I think the coffee's boiling." She pulled two mugs from the cupboard. Both had unique flower patterns and both were cracked. In the short time that the doors were open Floyd noticed that the cupboard was virtually empty. Polly set both cups on the table, then poured each to the top with the steaming liquid swirling with coffee grounds.

Floyd decided to let the coffee cool and settle a little before sampling it. "You didn't answer my question," he said. "Are you okay?"

Polly took two unmatched teaspoons from the drawer and set them beside the cups. She pulled a cottage cheese container marked "sugar" from the cupboard and opened it before she sat down. She dipped two spoonsful of sugar and stirred them in her cup. She then looked up as if she expected him to move onto another topic.

He put on his delicate smile while he sipped from the mug, letting the silence linger in the hope he'd get a response. She stared into her cup, then started to shake, spilling her coffee, as tears rolled down her cheeks.

Floyd pulled a handkerchief from his pocket and handed it to her, resisting the urge to pull her into his arms. She covered her face with the handkerchief and sobbed. When she finally got her breathing under control, she looked back up at him. "You're pretty sly." Her breath came in short gulps. "I wasn't going . . . to tell anyone. But you got . . . me going without saying . . . anything."

He sat quietly, waiting for her to find her own timing and words.

"The doctor looked at me when I took April in. He wasn't supposed to examine me or anything, but he started asking questions as he poked and listened to April." She paused and drew in a deep breath. "He asked if he could take a blood sample from me. He said I've lost too much weight since the baby was born."

"What did the blood test show?" Floyd asked.

Polly took a large sip of coffee and shrugged. "They have to send it to a lab. The nurse said she'd call with the results.

I was too embarrassed to admit I can't afford a phone, so I made up a phone number and gave it to her."

Floyd's brow creased with a deep furrow as his concern grew. "So you don't know the results? They might be okay."

She shook her head. "I'm sure they're not. April's father was real sick and I imagine I got whatever it was he had."

"Ronny's sick?" Floyd asked.

Polly dismissed the comment with a wave of her hand. "Ronny's not April's father. He's just a nice guy who helped us out. He stayed here 'cause he's got no place else to sleep except his car. We give him free rent and he shares his food money with us when he can."

Polly sipped the coffee and considered her words carefully. "I met April's Dad at the restaurant in Braham where I was working. He was a trucker who stopped in for lunch a couple days a week." Polly stared at the ceiling. "It was so stupid. We got real friendly and I got pregnant. He got sick about five months into the pregnancy. He stopped coming to town about the same time my folks found out I was pregnant. I told them I didn't know who the father was and they threw me out." Her voice cracked.

Floyd leaned across the table and squeezed Polly's hand. "Do you know what April's father had?"

"Something with his liver, I think," she said between sniffles, "He drank a lot."

"Cirrhosis? Hepatitis? AIDS?"

Polly shrugged. "Those might be it. I don't really know. I haven't seen him."

Floyd took a long drag from his coffee cup and got a teaspoon full of grounds with it. He quietly ran is tongue around the inside of his mouth, dislodging coffee grounds from between his teeth while he thought. He set the cup down and stood up.

"Come on. We're going to the doctor's office to see about your test results," he said, carefully releasing April from the highchair and taking her into his arms.

"Now?" Polly asked with surprise.

"Yes, we're going right now."

Floyd called the doctor's office from his cell phone as he walked to his cruiser. Polly found a battered car seat on the porch and rushed to catch up. He warned the receptionist he was on the way with Polly Hanson. She agreed to find a time for Polly to discuss her lab results with the doctor.

While Floyd waited in the doctor's office, he phoned Mary at the flower shop. "Hi, do you know if there is a Welcome Wagon-type group in Braham?"

"What?" Mary asked, confused by the obtuse question.

"Do you know if there is a Welcome Wagon in Braham?"

Mary blew out a breath as she thought. "Not off hand. I guess I can call the Chamber of Commerce to see if they have one."

Floyd closed his eyes and considered options. He said, "If they don't, you have just been elected to start one on your own."

"What are you talking about?" Mary asked.

"There's a single mother who's living with a baby in a broken-down farmhouse near Braham. She really needs food, a few decent dishes, and clothes for herself and her baby. And maybe something that'd be a little special . . . like flowers or some candy."

"Doesn't she have any family?" Mary asked.

Floyd struggled with the lump in his throat. "They threw her out when she got pregnant." He paused for a second, then asked, "Can you do it?"

"You old softy," Mary laughed. "I'll make a few calls and see what I can do."

Floyd did a Google search for the Pine Brook Free Church on his smartphone. Their website popped up, giving him all the pertinent information. The telephone rang a few times before a man answered.

Floyd asked, "Is Pastor Abbott in?"

"This is Pastor Abbott. How may I help you?"

"Pastor, this is Deputy Swenson. I was wondering about something that was mentioned during the investigation. Someone told us that the contributions to the church had gone up significantly in the recent past. Is that true?"

"Well, yes. That's part of what upset George Brown."

Floyd pulled out a notebook and started making notes. He asked, "Why did that upset George?"

"George thought we shouldn't include the extra collections in the budget since they weren't pledged. He argued that they were a windfall and should be set aside for a rainy day."

Floyd wrote *collections without pledges* in his notebook and underlined the phrase. Then he added *rainy day?*

"Did you get some new members or something else that would trigger an increase?"

"Not really. Contributions jumped about the time we started the mission church in San Miguel. I assume that some of our membership found inspiration in the project and made larger contributions to reflect that new-found commitment." The pastor went on about being proud that his parish had found depth in their pockets to match the depth of their convictions.

"Do you know if the contributions are from one person, or if they're from a group of people?"

"We have no way to track cash contributions that aren't in pledge envelopes. I just know we have more cash in the offering and it seems to show up after the trips to San Miguel. You might ask the treasurer, Bud Nordquist, or the ushers. They might have noticed who was dropping the extra money in the offering plate. It would be a little unethical to share that, but if it's tied to George's death, they might consider bending the rules a bit."

Floyd smiled about the ethics of tracking anonymous giving. "Thanks."

● ● ●

Polly Hanson came through the hallway between the examination rooms and the waiting room with a white bag in one hand and April on her hip. The nurse had her arm around Polly's shoulder, like a protective grandma. When Polly turned toward Floyd, her eyes were rimmed with red and she dabbed her nose with a tissue as she sniffled. When she saw Floyd, she pulled herself together and stood up straighter.

Floyd slipped his cell phone into a pocket and nodded to Polly, "Ready to go?"

"I think so." She checked to make sure April was asleep and thanked the nurse. "Is there any chance that we could stop by the store and pick up a box of laundry detergent?"

Floyd shrugged. "Sure."

They drove in silence to Chris' Foods in Pine City. They walked together to the store and Polly went directly to the household goods while Floyd bought two Snickers bars. The clerk rang up Floyd's purchase as Polly walked up to the counter with what was obviously the smallest box of laundry detergent offered.

"That won't last very long." As the words passed his lips he realized that she probably couldn't afford any more.

"It'll get me by for a while." She dug in her pocket and pulled out three bills and a handful of change, which she carefully counted out, leaving a scant few coins in her hand. He was tempted to offer assistance but didn't want her to feel guilty.

In the car, Polly strapped April into the infant seat. When she'd buckled her own seatbelt, he handed her a candy bar. Polly shook her head. "I won't take charity."

"I won't eat candy bars alone," he said as he peeled back the wrapper and took a bite.

April stirred as the car engine started. Polly unwrapped the candy bar, broke a piece off the corner, reached over the back of the seat and put it in the April's mouth. Polly took a bite and closed her eyes, savoring the chocolate as she chewed slowly. Her rapture was so complete she didn't notice that April had taken the chocolate out of her mouth. In the rearview mirror Floyd watched April examine the now slimy candy. An instant later, the piece slipped out of her fingers and onto the seat.

Floyd laughed. Polly's eyes popped open and she looked nervously around to see what was so funny. She quickly saw the chocolate on the seat and looked about for something to use for cleanup.

"There are some napkins in the glove compartment," Floyd said.

She quickly retrieved them and made a futile effort at cleaning up the stain. "I'm awfully sorry. I think chocolate stains won't ever come out."

"Don't worry. The sheriff has been trying to get me to take a new car anyway." They drove in silence again while Polly shared bits of the candy with April. When they finished she carefully folded the wrapper and slipped it into the pocket of her jeans.

When they were off the interstate Floyd asked, "What did the doctor say?"

Polly wiped her face with the remainder of the napkins and tucked them into her pocket. "I'm fine," she said folding the wrapper and jamming it into her front pocket.

Floyd sounded surprised. "Really? Nothing wrong at all?"

"Nope. Just fine." Polly stared out the window without meeting his gaze.

"I can ask the doctor. He has to tell me if your bill is paid by the county." He lied.

Her head turned toward him. "That'd be an evil thing to do." There was a strong air of indignation in her voice. "Why do you care?"

"I hate to see you deal with this by yourself. Maybe I can help."

Polly stared straight ahead and asked, "Do you know anyone who has hepatitis or AIDS?"

Floyd froze, wishing he hadn't asked the question. With Pandora's Box open, he forged ahead. "The blood tests indicated you have AIDS?"

Polly shifted uncomfortably in her seat. "This test didn't, but it may not be long enough since I was exposed." She sat quietly for a few seconds and Floyd saw tears rolling down her cheeks. "But April's father probably does and it's going to take a while before it shows up in me."

CHAPTER 23

ST. PAUL MINNESOTA

Laurie Lone Eagle knocked on the BCA director's office door. He was reviewing first quarter spending in preparation for a budget meeting with the legislature when Laurie walked in.

"I got an e-mail saying I was off the Tommy Martin kidnapping case. We're making good headway and I want back in." Her tone was assertive and when the director looked up, she was standing akimbo.

"What are you talking about?"

"I told you. The deputy director sent an e-mail saying I was off the Tommy Martin kidnapping and I want back in."

The director leaned back in his chair and looked her over. Laurie's body language was clear. This was a fighting matter. He took off his glasses and set them on the desktop. "I'm not up to speed on the individual cases. Could you give me a few more details?"

"The FBI is taking over my case and I'm making progress." Laurie said, taking a chair across the desk from him. "They shouldn't be allowed to steal the glory like this. Tell them to go screw themselves. It's our case. We're going to solve it and take all the credit."

"Ohhh." Recognition swept the director. "You're talking about the kidnapping of the little boy in White Bear Lake. The regional FBI director called and explained that it was an interstate case. They took control in order to act as liaison among all the different states and municipalities. I agreed."

Laurie slid the chair to the edge of the desk and set her elbows on the desktop. "I'm the one who found the connections to the other states. I called the other municipalities and arranged the NCIC fingerprint check that identified Ernesto Gonzales as the kidnapper. I told the FBI that there were two kidnappers, that they drove up in a gray Olds, and that the Olds had license plates taken from a scrapped car in a Texas salvage yard." She paused, then added, "I think it stinks! They step in now that the case is all wrapped up based on my work. They'll arrest this Gonzales guy and waltz off to make an announcement at a press conference."

The BCA director got up and closed his office door. He walked back and sat down. "I'm going to tell you some things that won't leave this room. Agreed?"

Laurie nodded.

"I wasn't aware of your contributions to this case. My FBI counterpart represented the accomplishments as theirs, but that does not surprise me, because he's no closer to the details of his agent's cases than I am. Technically, they do have jurisdiction. However, there is no way I will take this case from you given your interest and the work you've already done. I'm obligated to give them our full support, but I will not direct you to stop working on the case." He leaned back in his chair. "But be careful of the bridges you burn because this conversation never occurred. If you screw up, I'll cut you loose."

He stood up and opened the door for her. As she passed he gave her a wink. "Let the FBI have their press conference. The FBI director knows that I have a friend at Channel 4 who will get the whole story, and who will call them out if they don't share the glory."

● ● ●

PINE CITY, MINNESOTA

Floyd collapsed into his desk chair. It had been a long day and the only progress he'd made was to discover that Polly Hanson may have contracted some disease that might not show up in her bloodstream immediately. In a small town, that was often a sentence to isolation. He rubbed his head and pulled the telephone over to call Bud Nordquist, the Pine Brook Free Church treasurer. A child answered the telephone. After a moment, Bud came on the line.

"Hi Bud. This is Floyd Swenson with the Pine County Sheriff's Department. I'm investigating George Brown's murder and I spoke with Pastor Abbott about the recent increase in collections. He suggested that you might be able to help me solve a mystery."

"Sure, Floyd" Bud replied, "I'd be happy to help if I can."

"Pastor Abbott thought the increased collections coincided with the start of the mission project in Mexico. Is that right?"

"Hang on for a moment while I open a spreadsheet on my laptop." Bud was back in a few moments. "That's right on. The

Sunday after the first work group got back we collected $200 above pledges. It's a little cyclic, but we've been over most of the time since then."

Floyd considered the information, then asked, "Is the unexpected contribution always $200?"

"Let me look." The line went silent for a few seconds. "I'm looking back about a year and it's always exactly $100, $150 or $200."

"How can you tell that precisely?"

Bud laughed. "It's easy because I find a few extra bills in the plate when I count the collection. They're folded together and they're always $50s or $100s."

"Have you ever noticed who contributes them?" Floyd asked.

There was a long pause. "You know, that's really strange. I often usher for the collection and I have never noticed a bill larger than a 20 in the plate until we count after the service. No one has access to the plates after we carry them to the pastor after the collection, and he sets them on the altar. But there they are when we count. I hadn't thought about it before. It's almost like manna from heaven."

"Is the extra cash *always* there?"

"Oh no. Some weeks they aren't." Bud replied. "But most weeks they are."

Floyd considered the collection plate information as he tapped a pencil on his desk. "Is there a pattern to when the money doesn't show up? Perhaps, the first Sunday of the month, or every sixth week, or something like that?"

"I guess I've never thought about it that hard. Let me look." Again the line went quiet as Bud apparently studied the data. "Okay, it's not random, and the extra money shows up more than three out of every four weeks."

"Do you keep track of collections against pledges?" Floyd asked

"Sure." Bud replied. "The congregation gets statements so they can deduct the contributions on their taxes."

"But these extra donations always come as cash, and you don't know who gives them?" Floyd asked. Then he surmised, "So, whoever is giving this money isn't concerned about claiming it on their taxes."

Bud thought for a second. "That usually means somebody really rich, who doesn't care about the deductions, or someone relatively poor who only takes the standard deduction. Not many people in our church who fall into either of those categories. Certainly whoever is doing this is pretty well off. They've dropped a few thousand dollars in the collection plate this year."

"Interesting observation," Floyd mused. "Please give me a call if you think of something that ties these things together."

"I sure will. You've got my mind working now. I'm going to study the dates we get the most money to see if I can tie them to some event."

CHAPTER 24

PINE BROOK FLORAL

A phone call to the Braham city offices told Mary Jungers there wasn't a formal Welcome Wagon group nearby. A call to the Braham Lutheran Church gave her the name of the chair of the women's club, Helga Ledin.

In rural areas there are no groups like the Salvation Army or Little Sisters of the Poor, who act as a safety net for people with financial problems. People rely on family, neighbors, their church, or county social services to be their support groups. In Polly Hanson's case, the first two had not come through. It took a while for social services to get moving on new cases. Some people were kept afloat by a local congregation.

A woman answered the phone at the Ledin house.

"Is this Helga Ledin?" Mary asked.

"Yes it is. May I ask who's calling?"

"This is Mary Jungers. The Braham Lutheran Church said you were the leader of the women's group. I was wondering if I could interest you in a goodwill project."

"We are always looking for appropriate opportunities to serve," Helga said with skepticism. "What did you have in mind?"

Mary spent the next ten minutes filling Helga in on Polly Hanson. "I'll twist arms with the Chamber of Commerce to assemble a "care package" to help tide Polly over until the county starts assistance. You might ask Polly if she's interested in attending church services. She may be hesitant because Floyd says she doesn't own a car."

Helga listened intently. "I think several of the ladies would love to do something like this. I imagine that we could even round up a few jars of canned raspberries and jam. I'll bet that Peggy Larson would bake up some fresh bread. Thanks for letting us know about this opportunity to serve."

Mary's spirits were lifted by the response. "Thank you. I know Floyd will sleep a lot easier knowing that Polly has some sort of a support network. Do you know her family? They seem to have abandoned her."

Helga thought for a few seconds. "I bet I do. They farm north of town. If it's the same Hanson family I'm thinking of, her mother is a bitter lady who acts older than her years. The father is sweet, but the mother wears the pants in that family. I think Polly's brother moved away the day he turned 18 . . . he couldn't stand his mother anymore. At least that's the story that I heard."

"I guess that would all fit with Polly's situation. I'll tell Floyd that she's in good hands."

● ● ●

St. Paul, Minnesota

Tubby and Ernie fell asleep beside the motel pool. When Tubby awoke, he thought about Dolores and Roberta. The longer he was away from Dolores the more heartsick he felt about leaving her with a refrigerator full of beer, the Domino's Pizza number, and strung-out Roberta.

At sunset they walked across the street to the Chi Chi's Mexican restaurant for dinner. Ernie pointed out that only stupid gringos would name a restaurant after a woman's breasts. He gestured with his hands emphatically and thoroughly embarrassed Tubby because some college-aged girls came out of the restaurant as Ernie was in the midst of his gesture. One of the girls thought Ernie was making fun of her and she flipped them the bird.

"The food isn't bad," Tubby said, sipping a Corona beer and eating tortilla chips dipped in salsa.

Ernie picked up a blue tortilla chip and turned it in his fingers. "This is strange. Do you think it's safe to eat?"

Tubby looked around. "There are dozens of people eating them. They must be okay."

Ernie broke off a corner and chewed it tentatively. "Tastes okay. It's just strange to eat something blue."

The waitress, a skinny blond college student, came for their order and when Ernie ordered in Spanish, she cocked her head. "I don't really know any Spanish. I just work here."

Tubby translated Ernie's order and ordered chicken enchiladas for himself. Within minutes their dinners were served and Ernie dove into his soft-shell tacos.

"Pretty good," Tubby said.

"If you like Swedish tacos," Ernie said, wrinkling his nose. "Do you think these people have ever seen a habanero pepper?" He removed the cap from the bottle of Sriracha sauce and poured it liberally over the tacos. Taking a bite, he nodded. "Better."

After stuffing themselves, Tubby and Ernie walked back to the hotel and fell into bed.

● ● ●

BCA OFFICE, ST. PAUL, MINNESOTA

It took Laurie Lone Eagle five phone calls to find someone in the Brownsville, Texas, Border Patrol office who would talk to her about Ernesto Gonzales. Agent Michaels dug through files while she was on hold.

The telephone came alive. "You still there? I found a file here that looks like your man. We've arrested him twice. Both times he made it quite a way inland before we caught him."

Laurie grabbed a pen and made notes. "What can you tell me about him?"

"He doesn't know exactly what year he was born, but we guessed he's about twenty-five. He grew up on the streets of Matamoros. Most of his education has been from the school of hard knocks by the looks of it."

"Does the file give you any hints about where we might look for him?"

Computer keys clicked in the background. "Last time we picked him up he was working with a ring smuggling illegal aliens to San Antonio. We shipped him back to Mexico last

July, but he could have been back to San Antonio in two days if he had good connections."

"Is there a picture in the file?" Laurie asked.

"Yes ma'am." Was the emphatic answer. "He's staring back at me from the computer right now. Would you like me to email a copy to you?"

"Yes," she replied. "We found his prints at a kidnapping scene. I'd like to show his picture around here to see if someone can I.D. him. Thanks for the help!"

"No problem. I just clicked send so you should see his face in a few seconds."

Laurie hung up and leaned back in her chair to think. She'd have the White Bear Lake Police show the picture to the people at the hotel. The suspect had obviously stayed in town after the kidnapping. "What do I do now?" she asked as the ICE email arrived in her in-box.

The ringing telephone jarred her from her thoughts. "Inspector Lone Eagle."

"Laurie. Please come back to Duluth." Her mother's voice cracked on the telephone. "The doctor says daddy's stomach is blocked and he wants to do surgery tomorrow morning. I don't know what to say. I suppose they have to do it. Your uncle says we should wait until after we know if the herbs are working."

"I'll wrap up some things and be home later."

She set down the receiver and asked herself, "Why does life pile things on me so fast?" She put her head in her hands, feeling guilty that she'd been so far away and was deeply immersed in "other people's problems."

Laurie studied the picture and asked, "Where are you, Ernesto?" Little did she suspect that he was drinking a beer only miles from her BCA office.

She walked back to her desk and made a telephone call. She arranged to meet Sergeant Bill Randall at the White Bear Lake Police Department on her drive to Duluth.

● ● ●

PINE CITY, MINNESOTA

Floyd Swenson had two messages waiting on his desk, one from the Duluth medical examiner's office and one from Cory James, the chair of the drug task force. He dialed the medical examiner first.

Eddie Paulson, the assistant to the medical examiner, answered the telephone. He handled most of the administration for the office. Eddie was unusually cordial. "Floyd, how are you doing on the explosion?"

"Not much information here. I got one four-year-old kid who saw two men stop in front of his house and one walked off with a shoe box size package. That's about it. No motives and no other witnesses."

"Well, we got a piece of the puzzle for you. BATF identified the fragments of the detonator we recovered from George Brown's body. They're from a manufacturing lot intended for construction use made in 1996. Most have been accounted for, but a bunch were stolen from a construction site in east Texas in December 1997, along with a case of dynamite."

Floyd stared at the note he had just made. "That's good work Eddie. However, I am still stuck. How would detonators stolen from Texas show up in George Brown's car?"

Eddie still sounded cheerful when he added, "I can't help you there, but the BCA says the blast residue from the car also matches the dynamite taken from the same theft. The manufacturers put trace elements in the different manufacturing lots to make them traceable."

It was obvious that Eddie's enthusiasm was not deterred, so Floyd egged him on, his own spirits lifting. "That's interesting. Did you pick up any fingerprints from the quarter inch chip of circuit board?" They both laughed.

"I'm afraid that's about all we can do right now." Eddie replied. "Next time you make it to Duluth I'll buy you a beer and show you my new apartment."

"I'll take you up on that. I don't have any trips planned right now, but I'll give you a call the next time I head your way."

"I'm counting on it." Eddie's voice was obviously lifted by Floyd's acceptance. "You and Dr. Oresek are really my only friends and it would mean a lot for you to see my place."

A line was blinking when he hung up with Eddie and the dispatcher's voice boomed over the overhead speaker. "Call for Swenson on line 3."

Floyd punched the button. It was Cory James, from the drug task force. "I've got a man to do that undercover work for you. Are you still interested?"

"I haven't made a bust yet." Floyd replied. "So, yes, I'm interested."

"You said you needed someone who wouldn't look out of place with a bunch of teens, so I lined up Russ Watson. He's a young deputy from Aitkin County. He's 25, got blond hair and is a little chunky, so he looks like maybe 19. When do you want him?"

"The big teen night is Wednesday. So, as soon as you can get him here on a Wednesday, I'll brief him and get him in there to take a look around."

"Tomorrow is Wednesday." Cory offered. "Do you want him tomorrow afternoon?"

"Great!" Floyd was surprised by the quick response. "Have him meet me in the courthouse at 2:00. Do you know if he can roller-skate?"

Cory laughed. "No. But I assume that he knows how to tie the skates on and sit around quietly without hurting himself."

Swenson scribbled a note to himself to be at the courthouse at 2:00.

• • •

ST. PAUL, MINNESOTA

Terry Preston loaded boxes of pump parts into the back of his Ford Ranger pickup and closed the tailgate and topper cover. He carefully locked the topper and then started north.

At the North Branch I-35 Exit he turned off and drove east to the downtown area. He stopped at the local pump repair shop, dropped off two boxes, and had them sign the delivery slip for billing. He drove back toward the freeway, pulled onto a side street, and stopped in front of a small house that looked like every other house on that block, differentiated only by their color. He knocked on the service door to the garage and waited. There were several clicks and clacks as the locks were released and a young, dark-haired man appeared from inside. Visible over the man's shoulder were a Red Camaro and a workbench with several pieces of automotive equipment lined up under the glow of a fluorescent bulb.

"Come on in."

Preston walked into the garage while the man closed the door and refastened several of the locks. Preston held out the box and the man carried it over to the workbench where he opened it using a razor blade. He carefully lifted the clear plastic bag containing white powder from inside the box and set it on an electronic scale. The green digits read 100.8.

After reading the scale the man reached into his pocket, retrieved a roll of currency, and peeled a stack of $50s and $100s into Preston's outstretched hand. "I assume that it's the same quality."

Preston nodded. "Same as always. You'll have to cut it yourself."

Back in the truck Preston pulled out his invoice book and wrote out a receipt for parts and labor marking the total as the amount he had collected in the garage. The money was now "clean." He would have to pay taxes on it, but no one would ever suspect that he was getting rich from running drugs. He was just a very successful small businessman distributing pump parts all over the Midwest.

Preston drove on to Harris, Moose Lake, Cloquet, and Duluth. In each town, he delivered pump parts to a repair shop, followed by a stop at a nearby private residence to deliver the methamphetamine. He arrived back in St. Paul late that night and made a large cash deposit in the night depository window at Midway National Bank on the corner of Snelling and University. He was very careful to keep the total under $10,000 so that it would not have to be reported to the IRS.

On his way home, he made another deposit, also under $10,000, at the Eastern Heights Bank in Woodbury. He drove to his $300,000 house in the posh Evergreen development east of St. Paul, driving past the houses of doctors, lawyers, and corporate executives before he parked his pickup in the driveway of his upscale house.

CHAPTER 25

MOOSE LAKE, MINNESOTA, TUESDAY

Floyd Swenson stopped off at the Shopko and bought five plaid shirts and two pairs of khaki slacks. He decided to keep wearing his Rockport Stalkers, but seriously looked at a pair of hiking boots.

At noon, he developed a craving for homemade meatloaf and drove to Art's Cafe. While he was eating and discussing an accident investigation with a Moose Lake police officer, Laurie Lone Eagle walked in and looked around.

"Laurie. Over here. At the counter."

She spotted Floyd and sat on the stool next to his and ordered a bowl of potato soup.

The conversation turned to "cop talk" and the investigations that each was pursuing. Laurie spilled her feelings about the Tommy Martin kidnapping and her frustration that the FBI was trying to take over the case.

Floyd gave a wry laugh. "Yeah, it's just like the FBI to take over when they can smell the kill. We do the work and they take the glory." Floyd asked, "Did I tell you the fragments of the detonator and the dynamite that killed George Brown were stolen from a Texas construction site last year?"

Laurie set down her spoon and turned to face him. "No shit? Exactly when was George killed?"

Floyd thought for a second. "A week ago yesterday. I think it was the fourth."

Laurie threw her paper napkin on the counter. "I'll be back in a second." She left the restaurant and returned with her laptop. She pushed the dishes back, opened the top, and pressed the power button. The hum started and after a few seconds, there were a series of beeps as Laurie's fingers started to fly across the keys. Floyd watched quietly.

Laurie spun the computer so Floyd could see the screen, then pointed to some dates. "The White Bear Lake kidnapping took place the day after George's murder."

Floyd was wiping the last of the gravy from his plate with a piece of bread. "Lots of crimes happen a day apart in Minnesota. What's so amazing about that?"

Laurie shook her head as she entered George Brown's murder in her database. "The kidnappers were driving a gray Oldsmobile with stolen Texas plates. They were both Hispanic, and the one that we have prints on is an illegal alien who was last deported from San Antonio. They checked into the White Bear Inn late Monday evening." She spun the opened a file and spun the laptop. "Here's a picture of one of the kidnappers."

Floyd smiled and pushed his plate away. "That's pretty thin evidence. You haven't convinced me."

Laurie glared at him, then asked, "How many Texans visit Minnesota in April?"

Floyd finished off his cup of coffee and signaled the wait-ress for a refill. He replied, "I can't buy it. What ties together a kidnapping in White Bear and a murder in Pine Brook? I doubt that George Brown even knew anyone in White Bear. Besides, that detonator and the dynamite might have been resold a dozen times since they were stolen."

"Give me your e-mail address. I'll send you a copy of the picture."

Floyd recited the address, then asked, "How's your father?"

With the e-mail sent she closed the laptop. "He's worse. My uncle wants to wait to see if the herbal treatments work before they let the white doctors treat him."

"How do you feel about that?" Floyd asked.

"I don't know," Laurie said with a shrug. "It may be a moot argument. He may not live until the decision is made."

●　●　●

Floyd walked to the ready room for a cup of coffee. Pam Ryan's head was down on the desk when he walked in. With the sounds of him pouring coffee, she woke up and stretched.

"I thought you'd never get in this morning," she said as she twisted the kinks out of her back.

Floyd glanced at the clock and realized that it was almost nine-thirty. "I had a meeting with the BCA this morning." He looked at the vile dark liquid in the cup and decided to add some dry creamer to lighten the color. He asked, "Why are you in so early?"

Pam pulled a report off the top of her desk and walked across the room to hand it to him. "I talked to all the deacons' board members. They had nothing new to add and I really cannot come up with a good alternate target for the bomb. For the most part, I would have to say they are a pretty boring bunch who wouldn't attract many assassins."

Floyd nodded. "I guess you're probably right about that." He set one cheek on the corner of a desk and stirred his coffee with a pen. "Let me run something past you. I talked to Laurie Lone Eagle this morning and she told me a couple of Hispanic men traveling in a gray Oldsmobile with stolen Texas plates apparently kidnapped a baby in the Twin Cities the day after George Brown was killed. I also heard from the medical examiner's office that the dynamite and detonator used in the Brown killing were stolen from a Texas construction site. I've got a kid who saw a man carrying a box get out of a dark colored car a couple of blocks away from the church shortly before the explosion."

Floyd quickly ran through the facts again in his mind to make sure he hadn't skipped anything. "So, what do you think the odds are that the two crimes are related?"

Pam pondered the question for a few seconds. "At first blush, I'd say that the odds are pretty long. However, the Texas link is intriguing. I don't think you can discount it." Suddenly Pam's eyes grew wide. "We've got the Hispanic guys in the bar and at the motel in Rock Creek. They had Texas license plates, too."

Floyd's mind had been such a muddle that he had completely forgotten those tidbits that Pam had found when checking around the bars. "I've got an e-mail with a picture of one of the guys. Check back with the Rock Creek motel. Show them the picture, and get the license number and description of the car."

Pam rubbed her eyes. "I'm off shift. Do you want me to do it right now, or when I'm back this afternoon?"

Floyd slapped her shoulder. "You're on overtime."

CHAPTER 26

The old farmhouse was quiet and lonely without Ronny. He had been in jail on contempt charges for a week, and without telephone or television, there was not much to do in the big old house except clean and play with April.

When Polly heard the car door slam in the yard, she quickly scooped up April and met the two women at the door. They were carrying boxes and each was smiling broadly. Although Polly didn't know either of them, they looked familiar. She assumed that she had waited on them at the restaurant sometime in the past.

The taller woman carried the biggest box. Polly guessed that she was as old as her grandmother. She set the box on the step and offered her hand. "Hi, Polly. I'm Helga Ledin and this is Mona Tidwell." Polly had to swing April to her left hip to shake hands with them. "We're from the women's group at the Lutheran Church and we're the Braham welcoming committee.

I understand that you are just setting up house here and we came to say hello. May we come in?"

Polly's face lit up. "C'mon in. I'll put some coffee on." Polly showed them into the kitchen and put the baby into the high chair while the two women sat in the only two chairs at the table. Polly pulled out the old porcelain coffeepot and drew water.

"We heard that you were out here all alone," Mona said, "so we thought we would stop by with a few welcome gifts from the Lutheran church and local merchants."

Polly measured the coffee grounds and dumped them into the water. She lit the stove and walked over to the table where Helga pulled items from the box. There was a loaf of fresh baked bread, home canned raspberries that the ladies called raspberry sauce, a canned ham from the grocery store, canned green beans, canned corn, and a mesh bag of potatoes, jars of homemade jam, jelly, and pickles. In the bottom of the box were a few baby clothes.

Polly was overwhelmed. "This is really nice, but I don't accept charity," she said with conviction.

Mona, who was close to 70 and had a grandmotherly air about her said, "Honey, these aren't charity. We bring gifts to our new neighbors as a gesture of our friendship. It's a part of our commitment as a church. We would also like you to join us for church on Sunday morning. Our service is at ten."

Polly heard the coffeepot boiling and quickly moved to turn it off. She retrieved the two cracked mugs from the cupboard and poured a cup for each of the women. They noticed that she did not pour for herself.

Mona asked, "Aren't you going to have some too?"

Polly blushed deeply. "I've only got the two cups. I'll have some later." She quickly changed the topic and asked, "Can I cut the bread and offer you a piece with the raspberry jam?"

The ladies glanced at each other and shook their heads. Helga said, "Oh no. We had lunch on the way over."

Polly walked into the living room and returned carrying a wooden box marked Washington apples. She turned it on end and sat on it at the table. "What's your church like?"

The ladies started telling her the history of the church and, then spent forty-five minutes filling her in on the various groups that were active and the things they did. The Bible study group met on Wednesdays at the church and the Ladies Club met every Tuesday at a different member's home. Polly listened intently. She cut a slice off the loaf of bread and spread it thick with jam for April. The three watched intently while April broke off pieces of bread and smeared her face with jam. When they laughed, April smiled with a toothless grin.

While they watched April, Polly asked, "Is everyone as nice as you?"

Mona glanced at Helga then smiled. "We'd like to believe that everyone is very nice, but we're all sinners in our own way and that's what brings us together. We all need each other."

Polly thought about Mona's words. "My family never went to church, so I don't know what it's all about. But I'm willing to give it a try."

"We'll love to have you." The ladies finished off their coffee while making small talk about the weather and raising babies on a shoestring. When they got up, Polly walked them to the car.

Mona asked, "Can we expect to see you Sunday?"

Polly started to say something, but stopped. She looked at the ground. "Maybe not."

"What's the matter, dear?" asked Helga.

Polly had tears on her cheeks when she looked into Helga's face. "I can't go to your church ma'am. I don't have a car, and I don't have any nice clothes. I've seen people going to church and they're always dressed up. All I own is this." She swept her hands over her jeans and tattered blouse. "You've been awfully nice, but I can't."

Helga felt the lump in her throat rise and started to offer her a ride and some hand-me-down clothes, then remembered Polly's comment about not taking charity. "Is there anything that we can do for you, dear?"

Tears streamed down Polly's face. "You gave me the nicest gift of all by just being here today. It's awfully lonely out here."

A light went on in Helga's head. "Let's ease you into this church stuff. The Ladies Club meets next Tuesday at Mona's house. She's putting on lunch and we're going to do some planning for a silent auction. Can I pick up you and April?"

Polly wiped the tears from her cheeks with the back of her hand. "That would be really nice. Is it okay for me to just show up without warning?"

Helga laughed. "We've been trying to get some younger members. The ladies would love to have you and April join us."

● ● ●

PINE CITY, MINNESOTA

When Floyd checked in at the courthouse, he found an e-mail from Pam. "I haven't been able to talk with Laurie Lone Eagle, so I left a message on her voicemail." Floyd kicked himself, because he knew that Laurie was in Duluth with her family. "I got the license number from the Rock Creek Motel and showed Ernie's picture to the maid. She wasn't certain but, she thought the photo resembled one of the men she'd seen leaving. The Rock Creek and White Bear Inn license plate numbers are the same. Yes!!"

Floyd called both hospitals in Duluth, trying to locate Laurie Lone Eagle. He found Edmund Lone Eagle at Miller-Dwan Hospital, but the nurse on the surgical floor had not been able to locate Laurie. He slammed the telephone down.

At 2:00 Floyd Swenson met Russ Watson at the courthouse. It was a welcome break from the frustration of the Brown murder. Floyd explained the tip that he'd had from Andy Peterson, one of his DARE kids, and the description of the drug dealer. They drove to the roller rink and drove the roads in the area to familiarize Russ with the location.

"Did Cory tell you if he wanted us to bust this guy or whether he'd prefer to try and trace him back to a supplier?" Floyd asked

Russ was watching the scenery, noting their direction of travel and the side roads. For the most part, this was a remote area, except for the fact that the freeway ran along the side of the roller rink. "Cory didn't express an opinion," he said.

"I thought we'd seen the end of meth when the cold remedy sales were restricted but, we're seeing a new surge in meth use," Floyd explained. "It's probably coming up from the Twin Cities, but we don't know the pipeline. The people we've arrested have been users and small players. We tried to make a large buy to bring the supplier in but, we've been unable to identify the big guys."

"So, does that mean I should try to make a buy from this guy?" Russ asked. "Or do I just keep an eye on him?"

Floyd shrugged. "Just check it out tonight. You might be able to get closer the next time."

"I'll go with the flow," said Russ. "If I'm offered a quarter or half, I'll buy. I won't wander around trying to buy a teener or 8-ball."

"I'm not into the drug lingo. What's a quarter or 8-ball?"

"A starter dose is a quarter. That's a quarter gram in a 1"x1" baggie that'll cost twenty or thirty bucks. People who want to score enough for a party or a weekend high look for a teener or 8-ball. A teener is 1/16th of an ounce and an 8-ball is 1/8th of an ounce. An 8-ball might cost two hundred fifty bucks or more."

They circled through some of the state forest and came back to the roller rink. "Park here in the lot," said Floyd. "I'll be back at the interstate exit ramp."

"Does the department have a car that's more discreet than this?" Although they were driving Floyd's unmarked squad, it still looked like a police vehicle. "I don't want to scare the guy off before we make it to square one."

"I'll drive my pickup and take a radio."

Russ nodded "You should park in a driveway past the roller rink entrance. I don't think anyone would be suspicious of a pickup parked in a driveway."

• • •

DULUTH, MINNESOTA

Tubby and Ernie checked into the Edgewater Motel in east Duluth after delivering the last Mexican package to a restaurant near the university. From their rooms they could see Lake Superior and could hear the waves crashing onto the shore.

A shiver ran through Ernie's body as he watched Lake Superior through the motel window. "This sure is a cold place to live. It was kinda warm when we were driving down the freeway. Then we came over the hill and had to turn the heater on. Do you think people here can grow gardens?"

"Who knows?" Tubby was dialing the phone and was irritated by the interruption.

Ernie asked, "Who you calling?"

Tubby finished dialing and waited. "I want to see how the girls are doing. We've been gone four days now and I was wondering if they are okay."

Ernie rolled his eyes in disgust. "So what you going to do if they aren't okay? Drive back tonight and help them out?" He asked.

"I don't know." Tubby snapped. "I just want to know." The telephone rang many times and there was no answer.

Tubby slammed the receiver down. "What a miserable day. We're freezing our butts off and we stick out too much here. Every time we walk into a store or restaurant, people stare at us. There's no way we can grab a kid here."

Ernie felt conspicuous too, but tried to quiet Tubby. "We've just got to find someplace with a parking lot, like a mall, just like before. We can sit in the car and watch the people. You're right. No way are we going to walk around here and have someone leave a kid long enough for us to grab. We'll scope it out tomorrow. Just chill. Okay?"

• • •

BRAHAM, MINNESOTA

At supper, Helga Ledin told her husband Henry about Polly and mentioned that she might be a good part-time clerk for his store in Braham. He said that would be okay, but only if Polly could arrange daycare and transportation. Helga thought for a while and started calling the members of the women's club. By nine o'clock she had sitters lined up for every day of the week and women to drive Polly to work. One suggested that Henry Ledin might pay them some token amount for the driving so it wouldn't be charity.

When Helga presented the plan to Henry, he was flabbergasted. "Why do you old biddies want to start babysitting and driving this girl around? All your kids are grown and your time is free."

Helga measured her words carefully as she followed him to the bedroom. "Maybe it's time for us to start paying back some things that we've gotten from this old church for all these years. Can't you remember when the Ericksons used to bring us all their hand-me-down clothes for the kids? And how about the time I was in the hospital and every night a different family brought you and the kids supper?"

"Okay, okay." Henry went to the dresser and wrote a note to himself to figure hours for a new part-time clerk. He asked, "You gonna tell her tomorrow?"

"I wouldn't miss it for the world." That night Helga went to sleep with a sense of contentment she hadn't felt in years.

CHAPTER 27

Willow River

The roller rink traffic cleared a little after midnight. Russ Watson drove his Firebird down the road to where Floyd parked, pulled alongside the pickup and rolled down his window.

"Oh, my aching behind. I don't think that I'll be able to sit or walk tomorrow."

"Fall on your butt a couple times?" Floyd shook his head. "I told Cory to find someone who could roller-skate."

Russ laughed. "I only fell about five times. Some high school girl from Sturgeon Lake took a shine to me and she kept dragging me out to the floor. I bet I got blisters on both feet and bruises everywhere."

Floyd asked, "How about our man?"

"He calls himself Wally." Russ pulled a tiny bag of white powder from his pocket and handed it to Swenson. "The kids called him 'Wally the dope man.' Log that as evidence and get it tested, please."

Floyd held up the bag and shook it. "I'm impressed. I was pretty sure the seller would need to see you at least a couple weeks before he'd feel comfortable selling to you."

Russ shifted in his seat uncomfortably. "Wally saw me talking with the locals and apparently thought I was safe. It helped that one of the girls was flirting with me so I looked like I was okay. After the rink closed he left in a red Camaro with a Minnesota license. He turned south on the freeway. I didn't want to make him nervous so I went over the bridge and then turned around and came back here. If we put someone at the Askov exit next week, we ought to be able to follow him home." Russ handed Floyd the license number he'd written on a scrap of paper.

Swenson picked up the radio and called in the license number. "Maybe we can find out where he lives now."

Russ shook his head and asked, "You don't think he's dumb enough to use his own car with his real address on the license plates do you?"

Floyd shrugged his shoulders. "There is no intelligence test required to become a drug dealer." He yawned. "I'm not used to these late nights anymore." He looked at his watch. "Nor am I accustomed to 16-hour shifts."

In a minute, the dispatcher was back on the radio with the registration information. The car was registered to Warren Adams at an address in North Branch. "I'll call the Chisago County Sheriff's Department tomorrow and have them check it out," said Floyd.

Russ spent the next five minutes sharing details about the evening, Wally, and the number of sales he witnessed.

• • •

Floyd's house was dark. After petting Penny in the kitchen, he stepped in the shower. The shower was partially to wash away frustration from a long day of limited results. It also helped to loosen his muscles from nearly twenty hours of sitting around. Floyd crawled into bed beside Mary.

She stirred slightly and rolled over to kiss him. "What time is it?" she asked.

He rolled against her back so their bodies nested like spoons. "About three."

Mary asked, "Is this one of the side benefits of being the county investigator? You get to work both day and night shifts in the same day?"

"I just had this investigation start up and I wanted to see it through."

Mary murmured, "You used to pass it on to the next shift."

"I guess."

Mary was drifting to sleep as she mentioned, "I left a note for you by the phone. Bud Nordquist has been trying to get hold of you all evening. He says he tried the sheriff's office, but they wouldn't put him through since it wasn't an emergency. He called here hoping you would be home. He said he found out something about the church collections."

Floyd closed his eyes. His thoughts drifted to fishing, his usual way to clear the days' events from his mind. "Hmm. I'll call him tomorrow."

CHAPTER 28

The telephone jangled in Dolores' dream and she tried to ignore it. It became louder and more persistent until she finally waved her arm at the annoying noise. When her hand hit the head of the bed, she was jarred awake and realized that the ringing telephone was real.

Dolores threw back the sheet and ran naked to the telephone in the kitchen. "Si . . . I mean hullo." Her accent and her sleepy haze made the words almost unintelligible.

"Dolores, where have you been?" Tubby's voice sounded angry.

"Tubby, is that you?" She asked though her mental haze.

"Yes. Yes. I tried to call you last night to see how you and Roberta were getting along and no one answered the telephone. Tonight I've been calling for hours. I was so worried about you."

Dolores rubbed the sleep from her eyes. "Oh Tubby, I'm sorry. Roberta is the devil. She cannot sit still. She stalks the apartment like a lion in the zoo. She is very angry all the time and she threatens me. We finally went out to a cafe last night and she found some men that promised her drugs. She went with them and I came home." Her speech rattled off as fast as she could find the English words. Then she asked, "Are you mad at me?"

Tubby tried to reassure her. "No, I'm not mad at you. I didn't want her to stay with you anyway. She is different from you and I didn't trust her."

Dolores asked. "Will Ernie be mad?"

"I don't think he'll care." Tubby dismissed her concerns about Roberta and went on, "Please stay in the apartment. I do not want you walking around the streets. There are bad people in San Antonio and you might get hurt or arrested."

Dolores seemed resigned to the situation and said, "Okay, I'll stay here until you get back. Are you almost through with your work? Will you be coming home soon?"

He hated Duluth, he hated the Minnesota cold, and he hated the next part of the job, but he also knew that it was the part where they would be most vulnerable if they weren't careful. "We finished part of our job, but the second part is going slowly. I really can't say for sure. I think it will take another day here, and then a day driving back. Maybe we'll be home Saturday."

"I miss you, Tubby. I was mad when you left, but now I feel so bad that I was not nice to you."

Dolores' words put butterflies in Tubby's stomach. For the first time in his life, he hadn't felt hungry when he arose from bed. "I have feelings I don't understand. I think that I miss you more than anything I've ever felt before. Please stay inside the apartment until we get back. I'll try to call again tonight."

"Tubby." Dolores hesitated for a second. "I have feelings too. My feelings are love."

Tubby hung up the telephone and looked at Ernie. He was still asleep and Tubby wondered if he would care that Roberta had run off with some other men while he was gone. Tubby thought he might be relieved.

● ● ●

Floyd Swenson slept until nine. When his eyes fluttered open Mary was already gone. He didn't remember hearing the alarm.

He got up, showered, and poured a cup of the dark liquid left in the Mr. Coffee. It tasted about the same as it looked— not good, but better than the average courthouse brew, and it supplied the required caffeine. His cell phone chimed, showing two messages from Mary, the first reminding him to call Bud Nordquist and the second said, "*Reminder. Steaks out for supper. Buy wine.*"

At the courthouse he found another note from Bud Nordquist taped to his telephone. He set it aside and called the church treasurer.

To his surprise, Bud was close to his home telephone and picked it up on the first ring. "Hello!" Bud's voice sounded like it was charged with energy.

"Mr. Nordquist, this is Floyd Swenson. You left several messages yesterday. I am sorry I didn't get back to you, but I didn't get home until 3am. I didn't get them until this morning."

Bud laughed nervously. "I guess I don't need to know what was going on, but I'm glad those are your hours and not mine." He went on, "I found something I knew you'd want to hear about. I went through all the church records for the last year and found a pattern to the extra giving. It stops for a week or two and then restarts at $200. After that one high week it stays at $50 or $100 a week until it stops again."

Floyd contemplated the information as he made a note. "It sounds like someone has a set amount of money set aside, like a budget. If they miss a week they try to make it up when they start again."

Bud agreed. "Exactly my thoughts. So, I tried to think about who might miss church in a pattern like that. I could not think of anyone. Then I tried to think of someone paid in a pattern. For instance, farmers tend to give after they sell crops. Then I started going back through the Sunday bulletins to see if there was something going on in the church that was part of the pattern. The extra giving always stops when our group is in Mexico, working on that mission church. Like whoever is giving it is mad about it and doesn't want to contribute while they're gone. Then, they feel bad when the group comes back and they catch up. I was actually wondering if George Brown was doing it. You know he was dead set . . . oh, bad choice of words. Sorry. He was against us doing the church down there."

Floyd asked, "Has that pattern continued since his death?"

"Well, the youth group was in Mexico last Sunday and there was no extra cash in the collection plate. If the pattern continues, there will be $200 in extra cash this week which would eliminate George, ooh, bad choice of words, again.

Anyway, George couldn't be the donor if the money shows up again this week."

Floyd offered encouragement. "Good work, Bud. Keep thinking about it and let me know if you come up with anything else."

Floyd's next call was to the Chisago County Sheriff's Department. After three transfers he spoke with a detective sergeant and explained the drug purchase at the roller rink. Floyd answered their questions about Warren Adams. Floyd told the detective the kids at the roller rink called Adams "Wally the dope man."

The detective apparently took careful notes as Floyd spoke. Then he offered, "We've had some methamphetamine sales locally, too. To be honest, I have never heard of Warren Adams before. I'll drive by the address and see what his place looks like. I have the description of the Camaro, and I'll see if any of our deputies recognize it."

"Thanks," Floyd said. He hoped for a return call.

A minute later Pam Ryan walked into the bullpen and set the booking picture of Ernie on his desk. "I caught Bud Ryberg at the Rock Creek Motel. He checked in two Mexicans. He looked at the picture and confirmed that Ernesto Gonzales was one of the guys who checked in. His companion, who signed the registration card and paid for the room, was much heavier and had a bad complexion."

Floyd looked at the picture and shook his head. "If they weren't connected to George Brown's murder, why were they here? Were they planning to kidnap a child around here?"

Pam sat down in the guest chair. "I've asked that same question a hundred times and I can't come up with an answer."

Floyd pushed the picture back across the desk. "Take this over to the Sinclairs. They live a couple blocks down from the church, in Pine Brook. They have a little son named Tommy. Show him the picture and see if he recognizes this guy."

Pam nodded. "I'm on it."

Floyd went to the sheriff's office to report the day's progress. The door was closed, but Floyd could smell cigar smoke. He knocked gently.

"Come in."

Floyd opened the door a crack. "Do you have a second?"

"Sure," The sheriff nodded. Sepanen set the cigar in the ashtray and folded the newspaper he'd been reading.

Floyd closed the door and leaned against it. "I think we have a suspect in the Brown case."

"Really?" The sheriff asked, straightening. "Who?"

"Ernesto Gonzales," Floyd replied. "He's an illegal alien from Mexico. The BCA got an ID on him from a kidnapping in the Cities. Pam got his picture and Bud Ryberg, at the Rock Creek Motel, identified him as one of the men who rented a room the day before George's death."

The sheriff leaned back and looked at Floyd through his bushy eyebrows. "That's pretty thin evidence. I don't think a jury would convict on that."

Floyd nodded. "True. But we also know that the detonator and dynamite came from a Texas construction site. Ernesto likes to hang around San Antonio."

The sheriff rocked back in his chair. "So, where is this guy and when can we question him?"

Floyd smiled. "I think the FBI is looking for him. They want to see what he has to say about a bunch of kidnappings. I'll ask the county attorney to issue a warrant listing him as a person of interest in a murder investigation. With that on the system, maybe someone will hold him until we get a chance to question him. He's been arrested twice by the INS and returned to Mexico."

The sheriff stood up, signaling the end of the conversation. "Keep me informed. And remember the election is Tuesday."

CHAPTER 29

DULUTH, MINNESOTA THURSDAY

Tubby had been watching people in the parking lot for nearly two hours while Ernie slept. He watched a young mother push a stroller across the parking lot on the north side of Duluth's Miller Hill Mall.

"Ernie, I think we got one. Wake up." Tubby punched his partner in the shoulder to get his attention.

Ernie rubbed his face with his hand and moved himself up so he could see over the dashboard of the car. The woman had just maneuvered the stroller off the curb, and was now walking across the parking lot, three rows away from them.

She pulled the stroller behind a red Ford Explorer, and then popped the rear hatch open to load several shopping bags. The woman moved to the passenger's side of the vehicle and spent four minutes strapping the pink-jacketed toddler into a car seat.

Tubby backed out of their parking spot and circled so that they could follow down a parallel driveway. As the Explorer pulled onto the loop road he had to rush ahead as the light was changed from yellow to red. A couple of cars honked as he sped through the intersection, but there was no police car in sight to ticket him.

The light industrial area around the mall drifted into pockets of swamp and forest, which spread for miles on the plateau above Lake Superior. A housing development appeared on the right, and a sign indicated they were passing the University of Minnesota, Duluth campus. At a stoplight, the Explorer turned left as Mount Royal Shopping Center passed on Ernie's side of the Olds.

Ernie was trying to follow their path on the navigation app on his phone, but the twisting and turning streets winding through the hilly Mount Royal neighborhood made it nearly impossible. A few more blocks of very expensive homes twisted past until the Explorer finally turned into a driveway.

"I don't like this, Tubby. This is a rich neighborhood and there may be too many people at home. I think we should go back and pick another." As he spoke, they cruised past the house. It was a huge two-story brick structure with a circular concrete driveway. Tubby stopped at the corner and made a U-turn. He parked where they could watch the house and driveway around a curve from half block away. Ernie expressed his concerns again.

Tubby blew up. "We've spent enough time farting around already. Rich people don't have many neighbors, and the ones that they do have don't care what happens next door. What was the name on the mailbox?"

"Robbins." Ernie replied. The anxiety added an edge to his voice. "The address was 35."

Ernie quickly typed the address into his phone. He found the telephone number, punched the numbers on the cellular phone keypad and handed the device to Tubby. Half a block away Nita Robbins fumbled with her keys as she rushed to open the front door.

Across the street from the Robbins' house, Elmer Morgan sat in his living room. "The Price Is Right" was blaring on his big screen television. He had been confined to a wheelchair since a slip on the icy deck of the ore freighter steaming across Lake Superior had left him with a severed spine and a large insurance settlement. He watched as Nita Robbins, the attractive wife of Professor Jonathan Robbins, struggled with her load of groceries. He always enjoyed watching her working in the yard, playing with the baby and running errands. She always treated him with the deference due a ship's captain. Or maybe it was because of his condition, or just deference to his age. She might be "Minnesota nice" for real, he thought.

Nita disappeared into the house with her bags. He watched for her to come back to pick up Christine who he could see strapped into her car seat. At the same time, he was watching a contestant, jumping up and down and listening to numbers shouted by the audience, while trying to guess the price of a new car.

"Mrs. Robbins, this is the Publisher's Exchange. You are one of our finalists, and I just wanted to verify that you had returned your latest set of entry documents." Tubby carefully suppressed his Texas accent and spoke as he slipped the transmission back into drive and started toward Robbins' house.

Nita Robbins set her bags on the kitchen counter and struggled to keep the telephone under her chin as she put her keys in her pocket and set her purse on the table. "Ah, yes. I believe I returned them. It was a few weeks ago. Haven't you received them yet?"

Tubby smiled, thinking he had her sufficiently distracted. "No we haven't. Perhaps we should send you another set." He stopped in front of the Robbins' house.

Ernie flew out the door and ran up the driveway to the Explorer. He flicked his Marlboro into the grass, then unbuckled the toddler from her car seat. The surprised baby started to cry. Before the first wail was out of her mouth, Ernie had her clamped to his chest, muffling her cries as he ran down the driveway to the Olds.

Elmer Morgan looked away from the TV as an old gray Olds rolled to a stop in front of his house. He watched in curiosity, then horror as a man ran up the driveway and started to do something to Christine's car seat. He picked up the cordless telephone from his lap and dialed the Robbins' telephone number. It was busy.

Ernie was running down the driveway with the struggling baby in his arms when Elmer looked up again. This time he punched "911" and wheeled his chair closer to the window. From his vantage point, he couldn't see the license plates.

Ernie was just ducking into the Olds as the 911operator answered. His name, address, and phone number flashed on the screen in front of the operator.

"Emergency operator. How may I assist you?"

"A man is kidnapping my neighbor's baby." He stopped and tried to see the license plate number on the back of the car as it pulled away. "They're just pulling away now."

The 911 operator quickly punched the number of the Duluth Police Department and the police dispatcher came on the line. "Mr. Morgan?"

"Yes, yes. Please hurry. The men are turning the corner with the baby." Elmer's voice was filled with tension as he blurted the words out.

"Sir, please start over."

Morgan let out a gasp of exasperation. "A car just pulled up in front of my neighbor's house across the street and they kidnapped the baby from my neighbor's Explorer." His heart sank as Nita Robbins walked out of the house toward the Explorer. She looked around frantically at the open passenger door and the empty infant seat.

"What is your neighbor's name and address?"

"I just saw her walk down the driveway and she ran back after she saw the baby was gone. She ought to be calling you any second now. Her name is Nita Robbins."

"Can you describe the car and kidnappers?" As the dispatcher spoke, he typed information onto the computer screen in front of him.

"I've never seen them before. Two men in a gray Olds from the middle 70s. I tried to see the license number but . . . my eyes aren't so good anymore." His voice cracked.

"Please stay on the line." The dispatcher called for a squad to go to Morgan's and issued an electronic bulletin reporting two suspected kidnappers in a gray Olds. As he finished, the second line flashed and his partner picked up the call from Nita Robbins.

"Mr. Morgan. There is a squad on the way to get the details for a report. Is there anything else you can tell me?"

A light flashed in Elmer's head. "The license plate was funny. It wasn't from Minnesota, unless it was one of our old ones. It was white, with dark numbers that were maybe dark blue or black. But it didn't have that blue bar like ours do across the top."

"That's good." The dispatcher said. "Can you describe the men to me?"

"They had dark hair and the one who grabbed the baby was wearing blue jeans and a gray sweatshirt."

"How tall was he?"

"I don't know. I suppose he was average height. He wasn't a teenager, but he wasn't a middle-aged man either."

"Thanks, Mr. Morgan. The officer should be there any second now."

Elmer wheeled to the front door and waited, tears rolling down his cheeks. He had failed. If only his legs worked . . . he could have stopped them. He punched the flaccid flesh of his right leg in frustration.

Tubby and Ernie were winding their way back through the neighborhood on streets they had traversed earlier. At the mall, they headed down Arrowhead Road toward the freeway.

The Duluth policeman took the information Elmer Morgan recalled. He notified the dispatcher to broadcast a statewide bulletin to watch for a gray Oldsmobile, with out-of-state license plates, involved in a kidnapping. By the time the broadcast was made the Olds was sixty miles away. The dispatcher quickly followed up her first broadcast with an Amber Alert that was sent to police vehicles and a civilian cellphone network.

CHAPTER 30

PINE CITY, MINNESOTA

Floyd Swenson had just crossed I-35 when he saw the gray Olds waiting to pull away from a convenience store north of Pine City. The license plates had black lettering on white background and immediately he thought "Texas." There were two male Hispanics in the car. One was holding a baby.

He steered the unmarked squad into the hardware store parking lot across the road and drove through the parking lot. He watched the Olds pulled back onto county road 11 and turned toward the highway. The Olds drove at the speed limit and its occupants didn't react as though they recognized the brown car with several antennae as a police vehicle.

Swenson waited for a break in the traffic and fell into traffic a few cars back. Floyd accelerated hard across the bridge without turning on the red lights and turned onto the I-35 entrance ramp four cars behind the Olds. After three miles of driving, he was close enough to read the license plate. He quickly eased off the gas and let a few cars settle in between his squad and the Olds.

"Dispatch, this is 608."

"Go 608."

"I am following a gray Olds with Texas plates." He read the license number to the dispatcher and waited.

"Ten four, 608."

The rattle of the highway expansion joints under the tires of the squad was the only sound inside the car while Swenson waited impatiently for a reply from the dispatcher. He watched the Olds cruise along about 200 yards ahead of him, keeping a conservative speed of seventy-two miles an hour. Most of the other traffic was passing them. Some passing cars reacted to the unmarked squad and slowed. Most flew past and ignored the antennae-laden brown car.

A few minutes later the dispatcher relayed the results of the query. "The Texas DMV lists that as a white, '89 Cadillac Seville that has been salvaged. Please recheck the plate."

Floyd's console-mounted computer chimed and displayed the Amber Alert. His heart quickened as he read the details.

"Dispatch, the number and state are correct. Please notify the Highway Patrol that I am at mile marker 178, southbound on I-35 in pursuit of the Olds with the Texas license number that I gave you. I believe this is the vehicle described in the Amber Alert."

Floyd's thoughts ran quickly to the earlier conversation with Pam Ryan. Was Ernesto Gonzales in the car he was following? Why would he come back to Minnesota again?

"Ten four. I will notify the State Patrol." He vaguely heard the dispatcher's voice switch to the statewide frequency to advise all law enforcement personnel that a Pine County squad was pursuing suspected kidnappers.

Swenson accelerated and advanced on the Olds. As he approached within 50 yards, he turned on the red and blue lights in the grille of his cruiser. When the driver failed to respond to the lights, he turned on the siren.

Pam Ryan's voice came over the radio. "I'm southbound, about a mile behind the pursuit." Floyd took a deep breath. At least there was one other officer backing up the chase.

Tubby and Ernie had been discussing the little girl they were taking to Texas. Tubby was still thinking of Dolores. Watching the little girl bounce on Ernie's lap was a reminder of what his future might hold.

Tubby started thinking out loud. "Dolores and I are going to have kids — maybe five or six. We both like kids and we can afford it."

Ernie was sick of hearing Tubby's talk about Dolores and had been seriously thinking about talking to Applewhite about finding another partner. "You're so full of shit, Tubby. You and Dolores aren't ever going to be anything. She'll probably have packed up all the nice stuff that you bought her and be shacked up with some other guy watching your big screen TV."

"Oh no." Tubby shook his head. "Not my Dolores. After this trip, we're going to get married and move into a real house. Then we'll start having kids. You'll see."

The argument was broken up by the sound of the siren behind them. Ernie shifted his eyes to the mirrors and looked in anguish at the brown car with the flashing lights behind them.

"Punch it, Tubby. Let's give him a run." Ernie's voice was tinged with excitement.

Tubby reacted instinctively and pushed the accelerator to the floor. He had spent many hours under the hood fine tuning the 350 V8. He had bored it out, ported and polished the exhaust manifold, installed a high rise cam, and put on headers. When Tubby pressed the accelerator the rear of the Olds dipped down and a puff of dark smoke puffed from the exhaust pipe as the car responded to the surge of power.

Swenson watched the Olds start to pull away and pressed the squad's accelerator to the floor. The Olds continued to accelerate for a few seconds, but their speeds were soon equal. Floyd maintained a comfortable buffer, hoping to not spook the driver too badly, endangering the child onboard. The Olds darted through the sparse daytime traffic on rural I-35 with Swenson back 125 yards.

"Advise the State Patrol and Chisago County that I am in pursuit at mile marker 173," Floyd announced to the dispatcher. "The Olds is now travelling 115 miles an hour and is not responding to my lights and siren."

"There is a state patrol officer at the Harris entrance ramp," the dispatcher replied.

Floyd swerved around a gray-haired driver who was traveling at the speed limit. The man was oblivious to the flashing lights until the squad flashed by. Floyd made sure he was safely past the car before responding to the dispatcher. "Ask him to get on the highway now and stay in front of the suspects to see if we can slow them down."

A mile ahead, Swenson could see the bridge over the interstate at the town of Harris. As they approached, he could see the flashing yellow lights of the rear of the cruiser as it pulled onto the interstate. The Olds slowed slightly as it approached the Highway Patrol car, but the Olds was still traveling nearly 100 miles an hour. The state trooper started to weave his squad as the last of the traffic between his squad and the Olds pulled to the shoulder.

Swenson was right behind the Olds when Tubby slammed on the brakes and Swenson rammed into the rear bumper. He lost control for a second, but quickly pulled alongside the Olds, swerving and narrowly missing a Ford Escort that had pulled over to the shoulder. Floyd looked up to see the flashing lights of Pam Ryan's squad approaching a quarter mile behind.

The Olds started to pull away and tried to get past the trooper on the left shoulder. The trooper pushed them to the side and the Olds briefly flew through the grass in the median then drove into the northbound lanes, still accelerating hard, but travelling into the oncoming traffic. Swenson quickly glanced ahead at the northbound traffic and saw the majority of the cars slowing and moving toward the right shoulder.

One car, an older blue Buick, kept going straight down the left lane. It passed within inches of the Olds, and Swenson watched as the blue-haired lady, who could barely see over the wheel, gripped her steering wheel with fear and cranked it hard to the right well after the danger had passed. She slammed into the rear of a rusty pickup that had pulled onto the shoulder.

Pam Ryan's voice came over the radio. "I'm stopped at an accident in the northbound lane of I-35. Approximate location is mile marker 169." Floyd looked back to see Pam's squad plunge through the ditch in a spray of muddy water. In a second she was back onto the freeway where the Buick was now at rest in a cloud of dust and radiator steam.

The Olds raced along the northbound lanes for a mile, scattering traffic. After a narrow miss with a northbound semi, they crossed back into the southbound lane in an area where the grass in the median was short. The northbound traffic had disappeared and Swenson switched his radio to the State Patrol frequency suspecting the northbound traffic had been blocked. There was a lot of chatter, including the state patrol and fire units responding to the fatal crash at mile marker 169. Swenson grimaced. Hopefully, Pam had it under control.

A radio message confirmed that the state patrol and the Chisago County Sheriff had blocked the northbound lane of I-35 at Stacy. All traffic was being diverted onto old highway 61, which paralleled I-35 for most of its length from St. Paul to Duluth. The dispatcher announced that three police cars blocked the southbound lane just before the Stacy exit, 3 miles ahead. Floyd calculated that at 100 miles an hour, they would be there in less than two minutes.

The passenger-side window of the Olds rolled down and a toddler was slowly extended through the open window. One hand was under her chest and the other hand was clutching her feet. Clearly, it was an implied threat. Swenson backed off the accelerator. The frantic child squirmed, screaming into the 100-mile-an-hour wind whipping past her tiny body.

The voice of a State Patrol sergeant announced, "He's holding the child out of the window. Open the roadblock and deploy stop sticks. We'll deflate his tires or run him until he's out of gas."

The squads opened as the Olds approached and one officer threw a yellow bar covered with hollow needles that skidded across the highway as the gray vehicle sped past, missing the tires.

Tubby was furious. "What the fuck do you think you're doing Eddie? Don't you hang that kid out there."

Eddie was not to be deterred. "What's your beef? It worked, didn't it? We got a trump card and as long as they think we might play it we're O.K."

"We're okay for how long? I can't outrun them. I don't know any of the back roads and they know them like the backs of their hands. I'm either going to run into something or run out of gas. Either way, we're done."

"You worry too much Tubby. You just keep driving and I'll think of something." Ernie was busily bouncing the toddler on his knee, trying to settle her down after her harrowing experience outside of the car.

Tubby's nerves were reaching their limit. "I got news for you, Eddie. I might go to jail for kidnapping, but no one is going to give me a lethal injection for killing a kid."

"Aww. You worry too much." Eddie mocked. "These Northern people are liberals. They don't put people to death for anything. They sentence you to life in prison, feed you good, and then apologize for the inconvenience when they let you out after five years. It's not like the South where they put an IV in your arm and pump you full of chemicals."

Tubby frowned. "Yeah? Who fed you that bullshit?"

"My cousin Emilio told me he never does crime in Texas anymore. He always goes north; No death penalty and comfortable prisons. He says they have TV lounges and steak for Christmas dinner. Hell, they don't even make you work if you are a little bitchy."

Tubby was working his way through the traffic that was starting to increase as they approached the Twin Cities. They stayed to the left as I-35 split: 35E, going to St. Paul and 35W going to Minneapolis. The police cars were staying a quarter mile back, but police vehicles blocked the entrance ramps, thinning the traffic.

As they passed under County Road H2 Tubby veered sharply to pass a semi on the shoulder. He misjudged the speed, and the back fender of the Olds touched the truck's tire. The Olds slid sideways on the asphalt shoulder. Tubby struggled to retain control, but the car slid sideways through the water-filled ditch, spewing mud and water 20 feet into the air. The right fender crunched as it strained against the chain-link fence and then the car was pulled back a few inches by the fencing.

Three police vehicles skidded to a stop on the roadway. Two troopers and Swenson flew from their cars and ran toward the steaming wreck. Before they got across the muddy ditch, the passenger door of the Olds flew open and Ernie struggled out on rubbery legs, clutching the bloody screaming child to his chest.

"Stay back! I don't want to hurt the baby no more, so just stay back." Ernie reached into his pocket and pulled out a lock-back knife. He fumbled to open it while the police struggled, their feet mired in mud and swamp grass.

Swenson circled to the left and looked into the car with his Glock drawn. He saw the driver rocking back and forth as if he might be badly injured. His face and hair were covered in blood. Seeing no threat from the injured man in the driver's seat, Floyd stood up. He spoke to Ernie across the top of the Olds.

Floyd said calmly, "We should call an ambulance for your friend. It looks like he might be badly injured."

Ernie squatted down and peeked at Tubby while holding the tip of the knife to the baby's throat. Tubby had stopped rocking back and forth with the pain, and slumped over the steering wheel. Ernie assumed Tubby was dead.

One of the troopers freed his feet free from the muck and moved slowly toward Ernie. He held his empty hands out and spoke softly. "Set the knife down. You and the baby need some medical attention. We've got an ambulance on the way."

Ernie was very confused. He had hit his head on the windshield and he wasn't even sure where he was. Blood from a gash in his brow obscured his vision and his right eye was rapidly swelling closed. He held the point of the knife to the throat of the child. "I told you. Stay back!"

The child had been whimpering softly, but she became quiet, her face turning waxy and white. Floyd leaned over the top of the car and focused on her. He couldn't tell if she was breathing. He thought back to his conversations with Laurie Lone Eagle and Pam Ryan. He remembered that the illegal alien they'd identified was named Ernie.

Floyd leaned his Glock on top of the Olds. He spoke softly, but with authority. "Ernie, I think the little girl just stopped breathing. If we don't give her CPR right now, you're looking at a murder charge. Set the knife down and give her to me before it's too late to save her."

Ernie was obviously rattled that Floyd knew his name. "Quit messing with my mind, Cop." He reached under the child's chin with his hand and lifted the baby's head up while pinning her body to his chest with his upper arm. "See, she's just fine."

Swenson circled around the front of the Olds. He was starting to get very anxious about the condition of the little girl. She needed immediate medical attention and he feared it might already be too late.

"Ernie! She's dying in your arms. Give her to me. Now!"

Floyd held out his left arm to accept her, but Ernie backed away.

Floyd had practiced with a variety of handguns for years as well as the department's shotguns and rifles. He had always been far above the minimum level for "Qualifying" to carry a firearm in his annual requalification. However, this was very different from firing at a paper target. His heart pounded as he looked at the man holding the small dying child. Floyd pulled back into his mind and focused as a master marksman would before a match. He raised the Glock and lined up the rear notch site with the front blade, and centered them on Ernie's right ear. As Ernie turned to face the state troopers, Floyd's finger tightened on the trigger.

One of the troopers was pleading with Ernie. As the trooper spoke to him Ernie lowered the girl a bit to gain a better grip. As he shifted, the tip of the knife moved away from the child's neck.

CRACK! Swenson's hands jumped with the Glock's recoil, obscuring his view of Ernie. When the gun came down, he saw Ernie falling toward the grass, his whole body slack. The little girl fell to the thick mat of grass. In the background, an ambulance siren wailed as it turned from highway 96 onto I-35E, a mile away.

Floyd put his finger alongside the trigger guard and pointed the gun at the ground as he edged closer to Ernie's body. He was aware of one of the troopers snatching up the little girl and checking her pulse, but focused on Ernie's inert form, lying on the grass. Blood seeped from a neat round hole behind Ernie's ear.

The trooper looked up at Floyd as he held a finger to the baby's neck. "She's unconscious but her heart is beating." The officer put the child's face close to his ear, listening for her breathing.

There was a sound inside the car and Floyd spun to his right, instinctively going into a tactical shooting crouch while keeping his finger outside the trigger guard. He brought the barrel down to point at Tubby's shoulder. There was a low moan as Tubby rolled his head and tried to lift his chin from his chest.

Swenson released a breath and realizing that he was shaking. He looked back at the troopers. One had checked for Ernie's pulse. He shook his head when Swenson looked at him.

Swenson holstered his gun and walked around to the driver's door of the Olds. He pulled at the handle, but found it jammed. Tubby was moaning regularly now. The steering wheel was pushed up over the dash. It looked like Tubby had taken the force of the blow from the crash on his face and arms. Blood flowed freely from his nose and mouth and the skin around his eyes was starting to take a dark tint that would eventually turn purple.

Floyd asked, "Can you hear me?"

Tubby tried to say something, but the blood and loose teeth in his mouth garbled the words. He started to cough, spraying more blood on the inside of the dash and windshield.

Swenson stood up and spoke to the troopers. "The driver's alive, but he's in pretty bad shape. It looks like we'll need a rescue squad to pull him out." As he finished the sentence, the ambulance pulled onto the shoulder of the road next to the five squad cars. The EMTs quickly pulled two boxes of gear from the compartments built into the side of the ambulance and they waded across the watery ditch. A state trooper waved them over to the little girl. They set the boxes down, opened one, and carefully donned surgical gloves, then made a quick assessment of her condition.

The EMT nodded at the trooper who had been standing protectively over the girl. "I think she'll be okay. How about the guy in the grass?"

The second trooper shook his head. "The coroner's on his way for him. But the driver is still alive." He looked around to make sure no one else could hear and added, "Don't rush."

With the girl in an ambulance and on her way to Regions Hospital, the EMTs carried their boxes to where Swenson was standing next to the Olds. Some of the blood was congealing on Tubby's chin and his head was up, but wobbling as he moaned. Tubby tried to touch his face, but the pain in his broken arms was too great. After a moan of pain he lowered his arms again.

"At least he had the seatbelt on. His extremities are pretty badly broken up, but my guess is that he might not have any internal injuries," the first EMT said as he took some gauze pads out of the box and started to wipe the blood from Tubby's brow. The other EMT tried the driver's door but it was jammed so he circled to the other side of the car and climbed into the passenger's seat. In the distance more sirens wailed.

Floyd leaned on the fender and spoke to the EMT who was assessing Tubby's injuries. "Can I talk to him for a second?"

The EMT shrugged. "I guess you can try. Looks like he lost a bunch of teeth and you might not be able to understand him, but his vital signs are stable."

"Is this the little girl who was kidnapped from Duluth?" Floyd asked.

Tubby tried to turn his head so he could see outside the passenger's door. Blood from a cut on his forehead had run into his eyes. "Where's Ernie?" The words were garbled, but understandable.

"Was Ernie the other man with you in the car?" Floyd asked. "Was he Ernesto Gonzales?"

"Yes." Tubby took a deep breath. The exhale gurgled. "Where is he? I want to talk to him."

Floyd saw no advantage or risk in telling Tubby the truth. "He's dead."

Tubby slumped slightly then picked his head back up. "Am I going to die, too?"

Floyd looked at the EMT, who shook his head. "No. The paramedics say you'll be okay." Floyd let that settle in before asking again, "Is the little girl the one kidnapped in Duluth?"

Tubby seemed to ignore the question. "Will you call my girlfriend and tell her that I'll be late. She expects me home tomorrow."

"Did you kidnap the little girl for her?"

Tears formed in Tubby's eyes. "No! Sweet Dolores will have my babies."

"Then who is the baby for?" Floyd asked.

"Mr. Applewhite." The name sounded like, "awful way," through Tubby's swollen lips, Texas accent, and broken teeth.

Floyd felt a hand on his shoulder. "Deputy, the rescue crew is ready. Can you please move aside?"

Swenson moved back and watched as the firemen worked with the "jaws of life" to pry open the door. "Mr. Awful Way?" Floyd asked himself.

CHAPTER 31

REGIONS HOSPITAL, ST. PAUL

The emergency room waiting area was alive with people. Amidst the coughing children and cries of pain sat a man with his hand wrapped in a bloody towel. A brown-shirted deputy sat at the entrance to the treatment areas, politely talking to people and directing them either to the waiting area, or dispensing orange labels, on which he wrote the room number of their loved one.

"How can I help you, Sergeant Swenson?" the deputy asked as he read Floyd's name off his uniform shirt.

"I was just behind an ambulance delivering a car accident victim," Floyd replied. "He's a material witness in a kidnapping."

The deputy's eyes quickly scanned the waiting area to assess any impending problems, then looked at a computer screen. He printed a room number on an orange label and handed it to Floyd. "They're unloading him now, and eventually they'll put him in this room. Right now he's identified as John Doe, so I'm sure the admitting clerk will want his name."

"There was a little girl who came in just ahead of John Doe. Can you tell me where I can get information on her condition?"

The deputy's fingers flew over the keys. "She's being prepped for surgery. They're scrambling to find her next of kin to authorize treatment." He scrawled a room number on a scrap of paper. "You might be a hero if you can help."

Floyd leaned over the desk and softly said, "Call the Duluth Police Department. She was kidnapped from her home a few hours ago."

"Do you know the number off the top of your head?"

Floyd recited the number from memory and watched the deputy punch the numbers into the phone on the desk. "Hello, this is Deputy Peterson, from the Ramsey County Sheriff's Department. I'm on duty at Regions Hospital and a Pine County Deputy just informed me that a recent admission was kidnapped in Duluth today. We need to contact her parents immediately."

Deputy Peterson made notes as he listened. When he disconnected, he pointed to an automatic door opening behind him. "Go check on your witness. I'll give the doctors the cell number for the girl's parents." A slight smile lit Peterson's face. "Thanks. I hope we can return the favor someday."

The smells of disinfectants and medicines mixed with the earthy odor of blood and sweat. Staff members were busy shuffling patients into rooms as muffled cries came from behind closed doors. A St. Paul police officer was interviewing an obviously drunk man holding a bloody towel to the side of his head. Swenson found the sea of humanity and cacophony, spread through a maze of hallways, overwhelming. He was relieved he didn't have to deal with anything this unruly on a regular basis in his jurisdiction. This hospital was only 75 miles from Pine City but it was another universe.

Floyd hailed a nurse at the first station and explained his interest in finding the accident victim from White Bear Lake. He was directed through a set of double doors. Outside he heard a siren wail as it approached the hospital. The sound stopped seconds later as an ambulance drew up to the outside door. Two orderlies went out to meet it.

Tubby lay unconscious on a gurney in the center of the room. Around him spun a flurry of activity, with four workers dressed in surgical scrubs flitting around in what appeared to be chaos. A short brown-haired woman gave crisp orders. As Floyd watched, it became apparent that he was observing a well-trained team, each member with specific duties. The team members moved in relation to each other like the gears of a watch, each having a function and gliding along with the rhythm of the others. The pace was intense and the activity focused only on Tubby.

He eased into a corner of the room and stood quietly until the doctor looked up halfway through an order and saw him watching. She spoke to the nurse who was cutting off Tubby's pants. "Get him out of here." The order was made as if he were a piece of the furniture.

"I assume you're talking about me," Swenson said.

Without looking up, she responded. "I am talking about you." She was trying to insert a stiff tube in Tubby's mouth. "You're not part of the trauma team and you are not adding to this effort. Leave!"

"Sorry to be in the way, ma'am. I'm Deputy Swenson from Pine County. You're treating a kidnap suspect. I want to be here if anything happens." No one looked at him.

The doctor finished inserting the tube and backed away from Tubby. "Listen, deputy," she said, adjusting a pair of safety glasses with her forearm, "This guy is in tough shape. He isn't going to run away. And, if you're trying to protect him, do it somewhere outside this room."

As she finished speaking the door opened and a technician tried to roll in a large, gray, X-ray machine. Swenson backed out of the room and stood looking at the door for a second.

Floyd retreated to the lobby where deputy Peterson said he'd contacted the girl's parents, who were now driving to St. Paul. They'd approved of whatever measures were best for their daughter and the girl had been wheeled up to a surgery suite. Feeling a little useless, Floyd started reading a three-year-old *Field and Stream* magazine. After realizing that he'd read two pages and couldn't recall what he'd read, he decided to call Laurie Lone Eagle and stepped outside to use his cell phone. The BCA informed him she was on family leave and he remembered she was still in Duluth. He made a call to Miller-Dwan Hospital and spent 10 minutes on hold while the staff searched for her.

She finally came on the line. "This is Laurie." Her voice sounded tentative.

Without introduction he said, "We caught your kidnappers."

Laurie's voice perked up. "What? Floyd, is that you? How?"

"Yes, it's me." He checked to make sure no one was close enough to hear the conversation. "I got the Amber Alert after the suspects were spotted leaving a Duluth kidnapping. I saw them in the parking lot of a convenience store in Pine City and then we chased them down to the Cities where they clipped a semi and ran off the road."

Laurie's voice took on a sudden air of concern. "They crashed? You said they kidnapped another child in Duluth. Is the child okay? I saw the Amber Alert, but didn't realize the child was found." Obviously rattled, Laurie fired questions without giving Floyd time to respond.

He tried to sound reassuring. "The kid is banged up and being treated. One of the kidnappers is dead and the other is unconscious in the ER."

Laurie's voice became very controlled and focused. "There really were two," she said as much to herself as to Floyd. "We need the second one alive to find out where the other kids went. You said the second suspect was unconscious. Will he be okay?"

Floyd looked at the dozens of sick or injured people awaiting treatment in the emergency room. "I'm with the second kidnapper at St. Paul Regions Hospital now. The EMTs at the scene thought he has a fighting chance." Floyd changed topics as he ran out of information. "How's your father? Can you come down?"

Laurie's emotions ran through another cycle as her mind changed tracks. "He had surgery and they found duodenal cancer. They pulled out a big chunk of his intestines and sewed him up. The doc says they'll do biopsies and a bone scan to see if the cancer has spread. Bottom line is there's nothing I can do here except hold Mom's hand. There are plenty of relatives doing that already." She looked at the gathering of relatives milling around the waiting room. "I'm on my way."

Floyd interjected another thought before she disconnected. "Laurie. I did talk to the suspect a little bit before they pulled him from the car. He said something about calling his girlfriend to tell her he'd be late, and something about Mr. Awful Way. Does that mean anything to you?"

Laurie's mind raced though the case files in her mind. "No. But I'll have a couple hours to think about it on the drive to St. Paul."

Swenson walked back through the security doors to Tubby's cube and peeked through the small window. A lone nurse was taking Tubby's blood pressure. A sheet covered Tubby's legs and torso, and his breathing was slow, but regular. A tiny green hose under his nose supplied oxygen and an I.V. line was dripping next to his bed. Above his head a heart monitor beeped out a regular rhythm.

The nurse noticed Swenson as she wound up the blood pressure cuff and walked out the door. "You're not supposed to be in here."

"I'm the arresting officer. Can you tell me how he's doing?"

The nurse shook her head. "You'll have to talk to Dr. Anderson. She's in with another patient now, but I'll tell her you want to talk to her."

"Just tell me if he's stable. Does he have any internal injuries?"

The nurse cracked a smile. "You *are* persistent. We won't know for a while." She picked up Tubby's chart and entered the blood pressure readings. "His blood pressure is holding steady. So there is no indication of internal bleeding. However, we're waiting for bloodwork and the X-rays before we say anything definitive. He'll need surgery to repair the broken bones even if there are no other significant injuries."

Floyd returned the smile. "Thanks. That gives me a little to work from. I need to ask him a few questions."

"He's unconscious," the nurse said with authority. "We gave him some I.V. Demerol for the pain and it will probably keep him asleep. Then, you'll have to wait until after the orthopedic surgeon is done before he can answer any questions."

He thought about the little girl and went to the main nurse's station. It took him a second to catch the attention of a woman working behind the desk. "There was a little girl hurt in a car accident. Can you tell me her condition?"

When his inquiry was met with a skeptical stare he pointed to his badge. "I chased her kidnappers from Pine City to White Bear Lake."

The woman considered the request for a few seconds then typed a few lines into the computer. "She's out of surgery and they put her in a pediatric room a little while ago. She's stable. That's about all I can tell you."

Floyd asked. "Have her parents arrived from Duluth?"

The woman shrugged. "I don't know. Maybe you can check with pediatrics."

An hour and a half later Laurie Lone Eagle found Floyd sitting in the hospital cafeteria drinking coffee and reading *Sports Afield*.

"How did you know where I was?" Floyd asked.

"I asked where someone would go to get a cup of coffee," she said, slumping into the chair across the table. "What do you know?"

Floyd set aside the paper cup and looked at his watch. "You must have set a new land speed record driving here."

"My car has lights and a siren just like yours," Laurie said. "How's the kidnapper?"

"The doctor updated me about half an hour ago. She said they didn't find any internal injuries. He has two broken arms, a concussion, and a broken jaw. He's going to be drinking his meals through a straw for a few weeks."

Laurie nodded. "How about the child?"

Floyd stretched and rolled his shoulders. "She's fine. A mild concussion, a broken arm they repaired surgically, and a few other cuts and bruises. Her parents are with her now. I stopped by the room on my way to purchase this fine cup of coffee."

"Have you had another chance to question the surviving kidnapper?" Laurie asked.

"No." Floyd shook his head. "They took him directly from the ER to surgery. The orthopedic surgeon is working on him now. The ER doctor said she thought they'd have to pin his wrists to repair them. After that they're going to wire his jaw."

"Do we know the names of the kidnappers?"

"This one told the EMTs he calls himself Tubby. His driver's license says Toribio Lasoya. His address is in San Antonio. The survivor called his friend Ernie. I assume the other one was Ernesto Gonzales. He wasn't carrying any I.D. but he looked like the picture you sent."

Laurie noted, "The guy who left the fingerprints in White Bear was Ernesto Gonzales. We'll have to contact the medical examiner for prints and then check them against the ones we already have." She made a mental note to ask the White Bear police to handle that. "Was Ernie killed when they ran off the road?"

Floyd picked up his coffee and swirled the last of it in the cup. "No." Floyd paused while he tried to find the right words.

"I shot him. He was holding the girl at knifepoint." Floyd's voice was strained.

Laurie's eyes got wide and she put her hand on Floyd's arm. "You shot him?"

Floyd nodded. "The girl was unconscious and he wouldn't let her go. He kept poking the knife into her neck. I was just afraid …"

Laurie patted his arm. "I'm sure it was the only choice." Then she asked, "Any word on when we can get to Tubby for some questions?"

Floyd shrugged. "He'll be doped up after surgery. I suppose we'll have to wait a couple of days until he is fully out of the effects of the anesthesia. If we don't, the lawyers will eat us for lunch…If he says anything incriminating."

Laurie frowned. "I'm all for keeping the lawyers happy, but if I can find out what happened to the other kids, I'd be willing to give up the chance at prosecution."

Swenson looked at her and she seemed genuine in her conviction about the kids being more important than the conviction. "You're getting soft. The only way to get ahead in the BCA is convictions. You throwing in the towel on your career?"

"No." Laurie shook her head. "I've discovered what's important in life and it isn't always convictions. Sometimes it's being human."

Swenson smiled. "That's true. But, good luck selling it to your boss."

"I'll give the U.S. Attorney in Minneapolis a call and ask him to send someone over to consult."

"Why the Feds instead of the Ramsey County attorney?" Floyd asked.

"It's an interstate crime." Laurie added, "It's better to look like we're playing nice and protecting their case. Give me Tubby's full name again. I've got a friend in San Antonio and maybe we can get some information before we talk to Tubby."

"Do you need anything else from me?" Floyd asked as he wrote down Tubby's name and address. "It seems like I just passed the baton here and you're the key player now. When you question Tubby, ask him if he and Ernie blew up George Brown. Maybe we can place them in Pine Brook the day of George's murder."

Laurie patted Floyd's hand. "To tell you the truth, you look like hell. Why don't you go home and have a couple of beers and I'll call you in the morning with an update."

"Shit!" Floyd dug in his pocket. He pulled out the note from Mary and read it. "I'm in trouble. I have to call Mary and head out of here. Is there a liquor store along the freeway somewhere?" He launched himself from the chair, leaving the note on the table.

"There's an Italian market on Payne Avenue. It's called Morelli's. They have a good selection of meats and wine, but they only take cash."

Floyd waved thanks as he ran out of the cafeteria.

Laurie picked up the note from the table, read it and laughed. "I hope she cuts you a little slack," she yelled at Floyd's back as he ran out.

CHAPTER 32

ST. PAUL, MINNESOTA

After fighting through the crowd to buy his wine, Floyd Swenson pulled out of the parking spot next to Morelli's with a bottle of Merlot and an Italian red wine he couldn't pronounce. A Mediterranean looking customer said he was buying, "the wine of lovers." Floyd figured even if it were swill, the title might win some points with Mary.

He followed Payne Avenue until he found a cross street to take him to the Interstate. He accelerated down the Maryland Avenue ramp to I-35E and pressed into the mass of Friday evening rush-hour commuters. He considered calling Mary on his cell phone, but the traffic demanded his full attention. "How do people live like this?" he said to himself as he idled along with the flow of cars.

The traffic crept along until he passed a fender bender on the shoulder near Highway 36, when it sped to 50 miles an hour.

The traffic snarled and slowed to a crawl again as I-35 crossed 694. It reached the 70 mph speed limit as he neared

the Ramsey-Washington County line as the commuters started to exit to their homes in the bedroom communities. He
glanced over at the spot where Tubby had plowed through
the ditch and was surprised at how little remained to tell anyone of the deadly events earlier in the day. He sped up to
nearly 80 and held the speed the remainder of the trip.

At 6:15 Floyd turned off at the Sturgeon Lake exit and
followed the road through the state forest and into town. He
took the jog through downtown Sturgeon Lake and went west
on the county roads to his house. Seeing a half-dozen cars in
his driveway, he shook his head. "Oh, no."

Floyd pulled the wine from the trunk and walked to the
door with trepidation as the dog ran circles around his ankles.
The aroma of grilled steaks hit him at the bottom step. And
Mary met him outside the door while voices carried on conversations inside.

"I picked a bad night for a surprise birthday party," Mary
said, hugging him and kissing his neck. "Barb and Sandy Maki
showed up with the news about the chase, so we knew you
were going to be late." She took his hand.

"My birthday is next week," Floyd said, peeking into the
house.

"That's why it's called a surprise party," Mary replied.

Conversation stopped when Floyd walked into the living
room. Sandy Maki raised his beer bottle and forced a sheepish
smile. "Happy birthday."

Sandy's wife, Barb, with freshly bleached hair and a new
tattoo on her ring finger, pushed past the crowd and put her
arms around Floyd, giving him a hug without saying a word
while he awkwardly held the wine bottles.

Everyone else was silent, not sure what to say.

"Sometimes, good people have to take a stand against the bad guys. "The Sheriff's bass voice boomed from the back of the room. Everyone turned toward him. "I had a call from Marcia Jesperson, State Trooper Captain for the Twin Cities. She told me that there's a little girl alive tonight because of your actions, and I was told to give you the highest award the county can bestow on an officer. She'd like to be in the front row when we pin it on you," The Sheriff tipped his beer bottle to Floyd. "Good work."

Pam Ryan took the wine bottles and nodded her approval as the others shook hands with Floyd and patted his back. A cork popped in the kitchen and Pam handed Floyd a glass of red wine. "You look like you could use this."

"Thanks," he said, taking a sip. "If you'll excuse me for a minute, I'd like to get out of these muddy clothes." He slipped into the bedroom as the conversations restarted.

Mary met him coming out of the bedroom. "I've got a steak and a baked potato if you're hungry."

"Give me a couple minutes, "he replied, pecking her on the cheek.

"I'm sorry I sprung the party on you," she said, pushing back a stray lock hair. "I was pretty sure you'd say no, so I decided to ask forgiveness instead of permission. My timing was pretty bad."

"No one knew how today was going to play out," Floyd said, hugging her. "But, next time, let's go out for a quiet dinner."

After two glasses of wine, and birthday greetings form all the guests, the sheriff took Floyd's elbow and steered him out the back door. Sepanen leaned on the railing and looked at the stars. "The State Patrol has to do a shooting investigation," he said. "Marcia told me that she's already spoken with the two troopers who were on the scene and they are convinced that you saved that little girl's life. So, the investigation with be a formality, but you may be asked to testify at the hearing."

"I thought they might have to take it before a grand jury," Floyd replied.

"The Ramsey County Attorney may do that discreetly, but the troopers are behind you, so it shouldn't be a concern." Sepanen paused, staring in to the distance. "I also had a call from the BCA director. Laurie Lone Eagle briefed him and they're going to press the surviving kidnapper. Laurie thinks the two guys in the car have kidnapped several children across the Midwest and the BCA and FBI are sparing no effort to locate the missing children, even if it means not being able to prosecute the man in custody.

"I've called a press conference tomorrow morning to announce your role in capturing the kidnappers and the possible link to the other missing children. I want you next to me on the podium."

"No."

"No?" the sheriff asked, unaccustomed to having his suggestions refused.

"You go ahead and say what you need to say. I'll be somewhere else."

"You're the hero in all this. People will want to see your face."

"I'm not a hero. I just happened to be in the way, and no one wants to see my ugly mug on television or in the newspaper. If anyone asks, tell them I'm trying to find a murderer."

"I could order you to be there."
"I could retire, effective tonight."
"You're a stubborn old coot," the sheriff said, smiling.
"Yes, I am."

CHAPTER 33

Laurie waited for Ray Pierce, the Assistant U.S. Attorney, in the hospital lobby. He walked in with a younger man she didn't recognize. Laurie had worked with Ray Pierce on several occasions and found him polished with an eye on political office or a federal judgeship. Her first impression of the man standing next to him was FBI, but she quickly ascertained his suit was probably a two for one special as advertised on television. That eliminated FBI and opened the possibility of the man being a public defender.

"Hi, Laurie," Ray Pierce said, flashing his professional smile at Laurie as they shook hands. "This is Toby Carmichael. I asked him to join us as counsel for the accused. He works out of the public defender's office in Minneapolis and I felt it was important everything be above board."

As Laurie and Toby shook hands he said, "Ray has great things to say about you. He makes me think I should keep an eye on you every second."

Laurie laughed. "I appreciate the compliment." They walked to the hospital elevator. "I spoke with the doctor this morning and the patient is lucid. His name is Toribio Lasoya, but he told the nurses to call him Tubby."

The elevator doors opened and they stepped in. Laurie continued, "Tubby is fully capable of talking to us. However, he's under the influence of narcotics and probably still has some hangover from the anesthesia. Just to warn you, he broke both arms and his jaw at the end of the chase yesterday. He's bandaged and his face looks like a swollen plum. His jaw is wired shut, but he can talk through his teeth."

The elevator slowed and the doors opened. Laurie led them to the left, toward a federal marshal who was sitting on a padded straight back chair in the hallway. As they approached, the marshal rose from his chair and set his magazine on the chair. He was slightly over six feet tall and had an athletic build that would make anyone think twice about starting a fistfight with him. He recognized Laurie and looked at the approaching group without apparent emotion.

Ray Pierce reached inside his suit jacket and proffered a wallet with his credentials. "We're going to question the prisoner. You can take a break if you'd care to," Pierce said, as Carmichael gave the marshal a business card.

The marshal nodded and walked off down the hall. Carmichael turned to Pierce and asked, "Prisoner? I thought you had him in protective custody?"

Pierce nodded. "He has not been arrested. Therefore, technically he's in protective custody. Realistically, he's apparently committed several federal and state crimes, and we intend to charge him when he's released from medical care.

However, we're also concerned about his personal safety. We suspect him of having ties to some less than nice people."

Pierce started to open the door and Carmichael stopped him. "Has he been questioned prior to this?"

Laurie jumped in. "He spoke with emergency personnel at the scene of the accident, but he hasn't been formally questioned by law enforcement." She stretched the truth, knowing Floyd Swenson had asked him several questions. She was certain Tubby would never remember it.

Carmichael added, "I assume you are going to question Mr. Lasoya now. I want you to Mirandize him first and if I object to the questioning or feel the questions are getting intimidating, I will warn you to stop. If you don't, you will jeopardize this entire case and I'll ask the judge to throw out anything he reveals. I'm not very comfortable with my client being questioned in his obviously incapacitated state and I feel we'll be walking a thin shaky line."

"Mr. Carmichael," Laurie's voice developed a distinct razor edge. "Your client was in possession of a kidnapped child when he tried to evade the police. His accomplice held the child outside a car window during a high-speed chase. His deceased partner's fingerprints were found in the van at another kidnapping a few miles from where the car crash occurred. We're awaiting a search warrant for the car and I can hardly wait to see what that reveals. Your client is guilty as sin. We don't need a single thing he may say to put him into a federal or state prison for the rest of his natural life."

Although she was six inches shorter than Carmichael, Laurie moved up so she was standing toe to toe with him. The veins in her neck were standing out. "I personally believe Mr.

Lasoya was involved in the kidnappings of *at least* five other children, all of whom are still missing. Your client had better provide the location of those children and then ask the mercy of a judge. If he doesn't cut a deal, he'll rot in prison until his body turns to dust."

Carmichael looked nervously at the federal attorney for support and saw him grinning broadly. "I told you she was tough, Toby."

Tubby's television was tuned to the cartoon network. He turned his head to look at them as the three visitors walked into the room. His eyes looked like two watery pieces of coal set deeply into the surface of a plum. Both arms were covered with white compression bandages, giving the impression he was being restrained. Although he could move his arms freely, his fingers were enclosed in cotton batting.

The lawyers were taken aback by the severity of Tubby's injuries. Laurie walked to the bedside and turned off the TV. She took a tape recorder from her purse, set it on the table next to Tubby's water pitcher, and punched the play/record buttons.

"Mr. Lasoya. I'm Laurie Lone Eagle from the Minnesota Bureau of Criminal Apprehension. These gentlemen are lawyers. Mr. Pierce is from the U.S. Attorney's Office and Mr. Carmichael is a public defender here to represent you. Do you understand who we are?"

Tubby nodded.

"For the sake of the recording, I interject that Mr. Lasoya's jaws are wired shut due to his injuries and he has just nodded his head indicating he understands what I have just said. Mister Lasoya, you are not currently under arrest, but there is a federal marshal on duty outside your room to protect you.

We'd like to ask you a few questions. You have the right to not answer them if you feel they would incriminate you. Mr. Carmichael is here to represent your interests, so you have a lawyer present. Anything you say can be used against you in a court of law. Do you understand those rights and are you able to answer some questions for us?"

Tubby let out a deep sigh. "Tell me what happened to Ernie." His words were difficult to understand because of the swelling and the wires immobilizing his jaws.

Carmichael asked, "Was Ernie with you in the car at the time of the accident?"

Tubby nodded, almost imperceptibly. "Yes. Ernie."

"Does Ernie have a last name?"

"Gonzales. Ernie Gonzales. Where is he?" There was almost a whine to Tubby's voice as the question came out.

Laurie waited for Carmichael to say something. When he didn't she said, "Ernie is dead."

Tubby rolled his head back so he was staring at the ceiling and a shudder ran through his body. "In the car crash?"

"You don't remember?" Carmichael asked.

"No. I don't remember much of anything before the recovery room after surgery. The nurses told me there was a car accident. I don't even remember that."

Laurie waited for the attorneys to add the final explanation. When they didn't she added, "Ernie was shot by a deputy sheriff. Your friend was holding a knife to the little girl's throat after you crashed."

Tubby closed his eyes. "The kid died too?"

"No." Laurie's voice was soft and reassuring. "She was banged up pretty badly, but she is okay." Laurie pressed ahead with the key question. "Tubby, a number of other children have been kidnapped over the past few months. I believe you have been involved in those kidnappings. I want to know where those children are. Will you tell me?"

Toby Carmichael stepped forward and moved up next to the bed. "Mr. Lasoya, I have to advise you not to answer that question, if you know the answer."

Tubby licked his lips. "Water." Laurie held a cup next to Tubby's face and slipped the straw between his lips. When he was through drinking he said, "I want to answer the lady's questions." Tubby paused, then asked, "Can I see my girlfriend?"

Carmichael turned to the other two. "Can I have a moment with my client while I discuss some legal technicalities with him?"

Laurie and Ray looked at each other and walked out. As they closed the door, Laurie heard the "click" as Carmichael stopped the recorder. "Damn," she muttered.

They waited in the hallway for a dozen minutes, listening to the buzz of voices from inside the room. When the voices stopped Carmichael emerged from the room and closed the door carefully behind himself.

"Tubby," he said, "has expressed an interest in assisting you with the recovery of the children, but his ability to help may be limited by the structure of the network. However, I think a little work will sort that out with the direction he can point you."

Laurie perked up. "He doesn't know where the kids are, but he's willing to point us to his contact?"

Carmichael measured his words carefully. "That's essential-ly right. However, we need some help from Mr. Pierce. I sug-gested my client cut a deal with the feds to provide evidence and testimony to bust this thing open. In return I'd like to have his immunity from prosecution, relocation with a new identity, and assurances he'll be reunited with his fiancé." Carmichael grimaced before the next words came out. "It appears his fi-ancé is an illegal alien." He smiled a weak smile and looked at Pierce through his eyebrows.

Pierce gave him a broad smile. "That's a great law school offer. But the reality is we don't hand out immunity, placement in witness protection for an illegal alien, and a clean record for peanut players like your client. I'm sure a federal judge will be deeply touched by your client's assistance in recovering the missing children. We may even suggest leniency in sentenc-ing. But your client just doesn't offer us enough to get excited about."

"Give me another minute." Carmichael disappeared into the room again.

Pierce looked at Laurie and whispered. "The kid is dying to tell us a story. I don't think it will cost too much to get it."

Minutes later, Carmichael emerged from the room again, his demeanor changed. His head was high and he seemed to have found renewed confidence. "If we could bust a major methamphetamine pipeline at the same time, would you con-sider my original terms?"

Pierce looked at him skeptically. "Where'd this cock-and-bull story materialize from?"

Carmichael was smug. "When you search the trunk of my client's car, certain items will leave a large question mark in your minds. Maybe we should talk again later."

Laurie worried as control seemed to shift. The issue of the children slipping aside in favor of legal bantering. "Can we go in now to ask a few more questions regarding the children?"

Carmichael shook his head. "I think you'll find my client is quite tired at the moment and will be very reluctant to answer any questions until he has some assurances about his future."

Laurie rolled her eyes and turned to the federal prosecutor. "Pierce, why don't you get on the horn to your boss and talk it through."

Ray Pierce was not a man who liked being pushed, and having a state cop and a cub lawyer doing the pushing particularly annoyed him. "I think we'll take the interstate kidnapping charge and run with it," he said to Carmichael. "We'll talk to your man after he's spent six months in Sandstone. Maybe he'll be less demanding then."

Laurie was getting exasperated. "Ray, he's got you by the balls. You can take down a petty crook for one kidnapping, or you can bust a kidnapping ring, recover the kids, and bust some dopers to boot. What'll look best on your resume?"

Carmichael smirked, sensing an ally in Laurie. "Don't take too long, Ray. These guys are slippery. If they get word Tubby's talking with the cops, the whole operation will be gone. Poof!"

Pierce shifted his weight. "I'll make a call. But I make no guarantees." He walked down the hall and disappeared around a corner.

Carmichael watched him round the corner before talking to Laurie. "Pierce seems a little bit testy."

Laurie reflected on her past dealings with the US Attorney's office. "The Feds run a tension-filled organization. Every attorney is trying to look better than the one next to him. If he can get bigger cases and higher conviction rates, he might get his face on TV more often. If he does, he can run for office or cultivate some political friends and get a federal judgeship. If he doesn't, he's forced to pick up more piddly cases as he watches junior people steal the glory and pass him by."

"It makes the public defender's office look like the bush league," Carmichael commented. "We all sit around hoping we can get one innocent person free while we deal with the scum of the earth and defend them just well enough so they can't appeal on the basis of incompetent defense. Some of the new people cry over the first few cases they lose. Ninety percent of the time we plea bargain down to a lesser crime and rush back to tackle the ever-growing pile of case files on our desks."

Pierce came walking back without expression. "The boss man says immunity from prosecution for every crime revealed to us in the course of questioning. No witness protection program for him or the illegal alien."

Carmichael shook his head. "He runs with his girl or he doesn't answer questions. Period."

Pierce gingerly patted his perfectly coiffured hair before explaining. "We're skeptical about his ability to reveal a drug ring of any magnitude. Give me some sort of hint as to the size of the business we're talking about and maybe I can offer him more."

Carmichael measured his words carefully. "He's aware of one leg of an operation and can give details about the supply line bringing several kilos of crystal meth from Mexico to Minnesota dealers every two to three weeks. I think you'll be able to get at least two or three other legs of the supply from his contacts."

Pierce turned to Laurie and asked, "What do you think?" He didn't need her opinion, but it gave him a little more time to consider how much he was getting for the deal.

Laurie had one objective. "I want the kids. The sooner the better, and if we get a few videos of joyous parents hugging their kids while the federal prosecutor who broke the case looks on, I won't mind."

Pierce smiled at her obvious pandering to his ego. "All right. Let's do it."

Carmichael raised his hand. "This means immunity and re-location? Including the girlfriend?"

"I'll start making the arrangements with the Federal Witness Protection Program on Monday. Yes, the girl too."

The three walked into Tubby's room together with smiles on their faces. Laurie started the recorder and Carmichael explained the deal to his client. Laurie, Ray, and Toby spent the next forty-five minutes listening to Tubby explain his connections with Mr. Applewhite, the vans coming back from Mexico, and the deliveries to the Preston Pump Service and several other outlets along I-35.

Pierce took copious notes, and when Tubby finished, he rushed from the room to call the Attorney General, the FBI, and the DEA. Laurie was disappointed Tubby didn't know where the children went after they were left with Mr. Applewhite. She asked the question about the children repeatedly, but hit the same dead end. Tubby never went any further than Mr. Applewhite's front door.

Tubby was contrite. "Miss Laurie. I really don't know. I'm sorry."

Laurie struggled, but couldn't think of another way to approach the same question. "Okay, Tubby. We'll have to catch Mr. Applewhite and get it through him."

Tubby turned to the public defender. "Mr. Carmichael, would you please call my girlfriend. Someone's got to tell her what happened, and assure her we'll be okay."

Laurie shut off her recorder and packed it into her bag as Tubby recited his home telephone number to Carmichael. He dialed the number and held the receiver to Tubby's ear as it rang. Laurie listened as Tubby tried to tell Dolores what had happened and that he was in the hospital, but he was going to be okay.

Laurie started to leave the room, but Tubby called to her. "Miss Laurie, can you help?" She turned to him. It was obvious Tubby felt some kinship with her, another person of color. "My girlfriend is afraid if police come to get her she'll be sent away to Mexico. Can you go to San Antonio and travel back with her?" His voice was pleading. "I trust you and I told her she could, too. You really care about the kids and that's important."

Laurie started to say no, and then thought about the chance to be part of the team who rescued the kidnapped children. "Sure. Tell her I'll do that. Just let me know how to find her. How will she know it's me?"

"That's easy." Tubby's eyes sparkled for an instant. "You look like one of us."

Laurie listened to Tubby talk more on the phone, and then he said good-bye. As Carmichael hung up the phone, Tubby was using the bulky cotton batting around his hands to wipe the tears from his eyes. Laurie started through the door again then stopped short and turned back. Carmichael was making notes on a legal pad and Tubby was struggling to turn the TV on with his clumsy bundled hands.

Laurie asked, "Tubby. What about the car that exploded in the church parking lot in northern Minnesota?"

Tubby turned his head to look at her. "Oh. You know about that, too?"

● ● ●

STURGEON LAKE, MINNESOTA

Floyd Swenson was on administrative leave while the Minnesota State Patrol investigated the fatal shooting along I-35. Floyd used the spare time to work on the engine of the 1952 pickup that had been gathering rust in his garage for nearly a decade.

The telephone rang at the Swenson house and Mary jumped up from her crossword puzzle to answer it. Laurie Lone Eagle identified herself and asked for Floyd. "I tried Floyd's cell but it rolls over to voicemail immediately."

"He's out in the garage tinkering with his junker pickup. Do you want me to give him a message?"

"Tell Floyd *he* caught the car bomber," Laurie said. "It was the kidnappers. Someone in Texas paid them and told them when they'd find that particular car in the church parking lot. We even found a map of Pine Brook with a description of the car and the license number." She hesitated, then added, "Listen, I'm heading to Texas and I'll be in and out of cell coverage for a couple days, but I'll talk to him when I get back."

Mary perked up with the news about the bomber. "Please hang on. I'll carry the phone to him. He'll want all the details."

"No." Laurie protested. "I really shouldn't get into this on a cell phone and I'm driving. Just give him the message and tell him it's not a joke."

Mary literally ran to the garage with Penny, the dog racing alongside her. Floyd, smeared with grease, he had the carburetor in several pieces on the workbench. He looked up when she came through the door.

"Laurie Lone Eagle was just on the phone. She says you caught the people who blew up George Brown's car. It was the kidnappers. They admitted it!"

"What?" Floyd asked, wiping his hands on a greasy rag. "Is she still on the phone?"

"No. She's on her way to Texas. She said she would explain it all when she got back."

She disappeared out the door and walked back to the house with Penny at her heels, leaving Floyd confused about a number of things. He followed behind, still wiping grease from his hands. Once in the house he called the sheriff's cell phone.

When Sepanen's deep voice answered Floyd said, "I just had a message from Laurie Lone Eagle. The kidnappers apparently admitted to bombing George Brown's car. The case is solved."

"Really?"

"Really," Floyd replied. "You can probably get the details from the BCA and make an announcement to the news media. I'm taking myself off leave; there are too many leads I need to follow for me to be sitting at home."

"Sure. Your leave is cancelled," the sheriff replied. "I'm calling the BCA." The dial tone followed instantly.

Floyd smiled as he thought about how the sheriff loved the limelight. He dialed the dispatcher again and asked for Pam Ryan this time. It took a few minutes, and the dispatcher said Pam would call him from her cell phone. Floyd hung up and within five seconds, the telephone rang.

"Hi Floyd, The dispatcher said you wanted me to call."

Floyd struggled to maintain his composure. "I just had a message from Laurie. You were right. The two guys at the Rock Creek Motel were the bombers. The surviving kidnapper admitted it this morning."

"Really? He admitted it?"

"I didn't hear it from their own mouths," Floyd hedged, "but that's the message I got."

Pam squealed with joy. "We got them!"

"Yeah," Floyd answered. "But why would two guys from Texas want to kill George Brown?"

Minneapolis, Minnesota, Saturday

A team of FBI forensic accountants were quietly going over the tax returns of the Preston Pump Service. They had discreetly audited the books of several suppliers and were reconciling shipments of pumps and parts against the reported earnings. All the data indicated Mr. Preston was making enormous profits on his parts and labor. One agent noted, "Loan sharks would be envious of the returns Preston gets on his investment."

A team of DEA agents shared their vans with St. Paul drug task force officers. One van watched the front of Preston Pump Service. Another team was parked across from the end of the alley.

In Woodbury, an FBI agent was making a pitch to the chief of police while two teams of agents took turns circling through the Evergreen neighborhood, trying to watch for activity at Preston's house. They wanted to set up surveillance on the home, but a quick cruise through the upscale neighborhood's narrow streets showed it would be very difficult to be discreet in any parked vehicle.

In San Antonio, a joint team of investigators was desperately trying to locate Mr. Applewhite and his bogus adoption service. A female FBI agent was making telephone inquiries to every adoption service with an online listing. The San Antonio police had five detectives trying to locate the Applewhite house based on Tubby's description of the property and directions based on landmarks — Tubby didn't know the street names. Another detective was searching Texas and national databases for the name Applewhite.

The DEA alerted all Mexico/U.S. Border Patrol officers to start discreet gas tank checks of vehicles for hidden compartments enclosing packages of drugs wrapped in foil ... especially vans.

The agents worked through Saturday, trying to put together the pieces of the Applewhite operation from drugs to kidnappings. There were holes, but slowly they were able to fit the pieces together. The Special Agent in Charge called the St. Paul police and advised them that they were going to obtain search warrants and planned to raid the pump service.

CHAPTER 34

At the Pine Brook Free Church, Floyd and Mary joined the family groups making their way from the parking lot to the building. Inside, an older couple greeted them and directed them to the sanctuary.

The service reminded Floyd of the Lutheran experience. The hymns were different, but the pattern the same. His singing voice had not improved, nor had his tolerance for hard seats. By the time the sermon was over, he was squirming like the nine year old sitting in front of them.

The offering plates were passed, and Floyd watched intently as it went back and forth through each of the rows on both sides of the aisle. He had purposely chosen to sit in the last row, and when the plate got to them he took it and carefully pushed a five-dollar bill back and forth through the contents. He saw nothing but pledge envelopes and smaller bills. Mary gave him a scowl that would have curdled milk. He shrugged in response.

When the music stopped, the congregation stood and sang. Floyd watched intently as the ushers carried the plates to the front of the church. Ed Abbott said a few words with bowed head. Then he and Tom Knight each took one plate, turned, and set the plates on the altar.

After the final hymn and a benediction, the parishioners filed out to shake hands with the pastor. Floyd quickly searched the crowd and spotted Bud Nordquist walking toward the altar. Floyd and Mary made their way through the people chatting and joking with each other and caught Bud as he was stepping down with the collection plates.

"Bud. Could I join you while you count the collection?"

Bud looked at him for a second, then recognition swept over his face. "Deputy Swenson. Hello."

"Are you going to count the offering now?"

"Well, yes. But it's more than counting the offering. I mark down all the gifts by envelope number so we can send reminders to people who aren't keeping up with their pledges. I send a quarterly statement for everyone's tax records."

Floyd repeated the question. "May I watch?"

Nordstrom hesitated. "I don't know that I feel comfortable with that. People are very sensitive about their pledges and we don't advertise who gives how much."

Floyd tried another approach. "I can respect the confidentiality. However, I'd like to see if your mystery giver made a contribution today. He never puts it in an envelope, right? It just sits loose."

Bud's frown turned to a smile as the plan hit him. "Sure." He said, "We can look at the loose giving."

Floyd squeezed Mary's hand and said, "Would you grab a cup of coffee and give me a little time with Bud?" Mary nodded.

Floyd and Bud went to the little office that served the finance chairman and the Sunday school superintendent. Bud started to organize the currency from the top plate. Floyd was about to do the same for the other plate and immediately spotted several crisp fifty-dollar bills. He recognized his own five-dollar bill, folded length-wise, immediately under the crisp fifties.

"Bud, they're here." Bud reached over to where Floyd was pointing and separated out the large bills.

"Right on schedule. He missed last week, so he makes up for it by putting $200 in this week. He'll be back to $150 next week."

Floyd continued with the task of arranging and stacking the currency. "I think I know who put them in." He considered the value of getting fingerprints from the bills and discounted it as secondary to the rest of the investigation now that he was sure of the source.

"Really?" Bud tapped the stack of bills in his hand to align the edges. "Who is it?"

"I think he's like your people who use the pledge envelopes. He wants it kept confidential. It's not up to me to breach the person's trust." Floyd finished stacking the currency and handed the bills to Bud to count.

Bud agreed, "You're right. However, it's such an interesting mystery. I'd love to know who it is."

Bud counted out the currency and entered the total on a slip of paper. "Thanks for the help. I have to tally the envelopes and checks now."

Floyd caught the hint that it was time for him to leave and stepped to the door. "Thanks for your help, Bud."

Bud smiled. "You know, the assistant treasurer moved to the Twin Cities and I don't have anyone to back me up when I go out of town. I think the deacons' board would trust you with that task."

Floyd laughed. "Bud, you are smooth. But, I work too many irregular hours to be reliable."

Mary took Floyd by the hand as he left the church office and led him to the door. "Would you be up to another church service today?"

Floyd scowled. "That seems a little excessive, don't you think?"

"I think we should check out the church in Braham too."

Floyd smiled. "You think the Welcome Wagon may be at work there today?"

Mary smiled. "A little bird told me they might be."

They arrived too late for the Lutheran service. The first parishioners were coming out the front door as they walked in. They were greeted cordially, but with obvious confusion until they got into the narthex, where a large group had gathered to talk.

As Mary and Floyd wound their way through the people, a voice called out to him. "Deputy Swenson!"

Floyd turned to find Polly Hanson in the center of a group of women. Polly pushed her way through the group and called his name again. "Deputy Swenson! Over here!"

He was unprepared for the hug she gave him, but shyly returned it. "Polly, how are you doing?" He slipped free and pulled Mary to his side. "Polly, this is my friend, Mary."

Polly shook Mary's hand politely. Then she grabbed Floyd's hand, and dragged him toward a group of women. "I'm doing great. You have to come and meet my new friends."

Helga Ledin was bouncing April on one hip, while the other women fawned over the baby. Polly tried to introduce all her new friends, who were mostly in their sixties and seventies. She quickly ran out of names after Helga, Mona, and Clarice.

Polly was almost breathless as she introduced Floyd and Mary, "They came to the house the day you drove me to the doctor and brought a gift box from the church to welcome me to the community."

Helga gave Mary a wink. She noted Polly and April's dresses looked like they had been hand sewn and knew one of the ladies is regarded as the best seamstress in Mora. Her "signature" embroidered daisy was on the collar of both garments.

Polly's enthusiasm had her bubbling like a child at Christmas. She went on, "Since then, they invited me to lunch and even drove me to church today. It's so great to get out of that old house once in a while."

Floyd smiled deeply, nodded to Helga Ledin, then said to Polly, "These ladies are a pretty special bunch. You better hang onto them."

CHAPTER 35

SAN ANTONIO, TEXAS

A man in a tan sport coat waved discreetly as Laurie exited the Jetway. She noted the badge hanging from the pocket of his sportcoat and acknowledged him with a nod. She followed the parade of passengers making their way to the concourse.

"Inspector Lone Eagle?" He offered a handshake.

She shook his hand. "Call me Laurie."

"Randy Lewis. San Antonio P.D. I'll be your liaison while you're in town." He was well over six feet tall, and well-muscled through the shoulders. The sportcoat obscured his waist, but it was 10" smaller than his chest. They walked down the concourse.

"Did you check any luggage?"

"I've just got my carry-on," she answered. "I wasn't supposed to be here very long."

They exited the terminal into a wave of heat. "Wow, this feels like a sauna,"

Laurie commented.

"Welcome to spring in Texas," Lewis said with a smile. "If you think this is warm, come back in August some time."

They found his white Chevy parked in a "police only" parking spot. The heat inside the car was unbearable. Lewis slipped behind the wheel and turned the air conditioning to *Max*. They leaned on the roof and talked while the interior cooled to the 90s.

They wound their way through the traffic in the industrial area near the airport and then caught an entrance ramp to I-35. Once on the freeway, Lewis relaxed.

"Have you been to Texas before?"

"This is my first trip," replied Laurie

"You'll have to come back as a tourist some time," said Lewis. "San Antonio has tons of tourist attractions. People here for a week are only scratching the surface of local culture."

"I'll add it to my bucket list," said Laurie, watching the outer suburbs pass as they approached downtown.

"We've been working with the FBI all night trying to locate Mr. Applewhite," he said. "There is no Mr. Applewhite in San Antonio. At least none who are tied to this ring. However, one of the female FBI agents was calling adoption agencies. She spoke with a Mr. Applewhite. She, and her real husband, have an appointment with him Monday evening to start an application."

"Did she get anything revealing from him?" Laurie asked.

Lewis smiled. "No. He didn't incriminate himself on the phone. He gave her their standard fees and told them the wait would be nine months to a year. That's pretty much in line with what everyone else told her. One thing that was interesting was he assured her she could get a white baby. Most of the other agencies were unable to give any assurance."

"So, we won't know anything before Monday?" Laurie asked.

"I guess that's the best I can offer. We've had some discussions about getting a search warrant to hit the office for records, but the Chief wants to wait until after the appointment."

"How about the address our informant supplied?"

Lewis chuckled. "It wasn't really an address, more like some vague directions. We found it and checked it out. It's in a blue-collar neighborhood with a mix of Hispanics and whites. The address is a private residence. The tax rolls list the owner as Thomas Hilliard. We haven't had enough time to find much on Mr. Hilliard. So far we've just got a telephone number and his car registration. The car is nothing special, an old Acura. The phone number is different from the cell phone number our officer used to contact Mr. Applewhite, but the phone company has verified Applewhite's business phone rings in the Hilliard house, and the cell phone GPS also pings at that location."

They exited into the downtown traffic and drove several blocks to the old stone-faced building that housed SAPD headquarters. After passing through security and getting a visitor tag, Laurie met a number of investigators. They were crowded in the small room that served as their headquarters for this investigation.

One man was wearing an expensive suit. Randy introduced him as the FBI liaison. Laurie sized him up as the "spy" who reported every success of the San Antonio PD to the FBI.

The SAPD officers spent several hours with Laurie reviewing the information they had collected. She played the tape of Tubby's interview while all the officers listened intently. After a short discussion, the SAPD detectives set up the relief rotation for the stakeout at the Hilliard residence and broke for lunch. It seemed like there was little else to do until the adoption interview with Mr. Applewhite on Monday.

As they walked down the steps of the police headquarters Laurie asked, "Are we close to the Alamo? As long as I'm in town I'd like to see it."

"Sure." Randy replied. "There's a great little Mexican cantina right across the street."

They drove in silence through back streets. He found a loading zone unoccupied and parked the unmarked car there. He pulled down the visor, displaying a *POLICE VEHICLE* placard. Randy led Laurie through a narrow alley until they stepped onto the sidewalk fronting a narrow street next to the Ripley's Believe it or Not Museum. There was a short line at the entrance and the windows were covered with posters reminiscent of a carnival. Other storefronts were taken by souvenir shops and other tourist traps. A man wearing a red beret was offering pamphlets and warning people that they might not have much time to find their savior before the end of time.

"There's the Alamo," Randy said, pointing to a stone building across a small park. Throngs of people milled around the front of the Alamo as the traffic passed by.

Laurie cocked her head and studied the structure. "I thought it would be bigger."

He pointed down the street and they walked down the sidewalk as he explained. "It was just a little mission church.

The low buildings to the left were a barracks. However, it really was not much more than a chapel. Not much at all by modern standards."

They finished lunch across from the Alamo while making small talk about their careers and life in Texas versus life in Minnesota. After lunch, Randy steered her around the corner, away from the Alamo. They stopped in front of a greenish statue depicting a soldier holding two dueling pistols. Laurie read the inscription, "Toribio Lasoya," and looked at Randy in surprise.

Randy nodded. "He fought with the Texans at the Alamo."

A frown crossed Laurie's brow as she noted, "Tubby told me a relative had fought at the Alamo. His family has been in Texas four or five generations, longer than most whites."

Randy pulled back the tail of his sportcoat and unclipped a buzzing cell phone. He stepped into the Visitor's Bureau building while Laurie enjoyed people-watching.

Two minutes later he emerged and grabbed Laurie by the arm. "Let's go! Something is up at Hilliard's." They ran to his car and pulled into the traffic. They were both breathless when they reached the car. Randy flipped on the lights and siren and pulled away from the curb before Laurie had her seatbelt buckled. She sat silently, letting him concentrate on dodging pedestrians.

Once on the freeway, the traffic eased and Randy accelerated hard down the left lane. Laurie grimaced as he narrowly missed an old man driving a dilapidated pickup. Randy evaded the collision by driving on the left shoulder of the highway.

Traffic opened again and she asked, "What's going on at Hilliard's?"

"He's loading the car and is looking around nervously." Randy answered. "The chief detective is with a judge now requesting a search warrant. If Hilliard sets foot in the car, the surveillance team is to arrest Hilliard and hold him until the deputy chief gets there."

Randy cut across the three lanes of traffic and flew down an exit ramp. Soon they were going through a residential area where Randy shut off the siren and lights. When they took the last turn, they saw four or five police cars parked in the street with lights flashing. Randy double-parked. They walked up to a group of plain-clothes officers who were talking quietly.

He asked the sergeant, "What's up?"

"Hilliard is in a squad over there." The sergeant gestured with his head. "He was loading personal stuff into the car, suitcases, briefcases and stuff like that when we arrested him. We've been sitting here waiting for the deputy chief since then."

The house was closed except for the garage door. Visible in the trunk of an Acura parked in the driveway were a suitcase and a briefcase.

"Any indication he was tipped off? Or was this just a sudden vacation or business trip?" Lewis asked.

"I don't have a clue," the sergeant replied. "He isn't saying anything except he wants to see his lawyer."

In the distance, another siren was approaching. As it got within a block or two it went silent, then a white Dodge Charger turned the corner. "That's the Chief." The sergeant said.

The Chief, a short, stocky fellow climbed out of the car, carrying a piece of paper in his hand. He joined the group.

"I've got a warrant to search the house, car, and grounds. It specifies cash, drugs, drug paraphernalia, firearms, ammunition, computers, cell phones, electronic data recording devices, photos, records related to adoptions, financial records, and any records or materials related to drugs or drug dealing. I'll serve it on Mr. Hilliard. Parker and Stevenson, start in the car. The rest of you get started in the house. "

Two detectives went to the car, and two other teams, plus Randy and Laurie, went into the house. The living room seemed unscathed, but in the bedroom every drawer was open and the closet was empty. Down the hall, Laurie found a small office that had been converted from a bedroom. The room was in shambles with drawers and papers strewn everywhere, reminding Laurie of a burglary scene.

Laurie watched the SAPD officers sift through the papers thrown everywhere. She walked around the rest of the house and found a door from the kitchen that led to the garage. The inside of the garage seemed untouched. She was about to leave when she noticed a piece of paper sticking out from the gap between the washer and dryer. The washer hummed in the background.

Laurie frowned and asked, "Why would someone wash clothes when they were running away?" There was no one there to hear the question.

She walked over to the washer and bent down, to pick up the piece of paper. It was a computer generated document and said simply, "Boy #3. Hauser, Ronald and Rebecca", with a street address and phone number. The final line said, "$15,000."

Nausea swept Laurie as the relationship of the note to the running washing machine hit her. Frantically, she pulled the selector handle on the washer to stop the agitator and flung open the lid. Inside was grayish-white goo, what was left of Hilliard's paper files.

"Randy! Come Here! I found the adoptions files!" Laurie yelled. She looked around and found an empty box of Tide laundry detergent. The water selector was set for hot water. Hilliard had dumped the adoption records into the washer. The combination of detergent and hot water had turned the sheets into pulp.

Randy walked into the garage and she pointed to the washer. He looked inside and in a few seconds, recognition hit him, too. "Aw, shit!" He pounded his fist on the frame of the washer.

Laurie handed him the one sheet that was intact. He read it quickly and smiled. "We got him!"

"Yeah." Laurie replied. "But without his cooperation we'll never find the other kids. I don't want him busted on one charge. I want all the kids back, however many there were. Then I want to hang his ass from a flagpole."

Randy looked at the piece of paper in his hand and snapped his fingers. "This is off a computer printer. I didn't see a computer in his office, but if it's still there, we may have a fighting chance."

They went back to the office and looked around. There were still two detectives searching through the loose pieces of paper on the floor. "You guys having any luck?"

"Not unless you want to know what he paid for utilities in 1999. Or the certified entry from the Reader's Digest Sweepstakes."

"Any sign of a computer?" Laurie asked.

One of the detectives stood up and stretched. "There's a printer by the desk. It has a cable for a USB connection, but no computer."

Laurie grabbed Randy by the arm. "Come on. Maybe he loaded it into the car. They walked out to the driveway where the other two detectives were going through the Acura. The contents of the trunk were roughly stacked on the driveway."

"Did you guys happen to find Mr. Hilliard's computer?" Laurie asked.

The taller detective, who Laurie knew as Parker, replied. "Yeah. A laptop. The cover looks like a black leather briefcase."

Randy pulled it from the pile and set it onto the trunk of a squad, then unzipped the cover and flipped open the lid of the Toshiba laptop. The lid was an LCD screen, and he felt around the outside for the switch. The little unit purred to life and after a series of beeps, the screen lit up. "<Enter Password>," flashed at the top of the screen.

"I don't suppose Mr. Hilliard would tell us what his password is." Lewis typed in a series of words; BABY. MONEY. ADOPTION. METH. METHAMPHETAMINE. HILLIARD". Each time he got the same reply, "<Enter Password>".

Laurie looked at him. "Now what?"

Randy shut down the computer and closed the lid. As he slid it into the case he replied, "I'll give the Chief the piece of paper you found and he'll get someone over to the Hausers' house and I'll sign a chain of evidence form to check out the computer. Hausers ought to be able to give us a good I.D. on Hilliard. You and I are going to the University of Texas computer lab where a friend of mine is going to break into Mr. Hilliard's computer files."

CHAPTER 36

BRAHAM, MINNESOTA

F loyd and Mary lingered at the church talking to people and drinking coffee until the crowd thinned. Everyone went out of their way to greet the visitors and to encourage them to come back again. Floyd smiled and said they would consider it. When the last of the cars cleared the parking lot, they walked to Mary's car.

"That was really nice." Mary said as she fastened her seatbelt. "The people were so friendly."

Floyd sat behind the wheel, thinking about something. He finally started the car and answered, "Yeah, they were very nice. Too bad you have to sit through an hour of church to get to the coffee and goodies."

Mary punched him in the arm. "What a cynic. I guess I don't have to worry about you falling for any of the women in their 'ladies circles.'"

"Probably not." He paused and asked, "What did Helga Ledin tell you about their visit to Polly?"

"Helga called Friday. They visited Polly on Tuesday and brought Polly a box of goodies. She accepted them and fed Helga some god-awful coffee." She smiled, then suddenly her face turned sober. "She only had two kitchen chairs and only two cups. Polly didn't have coffee and sat at the end of the table on an apple crate. They offered to drive Polly to Sunday church, but she said no because she didn't have anything to wear. She got together with the ladies club and they were going to take a clothes collection, but she knew Polly is dead set against charity. So they mulled it over and they're teaching her how to sew her own clothes with a loaned sewing machine and a lot of coaching. Helga coerced her husband into giving her a part-time job at his store. The ladies in the club are going to babysit for her until she gets on her feet. I bet that little kid ends up spoiled rotten with all those grandmas hanging around her like flies at a honey jar."

Floyd smiled and started the engine. They drove down Main Street in Braham.

"Aren't we going home?" Mary asked.

"Eventually. Maybe I'll treat you to lunch." They drove to Pine City in silence. A block before the cafe Floyd turned right and slowed as they passed an alley. He sped up, went around the block, and slowed as they crossed the other end of the alley.

"What's up? You turned three blocks before the cafe and then looped the block." She didn't get an answer.

At Main Street he turned left and drove slowly past the businesses. He stared intently at Brown's hardware store. Above the store, curtains moved in the apartment as someone walked past them.

"Floyd, the cafe is the other way," Mary offered. "What are you doing?"

"I decided A&W sounded better. He sped up and they drove several blocks and went inside for lunch."

• • •

SAN ANTONIO, TEXAS

Laurie and Randy found a parking spot on the street near the university computer science building. They walked through the evening heat to the front entrance and climbed two sets of stairs.

"What makes you think your man is going to be here on a Sunday night?" Laurie asked. "Doesn't he have a family or a girlfriend?"

Randy chuckled. "Ron is a computer geek. His computers are his life. He prefers to work on mainframes, but he's helped us out with PC problems, too."

They entered a dark, narrow corridor. Halfway down, Randy pulled open a door. An emaciated man inside spun in his chair at the sound of the door.

The man was obviously rattled. "Jesus, Randy. You scared the shit out of me!"

Laurie noted the room looked like a haven for vermin. Potato chip bags and soda cans surrounded the wastebasket. The entire floor was littered with pieces of chips and spilled liquids. The room smelled of mildew and rot.

"Sorry, Ron. I have a project and I need some expert advice." Randy walked over and set the Toshiba on the cluttered table behind Ron. He unzipped the leather case and flipped open the lid. Ron was totally focused on Randy and the Toshiba computer. In Ron's world, Laurie didn't exist.

Ron slid his hand down the side as if he was admiring a fine antique. "Ahh. A Toshiba ... cute little things. You should upgrade, though. These don't have half the RAM of the new ones and they are slow." He flipped up the screen and ran his hands around the outside of the base. "Not much I/O capacity either. Very limited."

When he turned on the power a hum started and beeps followed. Finally, the screen lit up and the <Enter Password> prompt lit the screen. "What's your password?" Ron asked.

"It's not my computer." Randy answered. "We seized it in a search today."

Ron smiled. His fingers flew over the keyboard and after a few moments, he turned it off.

"You can't get into it? Randy asked.

Ron shook his head and pulled a CD ROM out of a pile. "Nah. We just need to do a cold boot." He slipped the disk into a slot hidden on the side of the computer and restarted the machine. When the machine came up in DOS mode, Ron executed some quick keystrokes. "SMUGGLER" appeared on the screen.

Ron turned the laptop so Randy could see the screen. "There you go. Is that all you needed?"

"Could you go in and see what he's got for files?" Randy asked.

Ron typed a few commands into the computer and it returned to the password prompt. He typed in SMUGGLER and waited. A *Windows* screen appeared and Ron selected a return to DOS where he typed DIR/W. The screen filled with the names of files.

"Not many data files here." Ron said. "Most of this is program stuff. Look here. Everything which is followed by an '.EXE' is a master file for a program. Looks like he's got some Excel data files. Do you want me to explore?"

"Hell yes."

Again his fingers flew over the keyboard as the computer flashed different screens which came up and disappeared in seconds. He stopped as a screen came up covered with dates and dollar amounts.

Randy leaned close and asked. "What's the title of this file?"

"It's right here at the top.'MNB.exl'. The dot EXL just means it is an Excel file. What do you think? Someone with initials MNB owes him money?"

"Could be he's running a bookie ring, too." Randy commented. "When do the dates start?"

"April of last year."

Randy looked at Laurie. "When did the kids start disappearing?"

Laurie paused a second as she considered the question. "At least a year before then."

"Damn." Randy exclaimed. "That doesn't answer anything. Pull up a different file for me."

"Do you want me to stay in the Texas subdirectory?" Ron asked, "Or should I try one of the others?"

Randy slid a pile of computer magazines off a chair and pulled it close enough to read the computer screen. "What do you mean?"

Ron sighed with frustration. "There are a number of sub-directories. You asked me to open a file. I picked one in the Texas sub-directory. I could open another one in this directory, or I could go to a different sub-directory and open a file. Which would you like me to do?" His voice had a condescending edge, like a parent speaking with a difficult child.

"If this one is named Texas, what are the others named?" Randy asked.

Ron punched a few keys and new screens flashed until a screen, which resembled a family tree, showed up. "You have your choice of TEXAS, ARZNA, CALIF or NCRLNA."

Laurie perked up. "ARZNA might be Arizona." She said. "Try that. It looks like the others are California and North Carolina."

The screen flashed and they stopped with a spreadsheet listing dates and amounts with a column of cumulative totals. The dates ran from 8/4/1998 to 1/10/2000. "What's the name of this one?"

Again Ron looked exasperated. He pointed to the top of the screen where it said, "PFSB.EXL."

Laurie snapped her fingers. "Go back to the list of the files in this sub-directory. I think I see a pattern."

Keys clicked and the list flashed onto the screen. "They're banks. Look. Every one ends with a 'B'. The 'FSB' ending is Federal Savings Bank, the 'NB' is National Bank, and the plain 'SB' is State Bank. We've got Hilliard's financial records!"

Suddenly, Ron started clicking keys and a screen came up and showed a series of numbers. "How could he be so dumb? He put the account numbers in as a footer. It doesn't show on the screen, but when he prints it out, it shows on the bottom of the page. I bet the hotshot thought he was pretty smart."

"We've got another problem." Randy added. "This guy was running an adoption agency for kidnapped children and we need to know who adopted the kids."

Ron clicked through the screens again to a master directory, but no data files showed except the bank records. "That's all there is on his hard drive. Maybe he's got the other files on a flash drive."

"There's got to be more." Laurie pleaded. "We have one sheet that lists a boy, the names of the adoptive parents and the address. It looks like it was printed out on his printer."

Ron shrugged. "He could have another computer with that information, unless he purged the files. Then they wouldn't show."

Randy asked. "Can you tell if he purged some files?"

Ron turned and smiled broadly. "Does a bear shit in the woods? Computer files are there until you over-write them with something else. Even if the directory is gone."

Ron's fingers started dancing over the keys and suddenly *Microsoft WORD* appeared on the screen. He punched more keys and a directory opened and listed all the files in the resurrected directory. They started with "Boy1, ran through Boy11, then ran through Girl1 through Girl7."

Laurie was leaning over Ron's shoulder to see the screen. "Pull up Boy11," she said, ignoring Ron's need for a shower.

A screen giving the name of the Peters family in San Antonio appeared. Laurie scribbled down the address and names.

Laurie was so excited she could hardly read what she had written. She grabbed Randy by the arm and dragged him toward the door. "Take me there while Ron prints out the others."

"We'll be back. Order some pizza to keep your strength up while you work." Randy left a twenty dollar bill on the desk. The two officers drove to the suburban San Antonio address on the slip of paper. Laurie had Randy stop once, at a Wal-Mart where she purchased a digital camera and memory card.

Randy knocked on Stan and Monica Peters' door. They waited for a few moments then knocked again. Finally, an attractive woman in her mid-thirties opened the door.

"Mrs. Peters, I'm Randy Lewis from the San Antonio Police Department." He showed her the folder with his badge and picture I.D. She glanced at it quickly and looked up curiously at Laurie. "This is Inspector Lone Eagle from the Minnesota Bureau of Criminal Apprehension. I believe you have recently adopted a boy from Mr. Applewhite."

Monica Peters blanched for a second, then regained her composure. "I don't know what could be the problem. They treated us very well, except the costs ran a little higher than expected. Is that it? Were they doing a pricing scam?"

Laurie pushed ahead of Randy. She asked, "May we come in and speak with you?"

"Heavens, yes. Where are my manners?" Mrs. Peters showed them into the living room. The room was spacious and decorated with expensive furniture. Toys were scattered everywhere.

"Please excuse the mess." Monica Peters apologized as she gathered toys in her arms. "I just put Andy to bed and

I haven't had time to pick up yet. Please, have a seat and I'll fetch my husband."

Laurie's heart sank as she looked around the room. The adoptive parents had spent thousands of dollars on toys and probably made plans through college for little Andy. Now she and Randy might have to tell them Andy has another set of parents who also had dreams for their little boy.

In the background they could hear Andy crying as Stan and Monica Peters entered the room and made introductions. "Stan was reading to Andy. So we put him in bed."

"Mr. and Mrs. Peters, I don't know how to put this delicately." Randy stopped for a second and cleared his throat. "It appears the children Mr. Applewhite was placing for adoption may have been kidnapped from other states."

The Peters' reached for each. Laurie jumped in. "We're not certain, Andy may have been kidnapped from a family in Minnesota a few days before Mr. Applewhite delivered him to you. It will take us awhile to verify all this, but we need to make sure. I brought a camera along. With your permission, I'd like to take a picture of Andy, and a small lock of his hair."

Monica Peters was sobbing. "You can't take Andy. We've waited years for our baby." Stan Peters was doing his best to console her, but he had paled and looked shocked.

Stan motioned for Laurie to follow him. She took out the camera and followed him into the bedroom.

The bedroom was the size of Laurie's entire apartment. The walls were decorated with baseball wallpaper and framed antique baseball cards. In a shadow box was a baseball with a signature. Laurie saw it said, "DiMaggio."

Andy was standing in the crib, clutching the rail. Stan Peters picked him up and held him close. The crying stopped immediately. Laurie loaded the storage chip into the camera, and took several pictures with the camera, then took two final pictures with her smartphone. Monica Peters stood at the door watching with her arms crossed over her chest. Her sobbing had stopped, but tears still streamed down her face.

Laurie collected her pictures and an idea came to her. "Do you still have the clothes Andy was wearing when you got him?"

Monica nodded and walked to a dresser. From inside a drawer she pulled a plastic bag with a red striped T-shirt and a pair of "Oshkosh B'Gosh" coveralls. Laurie spread them on top of the dresser and took a photo of them with her smartphone.

"Do you have to take him now?" Monica Peters asked, almost in a whimper.

Randy Lewis clenched his teeth for a second. "I don't think that will be necessary. Andy appears to be well cared for, and we have not established he is definitely the missing child. We'll be in touch as soon as we know anything either way. I promise. But please don't remove him from San Antonio."

Randy drove in silence while Laurie e-mailed the pictures of Andy and his clothes to White Bear Lake. Finally, he said, "You don't have a hotel room yet, and my stomach says it's feeding time."

"I don't much feel like eating," Laurie replied. "Can we go somewhere so I can make a few calls?"

"Sure. If you'll let me pick up a couple of burgers."

"It's a deal."

Randy Lewis ordered Whataburgers while Laurie called the BCA from a booth in the back of the restaurant. Everyone was gone for the day, so she left numerous voicemail messages. She scanned though her phone contacts and called Sergeant Bill Randall from the White Bear Lake Police Department. The dispatcher answered, but said Sergeant Randall was off until morning. She hesitated, then decided he'd prefer an interruption at home rather than waiting for tomorrow.

As the phone rang, she looked at her watch and realized it was 9:30 at night. "Hello," a female voice said.

"Is Bill Randall there, please? This is Inspector Lone Eagle from the Minnesota BCA."

The woman was polite and probably accustomed to police calls at home. "Just a moment, Inspector."

A few seconds later a voice said, "Laurie?"

"Hi, Bill. I think we have found Tommy Martin." Her voice sounded dead tired from the extremely long and emotional day.

"You don't sound very happy. I take it he's not okay?"

"On the contrary." Laurie answered, "He's very alive and well. He was placed with adoptive parents who are spoiling him rotten. I took some pictures of him and the outfit he was wearing when he was delivered to the adoptive parents. Give me your e-mail and I'll send you the pictures."

Randall recited his e-mail address. "I'll look for them in a couple minutes," he said with excitement in his voice.

"Here." Randy handed her a hamburger wrapped in a greasy paper. "Eat one of these. I've got to update the Chief."

He walked away, dialing his cell phone. Laurie pushed the hamburger aside and lay her head down on the table. She had just fallen asleep when the telephone rang next to her head. She jerked her head up and looked around, trying to get her bearings. It all came into focus in a second and she picked up the telephone. "Inspector Lone Eagle."

"Laurie, Randall here. "The Martin child was wearing red and white striped T-shirt. Stripes running horizontally. Blue denim Oshkosh B'Gosh coveralls. I called the Martins and they want to know when they pick him up." His voice was filled with excitement. "By the way. Where are you?"

"San Antonio, Texas." Laurie took a deep breath and considered the Martin's interest in moving quickly. "It'll take a few days to get the legal paperwork done. I'll call tomorrow after everything gets rolling and give you an update. If I get tied up, contact Randy Lewis in the San Antonio P.D."

"Sounds great!" Randall's voice was exuberant. "By the way, good job. You should get a medal."

Randy sat across from Laurie and took a huge bite from his burger. "The Chief is excited. He's got the lab combing the evidence they collected at the house. He wants to know when we will have the names of the other adoptive parents."

'Back to the University," she said. "But let me eat some of this burger. Maybe it'll recharge my blood sugar."

Randy pushed a cup of Coke to her. "The caffeine and sugar will work faster."

Ron, the computer geek, was sitting at his desk. A pizza box sat next to his keyboard and he was pushing a cursor around the computer screen with his right hand. A slice of pizza dangled from his left.

"Hey! You're back." He took a final bite of pizza and threw the crust into the box. "I put all the information on a thumb drive," he said, holding out a memory device.

"What's on it?" Asked Laurie.

"Names, dates, addresses, finances, bank accounts," he said, then paused to swallow. "Was this guy into drugs, too? I mean, some of the files are really cryptic and he talks about bricks going to Kansas, Iowa, and Minnesota. I assume that's some variety of drugs."

Laurie, looking bone weary, took the thumb drive. "I can't thank you enough."

Ron pulled out his wallet and held it to his ear. "I'm sorry, I can't hear you."

Randy waved his hand. "Submit an invoice. I'll see that it's paid."

"I'm expensive," Ron replied.

"Your information is invaluable," Laurie said. "You're going to help us repatriate a dozen kidnapped children with their parents."

"Cool!"

CHAPTER 37

SAN ANTONIO, TEXAS

Randy Lewis dropped off Laurie at the hotel after 11 p.m. The crowd of sightseers had thinned and the lobby was almost empty when she crossed to the elevator. In her room she stripped off her blouse and slacks, took a three-minute shower, then collapsed onto the bed. The bed was too hard, and the pillow too soft. Visions of missing children and bloody kidnappers ran through her dreams. When the wake-up call came at seven a.m., she felt like she'd only had two or three hours of sleep.

After showering again and drying her hair, Laurie called her parents. She hoped her father would be home from the hospital. Regardless of his hospitalization, she expected some member of the extended family to be at the house to answer the telephone.

"Hello."

"Hi Mom," Laurie replied, surprised her mother was answering the telephone. "How's Dad doing?"

There was a long pause. "The medicine the hospital gives makes him very ill. He still can't keep food in his stomach, and they feed him through the tube in his arm."

Laurie sighed. "Is he getting chemotherapy?" She had a terrible feeling of helplessness trying to deal with her mother from a thousand miles away.

"I don't understand what they do to him," her mother replied. "He gets this and he gets that. They tell me, but I can't understand except he gets sicker." There was a pause before she asked, "When are you coming back to see him? Are you still in Minneapolis?"

"No, Mom. I'm in Texas. We tracked down a man who steals babies. Now we are going to find the babies and bring them back to their mothers."

"I had a baby once." The voice was filled with spite. "I thought she would marry and give me many grandchildren. Now she forgets her family and works for other people. Do you think you could bring *her* back? Her father needs her."

Laurie let out a deep sigh. "I understand, Mom. I have one more thing to do, then I'll fly back to you and Dad."

"Children forget the people who bring them into the world." Laurie's mother paused to consider her words carefully. "They worry about other people's families, like they should worry about their own. It's a sad world. It is good your father should not have to endure much more of it. Will you be able to see him when he departs this world, or will you be too busy with the problems of others then, too?" The voice was very controlled, almost resigned. "I was not happy when you went to school to be a policeman, but I didn't speak. I hoped you'd come back to the tribal police, but instead you went to Pine

City. Now you go even further away and you don't come home when we need you."

"I'll be home soon. He has wonderful medical specialists caring for him. There is nothing I can do for him. But, I will come."

There was no further response. The line just went dead.

Laurie felt bitter bile rise in her throat. She briefly reflected on her interview with the tribal police shortly after graduation. She would have had to arrest people she'd known for years, friends and relatives who would expect her to look the other way. She's seen the poverty, the abuse, the effects of alcoholism and drugs all her life.

Her interview with Pine County had been with a previous sheriff who'd made her feel comfortable and respected. He'd sent her off to ride with Floyd Swenson, who was pleasant, paternal, and supportive. He'd agreed with her when they talked about the difficulties of policing your hometown, and by the end of the ride she felt she'd found her new home.

The BCA was a big step up where neither her gender nor her Native heritage were issues. The pace of life in the Twin Cities was faster and the job pressures intense, but she loved it. She dove into the searches for missing children and experienced an incredible rush each time a child was found and returned to his parents. The flip side was the dark gnawing feeling of defeat when a child was found dead. At first she'd felt inadequate and guilty, questioning whether she could have done something different or something more. With time, she'd learned that she had no control over the criminals and the only role she could play was to expedite a solution. She found energy in her continued optimism that kept every case could be solved. She also learned that the parents needed closure. Even bad outcomes gave some degree of solace to the parents.

Laurie had agreed to meet Randy Lewis in the hotel restaurant at eight. By the time she got packed and checked out it was five minutes to eight. Randy was already sitting at a table drinking coffee and reading USA Today.

When she slid the chair out, he looked up and said, "You look like hell. Didn't you sleep?"

"Good morning to you, too," Laurie replied as she hung her bag over the back of a chair.

"Oh. Sorry." Randy backtracked, realizing Laurie wasn't used to his sarcastic banter. "I've been told I tend to speak my mind a little too much sometimes."

Laurie sat down and signaled the waitress for coffee. With the assurance of coffee she replied, "I always have a hard time sleeping the first night in a strange bed." The waitress poured the coffee and refilled Randy's cup. When she left, Laurie added. "To top it off, I spoke with my mother this morning and my father isn't doing well. He is having chemotherapy for stomach cancer. She thinks he's declining because his only daughter, who hasn't given her grandchildren yet, isn't at his bedside for the vigil."

"Boy. That's some pretty heavy guilt," Randy observed. "Even my Catholic mother can't come close to piling it on that thick."

They ordered from the menu when the waitress came back to refill their coffee. After ordering Laurie asked, "What's the plan for today?"

"The Chief says we wrap up some of the loose ends of the Hilliard arrest," Randy replied as he folded the newspaper. "It looks like we can nail him on a bunch of stuff. We can nail him with what was on the computer and Tubby's testimony. It looks like he'll face charges for manslaughter, interstate transport of controlled substances, and kidnapping. That's just for starters. The IRS and FBI are here to go through his financial records and that may open a whole new line of prosecution, money laundering, tax evasion, illegal transfer of funds and more."

"Sounds like they should be able to keep him locked up for years." Laurie was impressed with the list of charges and the quick response of the feds. She asked, "Is Tubby still under protective custody?"

"Yup." Randy nodded. "They moved him to a nursing facility that's more secure. I don't have a clue where."

Breakfast arrived and as Laurie ate a spoonful of oatmeal Randy asked, "Are you hanging around until we find all the kids?" When Laurie didn't jump at the question he went on. "It would only be fair that you hang around and see the benefits of all your hard work."

Laurie turned somber. "I need to pick up Tubby's girlfriend this morning," She stirred some brown sugar into the cereal slowly as she continued. "Tubby specified it could only be me who collected Dolores. After that, she and I can catch a plane back to Minnesota and I turn her over to the U.S. Marshals for protection and go home."

Laurie called Tubby's apartment twice before leaving the restaurant, but the line was busy each time she dialed. After the last attempt, she asked the operator to check the line. The operator reported the line was out of order. When she arrived at Tubby's door, she knocked. The door edged open with the force of her knock. Laurie's heart started to race as she reached in her purse and pulled out her Glock. She listened, but there was no sound from inside. She pushed the door open slightly and saw the doorjamb was splintered around the deadbolt. She thought briefly about investigating further by herself, but decided to get Randy for backup.

When Randy saw Laurie running from the apartment complex with her gun drawn he immediately called for backup, pulled his Glock, and met Laurie halfway across the parking lot.

"Someone broke in." Laurie gasped. "The door jamb is splintered and there's no sound inside."

Randy passed her, ran up the stairs two at a time, and paused at the door while she caught up. He peeked through the small opening of the door, then turned back. "I'm going in on three. I'll go left," he signaled.

Laurie set her purse down and rifled through it to remove the badge holder. She slipped it onto the waistband of her slacks and held her gun at her side. She had no jurisdiction, but at least another cop would see her badge and wouldn't mistake her for a bad guy.

Randy watched with a degree of frustration until she was ready. By then, he had stopped breathing heavily. When Laurie gave him a "thumbs up," he mouthed the words. "One, Two, Three."

"POLICE!" The door crashed open with his kick and he lunged into the room in a low crouch. She swung the Glock around the corner of the door and braced herself in a Weaver stance, her shoulder against the right jamb. The room was empty. Laurie's pulse was racing.

Randy plunged into the kitchen. Laurie moved up to the opening to the hallway and braced there. She pointed the gun, prepared to shoot anyone who came out of the bedrooms or bath. She glanced behind her and saw the living room furniture had been pushed around a bit.

Her eyes froze on a dark spot on the couch. She yelled out, "Blood on the couch. It looks old!"

He came up behind her with his gun held low, still gripped in both hands. He looked where she indicated and commented, "We might be too late." In the distance, sirens wailed.

"Let's do the other rooms," he whispered. Randy stopped at the edge of the hallway and took a crouch for a second before he lunged into the bathroom, using his shoulder as a battering ram.

The bathroom door crashed as he flew against it. In two seconds he was back at the door and hesitated to make sure Laurie was in position. He crashed into the first bedroom as the sirens stopped in the parking lot.

He came out and said, "It's clear. Are you ready?" She nodded as she moved further down the hall. He crashed through the second bedroom door and disappeared. A low moan came from the room.

"In here!" he shouted.

Laurie raced into the room as footsteps pounding down the hallway outside the apartment.

Dolores's naked and bruised body was smeared with blood. She moaned pitifully as she lay on the floor, hidden behind the bed. Laurie went to her side and looked at her face. It was as bruised as Tubby's had been after the car accident. Laurie slipped her Glock into the pocket of her slacks.

"Dolores. Can you hear me?' Laurie knelt down in the narrow space between the beds. "I'm Laurie. Tubby sent me to bring you to Minnesota."

Dolores replied in moans and weak coughs.

Two uniformed officers stood at the door with their hands on their holstered guns. Randy looked up at them. "Call an ambulance and get a crime scene team here."

One officer lifted the portable radio from his belt and relayed the request to the dispatcher.

Most of the blood had dried on Dolores's skin and the bruises were already deeply colored. "When did this happen Dolores?" Laurie asked. "Who did this to you?"

She moaned as Laurie pulled a few strands of blood-caked hair from where they were plastered against Dolores' forehead. "They came in afternoon."

Laurie looked at Randy and he mouthed, "Yesterday." He rolled his eyes in frustration.

Laurie asked again, "Who did this to you?"

"Two men." Dolores was becoming more lucid as Laurie spoke with her. "They told me they were friends of Tubby's and wanted to know where he was. I told them he was gone to work and they got mad. They pushed me and told me he owed them money. When they couldn't find him here, they punched me. They pinched my breasts and twisted them. I screamed and then they punched me."

Laurie looked at Dolores' bare breasts, they were bruised and scraped. She looked down and saw there was blood in her pubic hair and on her thighs. She wondered if Dolores had even been conscious when they raped her.

"Can you describe the men for me?" Laurie looked at the bed. The sheet was smeared with blood.

"They were mean and ugly. Both were Mexican, but one spoke good English. The other spoke with an accent, like me."

"Had you ever seen the men before?"

"I don't know. Maybe. One might have been from the bar where Tubby met me."

"Did you tell them Tubby was in the hospital?" Fear was creeping into Laurie's voice.

"I'm afraid." Dolores started to cry. "They said they'll kill Tubby. I said he was in the hospital in Minnesota, but I didn't know where. Then one of the men kicked me in the stomach and I don't remember after." Dolores was becoming more lucid and she realized she was naked. She tried to cover her breasts with her hands.

Randy pulled a sheet off the floor and covered Dolores while they waited for the ambulance. "I'll lay you odds Hilliard is behind this." Randy whispered to Laurie.

"Tubby and Ernie are probably late," said Laurie, "so he sent his boys to see what was going on. When he got word from the thugs that Tubby is in the hospital, he put two and two together, and decided it was time to bug out and start a new life."

The ambulance siren whined, then stopped in the parking lot.

"We'll get her to the hospital and they'll run a rape kit," said Randy. "The crime scene techs will have a field day with the mess in this apartment. With any luck, they'll find some fingerprints and DNA to compare in the database."

CHAPTER 38

PINE CITY, MINNESOTA MONDAY

Floyd left a voicemail message for Russ Watson, the investigator from the drug taskforce. Then he leaned back in his chair and tapped his pencil on the arm while he thought aloud. "Laurie said the kidnappers planted the bomb that killed George Brown. But why? What's their connection to George Brown?"

He dialed Laurie's cell phone and left another voicemail. He started to write his report of the chase and shooting in White Bear Lake. As he was wrapping up the report his cell phone rang.

"Swenson."

"Hi, Floyd, I got your message." The line crackled and he assumed Russ Watson was calling from a cell phone.

Floyd asked, "I was wondering if you guys got anywhere with the drug dealer in North Branch?"

"The guy is really weird." Watson replied. "He gets up in the morning and walks to the garage. He has like seven or eight locks on the door and he looks around after he unlocks each of them. He's motion activated lights all over and cameras mounted under the eaves that give him a 360 degree view of the house and garage. He's paranoid.

"When he goes into the garage, he spends the whole day there. Never comes out to eat, piss, or answer the telephone. Every night he carries a toolbox to his car and drives to some teen place. He goes to a different one every night of the week. When he gets back to North Branch he puts the tool box away, locks the garage, then goes in the house. The lights are out in fifteen minutes and there's no sign of activity until the next morning. He opens the living room blinds, eats a bowl of cereal, then goes back into the garage."

Floyd pondered the information. "Do you think he has a lab in the garage?"

"We've had it under surveillance for almost four days now and there is no indication he's bringing in or disposing of any quantity of chemicals. His electrical usage is normal, so he doesn't have a pot farm. There's a furnace vent on the garage, but it doesn't smell like it's spewing fumes from a meth lab."

"No sign of where he gets the stuff he's selling?"

"Not so far." Russ answered, "But it's been less than a week. He might make a pick up, or get a drop once or twice a month."

"Let me know if there's anything I can do to help." Floyd said, having nothing else to offer.

"I don't know of anything you can do right now. You can ask your deputies to keep clear of the roller rink so they don't screw up the surveillance."

"Consider it done."

Floyd wrote an email regarding the drug surveillance and sent it to the Sheriff and all the deputies. After that, he proofed the shooting report and printed a copy. The paper went into the files. Then he e-mailed a copy to the Sheriff and poured a cup of coffee.

As he was shutting down the computer, the sheriff walked in. "Floyd. I saw your report. How are you doing?"

"Fine. How about you?"

The sheriff smiled as he walked to the visitor's chair. "It's not a social question. You were involved in a fatal shooting. You're supposed to be on administrative leave—two weeks off, with pay."

Floyd sat in his chair. "I'm okay. I was a little rattled at first, but I'm fine with it now."

"Just so you know. I had a call from the Ramsey County sheriff and I've talked to the highway patrolmen at the scene. They fully support your actions. But the county attorney is obligated to go ahead with the grand jury anyway."

The sheriff pulled a cigar from his breast pocket and carefully made a ceremony out of unwrapping it and rolling it between his fingers. He asked, "Would you like me to have the Pine County attorney go down and sit in on the hearing? He can't offer any defense, but he can listen and ask procedural questions."

"I never thought about it." Floyd sat uneasily waiting for the sheriff to say more. When it was apparent the conversation was through he said, "I'd like to ponder that a little bit."

"Take whatever time you like. The offer stands. And so do I." The sheriff got up and walked toward his office. As he stepped out the door, Floyd could hear a match strike. The odor of burned sulfur, followed by a wisp of cigar smoke wafted by.

Floyd looked at his watch and decided go out for a cup of coffee and a sweet roll. He parked on Main Street and met Dan Williams, the undersheriff, coming out the café door.

"Floyd said, "Can I buy you a cup of coffee?"

Dan smiled. "I just had one. But if you want to talk, I can force myself to have another."

They sat in the booth and talked about the shooting and the pending grand jury in Ramsey County. Dan listened attentively and asked a few pertinent questions until Floyd ran out of talk.

"Let me tell you," Dan said. "I had to draw my gun and shoot a man once. I was lucky. He was running out the back door of the cowboy bar in Willow River when I was running in." Dan paused as he closed his eyes to replay the scene. "He got a shot off before I ever got my gun out. He shot high and missed me. He was getting set to shoot again. My first shot hit him in the chest. He was aiming again and I was so pumped with adrenaline that I emptied all six shots on him. He was still struggling to get the gun up when I dropped the hammer on the empty chamber and heard the click. I was shaking so badly I couldn't reload. Luckily, he dropped the gun when he fell."

Floyd swirled the coffee in his cup and asked, "How'd you feel the next day?"

Dan opened his eyes and stared at the Formica tabletop. "Scared, embarrassed for being scared. I felt stupid for standing there, blazing away without knowing if there was a bar full of people behind him." He paused and looked down into his coffee cup as he mumbled. "And sorry for a mother who wouldn't have a son to send her a card the next Mother's Day."

Floyd was surprised at the depth of Dan's remorse. He asked, "Do you think he would have sent her a card? Or, was he a schmuck who spent his whole life in prison or on the way there?"

Dan shook his head. "Does it matter?" He signaled the waitress for a refill, then said, "It took me awhile to realize I'd done what I was trained to do, my job. Sometimes it's a damned shitty job, but I had no more choice to shoot than you did."

They waited for the waitress to finish filling the cups, then Dan went on. "We took an oath to uphold the law, and they've trained us how and when to use our weapons. They hope we'll never need to, but expect us to do it if we have to. I had to. You had to. You had a little kid dying before your eyes. The child would have died if you hadn't pulled the trigger. Your conscience made a choice. It was a good choice. Don't second guess yourself."

They got up to leave, and Floyd left a five-dollar bill on the counter. As they walked out the door Floyd turned to Dan. "Did you talk to someone after you shot the guy in Willow?"

"I never did and it was plain dumb to keep it inside." Dan held the door open as Floyd walked out. Then he added, "There are only three deputies in the history of Pine County to ever fire their guns at another person."

"Lucky I ran into you. You helped me get my head straight."

Dan smiled and put his hand on Floyd's shoulder. "Luck had nothing to do with it. I've been sitting in the cafe all morning waiting for you. I was just giving up and coming to get you when you showed up."

Floyd checked his cell phone as he walked out of the restaurant and saw that he'd missed a call. The call log said, "Laurie Lone Eagle" He touched "call back" and waited.

"Inspector Lone Eagle."

"Laurie. What do you mean the kidnappers were the ones who set the bomb in George Brown's car?"

"What happened to Hello Laurie, how are you?"

"Sorry," Floyd stammered. "I'm a little preoccupied."

"You're excused." Laurie switched to her business voice. "It's just like the message I gave to Mary. You told me to ask Tubby if they killed George Brown. The answer was affirmative."

"I got the message, but it seems so incredible."

"They had orders from a guy, who called himself Mr. Applewhite, to take out George's car. They didn't know who it belonged to, but they had the description, the license number, and a map to the church. They were given the dynamite, the detonator and directions on how to use it."

Floyd was dumbfounded. "Why?" He asked.

"They didn't know why." Laurie answered. "They were just the hit men. They made an extra $500 for the job."

"Do you see any connection between George's murder and all the other stuff going on?"

"Not right offhand. However, they were also delivering drugs to St. Paul every trip. It was smuggled across the Mexican border under unsuspecting vehicles. They'd pull the drugs off in San Antonio and deliver the packages to St. Paul. They had a neat setup. There was a UPS uniform in the trunk of Tubby's car and a couple of pre-addressed boxes. All they did was load the drugs into a box with a UPS label, get dressed up like a UPS delivery person, and deliver the package to Preston's Pump Service in St. Paul. By the way, the pump service is under surveillance and we expect to bust them after we find out how wide their distribution network is."

"Quite a neat operation. Delivering drugs going north and kidnap kids for adoption going south."

"And a little capital murder for spice." Laurie added.

Floyd digested the information and then asked, "Is our friend Tubby going to Leavenworth or Sandstone for a long time?"

Laurie paused before answering. "Tubby's going into witness protection while he sings. That is unless he spooks. They almost killed his girlfriend yesterday trying to find him."

Floyd shook his head. "Nice guys."

After he got off the telephone with Laurie, Floyd wandered to the ready room for another cup of coffee. Pam Ryan was talking to Sandy Maki over a pile of papers. Floyd filled his cup, then joined them at the desk.

"Excuse me," Floyd interrupted. "I just had a call from Laurie Lone Eagle." He took a sip of coffee as he sat down in the metal guest chair. "The two Mexican guys were running drugs north and kidnapping kids on the return trip. In Texas, they had a guy running an illegal adoption agency which was placing the kids for big fees. It seems the Brown murder was just a sidelight. The guys who placed the bomb were just hired thugs. They didn't even know who they were going to kill, or why. They just had a description of the car and they knew it would be at the church that night."

Pam stared in disbelief. "They didn't know it was George Brown's car?"

Floyd shook his head. "Apparently not."

"Then it was someone else who knew George would be at the meeting," said Pam. "That still leaves someone else as a co-conspirator in first degree murder."

"Right." Floyd nodded. "That leads us back to the original questions; who wanted George Brown dead, and why?"

Floyd squinted into his coffee cup. "Um, Pam, would you do one thing for me?"

"Sure."

"When you make your rounds today, stop by Polly Hanson's farm near Braham. She's been living there alone. Stop off to see how things are going."

Pam smiled. "And maybe talk a little girl stuff?"

"Right."

CHAPTER 39

Floyd made an appointment to see Glen Bergstrom, the family doctor. At four-thirty, he was sitting in the waiting room reading a comparison of the 10mm and .45 ACP in *Guns and Ammo* when the receptionist called his name.

He sat in the padded chair, across from the doctor's desk, reading the diplomas and society memberships on the walls until Glen Bergstrom swept into the office ten minutes later. He was tall and lanky. He hung his white smock behind the door and closed it in one motion.

Bergstrom threw his slender frame into the desk chair and took a deep breath. "What's up, Floyd?"

Floyd studied Bergstrom's wire-rimmed glasses as he adjusted them on his nose. The gray at his temples had become more pronounced since Floyd's last visit. After a few seconds Floyd said, "I need to talk."

Bergstrom searched his desktop for Floyd's medical file. Not seeing it, he asked, "Is this professional or social?"

"Let's get into it, and you can decide." Floyd shifted in the guest chair before going on. "The sheriff suggested I see the county shrink. I'll let you decide if I need more than just a discussion with you."

Bergstrom blew out a deep breath and sank in his chair. "I'm not much of a psychiatrist, but we can talk. What's up?"

Swenson smiled. Glen Bergstrom was not a psychiatrist, but he was the community confidant and that seemed more important than psychiatric training to many people in the small town. Besides, everyone quickly knew when anyone went to Duluth to seek psychiatric assistance. A visit to Dr. Bergstrom could be for anything.

Floyd wiped his sweaty palms on the legs of his pants, then said, "We had a hostage situation yesterday. Two men kidnapped a little girl from Duluth. I saw them pulling out of the Tom Thumb and chased them to the Cities. They ran off the road and one of them was holding a knife to the kid's throat when she went limp and looked shocky. I made a decision." He drew a deep breath and blew it out. "And I pulled the trigger."

Dr. Bergstrom listened and watched Floyd's body language closely. He could see Floyd was withdrawing; the failure to look him in the eye indicated feelings of guilt and doubt.

Bergstrom asked, "What happened to the child?"

Swenson looked up. "She was unconscious, but she's okay."

Bergstrom nodded, hoping Floyd would find his nods reassuring. "How would you have felt if you hadn't shot and she'd died?"

Swenson squirmed. "I don't know." He paused and thought for a second. "I suppose I'd be mad. I'd blame myself for a poor decision. I'd want to kill the guy. I'd complain about life and the sad state of our criminal justice system."

"Do you think the girl would have died if you hadn't shot?"

Floyd shrugged "Maybe. Probably. Who knows? She was in shock. She had a couple of minutes, but not too much time. The Troopers were approaching him, trying to talk him down. Maybe he would've surrendered and handed the girl over."

Bergstrom asked, "Did the guy look like he was about ready to give up and turn her over?"

Floyd shook his head. "No. He was agitated and getting more frantic. I think he'd banged his head pretty hard when the car crashed. He wasn't thinking clearly." Floyd rubbed his hand over his face. "Hell! That'll probably come up in the hearing too. I shot a guy who was impaired after an accident. He probably wasn't able to make a rational decision."

Bergstrom picked up a pencil and started to scribble notes on a yellow Post-it Note. "Mm. The guy had a knife at her throat. If you hadn't shot, the child would have died. You did shoot and she lived. Is that right?" He set the pencil aside.

Swenson gave a so-so nod. "I guess."

"What happened to the guy you shot?" Bergstrom asked. "Dead?"

Floyd pointed to a spot behind his ear lobe. "I hit him here with a .45. He never wiggled."

Bergstrom nodded. "He probably had massive brain stem trauma...Never heard the shot. Never felt a thing. I assume he fell like a rag doll?"

"Uh huh."

"He was dead before the bullet exited his body." Bergstrom leaned his elbows on the top of the desk. "Floyd, it was as humane a death as is possible. However, that doesn't console you. Does it?"

Floyd shook his head. "Uh uh."

Bergstrom asked, "What would you do differently? You've already lived through it a couple hundred times I'll bet."

"A few thousand is more like it," Floyd said, shifting in the chair. "I don't know. I could have not shot and then the kid's death would be on my conscience." Floyd shook his head.

"I don't think you could have done that. What does your oath say? You are to enforce the law and protect the people, or some words to the same effect?"

Swenson nodded. "Something like that. It's been a couple of years since I swore it."

Bergstrom stood up and paced between his desk chair and the door. "You had to protect the life of an innocent child. Does the law offer you any option? I can't think of any. And when the kidnapper left you with only one option, you exercised it."

Swenson shrugged. "Maybe. But why do I feel so shitty?"

Bergstrom sat back in the desk chair and took a deep breath. "I've never told anyone in town this, and I'd prefer to keep it between us." He waited until Floyd nodded. "A woman came in to the hospital by ambulance and was about to deliver a baby. I was the doctor on-call and I was full of self-confidence and thought I knew it all. I'd help deliver a dozen babies. Consequently, I didn't call the resident up from the cafeteria. I took her into an examining room and checked her cervix."

Swenson sat up straight in the chair and listened intently.

"She was dilated to seven centimeters and I could feel the baby's head when I put a finger up the cervix. So, I didn't bother putting on a fetal monitor. I knew the baby was on the way and I told the woman to push. She pushed and pushed, but the baby wouldn't come down any farther. She and I sweated and waited for the baby and I failed to realize how tired she was getting. I was totally focused on getting the baby out."

Floyd nodded and asked, "How long did you keep at it?"

It must have been close to an hour before the resident showed up. He looked at the woman and asked how the baby was doing. I said it was almost crowning. He checked and asked me if the baby had progressed. I said, 'not much'."

Bergstrom rocked back in his chair and stared at the ceiling. The scene replayed itself in his mind. "Bottom line is the woman was small, the baby was big. It wouldn't pass through the birth canal. The resident rushed her to surgery and he did an emergency C-section and I assisted him."

"What happened to the baby?" Floyd asked.

"She and the mother were both okay, but only because the resident intervened when he did. If I would've continued, the baby would probably have been stillborn."

"What happened to you?"

"I was beside myself with guilt. First I wanted to quit, then I thought they'd throw me out. The resident chewed my ass royally, then he told the head of the ER that anyone would have done the same, given the conditions."

"You've learned to live with all this?" Floyd asked.

Bergstrom shook his head. "It's made me one hell of a better doctor. I go to church every Sunday, and I pray to God to remind me I'm mortal and no better than the lowliest indigent who walks through the door. I'd also like to believe I'm less arrogant and more concerned about my patients than most of my colleagues."

Bergstrom paused, then asked, "How about you, Floyd? Can you live with the decision you made? A scumbag forced you into a decision. In return, you saved the life of an innocent child so she can live a rich life with a loving family. I don't see any comparison."

Floyd stared at the wall over Bergstrom's head. "I don't like playing God."

"Neither do I." Bergstrom picked up a pencil and doodled on the Post-it Note. "But the jobs we have sometime leave us with no option. You didn't make the choice. The kidnapper did."

Swenson stretched his legs and then leaned over the desk. "When do the nightmares go away, Glen?"

Bergstrom snorted. "With time. Our minds are funny things. They search out the positive, fun, and exciting things we have done in our lives. Our minds keep them at the surface. The bad, sad, and disgusting are at a different level, there for reference, but not easily accessible. That imbalance keeps us sane."

Floyd stood up. "I think I can get it back in perspective." He put a hand on the doorknob and stopped. "Doc, I drove Polly Hanson here for the baby's checkup. She told me you seemed more interested in her than the baby."

Bergstrom smiled. "The baby was fine, but I was afraid Polly was anemic. She let me run some blood tests."

"She told me she probably has AIDS"

Bergstrom's smile turned to a somber frown. "I can't discuss my patients with you, Floyd."

"So," Floyd pressed, "she does have AIDS?"

"Floyd," Bergstrom rolled his eyes back then started tapping his foot. "I told her to come back for a second test in a month or two. She was negative, but her blood test might not be positive that soon after exposure. She was convinced that April's father has full blown AIDS. She told me about his weight loss and jaundice. I can understand why she's paranoid, but there are a hundred medical things that could've been going on with that guy. Sure, AIDS is a possibility, but he was a heavy drinker, and he might've had cirrhosis or hepatitis. I can speculate all day, but without having him here, all I can do is guess, test her blood, and hope for the best."

Floyd closed his eyes. "She won't be back. She doesn't have any money or transportation. I can't drag her in and she won't take charity."

Bergstrom thought for few seconds then said, "She'll do anything for the baby. Bring her in for April's booster shots and I'll take Polly's blood too."

Swenson smiled. "You are devious." He opened the door to the darkened hallway and walked across the empty waiting room.

An idea flashed through Floyd's head and he turned back to the office. Bergstrom was making notes when Floyd stepped through the door. "Doc, when was the last time you saw George Brown?"

"I don't know." Bergstrom shrugged. "A week or two before the explosion. I think he hurt his hand on some barbed wire. Yeah, that was it. I gave him a tetanus booster."

"Did he come to you for counseling too?"

Bergstrom laughed. "I have been known to provide and accept philosophy during office visits."

Floyd asked. "Did George say anything about problems at the church?"

Bergstrom moved Floyd to the empty waiting room and turned on the lights. He sat in one of the chairs while he thought. "Boy. That was a long time ago in terms of my memory."

Swenson sat in a chair, too. He tried to refresh Bergstrom's memory. "George was upset about the church spending and he told the deacons' board something was wrong. He said he was withdrawing his pledge. He also changed his will to exclude the church."

Bergstrom listened intently, then replied. "Pretty strong stuff, but George didn't pull his punches. He said he'd been distracted when handling the barbed wire. While I bandaged his hand, he mentioned the renter who lived over the hardware store who was entertaining a married woman. However, he never mentioned names. I got the impression he was trying to evict the guy, but he couldn't because the guy always paid rent on time and wasn't doing any damage. But that may not have anything to do with the church."

A small smile crept over Floyd's face. "I've got a hunch it ties together. Thanks."

● ● ●

Central Minnesota
The fields flew by as Laurie Lone Eagle traveled I-35 to Duluth. A big pond on the east side of the highway was covered with geese.

She had cleared her desk of messages after the trip from Texas and found out the U.S. Marshal's Service had hidden Tubby at Hazelden, a substance abuse treatment center in a rural town outside of St. Paul. He would be secure and the staff was renowned for being discreet.

She called San Antonio and found out Dolores was recovering in a hospital. Dolores had a few internal injuries, which were healing. She had been brutally raped. The semen samples were being DNA tested for identification of suspects and the few fingerprints didn't match anything in the NCIC database. So far, Dolores had been unable to give them much help in identifying the intruders.

As Walmart passed the passenger window at the Pine City exit, Laurie thought about turning off and talking to Swenson, but decided she'd spent too much time fooling around already and stayed on the Interstate.

At Hinckley, she drove up the exit and went through Hardee's drive-through for a chicken sandwich and coffee. It had already been a long day and the end was not in sight.

She balanced the sandwich on her lap, set the coffee in the cup holder, and turned back on the interstate. After the sandwich was gone, she wiped the crumbs from her slacks. She remembered the DEA/FBI investigation of the St. Paul pump service. She keyed a phone number into her cell phone and waited for the answer at the FBI office.

After being transferred to three different lines, she reached Randi Pitt, the agent assigned to the pump-service investigation. "Randi, this is Laurie Lone Eagle. I was wondering if you are making any headway on the Lasoya case."

"The accounting boys are still digging into the IRS records, but we have a lot of information. It appears the pump repair business is extraordinarily profitable. We've found several bank accounts for Mr. Preston where he makes regular deposits."

Laurie asked the critical question. "So you can nail him?"

The answer was preceded by a sigh. "If we could find him."

"What?"

Randi replied. "He apparently had some discussions with his friend in San Antonio. We had the business and his home under surveillance but he disappeared. When we got word the raid had gone down in San Antonio, we decided to grab him. The place was empty. He left so fast the safe was left open . . . and empty."

Laurie's heart sank. "So now what?" She asked.

"We've got the U.S. Marshals searching for him. But a man with a pile of cash can be hard to trace . . . for a while."

"I assume you've frozen his financial assets. That leaves him with just the cash in his pockets."

"And whatever he's got offshore. He may have some in the Cayman Islands or the Far East. However, he's going to have one hell of a time getting to it. We've got the INS and Border Patrol alerted so he'll have a hard time getting on a plane or crossing at a controlled border entry."

"Anything I can do?" Laurie asked. She expected the standard FBI response that they had it all under control.

"Not that I can think of. If I do, I'll give you a call."

• • •

Braham, Minnesota

It was well after dark when Pam Ryan pulled into the gravel driveway at the farmhouse. She notified the dispatcher she would be out of service, and as she turned off the ignition, a woman appeared at the kitchen window. The door was open when she got to the house and Polly Hanson met her.

"Hello, Officer."

"Hi," Pam smiled. "Floyd Swenson is off, and he asked me to stop by and see if you were okay."

Polly smiled. "I'm fine. Do you have a second for a cup of coffee?" Polly pulled the door open and stepped back for Pam to enter the kitchen.

"It's been a long shift, and a cup of coffee would taste great." Pam stepped into the neat kitchen and sat in a chair at the table.

"I understand. The nights get pretty long around here too with only April for company."

As Polly turned to make coffee, Pam looked to see if there was a television or a radio anywhere. The house was silent, and the living room was empty except for a moth-eaten couch and a couple of fruit crates. The only items that might provide entertainment were a couple of children's toys on the living room floor.

"I hope you take your coffee black because I don't have any cream," Polly spoke over her shoulder as she measured coffee into the porcelain coffeepot.

"Black is fine."

With the pot on a burner, Polly sat in the other chair. "I feel so stupid. I didn't even introduce myself. I'm Polly."

"I'm Pam Ryan." Pam offered her hand for a handshake.

Pam looked around, "Where's the tot? I heard she's very cute."

"She's in bed. This is the only time of day I get a few minutes to myself." The conversation lagged and Polly asked. As if on cue, there were cries from the other room.

Pam looked around at the shabby kitchen and tired furniture. "Is this how I'd live if my parents had thrown me out when I was sixteen?" she thought.

Polly popped up and disappeared. She was back in a minute and slid April into her highchair. "This is April. Apparently she wanted to meet you."

Pam leaned forward and stuck out a finger, which April immediately seized. Pam touched April's nose and asked, "Is this April's nose?"

The baby laughed.

Polly watched Pam play with April and asked, "Do you have any kids?"

April flirted with Pam. "Not yet. But I suppose someday I'd like kids."

The coffee started to boil and Polly jumped up. She set the pot aside, took two cups from the cupboard, and poured them full of the steaming brew. She set one in front of Pam and then got the container of sugar from the cupboard.

As Polly stirred several teaspoons of sugar into her coffee, she asked, "But you must have a couple of boyfriends?"

Pam shook her head. "My hours are pretty strange, and a lot of guys are put off by my job. They aren't comfortable dating a deputy sheriff."

Polly nodded. "Oh, I bet that makes them nervous. But at least it should help sort out some of the jerks." She sipped her coffee, and then added more sugar. "Now you take me. I was waiting tables and every jerk that walked through the door thought he could get into my pants. Let me tell you, that's no treat."

Pam nodded her understanding. "It's gotta be tough."

Polly shook her head. "Most guys are okay. However, look out for the ones who have been drinking. They all think they look like Brad Pitt." They both laughed.

"Were you married to April's father?"

Polly got quiet and stared into the coffee. "No."

Pam regretted the question. "Sorry."

Polly waved it off. "It's okay. He was a smooth talker and I thought he might have been the right one. Turned out he was already married."

"Yeah," Pam agreed. "I've stumbled across a couple of them myself. Seems like there are a lot of 'the wrong guys' out there."

Polly nodded. "I've been smarter lately. But it took a couple times of getting burned before I figured out there were guys who'll lie to you just to get you into the sack for a night."

Polly started to say something else, but cut it off.

"What's the matter?" Pam asked.

"I just get so little company sometimes I run off at the mouth. It was really nothing."

Pam tried to restart the conversation. "I dated a guy in my hometown. He was the undertaker and he took me to the mortuary to make out after a movie. I was so appalled, I ran all the way home."

Polly turned up her nose. "Oh, that's gross." She thought for a second then said, "I dated a guy who was a minister. I thought he was pretty cool, but it turns out he was also dating one of the married women from his church. I was at his apartment one night when she called and wanted to come over. I heard it all from the bedroom and I got really mad and wanted to leave. The problem was he'd driven me to Pine City and

I didn't have any way to get back home. I threw a fit and he had to drive me back to the farm. He apologized the whole way back, but I never had anything to do with him again." They laughed, and then she added, "That's not quite as weird as necking in a funeral home, but it was strange making out in an apartment and hearing voices from the hardware store downstairs."

Pam's mind seized up with that piece of information. She tried to retain their banter without seeming too interested. "Yes, that'd be a romance killer."

"He was kind of strange, you know, with his methamphetamine and all. I could deal with the meth. But dating a married woman at the same time, well, that was too much."

Pam rolled her eyes. "Boy, any of those things would be too much for me." She glanced at her watch and exclaimed, "Oh! I've got to check in with the dispatcher."

Polly saw her to the door. "Well, it was sure nice having you stop by. Come around again sometime. I'm always here."

Pam waved. "I'd love to stop again." Inside the squad she said to herself, "Tom Knight was dating a married woman from the parish and was dabbling in drugs. That's way too coincidental."

CHAPTER 40

Terry Preston had spent a night and a full day on the roof of his one story office building with a sleeping bag and a cardboard box. The overnight temperature dropped to thirty degrees, and he felt half frozen. In the box was $100,000 cash, a 9mm Browning pistol that matched the one under his leather coat, a kilo of methamphetamine, and a box of ammunition. He had heard the commotion under him as cops rattled through his office searching for him and evidence. They had even moved the box he'd set on the shelf behind him as he went onto the roof, but they hadn't seen the carefully fitted trapdoor to the roof above the box. If they had seen it, they had apparently reasoned no one would go onto the roof of a single story building, which wasn't connected to any others. They'd found the hidden stairway in the back, built by the bootlegger baker who had been the tenant during prohibition. They had rattled the door, but the rusty nails had given justification to pursue that exit no further. Preston's time investment in reopening the old exit and camouflaging the function had paid off.

At ten o'clock the second night, a cold spring rain started to fall. The insulation in the sleeping bag started to get soggy, losing its ability to hold his body heat. Preston decided it was time to leave. He carefully peeked over the edge of the low brick wall that hid the flat roof from view. The grocery store immediately across the street and all the other visible businesses were closed. There didn't appear to be any police surveillance. He had reached the point where he no longer cared if the police were watching. He was cold and hungry and decided he was either climbing down or he was going to die on the roof.

The steps of the rope ladder, which was stored on the roof as a fire escape, clattered against the side of the building, preceding the *thud* of the box hitting the asphalt in the alley. Preston slowly climbed down the ladder, twice losing his footing on stiff legs.

He picked up the box and walked toward the old Wilson High School, a few blocks away. His clerk lived on a side street where the view from down the alley was of the old brick high school building.

He walked past a couple of groups of young tough kids who made some comments about the "honky" walking the streets after dark. He slid the box under his left arm and placed his hand on the butt of the Browning. The kids didn't challenge him, just watched.

He was sure the girl who worked for him probably wouldn't be under surveillance. She thought she was working for a legitimate business and was so innocent the police would buy her story right away. He walked to Simpson Street and went to the old bungalow in the middle of the block. The lights were on inside.

His knock on the door stirred some activity. The thin drapes over the door parted and a middle-aged female face looked out. "What do you want?"

"I need to talk to Patty." He was tempted to identify himself as her boss, but he decided if the police had connected her with the pump service Patty's parents might dial 911.

"It's late. Who wants her?"

"Tell her it's Terry," he said with exasperation.

There were footsteps and voices inside the house, then the door opened. Patty looked at his whiskered wet face smeared with dirt, and took a step back, her mouth open.

"Don't scream." Her expression made Preston realize he gave the appearance of being a street person. This might work to his advantage if anyone spotted him. "It's me. Terry."

Patty put her hand over her mouth. Terry took her by the arm and guided her onto the porch. He closed the door behind them and whispered, "Listen. Have the cops talked to you?"

She nodded.

"I want to buy your car. Will you sell it to me and not tell the cops?" He could see she was very reluctant to comply and decided to soften the request. "Call them in two days and tell them it was stolen. I'll be gone."

He reached into the box, pulled out a neatly bound stack of $20s, and handed it to her. "Here's five grand. Is that enough for the car?"

She stared at it with her mouth open, then looked up at him.

"Isn't that enough?" He reached down and handed her another stack. "That's ten. Go get the keys." He took her elbow again and steered her into the house.

In two minutes, she was back with a keychain dangling from her fingers. "It's in back. There isn't much gas."

Before she had the words out of her mouth, he was bounding down the front steps and rounding the corner of the house. The green '73 Malibu was sitting on a dirt patch near the alley. He pumped the gas and called the engine to life. The car started with a low rumble. He backed into the alley and the tires spit gravel after he gave the engine a little gas. Within a minute he was on Snelling, and two minutes later he was on the entrance ramp to I-94. In 20 minutes, he was at the I-35 and 694 intersection, then on to I-35 north. With each mile behind him, Preston felt more secure.

Sleepy intersections buzzed past as the Malibu made its way north on I-35. Each had a few ramp lights, some had a gas station or two. Preston didn't need gas. Putting miles behind him was more important. He passed the rental place that used to be Fred's Red Shed as he pulled off the freeway and turned east toward downtown Pine City. In town, he slowly cruised Main Street until he spotted his landmark. He parked in a little lot behind the commercial buildings. The gas gauge was on "E," but he didn't care. The Malibu had gotten him to Pine City. He would find other transportation from here.

The parking lot was deserted. After a few minutes, he was convinced no one had followed him and he climbed out of the car and walked across the pavement. Behind an unlocked door, a set of stairs led to the second floor apartment.

Tom Knight was asleep when he thought he heard a muffled knock on the door. He rubbed his eyes and searched for his glasses. The clock said two-fifty a.m. He put on a robe and walked across the tiny living room to the door.

"I wonder which of the kids is afraid to go home tonight?" he asked himself. In his role as youth minister, he had held many midnight counseling sessions with one or another of the teens. He opened the door and was astonished at the sight of the grubby pump service owner. "Preston, is that you? What the hell are you doing here?"

Terry Preston pushed past Tom Knight as he spoke. "It's time to pack your bags and go. The whole thing blew up over the last three days. I'm on my way to Canada until it cools off. You might as well come along."

The shock of the news, combined with the late hour clouded Knight's mind. "I can't go. I'm only weeks away from finishing up at the seminary." He closed the door and watched Terry Preston open the refrigerator and rummage through the contents. Knight went on, "I'm a respected member of the community here. I can't just up and leave right now."

Preston selected an apple and took a big bite, savoring the sweet juice. "That's all bull." Preston had been so focused on escape he'd forgotten how hungry he was. The apple sent waves of hunger through his stomach.

Knight started to walk away from Preston, but Preston grabbed him by the sleeve. "It's all gone, Tom. Everything."

Preston let go of the sleeve and walked to the couch, where he took the last bite off the apple as he collapsed. "They arrested the couriers. Hilliard got nervous when they didn't show up in Texas with the package. His men found out from the girlfriend that Tubby was in the hospital in Minnesota and Ernie was dead. Hilliard was packing when he called me. I barely got out before the cops were all over my place. They apparently know it all. Tubby must have told them everything. We're all through."

Knight was in shock. "Wait! They don't know about me. I never had any contact with the couriers, and I had nothing to do with the distribution. They've never connected with me."

Terry Preston looked at the ceiling and gestured with his hands as if imploring God to intervene. "Tom, they know the bomb that killed your landlord was part of this. Do you think the cops are dumb? Eventually, they're going to put one and one together and come up with Tom Knight as the answer."

Knight held his head in his hands as he paced back and forth across the room. "I can't just leave right now. I've got things to wrap up here. Damn."

Preston stood up from the couch. "You do what you want. I'm outta here." He started for the door.

"Wait!" Knight blocked Preston's path to the door. "Spend the night. Let me wrap up a couple of things in the morning. Then I might be able to go with you."

"No way." Preston stated emphatically. "I've got a car that'll be hot in a day or two and I need to put some miles behind me ASAP. You come with me now, or you go it alone."

"Take it easy." Knight paced like a caged animal. "We'll leave your car in the lot here and take the van. But give me until morning. Sleep on the couch. You look like hell. Catch six hours of sleep. That'll make it nine in the morning. I can get things wrapped up here and I'll be ready to go by then."

Preston let out a deep sigh. He looked at the couch and thought about how heavy his eyelids had become. Sleep did sound good, but he was scared to death. "All right. But at nine we're out of here. No matter what."

Knight walked into the bedroom and pulled a pillow and a blanket off the closet shelf. He threw them at Preston. "The bathroom is next to the kitchen. Help yourself to anything you need."

Knight slipped back into the bedroom. After closing the door, he dropped his robe on the floor. He slid under the covers and snuggled up to the bare buttocks that jutted onto his side of the double bed.

"Mm. Who was at the door?" Judy Arend asked sleepily.

"An old friend from the Cities. He's sleeping on the couch, so don't run to the bathroom without putting something on."

"Don't you think he's ever seen a naked woman before?"

Knight ran his hand up over her breast and gave it a gentle squeeze. "He's never seen one as luscious as you."

Judy rolled over to face him and planted a warm kiss on his lips, eliciting a basal response from his groin. "You are such a sweet-talker." She pressed her pelvis tighter against his and repeated the kiss.

He nibbled her ear. "Have you ever been to Canada?" he asked as he ran his hand down to her hip.

"What's Canada got to do with anything?" she asked.

"We're going there tomorrow."

She sat up and snapped out of her semi-consciousness. "WHAT?"

"Shhh!" Knight shushed her. "I have an emergency. That's why my friend came here. He and I have to go to Canada tomorrow morning. I want you to come along, too."

"What about my kids?" She asked. "I can't leave them." She pushed herself up on one elbow.

He chuckled. "Just the kids. You're not worried about your husband?"

She fell back onto the bed. "That bridge is already in flames. But the kids are different. I can't run away from them."

"You said you wanted to get a divorce. This is all going to come out and I bet he gets custody."

"Aw crap," she uttered. "This is really a mess." She edged away from him and pulled the covers over her head.

CHAPTER 41

Floyd Swenson was at his desk early, reading reports. Bleary-eyed, he poured two cups of bad coffee and walked into Dan Williams' office with a cup in each hand. He set one next to Dan on the desk.

"Things going better?" Dan asked.

"Yeah. I guess," Floyd replied. "I talked to Doc Bergstrom after I talked to you. Now I think I've got my head on straight."

Dan nodded. "Good deal. But keep talking about it. Don't let it get in your guts and fester. Did you hear that Kerm Rajacich found a stolen car downtown last night? It was parked in the lot behind the hardware store and dry cleaners."

Swenson leaned back in his chair. In the Twin Cities, stolen cars were no big deal. Pine County, however, had very few stolen and Floyd couldn't remember more than a handful in his career. "A local," Floyd asked, "or someone from out of town?"

"That's the weirdest thing. It's from St. Paul, but the bulletin came from the Feds. It must be tied to something heavy."

"The Feds are involved? What is it? A stolen Rolls Royce or something?"

Dan laughed. "It's an old Malibu that was stolen in St Paul."

Swenson jumped forward so fast he startled Dan in his grab for the phone. "Hang on a second," Floyd said.

Floyd dialed Laurie's cell that immediately rolled to voicemail. He pounded the number for Laurie Lone Eagle's office and waited impatiently for an answer. After five rings a receptionist came on the line. "This is Deputy Swenson from Pine County and it's of the utmost importance I speak with Laurie Lone Eagle as soon as possible."

The receptionist at the Bureau of Criminal Apprehension was taken aback by the rush of words. She fumbled through the notes on her desk for a second. "Just a second, Deputy Swenson. She's at Miller-Dwan Hospital in Duluth. She can be reached at this number." She gave him the number for the nurse's station in the oncology unit.

Floyd pushed the button on the top of the phone and got a new dial tone. The numbers for Miller-Dwan were pounded in furiously. After speaking to a receptionist and a nurse, Laurie was finally brought to the telephone. "What's up, Floyd?"

"The Pine City PD found a stolen car in town. The funny thing is the FBI put out the bulletin. Is there any chance this is related to the kidnapping and bombing? The car was found behind George Brown's store."

Laurie scrambled to find a pen and a scrap of paper to write on. "Give me the license number."

"Hang on while I get it."

Laurie found Randi Pitt's FBI office number in her contact list. She dialed the number in Minneapolis and waited. Randi picked up the phone on the second ring.

"Randi. This is Laurie Lone Eagle. I understand the Pine City police just found a stolen car wanted under an FBI bulletin. Is this something related to the kidnappers?"

There was a long pause. "Ah, Laurie. I'm afraid the investigation is at a very sensitive stage right now and I can't discuss it without direct approval from the special agent in charge."

Laurie let out a sigh. "Listen Randi. I've got people who have stuck their necks out a mile for you. The person who made the inquiry risked his life to capture the two kidnappers. If you can't tell me, I'll call the *St. Paul Pioneer Press* and the *Minneapolis Star Tribune*. They'll have a field day dragging your ass through the editorial pages." Laurie's voice was past hostile. "Have I made myself perfectly clear?"

"That would be the end of your career, too." Randi's chair creaked as she shifted nervously. "I don't think you'd risk it."

"Randi, I've got a lot going for me. I'm a woman. I'm a Native American. I went to law school while working full-time at the BCA and graduated at the top of my class. On top of all that, I'm damned good." Laurie drew in a deep breath as she let the FBI agent ponder her seriousness. "All I want is a simple yes or no. Is that car a part of this investigation?"

Randi Pitt sat at her desk and looked around the room to see who might be listening to the conversation. Her face was beet red and she was grinding the tip of her pen into her daily planner. Finally, she whispered, "Yes. However, you didn't hear it from me. Agreed?"

There was no answer. Laurie was already dialing the number for the Pine County Sheriff's Department.

"Floyd, It is tied to the kidnappings." Laurie shared. "What are you going to do?"

Swenson smiled. "We're going to catch the SOB. If you can get here within the hour, you can help."

Laurie looked at her watch. "I'll be forty-five minutes, tops. You need the state patrol for back up? I can have them there in a few minutes."

Floyd pondered his next steps and then answered, "Sure, but keep it quiet. Have them come into the courthouse from the north end of town."

Laurie was already dialing her cell phone.

"Dan, unless I miss my guess," said Floyd, "we've got a drug dealer and a murderer in the apartment over Brown's hardware."

"No shit?" Dan jumped up. "I'll have Jodi notify our deputies and tell them to stay clear of downtown until we get a plan together."

A button on Dan's phone was blinking as he stood up. Jodi, the dispatcher's voice came over the intercom. "Floyd Swenson, call on line one."

Floyd snatched up the phone. "Swenson."

"Floyd," Pam's voice sounded sleepy. "I just got up, but I had to tell you about the conversation I had with Polly Hanson last night."

"Can it wait until later?" His voice was strained.

"No, it can't wait. I sent you a text last night, but you didn't respond."

"Oh, sorry. I haven't really mastered texting yet. What did it say?"

"It may have implications to the Brown murder investigation. Tom Knight, the youth pastor, was dating Polly Hanson before April was born. He was also having an affair with a married woman and had some packages of white stuff around his apartment." Pam let that settle in for a second. "I think that's the motive for the murder. George Brown saw Knight with either the married woman or the drugs."

Floyd was astounded. "I came to the same conclusion. On top of that, a car wanted by the Feds is sitting behind Brown's hardware. We were just going to set up a raid to arrest Knight and whoever else might be there."

Pam dropped the telephone as she reached for her bulletproof vest. When she picked it up again she was very brief. "I'll be there in fifteen minutes. Don't go in without me."

Dan was out of the sheriff's office and he shouted down the hall toward the ready room, "Floyd, call the afternoon shift deputies in. I'll call Carlton and Kanabec counties for backup."

They each went different directions and within five minutes two dozen law enforcement personnel were being mobilized. A command center was being set up in the ready room.

The Sheriff was on the phone when Dan flew into his office. Sepanen waved Dan to the guest chair and continued his conversation. "Thanks, I appreciate the notification. I'll make sure our people don't get in your way."

"That was the FBI," said the Sheriff. "They've got an interstate drug dealer at large. He was driving the stolen car Kerm found last night and they want us to impound it until they can get an evidence team up here to examine it this afternoon."

"That'll be too late. Here's what's going on . . ."

• • •

Tom Knight was eating toast coated with peanut butter as he searched his closet and cupboards for important contents to put into boxes. He loaded several stashes of cash from different locations around the apartment. He found the Colt .45ACP he'd bought a decade earlier when he and his partner, Preston, had been running an operation in Arizona. He hadn't needed it for years and it felt cold and uncomfortable in his hand. He turned it upside down and released the clip. The shells showed dark brown fingerprint stains, corrosion from when he'd last loaded it. The gun itself was speckled with rust. He pulled back the slide and let it "snap" into place leaving the hammer ominously cocked waiting for a trigger pull to unleash its power. A well placed shot was deadly. A near miss could disable a man, even a man high on drugs.

He sighted down the barrel and thought about the one time he'd fired at a man during one of their Arizona drug deals. The guy was higher than a kite on something, and had decided he wanted the methamphetamine and the money. Preston had distracted the man, and Tom had fired once. The .45 caliber bullet hit the druggie in the shoulder. In slow motion, the scene replayed itself in Tom's mind; again he witnessed the impact spinning the man a quarter turn. Blood, bone, and tissue spewed from the exit wound and splattered the wall. They had run before they knew if he was dead.

Tom shuddered and eased the hammer down. He wrapped the gun in a rag, placing it on top of a pile of fifty-dollar bills in a box. He buttered another piece of toast and ate while pulling several cans of Spam and a loaf of bread from the cupboard. He dropped them into a box along with a partial bag of apples and some Hi-C drink boxes. He set out a new 12-pack of Pepsi.

In the bedroom, Judy Arend was sitting on the wrinkled sheets making a list of things to pick up when she went to her house. There was nearly a full page of items, half of them scratched out. Tom had instructed her to make sure she was only going back for the essentials. They wouldn't have much time or space. Tears streamed down her cheeks as she contemplated leaving her children behind.

Tom peeked around the doorframe as he finished off the last bite of toast. "Are you ready?"

Judy sniffed back a tear and wiped her cheeks with her forearm. "I wish I could have gone to the bus stop and given the kids a hug." Tears welled again in her eyes. "But it's probably better this way." She shrugged and reached for the box of Puffs next to the bed. She blew her nose and threw the tissue in the direction of the wastebasket where it fell among the pile of others on the floor.

"You'll see them in a couple of weeks," Knight tried to reassure her. "And you can send them a card when we get settled." He lied. He knew she would never see them again. Eventually she would come to understand, or she would be dead. Either way, she had become too much of a liability to leave behind. He'd tell her whatever lies he had to so she'd get in the van quietly and across the Canadian border.

"Forget it!" She threw the pen and paper on the bed. "I can't set foot in the house. We'll just have to buy me new stuff as we go along."

Knight let out a huge sigh of relief, then walked over and gave her a hug. "That's more than fine. Cash is not a problem."

"Good," she said as she wiped away another round of tears. "I like to shop."

"Go do your bathroom thing. When you're done I'll wake up Terry."

She picked up a pile of clothes from the floor and disappeared through the bedroom door. He watched her walk out. She was great in bed, but she had a way of grating on his nerves. That was a problem for another day. Right now, he had to get the three of them on their way before the roof caved in on their escape.

Tom felt strangely uneasy about his relationship with the church. Over time he'd begun to enjoy the respect the congregation showed him. The kids loved him because he could talk their language. Too bad old George Brown had gotten his nose out of joint about his weekly liaisons with Judy. The night he tried to catch Judy in the apartment was definitely the beginning of the end. Instead of catching Judy in the apartment, George had caught Terry Preston making a big cash delivery and George didn't understand what was going on. Mr. Hilliard had demanded they not take any chances, so he ordered Tubby and Ernie to eliminate George. Tom Knight had supplied the logistics for the extermination since he knew George would be at the deacons' board meeting. He was very surprised to hear about the explosion. He thought they might make it look like a botched robbery. Instead, they made a big mess.

Floyd was briefing the group of 19 law enforcement officers from seven agencies in the ready room. "I believe the driver of the stolen car is in the apartment over Brown's Hardware." Floyd had a hand-drawn map of downtown Pine City spread across the desktop. He had highlighted the courthouse and was pointing to the hardware store. "There is every reason to believe both men are well armed and desperate. The one advantage we have is they don't know we're on to them."

He moved over to a chalkboard where he had roughly sketched the blocks around Brown's hardware store after making a discreet drive around downtown in his personal pickup. "The apartment is here. The first suspect parked the stolen car here and the second suspect's vehicle is a van parked here." He indicated rectangles on the board.

"I want to have the businesses on either side empty. Luckily, we were able to get the owners at home. We asked them to contact their workers and not open until they hear from us. Our deputies," he nodded to the day-shift deputies, "have discreetly evacuated the people from the second story apartments on either side of the hardware store."

Floyd moved back to the chalkboard and indicated a spot. "We have an observer across the street with binoculars and a sniper rifle. He has been watching, but so far the shades have been drawn and he hasn't reported any activity."

A line started blinking on the telephone and the dispatcher waved at Floyd to pick it up. He spoke for a second and an obvious wave of relief washed over him. "That was the observer. The shades are up, and we have at least one person moving around."

Floyd went back to the board and explained where he wanted each two-officer team deployed. "The plan is, we deploy teams as marked on the chalkboard. That should have them boxed in. I'll call the apartment in 30 minutes and try to negotiate them out. I want everyone prepared in case they make a break."

A hand went up from one of the highway patrol officers. "What if they break and make it to the van or car?"

Swenson smiled. "We had our ace mechanic disconnect the van's battery. The Malibu has two flat tires on the side away from the apartment." Heads nodded around the room.

"No other questions?" Floyd waited a second. "Then deploy. Let's keep this discreet and quiet. Don't spook them or shoot up the town if you're left an option. Everyone is wearing body armor."

The group left the room and headed for their assigned positions. Pam and Floyd were paired and had been assigned a position behind the van.

A man from the phone company rounded the corner carrying a phone attached to a long cord. He handed it to the sheriff. "Here's your direct line to the apartment. You lift the receiver and it rings in the apartment. They can't call anyone but you."

Sepanen nodded. "Thanks." He settled in and looked at his watch. Twenty-three minutes to go.

Tom Knight raised the shades on each of the three windows which faced the street. The morning sun flooded the room and shone directly in Terry Preston's eyes. "Time to get up. We're packed and ready to go."

Terry sat up and rubbed his eyes. The few hours of sleep he'd had helped, but he was still groggy. Out of the corner of his eye he saw an apparition float past in a white robe.

Terry threw an arm over the back of the couch and watched Judy disappear into the bedroom. "Where'd she come from?"

"She's been here all along," Knight replied. "Just in the bedroom. She'll be ready in a couple seconds."

"WHAT?" Terry's head snapped back to glare at Tom Knight. "She's not coming with us?" It came out more as a question than a statement.

"Sure she is." Tom started piling boxes next to the door. "I'm bringing her."

"Bullshit!" Terry exclaimed." I'm not dragging one of your bimbos along. Dump her. Give her a little kiss on the cheek and say it's been fun, but it's over."

"Sorry." Tom shook his head. "I can't. We need her to come along."

"I ain't bringing your love interests along on this trip," Preston said.

Knight looked over his shoulder at the bedroom door. He whispered, "Geez, Terry. Keep your voice down. She's just be-hind the door getting dressed. She knows too much to leave. We'll bring her along and deal with her later."

Terry Preston was pacing back and forth with his hands dug in his pockets. "I don't like it Tom. Let's deal with her here and be through with it. That puts an end to the evidence trail here instead of farther down the road. I'll do it if you don't have the guts."

"Take it easy. She's my liability. I'll take care of whatever happens."

Preston stopped and a smile crept over his face. "I get it. This is the one you were screwing on the last trip to keep the kids distracted while the package got placed. You weren't a good enough actor."

Knight's face burned crimson. "We're ready to go."

• • •

Floyd jumped when the telephone rang. He looked at his watch. There were still eight minutes before he was supposed to call, but the phone to Knight's apartment was ringing in his hand. He remembered any outgoing calls would ring only to him, and he pondered the prudence of answering.

He decided to pick it up and roll with the punches. "Hello."

"Hello. Hello. Who is this?" The female voice sounded very agitated, but was barely a whisper.

"Who are you trying to call?"

"911. Is this the police?"

"Yes." Floyd replied. "Who is this?"

"This is Judy Arend. I'm in Tom Knight's apartment, over Brown's hardware. There is another man here and he's trying to talk Tom into killing me."

Swenson's heart sank. "Listen carefully. Hang up as soon as I'm through talking. You'll be fine. Pretend you don't know anything about what they said. Act nonchalant. I'll have an officer there in a minute or less." As soon as he stopped talking, the line went dead.

"Now what?" Floyd asked himself.

CHAPTER 42

The dispatcher broadcast a radio message to the police teams indicating a potential hostage situation, asking them to sit tight and respond to developments as they saw fit. Floyd sprinted from the parking lot behind the old courthouse to the block that housed the hardware store. He turned down the side street, nodded to two State Troopers, then walked to the door that led to the apartment over the hardware store. It was a cool day, but Floyd's forehead was beaded with sweat. He caught his breath at the bottom of the steps. His hand on the butt of his pistol as he considered the options. He could call the kidnappers and hope for a good outcome, knowing they'd use Judy as a hostage, or he could gamble that they were oblivious to what was happening outside and . . . And what?

He saw Judy Arend's car a few feet away and thought about her children. His legs felt weak and his brain was telling him he was insane, but after a deep breath, he opened the door and walked up the stairs. "This tops the list of the stupidest things you've ever done," he said to himself.

The knock on the apartment door startled Terry Preston. He grabbed his 9mm Beretta pistol and spun to face the door. Tom Knight lunged and grabbed his wrist to keep him from firing through the door. He put a finger to his lips to silence Preston.

In a carefully modulated voice, Knight asked, "Who's there?"

"Floyd Swenson. Can I talk to you for a second, Pastor Knight?" He threw the "Pastor" in to make it sound like a church related visit.

Knight pushed Preston toward the bathroom. He looked around and saw no sign of Judy. "Just a second." He grabbed his pistol from the table and cocked the hammer before jamming it into the small of his back.

Knight unlocked and opened the door a crack. Preston watched from behind the bathroom door. "Floyd, what can I do for you?"

Floyd, heard the unmistakable click of the gun cocking and had steeled himself for the gun muzzle to show up in the crack of the door. Not seeing a gun pointed at him, he put on his game face. "I hope you can help me find Judy Arend," he said, his mind racing for a plausible reason to be there. "The school bus had an accident this morning and her kids are in the hospital. Looks like they'll have to transport one to the Twin Cities by helicopter. We can't find her husband and someone has to give permission." He projected his voice as much as he dared, hoping Judy wasn't already being held hostage and she'd hear him and react. "Her car is in the parking lot behind the building and I thought maybe she was here for counseling."

Before Floyd got out the last word, Judy flew from the bedroom with tears streaming down her face. She brushed past Knight and pulled open the door. She grabbed Swenson by the arm. "Please take me to them."

Floyd pulled Judy past him in the narrow stairwell and positioned her body behind him on the stairs. Then he asked, "Would you like to come too, Pastor?"

Knight was dumbstruck by the turn of events and the offer to leave. He sputtered. "Sure, I'll be right down."

Without waiting for further response, Floyd quickstepped down the stairs with Judy in front of him. Once out of the stairwell, he grabbed Judy's arm and pulled her against the side of the building. He drew his Glock as he waited for the sound of footsteps on the stairs. His legs felt like they'd turned to jelly, and he realized he'd been holding his breath while trying to hear noise from the stairs. He inhaled deeply and felt a sudden calm wash over him. After a few moments he nudged Judy and said, "Run to the corner."

Staying against the brick wall, he followed her down the block, his back to her, ready to fire at any threat coming out of the door. They were at the corner when the sheriff pushed Judy past him and into the arms of a Carlton County Deputy.

The sheriff pulled Floyd by the arm and whispered in his ear. "What the hell kind of fool stunt was that? You could have both been killed." Then he smiled.

The armpits of Floyd's tan uniform shirt were soaked with nervous sweat despite the cool morning. He took a deep breath and nodded. "Yeah, well . . . sometimes you do what's right, not what's smart. Make the call to the apartment."

Preston peeked out of the bathroom. Seeing the stairwell door closed, he walked into the living room. "That was a crock of shit and you know it."

Knight looked at him with his mouth open. "What do you mean?"

"Have you heard any sirens this morning?"

Knight shook his head and Preston went on. "Tell me. What are the odds there'd been an accident like that and we didn't hear a single siren?"

"Why didn't you stop her?"

Preston shrugged. "She was a liability and we have a better chance without her. Grab your stuff. We're outta here." As he picked up a box of money, the telephone rang.

Knight looked at the telephone tentatively, then picked it up. "Hello?"

"Hi Tom. This is John Sepanen, the Pine County Sheriff. We have an army of police around you and we've evacuated the building. Put down your weapons and come out with your hands up. If you do as we ask, you won't be hurt."

Knight's jaw fell open and he stared at Preston without saying a word. Preston walked over and took the phone from his hand. "Who is this?" As he gave up the telephone, Knight raced to the window and stared down at the street.

"This is Sheriff John Sepanen. The building is surrounded. Put down your weapons and walk out with your hands up."

Preston raced to the window and stood beside Knight. He looked up and down the street. There was not a person visible. "What are you trying to pull? There's not a cop anywhere. Is this a joke?"

"There is a sharpshooter in the window across the street. He has you in the crosshairs as we speak. If I give the word, you'll be dead before you hear the shot."

Preston looked across the street at the old courthouse on the opposite side. He caught a glint of light, like sunlight reflecting off a lens . . . or a rifle scope. He dropped below the line of sight.

"I've got a hostage up here." Preston threatened. He looked at Knight sitting on the couch.

"Sorry. That won't fly. Judy Arend is under our protection and we know that Tom Knight is part of the whole operation."

Preston looked around frantically. The only exits were the windows, covered by the man with the rifle, and the back stairs, leading to the parking lot. They had to have someone in the lot, too, he thought. He sat down on the floor and hung up the telephone.

Knight stood and started walking toward the door. "Come on Terry. Let's give it up. We'll get out in a couple of years."

Preston threw his head back and sighed in exasperation. "I've got priors. They'll lock me up and throw away the key. You can give up if you want to, but I'm going to make a run for the car." Then he remembered. "Shit, the car's nearly out of gas. Where are the woman's keys?" Preston asked.

"Probably in her purse," Knight replied. "They're probably in the bedroom."

Preston disappeared and then returned with a keyring that had a huge plastic daisy hanging from it. He fingered through the dozen keys. "I've got one GM key here. What does she drive?"

"I don't know. Maybe a Chev," Knight replied. "No, I saw her driving around with her kids in a minivan."

Preston fumbled through the keys again. "I can't tell what the hell these are for. I don't see a Chrysler or Dodge key. What kind of minivan was she driving?"

"I don't know. Maybe an old Ford Aerostar or something like that."

Preston threw the keys against the cupboard. "This is crap. I won't have time to run from car-to-car in the parking lot trying to find a key that works in some unknown car or minivan. What do you drive?"

"I've got the church's van."

Suddenly, Preston liked the plan. "That's it. You want to give up anyway. Give me the keys, then you go out and distract them while I make a run for the van." Preston stood up and stuffed his coat with stacks of cash while Knight watched listlessly.

"Where's the rest of your cash, Tom?"

"In the box."

"This is it? Where's the rest?" Preston pulled the rubber band off the stack and leafed through the fifty-dollar bills. "This is only like five thousand dollars."

"I had to use it." Knight shrugged. "George Brown kept threatening to stop the church project in Mexico. As long as everyone else thought it was drawing huge contributions they outvoted him to keep it going. Hilliard was going to reimburse me. He knew we had to keep the van going back and forth to ferry the kids and drugs."

Preston shrugged and stuffed Knight's cash in his jacket. He tucked the pistol into his waistband and pushed Knight toward the door. "You go down the stairs first." He motioned Knight to go through the door.

They shuffled down the steps together and stopped at the outside door. Preston peeked through the grimy window. "Where's the van?"

Knight pointed to the left of the door, where a white Dodge van was parked a half dozen spots away from the door.

"Go out with your hands up," Preston said, getting the correct key in his hand. "Walk toward the corner away from the van. When someone comes out you yell, '*I give up.*' That'll be my signal to run for the van."

Preston pushed and Knight popped out the door and quickly raised his hands over his head. He looked around, but there wasn't anyone in sight. He started to walk toward the right. After 15 yards he came to an open alley and a strong arm swung him against the wall and pinned him there.

"I give up!!"

Preston flew from the doorway, ran across the alley and into the parking lot. He stopped next to the door of the van and briefly watched as an officer held Knight against the wall.

"Drop the gun! Drop the gun!" a state trooper yelled as he ran across the lot toward him.

Preston pulled open the door and jumped into the driver's seat. He fumbled with the key, grabbed the steering wheel and turned the key to start the engine as the Trooper stopped. He watched a highway patrolman, only 20 yards away through the windshield. Preston thought he would have to drive toward the cop to get clear. He turned the key, and nothing happened.

Preston felt the cold steel of a pistol behind his ear. "Keep your hands on the steering wheel." Hidden behind the driver's seat, Pam Ryan was so close Preston could feel her breath on his neck. He had been so focused on the diversion provided by the Trooper he hadn't sensed Pam's presence behind the driver's seat. Dan Williams stepped to the passenger window, his gun pointed at Preston's chest.

Floyd threw the driver's door open and pointed his Glock at Preston's chest from a foot away. "Put your hands behind your head, and step out of the van, slowly."

Preston, his hands still on the steering wheel, hesitated. "Jail or a gunfight?" he said to himself.

Sensing the hesitation, Pam pushed the muzzle of her gun tighter against the skin behind Preston's ear. "If you even twitch," she whispered, "your brains will be splattered all over the windshield."

"You can't . . ."

"You're an armed fugitive with outstanding Federal warrants. They'll give me a medal."

"Okay. I'm raising my hands and putting them behind my head."

As Preston stepped down from the van, Floyd spun him and pushed his face against the side window. He kicked Preston's feet apart and then clipped handcuffs on his wrists, before removing the gun from his waistband. Patting him down, Floyd removed stacks of currency from Preston's jacket and threw them on the van's seat.

"There are hundreds of thousands of dollars here," Pam said, straightening the money into stacks as Floyd pulled out more and more money.

The sheriff saw the stacked cash and his eyes grew wide. To the trooper, he said, "Craig, I'd like you to witness the counting of this cash. I don't want any questions about how it was handled and secured."

Craig Downing, the Trooper, stepped up to the front bumper and looked through the windshield. He let out a whistle. "That's a lot of money."

CHAPTER 43

Floyd eased into his desk chair and flipped through the Post-it notes stuck to the telephone. The top message was from the sheriff, and he pushed it aside. The second was marked "Urgent." It was from the U.S. attorney in Minneapolis. The third was from Laurie Lone Eagle. The phone number was from the Fond du Lac reservation.

He decided it was too early for the U.S. attorney to be in, so he called the number in Fond du Lac. An elderly woman answered the telephone. She sounded very tired.

"I had a message to call Laurie Lone Eagle at this number."

"Yes. She left many messages. I will get her." The telephone receiver clunked against a hard surface as it was set down while the woman went to search for Laurie.

"This is Laurie." Her voice sounded flat.

"Swenson here. You left a message?"

"Oh yeah." Laurie's voice lifted slightly. "Is the sheriff basking in the glory of being re-elected?"

Floyd sat up and looked at the message from the sheriff. In the hustle of the murder investigation he'd forgotten Tuesday had been Election Day. He hadn't even voted.

"I can't really say." Floyd stammered. "I had kinda forgotten it was Election Day. Sepanen won?"

"By a landslide." Laurie replied. "With your performance saving the baby and cracking the Brown murder, there was hardly a person in Pine County who wouldn't vote for him after the news broke about the hostage rescue story. It was the lead story on every Twin Cities news broadcast last night."

Swenson became uncomfortable with the conversation and searched for a new topic. "Speaking of the murder and kidnappings, have the people in Texas found all the kids yet?"

Laurie let out a sigh. "They've done pretty well. A couple of the families have moved, so they were tougher to track down. However, I think they've found all but one. The little boy from White Bear Lake was back home the next day. I'll bet his mother never lets him sit in the car alone again," Laurie added as editorial. "The FBI has also been locating kids in Arizona, North Carolina, and New Mexico from scams run over the last seven years. Some of the kids have been with their adoptive families for that long and leaving them is presenting some real heartbreak."

"Wow," Floyd said, "I'd never thought about that aspect of it. I suppose the courts are supporting the return to the biological parents, but it's got to be hard on the kids." A light went on in his head. "Speaking of that, I assume things aren't going well with your father, since you're back in Fond du Lac."

There was a long pause. "He passed away Monday. We have the funeral today."

Floyd was speechless. He hadn't looked at the obituaries in the newspaper. "I'm so sorry Laurie. Is there anything I can do?"

"No. It's a family thing. But thanks for asking." With nothing left to say, they said their good-byes.

Swenson checked. It wasn't quite eight o'clock. He walked down the hall to the sheriff's office. The light was on and he could hear John Sepanen's booming voice on the telephone. Swenson stood in the hallway, waiting for the conversation to end, then rapped on the doorframe.

"I hear congratulations are in order on your re-election." Swenson entered the office and offered his hand.

Sepanen pulled the big cigar out of his mouth and set it in the ashtray. "Thanks. And a large part of the election outcome is due to your solving the George Brown case." Sepanen shook his hand firmly.

By the time Floyd got back to his desk, it was eight-thirty. He was reaching for the phone to call Mary when he saw another pink message slip. It was from Polly Hanson at Ledin's store.

He dialed the Braham number and Polly answered the telephone.

"Deputy Swenson?" Polly's voice was tentative.

"Hi Polly. What can I do for you?"

"Umm. I'm in a pinch. I have this job at the store, and everyone is being really nice to me, babysitting and all. But I had a call from Dr. Bergstrom's office. I need to get April to them for another vaccination, but I don't have any way to get there. Dr. Bergstrom told the receptionist to have me call you. I feel so . . . embarrassed to ask. If it weren't for April, you know I wouldn't ask. I can pay you for gas!"

Swenson smiled. "It's no bother. What time are you supposed to have her there?"

"I get off at three, and he asked me to come as soon as I could get there after work."

Floyd rubbed his eyes. Doc Bergstrom wouldn't have suggested Floyd drive unless there were a reason. He let out a deep breath. "I'll pick you up at three o'clock."

Floyd had been playing with the note from the U.S. attorney as he spoke to Polly. He decided to make the call despite his misgivings about the possible topic of Tubby Lasoya. Ray Price, the assistant U.S. attorney answered his own telephone.

"Hi Ray. This is Floyd Swenson, from the Pine County Sheriff's Department. I had a message to call you."

"Floyd, hang on for a second while I pull the file out of the pile here." Floyd heard computer keys clicking and the creaking of a chair. "Ah, yes. We've been talking to the attorneys for Terry Preston and Tom Knight, which incidentally aren't their real names. Both are charged with multiple felony counts. We've got a good case against them with the testimony of Toribio Lasoya. I think they're going to cop a plea and maybe help us put the ringleader away in Texas. I wanted to pass this by you before we got too far into the process. They're asking us to drop the kidnapping charges in exchange for guilty pleas on the drug and tax evasion charges. They'll also help the IRS find some of the cash assets and forfeit them. They've also requested that we talk to the Pine County attorney about dropping the kidnapping charges, especially since no one has actually implicated the two of them."

Swenson shook his head. "Don't you have enough to lock them away forever? Lasoya laid out the details of the drugs and murder. Even though they weren't a party to the murder, it's obvious that they were the ones who pointed out the risk in George's anger over the Mexican church project and targeted his car. Why not take them to trial and fry their asses?"

There was a pause. "It's not easy. We'll take them to trial here, in Minnesota, and a Hispanic informant, who is an admitted co-conspirator, won't sell well to a Minnesota jury. Besides that, the IRS wants the money, and we're talking about pulling millions out of accounts in the Caribbean and Europe. Mr. Lasoya can't implicate either of them directly in the murder. All his dealings were with the man he knew as Applewhite in Texas." Price paused as he put his argument together. "They'll be gone for a long time. And they'll be broke when they get out."

Swenson sighed. "How about Lasoya? You still going to put him in a witness protection program?"

"He's in a safe house with his girlfriend now. Once the Hilliard trial is done, they'll be off to a cushy setup somewhere in the Southwest where they'll become invisible. In case you're interested, they got married last week."

Floyd let out a weak laugh. "Well. Thanks for the update. I can't say I'm pleased about letting them off on so many charges. I guess you gotta do what you gotta do."

Swenson hung up and went through the obituaries in the Duluth newspaper. He found the listing for Lone Eagle. The memorial service was being handled by a funeral home in Cloquet with interment on the reservation. He noted the times on the back of Laurie's pink note, then he called Mary.

"I need a floral arrangement for a Cloquet funeral," he said, flatly.

"Is it someone I know?" Mary asked.

"No. It's Laurie Lone Eagle's father. She's been a close friend since she was with the sheriff's department, and I'd like to send something . . . substantial."

"Are you paying for it, or are you passing the hat?"

"I don't think there's time to pass the hat," he replied, sounding tired. "I'll give you my Visa card number."

"I'll put both our names on it," she said firmly. "You can buy me supper."

"But . . ."

"This is not negotiable," Mary said firmly. "Let me do this. There aren't a lot of things I can contribute to our relationship and I will do this. Period."

"Yes, dear," Floyd said with a smile.

● ● ●

At one o'clock Floyd walked into the rear of the funeral home. It was crowded with people. The other non-Natives were dressed in dark suits and seemed to be employees of the funeral home. He felt a tap on his shoulder and found Dan Williams, the Pine County Undersheriff, beside him. They stood in the back of the chapel through the service and watched as the teary-eyed intermixed with the stoic. They followed the coffin to the hearse.

Floyd and Dan drove together to the cemetery and followed the mourners to the gravesite. Several people said a few words before the crowd started to mingle and head back to their cars. Floyd walked toward the group closest to the coffin, while Dan got cornered by people who wanted to talk about the election. Sepanen's re-election meant Dan had continued employment as the sheriff's appointee. Floyd picked his way slowly to Laurie's side. She hadn't noticed him until he touched her shoulder.

"Floyd!" She threw her arms around his chest and buried her face into his shoulder as he stood helplessly patting her back while she sobbed.

After a few seconds she stopped and looked up at him, oblivious to the crowd who was staring at this out-of-place cop. "I'm so glad you came." She turned and searched for her mother, who was talking to some others nearby. She dragged Swenson by the arm.

"Mom, this is Floyd Swenson. He's the one who caught the kidnappers." She looked at him, and then back to her mother. "He was my partner when I worked for Pine County and we're still close friends."

Floyd blushed and looked helplessly at the crowd. Smiles started to crack sad faces and a few men walked forward to shake his hand.

Laurie took her mother by the arm and pulled her to Floyd's side. "Please come to the house and share lunch with the family. We have some fresh venison roast (she emphasized the fresh, meaning it had been recently killed, far out of the state hunting season) and a lot of other special dishes you've probably never tasted."

He smiled. "I'd like that very much. I have another chore in Braham at three, so I can't stay long."

Laurie kissed him on the cheek. "The flowers were lovely. The card said they were from you and Mary. I take it you two are getting along?" Laurie's face showed no hint she was kidding, but Floyd knew she was yanking his chain.

"We're getting along very well," he said.

•   •   •

At three, Floyd parked at the front door of Ledin's store. Polly ran out of the store and climbed into the squad. "This isn't too much to ask, is it? If it is, I'll figure something else out."

He eased the squad away from the curb. There was almost no other traffic in sight. "It's no problem at all. I'm happy to do it for April." He thought to himself, "And you."

They stopped at the farm and released one of the church ladies from her babysitting responsibilities. In the kitchen there was a different, but not new, set of chairs around the table. There was evidence of groceries on the counter, too. Polly wrapped April in a quilt while Floyd surveyed the second-hand living room furniture that had replaced much of Polly's fruit crate décor.

They strapped April in a used car seat and drove to Pine City, with Polly talking about the wonderful church ladies and the wonderful new job at the store working for wonderful Mr. Ledin. April chortled and laughed the whole ride. There was no mention of Ronny Benson, although Polly did tell him about the wonderful conversation she'd had with the new deputy, named Pam something. Swenson had heard through the grapevine Ronny had returned to his wife rather than suffer further jail time under the contempt order.

Floyd sat in the waiting room, reading an old *Field and Stream* magazines while April and Polly went into the examining room.

"Deputy Swenson?" Floyd was beckoned to the receptionist's desk by a soft voice. "Dr. Bergstrom would like to see you in his office for a moment." The nurse directed him into the back hallway.

Floyd had hardly settled into the guest chair in Doctor Bergstrom's office when the doctor breezed in and closed the door and collapsed into his chair. "How are you doing? The last time we spoke, you were a little rocky."

"Things are a lot better. I sleep again. Everything's coming back into perspective. I went to a funeral today, and it was okay. I heard from the Ramsey County Attorney they had presented the shooting at the car wreck and they didn't find grounds for an indictment."

"It's going to take time, Floyd. You'll never get entirely over some of the emotional aspects of a traumatic event like shooting someone. Like I told you, it all becomes a part of you and makes you a better person."

"I hope you're right." Floyd hesitated for a second.

"I heard you were mentioned on the news," The doctor said as he rocked forward in his chair. "Really? What happened?"

Swenson talked through the entire scenario, including standing at the top of the stairs, shirt dripping with nervous sweat, and hearing a pistol hammer "click" before the door opened.

"Holy shit, Floyd. That must have taken nerves of steel. Were you at least wearing a bullet-proof vest?"

Swenson shook his head. "No."

Bergstrom's eyes grew wide with surprise. "Why not?"

Swenson shrugged. "Just stupid I guess. I didn't draw the gun either, because Judy was inside." He paused. "But, the real reason was because I didn't think I could pull the trigger."

"Whew!" Bergstrom let out a low whistle. "That's bad news when you're a cop."

There was a long pause. "Pam Ryan had a gun behind that guy's ear in the van . . ." Floyd hesitated. "I was at the driver's door and if he had even twitched . . . Luckily, Dan was there too. He wanted to make sure I was up to it. He's been through this before."

Bergstrom asked, "What was George Brown's link to the whole thing? You said something I told you last time we spoke clicked."

"George didn't like Tom Knight. He was suspicious because he knew Tom wasn't making enough as the assistant pastor to even pay rent, but as Tom's landlord, he knew Tom was making the payments regularly. One night he caught Judy leaving Tom's apartment late and that crossed the line. That's what you knew about. Tom told the FBI that George caught the drug deliveryman, dressed in a UPS uniform, making a payment to him a couple days later when George went up to confront him over the affair with Judy. That sent him searching for answers and was behind his tirade about money at the board meeting before the explosion."

"So, George had all the pieces but couldn't see how they fit. In the end, it cost him his life." Swenson got up to leave and shook the doctor's hand. "Thanks for the talk, doc. How's Polly?"

"I can't tell you anything. She was in last week and I drew blood and sent it to a lab in Duluth. I'm reviewing the results with her in a minute."

"No hints?"

Bergstrom glared and held the door for him. "Polly can tell you if she chooses."

Ten minutes later, Polly came bubbling out of the exam room with April in her arms. Swenson guessed the news was good, but they walked to the squad in silence. Polly buckled April into the car seat, then sat in the front. She leaned across and kissed Floyd on the cheek as he reached to start the car.

"What's that for?"

"You and Dr. Bergstrom have a conspiracy. Don't you?"

"What?" He feigned innocence.

"My test came back. I don't have AIDS or any of the other nasty stuff the doctor checked for." Polly paused, then added. "Mrs. Ledin told me that your friend, Mary, mobilized the church ladies. That was really sweet." Polly's voice started to crack and she pulled a tissue from her purse. "You pulled my life out of the toilet. I can't ever repay you."

He smiled and drove out of the parking lot.

"Polly, I deal with people who are the dregs of this earth every day of the week. You were a bright spot with potential. All the thanks I will ever need is the smile that's been on your face. It makes the rest of my job okay."

This is a work of fiction. The people, events, and places depicted herein are creations of the writer's imagination, or are used fictionally.

Any creative work is a collaboration of many people and I have to acknowledge the assistance and contributions of a number of special people.

- Pat Morris has done her usual, outstanding job of editing and fact checking. She makes me, and the final book, so much better.
- Fran Brozo, Nancy Mohr, and Craig Kapfer have proofed and/or corrected manuscripts. I owe you all my thanks for your contributions, corrections, suggestions, and constructive criticism.
- Julie, my wife, continues to offer support and medical comment on the manuscripts. She has regularly reminded me that her role is to keep my humble - she excels at that task.
- Dennis Arnold (Carlton County Sheriff's Department, retired) offers suggestions and corrections to the police procedures. I accept most of his suggestions...

62925771R00216

Made in the USA
Lexington, KY
21 April 2017